"Terrifying, but so beautifully, dreamily written."

— Elizabeth Farrelly

"The reader is hurtled pell-mell into a febrile world of strong and desperate characters, alien lore and changing loyalties. As Pearl and Mica avoid 'attaining Perfection' and the Orchid Nursery, they make their separate difficult journeys through a dystopian world that Katz presents with luminous, edgy and at times almost unbearably vivid descriptions. Mysterious and compelling, the narrative is etched with a grim humour in its dark evocation of a world both eerie and strange and yet also disturbingly familiar."

— Libby Hathorn

"A powerful story, so visual and present it feels like a cross between a painting by Hieronymus Bosch and M C Escher ... if they'd both read *Riddley Walker* and *The Road*. A fundamentalist ruling class and its deformed creed are the brutal gardeners in the nursery; meanwhile, one young woman escapes, knowing only what she can*not* live with. Confronting in its truths, *The Orchid Nursery*'s richness of language also layers it in warmth and humour."

— Stephanie Smith

"A superbly crafted vision of a toxic cultural wasteland. Three women: rebel, zealot, hag. Three journeys through a disintegrated future. Check current news reportage before claiming the horrors of *The Orchid Nursery* could never come to pass within our lifetime."

— Cat Sparks

the orchid nursery

louise katz

[Lacuna]
2015

Published in 2015 by Lacuna
   http://www.lacunapublishing.com

   Lacuna is an imprint of Golden Orb Creative
   PO Box 185, Westgate NSW 2048, Australia
   http://www.goldenorbcreative.com

Cover design by Golden Orb Creative.
Close up shoot of a beautiful orchid blossom photo © A41cats | Dreamstime.com
Girl with bandages photo © Nikita Vishneveckiy | Dreamstime.com
Black dog photo © Chris Doyle | Dreamstime.com

Text design and typesetting by Golden Orb Creative. Typeset in 11 pt Adobe Caslon
   Pro (text) and Avenir (titles).
Mica image © Dave Dyet | Wikimedia.com
Pink Akoya pearl image © Uwakoya | Wikimedia.com
Cauldron with potion image © Mariia Pazhyna | Dreamstime.com
Louise Katz photo © Lucy Le Masurier.

National Library of Australia Cataloguing-in-Publication entry

   Katz, Louise, 1959– author.

   The orchid nursery / Louise Katz.

   9781922198204 (paperback)

   9781922198211 (ebook : epub)

   A823.3

Over the past few years, the revival of religion has taken on spectacular and, in many ways, frightening dimensions ... Is it a revival of spirituality? If it were, we could only welcome it with open arms. Is it a revival of faith? That wouldn't be a problem either. Unfortunately, it is all too often accompanied by dogmatism, obscurantism, fundamentalism – and sometimes fanaticism. It would be a mistake to leave the field to these forces ... it is a struggle for freedom ... in favour of the separation of church and state, in favour of the freedom to believe or not believe.

Andre de Compte-Sponville, The Little Book of Atheist Spirituality,
Viking Press, 2006.

Ideological purity. Compromise as weakness. A fundamentalist belief in scriptural literalism. Denying science. Unmoved by facts. Undeterred by new information. A hostile fear of progress. A demonization of education. A need to control women's bodies. Severe xenophobia. Tribal mentality. Intolerance of dissent. Pathological hatred of the U.S. government. They can call themselves the Tea Party. They can call themselves conservatives ... But we should call them what they are – The American Taliban.

'The Greater Fool', episode 10, series 1, The Newsroom, HBO Entertainment, 2012.

How confident can you appear at being lascivious? How credible is your air of lewdness? A girl who is just a try-hard will lose credibility and become an outcast. So a lot depends on how much support you can get from other girls ... Girls spray their "likes". They comment: ... "F--k you're hot" ... [G]irls have to conform to what boys see in pornography. And then girls post photos to "out-hot" the other girls by porn star criteria.

Olympia Nelson (age 11), 'Dark undercurrents of teenage girls' selfies',
The Age, 11 July 2013.

The parts that are cut away are disgusting and hideous to look at. It is done for the beauty of the suture ... An uncircumcised vulva is unclean and only the lowest prostitute would leave her daughter uncircumcised. No man would dream of marrying an unclean woman. He would be laughed at by everyone.

Cited in Hanny Lightfoot-Klein, Prisoners of Ritual: An Odyssey
into Female Genital Circumcision in Africa, Routledge, 1989.

They wore blouses with buttons down the front that suggested the possibilities of the word *undone*. These women could be undone; or not. They seemed to be able to choose.

Margaret Atwood, The Handmaid's Tale, Virago, 1987.

 MICA

1.

The door is thick and made of iron. The key is so big and heavy I must hold it in both hands. It's more like a bolt really, a long, hard shaft of black metal, scored and notched along its whole length. I quake at the blasphemy I am about to commit, then insert the key and push until I feel it bite. I turn it with both hands and the door opens.

The smell is powerful, raw, ammoniac. My breath catches in my throat and my eyes water. I am angry with myself for this simplistic animal response, so typical of weak (wo)Mankind, and make myself take a step forward into the close atmosphere. I have smelled similar in the stables, this reek of straw, of livestock and vegetarian excrement. It should not upset me so much. Of course the womanidols are made of flesh. This cannot be helped. But I had not expected this, our hallowed citadel, to smell like shit.

The Orchid Nursery is set into the centre of the corp-yard. The high, round dome is made of segments of lovely pink-hued glass, a rare flesh colour created by masters of the art of isolating and manipulating fundamental aspects of the elements, water, air and the earth, our wild mother, whose unreliable humours must be subdued and made to obey the dictates of Men lest we all fall pray to the exigencies of her whims. The shimmering half-globe rises from a circular stone wall inscribed with the sacred maxim, FORM FOLLOWS FUNCTION. This wall is twice the height of a Man, the granite surface obscured by the boughs of espaliered pear trees, their limbs splayed flat against the wall.

Most of the Nursery is under the earth; the mysterious lives within enjoy the filtered sunlight, safe against the extremes of seasons and the gaze of profane eyes. Before the western face of the Nursery is the stone altar with its Plea Box for annual Beseechings. It is a sacred secret/ un-secret, a mystery, but one we all see every day. It lies at the heart of all the concentric circles of our Perfect State.

We pass by the Nursery all the time on our daily rounds and some-times a girlie will stop to pay her respects to the womanidols within, who we know to be there though we never see them. We leave small offerings sometimes, a comb we have made, a piece of fruit. These are always gone by morning. But we don't go in, ever. The careforcers do, but they never tell, having sacrificed their voices to their sacred tasks when they are first commissioned. The Seed-Bearers enter the Nursery too, when they are selected for service, but they are Men so naturally we rarely speak to them. And of course those destined to become womanidols go inside; they go inside once only and they never, ever come out.

But I needed to know if Pearl was there. I was so very angry with her when first she went missing. When the anger passed, as of course it had to, I found that it had misled me, obscured my deeper feeling: a terrible fear for my friend. My anxiety was raw and red and had to be salved, for I had come to fear for my wits. So I stole the key from the Careforce office. I did not know what would happen to me if I were found out, did not know if a punishment had been invented for a crime nobody had ever committed before. I went by way of the underground passage from the office, the only way in or out, at least as far as I know. I was shaking violently and I could smell the acrid pungency of fear on my skin and my breath.

Yet all my life I have imagined being here, the place that all little girlies desire to end their childhood. The highest privilege is to be among those chosen to serve as a womanidol, clean and Perfect. Females born of unPerfected (wo)Men become foot-soldiers, gardeners or house-mothers if they are not themselves graced through a successful Beseeching for Perfection; the boys become Craftsmen or Scholars, Seed-Bearers or Ecumen. But the sons born of womanidols become our Properganders, Men of Right-Sight and Construers of the sacred DoppelBook, and are destined to succeed our Brother Ministers, the wise and mighty heroes of Liberation, for they are marked as Elect by GodFather (Blessed Be His Cock-and-Muscle, alive-alive-oh-oh ever amen). They devote their lives to prayer and interpretation of the Holy Strictures from the age when their tender lips can first form words until the day they are taken by merciful death into the embrace of GodFather (BBHCM) in Heaven above to live forever in blissful oversight of many farms and factories, with cunny aplenty trained perfectly in all the sexual arts, five-hundred apiece, that they might always be sated and (wo)Men need not be overtaxed.

The Properganders of Art & Pain, of Yearning & Duty, of Instruction & Destruction, guide us within the blessed order established after the long, hard-won Liberation. They teach us with righteous words and show us the way through this evil world that exists in tension of oppositional forces that *must* ever be kept separate. Evil is always ready to assail the good by seeking ingress to the minds of Men and (wo)Men through our ears and eyes and mouths and very skins created by GodFather (BBHCM) to seal us off from the world's profanity. Oh, the evil ones have soft phrases and pretty images to seduce us. The sensuous touch of the light-fingered breeze who cools the sweat risen to the skin from righteous labour, and she says, *Only rest awhile* – such temptations are sent to test us, and must be resisted. Or the wicked magic of the twilight, arousing the passive air as if it were the exposed skin of a virgin, but then comes the inevitable setting of the sun, filling the sky with blood. Our Properganders are our guides through this world of art and pain, yearning and duty, and they maintain harmonious relations between the Houses for they are the safeguards of Civilisation itself.

The week before had been our birthday. Mother Oblation 7th came into our cunnydorm to wake all the new Oblation Fifteens of Stone House: Anapaite, Antimony, Galena, Nickeline, Opal, Pearl and me. All of our stone names have meanings. Like my name, Mica, which means 'crumb'. So there stood MaOblat at the door on the first day of my life as a (wo)Man. The light from the kitchen haloed the frizz of hair escaping her cap so that it shone brightly. The smell of nutmeg from the kitchen was making my belly rumble and my mouth water. MaOblat's face had on its usual look that Pearl calls 'poo-jammed', and it is true that while MaOblat might want to be pleasant, her feelings are all blocked up behind a plug of hard scale. Of course I never let Pearl know I agreed with her about that because she did not need any encouragement in her irreverence. I have a duty to my friend and I have kept her safe so far – or so I thought last week.

'Fifteens,' said MaOblat from the doorway, 'As you know, today is your Day of Attainment. The Plea Box on the Altar awaits. You may Beseech. Then cake.' She had forgotten to detach her electric whisk-aug from her right wrist-branch with its multi-purpose connectors. Cake mix dripped onto the floor while the safety light flickered through the thin weave of her crone's opaque dressless. (It had only been last year that she'd finally given in to a decent matron's garb – someone must have told her – at last – that it was simply not enough just to have her fat surgically removed and redistributed and her pendulous labia tightened to disguise the ravages of age, thank GodFather, Blessed Be His Cock-and-Muscle!) I wrapped my arms around my body and hugged myself against the cold of the morning, perhaps for the last time. By this time next month, GodFather willing (BBHCM, alive-alive-oh-oh ever amen), I might well be Perfected, *inshallaweh*, or at least augmented like the mothers and the soldiers. I felt nervousness and pride uncoiling below my heart and spreading like tentacles of hot magnesium wire through my body from heart to cockslot.

But Pearl wasn't having any of that. 'How festive,' she murmured quietly to me so that no-one else could hear. 'Maybe she'll let us watch a bit of telly with the careforcers later,' she added, 'even stay up for the Late News post-Anthem. Yay.' Pearl has always been a sharp one, but this level of sarcasm was new.

Oh, I worry about Pearl, for she is the most porous of girlies, always listening and touching, always looking at everything around her, availing her senses to any assault, leaving herself open to the fleshly fallacy. Her eyes are bright with curiosity like the little cat we learned of so long ago when we had only been in the world four years, at Minus-Eleven from Attainment. We had this story from Bobander A/P, child-instructor of the Propergandery of Art & Pain, a most edifying tale about the little cat who poked her inquisitive nose into cupboards and behind doors ... 'Until the day came,' said Bobander, 'the day came when she learned her lesson, oh yes.' He smiled upon us benignly, so that we knew that he loved us. And the brightest of us thought hard about which lesson of all the many lessons this one would be. We were on the edges of our seats.

'It was a day of filthy rain like Satan's buckshot, rain that rattled the skulls of the fledglings in the trees, braining them! Braining them so that they fell down; they fell down *dead!*'

'*Ah* ...' we said with one voice, awed and terrified as we watched with our minds' eyes the falling chicks.

'They fell down *hard*, their little corpses dropping from their nests like cherry stones spat from the pursed lips of devils' imps ...' He paused, seeing our eyes wide with horror at the devils' imps, and also with a terrible guilty wanting-to-know, for Bobander was a wise one; he tempted us to the brink of sin then drew us back with a lesson ... oh, he was good. 'On this day, the little cat watched and watched the rain and thought and thought her kitty-thoughts when she should have been … when she should have been *what*, girlies?'

The quickest got our hands up so fast it was as if we punched holes in the air in our keenness to show our knowledge. I remember he chose Anapaite. I remember because I was envious and I was frightened of my feeling because only the week before we had learned about GodFather's preferred punishment for the envious. So I tried hard not to mind. Oh, no-one was better than her at repeating back the semenal texts of the Holy Strictures word for word, or at adapting the lyrical phrases and gentle rhythms of the Doppelbook into daily life. And not only that, but Ana was *fast*. '*Working*, sir,' she said. 'That little kitty should have been working!' I was relieved for so clever-clever Ana had got only half the answer! I had my chance to shine brightly in the eyes of lovely Bobander, so quick as a shot I had my hand up in the air again. He nodded towards me and I was so honoured and nervous I almost forgot my answer. Almost, but not quite: 'And *praying*,' I said, 'She should have been *praying* very *hard* in *silence* as she *worked!*' He smiled on me and I felt warm from head to toe. Then he said to us all, 'Good girlies. Yes. Praying and working with all the other little kittens of the House. But no! Not *this* little kitten! *This* little kitten was watching and prowling and thinking about pretty-this and funny-that and when will I have my dab of cream to lick off my whiskers?' Here Bobander did a very funny impression of the kitten looking sharply left and right, then licking lap-lap-lap so quick and kitteny we all laughed aloud.

His gaze became stern because some of us had giggled overlong, and the end of the story was coming, and he needed our full attention. 'And *then*, GodFather's (BBHCM) Angel of Righteousness descended upon her!' Bobander acted out the shock of the Curious Kitty with wide eyes and stiff hands held up in front of his face, like a creature blinded with fright. 'The Angel descended upon her and he slit her gut from throat to arsehole!' Slash-slash went Bobander's hands. 'And the Angel spread her innards out for her old enemy the Rat to take to feed to his children, for this is the punishment for the curious.' And the girls who had laughed too long looked down at their shoes in shame and fear. '*This*,' he said solemnly, 'is the fate of those curious girlies so taken with pretty and funny, with this and that, that and this, that they fail in their duty.'

There were other cat stories too that Bobander invented for us and told as we gathered around the heater with its friendly stink of kerosene, and the raindrops marking their paths down the window, so cosy inside. After a while there were so many cat stories we came to call them the Naughty Kitty Tales: Cheeky and Saucy, Wayward and Waggish were my favourites. He was a great orator, so good that some girls had bad dreams after his stories. They tried to hide it, but we others heard them weeping or crying out in their beds. Especially Nickeline. She was the most soft-headed of all the stupidest girlies in Oblation. In the morning we dutifully reported her and she was punished in Supervised Peer Slapping and Kicking so that she would remember with her body if her mind was too flighty to retain the lesson. We were so well taught by Bobander that after he was taken by death a memorial to Truth was erected in his honour at the South Gate which we all visit each Sorrow and Penitence month.

I know I should not waste my energies on concern for Pearl, for my duty lies with the work I do in the gardens, with my training with the girlie-guards, and the prayers I must repeat silently always to keep distractions of the world and the mind at bay that I may one day be worthy to perform the act of sacrifice, that is, to *make sacred* my own life. But I love Pearl dearly. We are different: I am careful; she is not. I am pious; she lacks a natural impulse towards devotion. But I can help her for she is the sister of my soul.

I remember saying to her then, as our House mother stood in the doorway dripping cake mix onto the floor of highly polished concrete, buffed daily to a high gloss by careforcers, 'Pearl, hush. MaOblat is a woman of virtue, our guide and mother.' Pearl rolled her eyes at me and gave me a quick kiss, flicking my ear with the tip of her tongue. 'Behave!' I hissed. And ducked my head so that she would not see my smile. Just a small smile. I could not help it.

We knew what to do. We had watched Fifteens' processions since the age of Minus-Ten from Attainment, which is when girlies become more or less sentient. We took off the sleeping-dresslesses we wore at night to keep us warm, drew our masks down over our faces, put on our high heels and tightly knotted broad-belts, and in the pure state of available nakedness made our way through the mild drizzle, two by two across the yard in a crocodile towards the sealed Orchid Nursery and the altar with its Plea Box, to Beseech. I could feel the heat of the boys' and Men's scrutiny of my body from the males' apartments that surrounded our corp-yard, for I had learned my lessons in Attracting the Gaze and

I felt so proud of my power to draw their eyes to my form. Pride again, I said to myself. Remember who you are: a palliation vehicle for the desire of Men, and if you are very, very lucky, in due course a vessel for a Seed-Bearer, a womanidol. You have a function to fulfill. No more or less. But then, I found even that made my heart swell … with pride.

 ## PEARL

2.

I have never been certain, or at least I cannot remember having been so. I know what it's for though, certainty. It's to give you a sense of purpose of course. It's to direct your energy towards an end that is of benefit not only to the female body corporate and thereby the rest of the State, but ultimately to Civilisation itself. Is this not right, is this not good? *Yes it is.* I know this to be so for it is what I have *always* known because I was taught well, so that even if I did not always attend to my lessons as I should, those drills still worked into my brain carrying their messages, and the messages settled there like – what? I have been told, and it is *true*, that a child's brain is an empty bucket and must be filled with information and knowledge of duties. This is how it *is*. Yet now an image comes to mind of silt caking the bottom of that bucket, bright green slime lining its sides.

And another image comes to meet it from some odd corner of my mind, based on pictures I have seen, I suppose, in the Museum of Iniquities. Behind my eyes I invent a street filled with energetic people talking to each other, Men and (wo)Men both, engaged in daily commerce, buying and selling, and conversing together about their work and their plans as if no-one was watching them, as if it was perfectly legal and correct. And there are children too. In dreams I walk down this street in this town although I know this dream world is *haraamasur*. I *know*. It is a corruption of reality, of righteousness, of the truth of how things are and must be. Isn't it? Yes, of course it is.

Oh, here in my mind, something has gone wrong, wrong, wrong. Some poison – no, worse – some *entity* – no, enti*ties* plural, *masses* plural, have entered my mind bearing poisonous notions that breed and spread like a green disease, so that now there is a great deal more material in my head than what was gifted me by my teachers. My mind still retains all my lessons, all the wisdom of the Men of Right-Sight, but they are getting rammed by the new notions, battered and cut by my mind's new population, my toxic invaders, my *demons*.

My demons debate among themselves the value of my learning, posing daring questions about the wisdoms achieved through effortful study, and I listen to them, and they lead me into temptation. They lead me into transgression. I follow, willingly.

 ## MICA

3.

As we made our way through the gentle rain towards the Plea Box, an occasional Craftsman or Scholar would come down from his apartment and avail himself of one of us, or even a Man from one of the Ecumenical Houses, Trojan, Gabriel, Usama or Caedmon. But more often it was a gamey young boy for, having just awoken, their needs were strongest. I looked over at Pearl. She was walking purposefully, as if by her demeanour she could avoid the glances of boys and Men and also their touch. As if she was exempt! Yes, Pearl is a proud one. Even worse than me. But her conceits take strange turns – taking pride in things that would cause me only shame. My closest friend, yet a conundrum as convoluted as the infolded female forms we had studied in The Labial Mystery as Metaphor for Life.

I watched with interest the coupling of one young Man with Galena, who had obligingly leant over and placed her hands on her widespread knees and tilted her arse upwards to make it easier for him to achieve access. The height of her heels was helpful in this regard also. Gal's dugs were bigger and plumper than anyone else's. She was *hot*. I noticed Opal looking on greedily, poor thing: Men rarely fucked her, she was so unappealing with her blue-white skin and that awful red-furred cunny, and she was so awkward and seemingly incapable of absorbing any of the advice in our many manuals, from Attracting the Gaze to Charming the Snake. Still, somehow she did manage to become pregnant at Minus-Three from Attainment – an uncommon piece of good fortune! But when her time came she made a horrible racket in the birthroom behind the latrine. It is one thing to remind us all of (wo)Mankind's necessary suffering for Eve's sin, but her howling and screaming was self-indulgent to a terrible degree. Unsurprisingly, she birthed a dudbub which, naturally, was taken to Spare Parts shortly after. This quietened her down, and she's been silent ever since. She'll be praying hard to be Chosen for Perfection to make up for her failure.

I looked back at Gal. Her dugs were shaking like jellies now that the Man was close to climax. I looked down at my own and thought they might be the smallest of all, hardly there really. Maybe when my bloods become more regular there will be an improvement. I hoped, *inshallaweh*, they would grow into such big round bulbs as Galena's, for the Men seemed to like them so very much. This Man now had one in each hand as he pumped away from behind her like an engine – so virile! – and he squeezed hard, his face all scrunched up in concentration, and her flesh bulged around his fingers like some ripe fruit, but with a thicker skin than any fruit. No mere peach could remain intact under such pressure!

We passed beneath the Way of Banners, erected especially to honour Fifteens on Attainment Day. First a series of small pennants banded with the colours of our House, sage green and violet; then our Flag with its representation of the Beautiful Man, Jesumuh, His sword in one hand, unfurled orchid in the other; finally a succession of inspirational passages from the DoppelBook, Romans 5:3–5, each phrase with a banner of its own to represent suffering, endurance, character, and hope:

> We rejoice in our sufferings …
> Knowing that suffering produces endurance …
> And endurance produces character …
> And character produces hope …

And oh, on that morning, we were all filled with such hope!

Then my attention was disturbed by Pearl's elbow in my ribs. One reason we are such close friends is because we were combed from the vessels of neighbouring womanidols on the same day and had been together from cradle to now: Attainment Day. (At last!) We even look alike – everyone says so – and there isn't anything we don't do together. It is funny how close you can be to someone, yet there are parts of them you never ever get, not really. I always try to get on with other people, but Pearl never cares to. She shows her bad feelings when she has them. At other times she gets very enthusiastic about something so that other girlies look at her in a funny way because her face gets flushed, and sometimes her eyes go all gleamy with a feeling she cannot hold in like a proper girlie learns to do. She has trouble getting the balance right, never really was any good at blending into the female body corporate. I look after her. It is a duty of love for the strong to look after the weak. And she tries to look after me as best she can, too, in her way. She never lets any girlie say anything unkind to me. If they did she would hit them, or at least spit. I did explain that this was not helpful, no-one likes a spitting girlie. But she'd do it anyway. Pearl has always been brave and foolish like that, led by her heart. And now we stood together, as we had done always, from earliest childhood through all our Minus-years from Attainment (as we counted them off, looking forward, year by year). The day had come.

'I'm not going to Beseech.' Pearl's eyes were bright and wild behind the mask.

I could not believe what I was hearing. I was glad for the mask that hid my face. But in any case, she rushed on before I had a chance to formulate any kind of answer. 'Mica. I have been thinking very very hard these last days,' she said, her voice low and hard. 'I have a question for you. Why be a womanidol?'

I had no idea why she would say such a thing. Orchids live and grow in beauty and fecundity in secret places. The greatest thing a girlie can *do* is to live that metaphor, to *be* the image, to live and serve and die in humility. 'Pearl, why ask? What else are we for?'

'House mothers. Gardeners. Foot-soldiers. You know this. And, Mica, you have excelled in all girlie-guard exercises since Minus-Ten! There are other things …'

Very few are able to attain the zenith of our ambition, but we are raised to aim for it at least. She knew full well that regardless of any other talents we may have (*inshallaweh*) this sacrifice is at the core of the meaning of our lives! 'There is nothing nobler than to aspire always towards the height of female Perfection, Pearl. You *know* this. Would you waste your life …?'

'Waiting in the dark for a Seed-Bearer to fuck a baby into me?'

I turned away from her then. She would have felt the chill of my withdrawal.

The foul heresy and the evil way she spat it out had rocked me so very badly. To denigrate the Attainment of life in death, flesh made spirit through the Sacred Blood Rites of Perfection to become what is no more nor less than a living goddess from whose loins may spring one of the next generation of Civilisation's leaders, arbiters of Truth, interpreters of the Holy Strictures of blessed Jesumuh! Yet she would spurn it! What had been going on in her mind? And for how long? It was horrible, and false, and arrogant … What sort of Cybelean imp had taken the place of my beloved friend? Where and how had she learned to betray? Even now I can barely bring myself to re-think her words even in the privacy of my own heart.

We of Oblation gathered at the base of the Nursery along with Sacricunt and Dutilove to hear the wisdom of the Son of the Son, the centre of all the circles, Elect of the Elect. He spoke in public on only the most sacred of occasions. And on this day of our Beseeching, he spoke to us Fifteens of Stone House. It was an annual ritual, but this year I was one of that 'us'. As I stood with head reverently bowed I felt all due humility, and yet … there was another feeling, an opposite feeling: pride. And it was clamouring to me to attend to it, to stand erect, to raise my head, to gaze directly into the eyes of the Son. I prayed silently for the strength to bear within my breast this paradox of conjoined opposites, one pure, the other a defilement that would ruin me if I let it.

I looked around at the row of pure and naked would-be vessels standing attentively, faces masked against the vanity of personal identity. I reached out to touch Pearl, but her body was rigid and unyielding. So I withdrew my hand and listened in silence to the Son of the Son, our representative on Earth of the Resolved Twins Jesumuh, only child of GodFather (BBHCM), deliver the prayer, The Way of (wo)Man:

> Forever hide thy face, O (wo)Man! Deflect thine abject gaze from that of your natural master. Be ever ready to serve the husbands whose land you till and protect. As nature's wilderness must be conquered, controlled and cultivated that its fruits may be brought forth to sustain us, so must (wo)Man's wildness be husbanded lest the corybantic frenzies of Cybele

lay waste to all that is clean and good and orderly in the world we have reclaimed from the mire. Indeed, the dumb earth yearns to be harrowed by the bladed till: so beseeches vegetal (wo)Man for the plough of Man. Rejoice, O Votives of the Flesh, Slaves of the Cannon, born of filth. Exalt now in the gift of redemption wherein all extraneous material may be sheared, sawn, sewn and smoothed into the purest form possible for the female repository to attain: the womanidol as holey Vessel of Man, molded by Man into the fulsome form of tamed fecundity, the Perfected incubator of the Sacred Seed of Man, given by the Father and sewn into the compost-rich mulch that is the essence of the female creature ...

And very soon, I knew, the Beseeching itself could begin. I knew, from having watched Beseechings since as far back as my memory extends, that it would be accompanied by music. Thus I was excited – undue, I know, unfitting – but music is rare, and for good reason, as it belongs to one of the categories of profane activities that are *haraamasur*. It was forbidden long ago by the wisest of Elders, first ministers and adminis-trators of the Dual True Faith. Not only is music a means of idling away time that may otherwise be spent in useful work or in prayer to God-Father (BBHCM), it is also likely to encourage disobedience by inciting, as it certainly does, untoward emotion in the listener. If the heart of a Man – but particularly a (wo)Man, so soft and biddable – should respond to that call, who knows where it might lead? However, music constrained and disciplined through repetition and monotone, using only drums and never *ever* woodwind or string, may serve a sacred purpose.

I knew the song we were about to sing. It was an old one from before Liberation, a song of self-sacrifice that anticipated the ideal of female Perfection, yet sung by an unPerfected (wo)Man, tragically common in those days. She had been mistreated in her lifetime in that wretchedly chaotic world, used and abused and finally martyred: forced to inject poison as punishment for her faith in her principles. The Son was intro-ducing the long-awaited climax of our day with the words: 'All rise and join me in song ...'

To the accompaniment of the big, deep bass drum reserved for ritual occasions we Fifteens chanted as one Billie Holyday's Hymn of (wo)Man, 'All of Me', in which she invites a Man to take her body, her arms, her legs – *all* of her – so demonstrating her profound understanding of how a (wo)Man may be fulfilled. My heart ached towards the possibility of self-realisation through sacrifice, oh take me, take *me* ...

And then the moment was here: in an orderly queue we mounted the granite steps, each with a hand on the shoulder of the sister preceding us and clasping that of the one behind so as to remain steady and dignified on our towering heels. We were proudly aware of the hot gaze of the boys and Men below us as their eyes followed the bulge of our calves up to our thighs and between them, our buttocks and waists bound in tightly cinched leather. And so, to the Altar before the western wall of the Orchid Nursery. One by one we prostrated ourselves before the Plea Box. Each girlie then rose and deposited her Plea in the slot – or at least, made that motion. Did Pearl indeed refrain? She made a pass towards the lip of the Plea Box. But was that a slip of paper in her hand, or a flicker of her light fingers to impress the notion of such on those who watched?

 ## PEARL

4.

I have confided a little – only a very little – of the turmoil of my mind to my friend, my sweet fierce Mica, who is so good at all the lessons, all the tasks, all the disciplines learned in the classroom, the Ways and Duties and Prayers, and all those practical skills for cleaning, gardening and military training. I do not tell the worst though. I do not tell her where it has led me. I do not tell her that I have been with a man, a single man, alone, with no witnesses. And we have kissed and we have touched each other in the vilest ways, unobserved by any other, as if we were a separate pair of people cut off from the body corporate. I told him I will go with no other. His face went pale, pale, pale at his Pearl's latest profanation. Then it went all rosy, rosy pink, so I kissed him again. And he held me to him as if I were precious.

The demons who possess me have found a comfortable home here among my cerebral folds and all that cosy cushioning brain-flesh. They have no desire to leave. Why would they? No, they say, very comfy, thank you, Pearl … it is very comfy in your mind, Pearl Stone. Bring me a cool drink scented with rosewater and a cinnamon stick to stir it, bring me a fragrant rollie-smoke in an ivory cigarette holder like the one Colander uses when he speaks to us after the News for Girlies and before the State Anthem of the Dual True Faith. Or actually, my pearly Pearl, why not bring me *his* ivory cigarette holder, *his very one?* You can hide it under your pillow with the pile of stories you stole the week before from the Museum.

Listen to me, say the demons in my head. And I do. I listen and I feel, I feel their bodies inside my own, and where their skin touches mine, bruises form, bruises of corruption that will rot me from the inside out ... *But,* says a big red demon with a face white as light, his finger raised imperiously, *but,* he says, it is from degeneration, from rot and corruption, that new life springs! When I heard that blasphemous twisting of one of our most sacred lessons, I laughed out loud! I felt not fear then, but joy! Oh, I'm a *goner.*

So, this is what is happening to me, to my soft mind. Yes – that is it – my mind is soft and pliant because all my lessons have failed to harden my edges – I feel I have no edges, and sense sometimes that I am slipping, slipping into some bright and dark place between certainties where there are no rules, no Ways, a lawless zone populated by monsters. And I no longer care. *No* – worse – worse and better – *I welcome them!*

How can I stay here, in my home? I am sickened by all that I see. I do not want the future that has been laid out for me. All the attributes that I once attempted to emulate, that I saw as noble, self-abnegating, dutiful, loyal, I now see differently. This new vision is the Devil's work for sure, isn't it? Yes, it is. Brought into my head by his imps and demons. And I welcome the Devil into my mind. I welcome the Devil into my heart.

I will find my chance. I will. Soon I will go. Soon, now ... and Asa will come with me. He will.

Something I know to be true: Asa will say he made his choice freely. That's true as far as it goes, as far as 'choice' goes. But if you start from a place of weakness or desperation, or hopelessness or love, you are *compelled.* There is no choice.

And here is something I learned from the Devil: in your life you can stay safe. If you stay safe you may live longer. But your spirit will shrivel and your heart will become a tight, dry little fist. Hard and wizened. But you can live with a shrivelled spirit, lots do. Or you can take a difficult way and die sooner. Though until that happens your spirit will be pumping full of life and you will die with a heart full and plump, full and plump as my blood-filled cunny-bulb!

Ah, Mica, my little darly. Mica. You looked forward so very very *hard* with all your heart. You looked forward to Attainment, always just around the corner, always just coming up, Four Years to Attainment, Three, Two, One (ah *one* diddly um-pum – pum*pum!*), when we'll all be standing together in our naked rows – chookies for the plucking, birdies for the fucking – and you so proud, but never for yourself, no, for you are so good good *good*. You are so proud of all this 'Perfection' we have.

She knows me so well, does Mica, so she does! She knows me well, my temper and intemperance, how I go all hot and cold and need to run run run … But how can a girlie run when everywhere she goes are the eyes?

The eyes of the mothers and the soldiers and the Men of all the trades, the Bearers and the Ganders and all the *idiot* boys. And the eyes of the rest of you stupid breeders, my sisters.

My sisters: I loved you all through my childhood and I love you still for I am still a part of you – though now *apart*. But if you knew, you with your trimmed quims and your sweet neat ways, if you only knew *how* to wish, wish for the ache, that delicious deep corrupting ache, then you *would!* But you do not know what I know. I know because they cocked it up, cocked up the operation we all have at Minus-Eleven from Attainment, all of us, Oblation, Sacricunt and Dutilove – Stone and Dirt and Bark – bark bark and howl at the moon! Oh my lovely butchers – you missed a bit! You missed a bit!

I have a man and his name is Asa, thank all the ancient gods, whoever you were before the Big Dual One came and knocked you sprawling so that all that's left of you is bits of broken limb and shattered ribs laid about the world. My gods – are you still breathing your dewy humours *somewhere?* Just over the lip of the horizon, some horizon somewhere! *Where?* Where are you now? Gone back to the heart of the sun that birthed you? Or deep in the ocean, in the cold, clean, salty sea, surging a hundred miles from the greasy greedy waters that lap at the shallows of Big River, choked with the filth from our godowns and manufactories?

Asa is mine. He is named after one of those ancient famous kings or kooks that the boys always get named for – and what do we girls get? Bark, dirt, and rocks. Let me pick up one of those rocks and throw it, throw it and hit you right between the eyes, you big old sunny Son

Twin Resolved, Child of GodFather, you big old manny Man from the pictures in the DoppelBook, you with your right foot forward and a flower in your hand.

I took Asa by the hand and I said, 'Let's go down where it's dark dark dark,' and he was scared, *dead* scared. And so was I, but I said, 'We're all goners – don't you know we'll all be dead soon? Death is by your side, your faithful friend and mine, always there to remind you to love what you have, take what you can …' And my boy Asa found my secret. He found it because he looked, looked and felt with his clever fingers, touched me all over, all over, for a long long time, and tasted me, tasted me with his slippery lips, slippery dip, dip and sway, dip and sway, against his lips and his questing tongue so that I cried to him, 'Never stop, I love it, I love you!' and he, he said, 'I love you, Pearl of All, my prize Pearl, my soft gleamer, light beamer in the dark …'

And we met again, and again, and only ever where it was dark dark dark, out of sight from the eyes that pry and stare and look up and down quivering on their stalks, all wavery and damp, then the body follows, drawn along behind, drawn by the stalk. The eyes, the stalks, the stalkers.

In the deep deep dark was where Asa and I lay together, his lean sweet hard body propped up on his hands looking down into my face, and his sly worm of a thing that can gather in on itself, then summon its nerve, become all hard, then slip into the secret place – *yes*, secret, my secret. None of those other horny little rodents got at it, and they won't. Our secret. Oh, I opened up to him and he moved like an angel, bumping up against that curious part of me, that little cunny-bulby thing that was so soft and now so tight and round and hard, bumping up against his sweet cock, so we moved in unison … and then, evil jez that I am – what did I do? I made like the original sinner, like the Hag from the stories, the foul harpy in her swampy hovel with her suppurating sores and her fiery loins and her burden of guilt! I did, I did! I rolled him over and climbed onto his body, his eyes widened with the shock and delight – yes, *delight!* He's not normal, no, he *isn't!* He's a Man among Men, anyone else'd be screaming for the guards, but not Asa. Asa was screaming for pleasure, only silently, and his eyes were on mine, and he held onto me like I was his only prayer, but silent we were, we were silent … moving together, a soundless storm, a noiseless sea … and here comes another silent breaker, and another …

 MICA

5.

A week passed.

I was not summoned to the audience with the Brother Ministers, though I know Anapaite had been. And Opal. Opal!

My Plea had not been accepted. I had not been chosen. How I wept when my name was not called! I supposed MaOblat had informed on me, told Tomander from Instruction & Destruction that I was yet to bleed regularly, or worse – told some other Propergander that I had been found wanting in one or more of the virtues of CHOM: Compliance, Humility, Obedience, Modesty. And I have tried so hard. Tried, and failed, imPerfect and still-fallen. Oh, what is wrong with me? Why *Opal* and not me?

I could – and can – only comfort myself with the knowledge that there will be other Beseechings. I am young yet.

And Pearl was gone. She said she would not Beseech, and if she had not, then how could she have been chosen for a vessel? Yet nobody has seen her since.

More weeks passed and no word. I could not rest and my eyes grew pouchy, the skin around them blue; I could not perform my duties well, so distracted was I with wondering and fearing. I needed to know for sure. So that is how I came to plan and then to commit this criminal transgression.

And now the last of the day's light filters through the rain and the thick glass of the dome over the Orchid Nursery, its grace unequalled by any other of the marvellous works of Man. The soft pink falls upon me from above: the knowing touch of my GodFather – Blessed Be His Cock-and-Muscle, alive-alive-oh-oh ever amen – caresses the skin of my hand, my face, my throat.

The walls of compacted earth reach to just above my head. They are the colour of the underside of very mature mushrooms, not quite brown for there is the faintest hint of now perished pink, and it is sweaty to the touch. To my right is another heavy door, behind which I assume lie the inseminated vessels of the gravidly successful womanidols.

The wall opposite me, about fifty paces from the entry, is broken into a series of curtained recesses. This area is the one I seek. I know each recess contains a sacred object upon a pedestal: fecund but as yet unimpregnated womanidols who share the Sacrament of Creation with those Men chosen to bestow upon them the Seed-Bearing Elixir of Life. Womanidols, who live out their allotted time in perpetual and glorious sacrifice. O, paragons of grace! Exemplars of femininity!

But inexplicably, here in this sacred citadel, I feel only dread. I know this feeling is heretical. I calm my breathing and tell myself not to be weak. But the chamber is filled with that terrible smell of rot and waste, so incompatible with its holy purpose!

I gather my straying sensations and thoughts and bid them hold their peace. I can hear the susurration of breath from behind the curtain, and the faint and intermittent beeping of the electronic filters and feeders, and the sound of my own, disobedient, unhallowed heartbeat.

I approach the cord that dangles at the edge of the row of niches and draw it across, slowly. Slowly, the heavy curtain pulls away from the secret place, and with the movement of the heavy fabric comes a dense exhalation of fetid air; the shit stink is concentrated and complicated with the smell of disinfectant, of sweet-scented ester and yeast. One by one the womanidols are exposed.

Each is encased in a glass container of fine Craftsmanship shaped like an hourglass. The Vessels themselves are clad in tight garments of silk, a different hue for each: apricot, violet, rose, salmon-flesh, scarlet ... Behind the masks that cover the upper part of their faces, I know their eyes are closed in silent prayer ongoing, for although the Properganders rule over us in the light, no order is possible without this complement of concentrated prayer below, in the dark earth, seedbed of creation.

I remember the orchid excursion we girlies of Oblation had been taken on when we were only Minus-Nine from Attainment, for Grade 3 Styles of Reproduction. Of course we'd been gardening since we were Minus-Ten, and so knew about pollination and sexual reproduction, as demonstrated by flowers, aided by the agency of gardeners with their long, feathered, pollen-daubed sticks; we knew about the potential for Perfectibility within the constraints set by flawed nature. But this time we'd hiked much further afield to the nearer edges of Yellow Swamp which infiltrates Stone Plain at its middle, by BigAmass. 'From the top of this tor,' said MaOblat, 'you can see far, almost as far as Hagovel, on a clear day.' We shivered in thrilled horror at the idea of Hagovel where the cursed one lives out her days in miserable solitude. The House Mothers don't keep the story of the Hag secret. She is an ugly truth for us to know about, useful to us as a moral lesson, an example of what can happen to disobedient, sexually profligate girlies and (wo)Men. Everyone knows her story.

But we had a reason to be there: to find a perfect orchid, to witness first-hand that perfectibility is possible even in the mire. Indeed, in nature, all life, fair or ill, is spawned from corruption. We girlies were old enough to understand this – and also to realise that nature can be corrected. If nature is allowed to burgeon, untrammelled prodigies may be created from the filth, but if we take control of her the exemplary becomes the norm, not the freak.

I was uneasy in that place with its oozes and tricklings and fishy stinks, its predatorial phantoms and shades who had been spawned in the moist, dark places by the matings of Lilith and her manifold demons. But we were in the care of MaOblat and two other Mothers from Dirt and Bark Houses; also a small posse of young foot-soldiers accompanied us so we felt almost safe from the influence of the fell phantoms with their reaching fingers and lidless, gobbling eyes and messy, noisome, un-pruned cockslots.

It was a trip broken by a night in tents that we erected to protect ourselves from the rain, the night-eyes, and evil humours, so when the twilight came we stopped to unload our packs. As we did I saw, all around, the air seeming to congeal, and small greenish lights like the campfires of imps began to be visible all around us. I hoped and prayed that we had nothing to fear, that it was just marsh gas and not the traps of feys. All night I lay awake listening to the soft rain pattering against the oiled skin of the tent, taking comfort in the knowledge that GodFather (BBHCM) smiled on us, on our task. Ah, but it was a beautiful ideal: the search for the rarest of orchids.

On the second day, in the bank of a rank rivulet of brownish tannin-stained water we found a fine bloom whose form echoed – as MaOblat had earlier described it – a set of labia plump and ready. 'This', said our Mother, 'is the form to which we all aspire, solitary and pure, unencumbered by superfluous foliage or limbs. Just a pure blossom on a single stem, awaiting the attentions of the wasp with his proboscis.' She looked around the ring of expectant faces. Pearl reached towards a fragile petal.

'You may not touch!' snapped MaOblat, slapping her hand away. Then, more gently, 'It is not for us to touch, to act, to do. Later, when you are of age, you may *be* touched. If you are chosen to serve.' A small breeze stirred the orchid so that it seemed to bob and dip in agreement with the Mother.

Now, here, deep beneath the corp-yard of our Perfect State, the orchid-like womanidol vessels are still. Where the glass containers curve inwards, so do the torsos of the womanidols. The silken corsets are smooth over their waists and edged with flounces like vestigial ball-gowns to remind the Men of the Olden Days of moral pollution before the Liberation and Separation of Our Perfect State from the Agnostics, long may they burn. Above and below these broad bands their breasts and buttocks blossom out from the centre, unhampered by limbs, which are superfluous to (wo)Man's ultimate purpose. The simplicity of the Perfected forms allows no distraction from their function.

The front of each plinth is concave so that the Seed-Bearers can easily press up against the glass containers of the womanidols and slip their cocks up and into the slots below. The womanidols' mouths, the only visible part of their shrouded faces, are densely tattooed in shades of blush, flush and fuschia, lips plumply swollen from the ministrations of the needle and childishly vulnerable beneath the covered eyes – covered for in darkness the mind readily turns inwards in ongoing vegetative meditation and prayer, so concentrated that the earth hums with its energy, and redemption is only a breath away.

I approach the glass-encased forms. I move slowly along, looking for my Pearl. I pray that she is here, a living shrine and testimony to Truth and Beauty of the Perfect sacrifice. For if she is not, then she has truly failed as a (wo)Man, is a traitor to Perfection and when she is found … but I could not think on that now. I must examine each womanidol with great care. But I cannot be absolutely certain, with the veils so dense, and the mouths so lovely, like ripe sugar-plums, yet so strange. The places where the extraneous arms and legs had once been are concealed beneath soft, silky cloth. I move a little closer until, like Pearl had tried that day, I could have reached out a hand and touched the glass that separated me from a pale womanidol in a frock of pearlescent rose. Could this be her? The stem of her throat rises above the burgeoning decolletage with particular grace. I see the slightly darker line at the top of the throat where the vocal chords have been severed. This womanidol is but newly Perfected, the wounds still edged in red. Oh Pearl, is that my darly girlie? Now in silence serving …

The flower (wo)Man now opens her mouth a fraction, as if to whisper … then she opens it wider, and I am looking into a black gash from which all the teeth have been pulled, leaving nothing but discoloured gums. From the throat there issues a guttural hiss. And now, all along the line of womanidols the sound spreads, each toothless hole joining in until the room resonates with the unholy sibilance of this mutilated choir, tiers of hothouse orchids silently screaming.

 ## PEARL

6.

Heh. Comic. How things turn out. It was just last week, after much wishing and loving and planning, that I'd sorted out what to do. I *knew* what I would do. I was certain. Good joke, that, and quite large. Cosmic.

One idiot girlie's certainty in the face of absolute crushing fact of the world as it is. Oh, you're sure of this are you? says the world that is shaped like a wall of water as big as anything ever was, as big as all space and time. Well, take *this!* And down crashes the wall. And what's left of the small person with the loving and the hoping and the certain plan? Nothing. Not a splinter of bone, not a shred of flesh. Not the whisper of a notion of shredness. All washed away and nothing left but a lovely clean beach.

Only last week the guileless, hopeful Pearl, incubating her silly certainty and her careful plan, lay by the side of her lover. See her as she pushes back a damp lock from his eye with its pupil so large and black you can hardly see the blue. We've finished fucking and lie a muddled bundle of humanity corded together like mangrove roots under the thin skin of swampy water that is our sour-sweet sweat. I say, 'Look at this map I found – no, never mind *where* just now, tell you later – we'll follow the way that leads to the edge of the treeline, on the edge of the world, edge of Civilisation. A crossroad, a forest, all the way to Hagovel where

Big River embraces the swamplands, rich in faeries, feys, and lil'im sprites. And from there I know it is not so far to the ocean, the clean, wide sea that goes on forever ...'

A little stray slip of moon gets in to where we lie and I see his eyes are alive with the hope and the terror, as must mine be also. I say, 'Anyone who is hated as much as the Hag has got to be our friend. Why else is everyone so frightened even by the thought of her? Got to be more to it. We'll find out what it is.'

By the look on Asa's face, which is now quite white, my audacity can blanch a Man's soul. I wonder what it feels like to have one of those, a soul, blanchable or otherwise? Like this? Like I feel? Oh, *haraamasur* ...

My infidelity has opened a chasm at my feet between what I always knew and what I have yet to discover. Between what was and what may be. I am terrified at my insolence and what it has done. Anything can happen now I have broken with the Lore, broken it in half and crushed it beneath my feet, and now I creep in my mind to the edge of the abyss and I peer over the lip at the end of the world, at the end of belief, and I see the bright and dark things within, flashes of possibility ...

And then what happens?

On the night of the Day of Attainment – or not – MaOblat came to me. I was working alone in the garden where I'd been sent – a mild and pleasant punishment for some pettiness, my slapping of a dullard for some irritating inanity, as is usual – to work late under the arc of light from the watchtower. I was here a lot, I liked my 'Solitary'. Alone amongst the rows of lettuce, turnip, silverbeet, their broad, dark leaves so thick and fleshy, lurid in the watch-light, I plucked the weeds that grew there, sly little stranglers. Then I saw her two feet in their brown felt slippers, all bulgy with aug-sockets for her useful appliances, her gizmos for dusting and brushing, for grabbing and grasping.

'Pearl,' she said in her crimple-crumpled little voice, her face bright and shiny as a septic carbuncle. At first I thought she'd reprimand me for having my dressless rucked up around my waist and my knees all muddy, but no ... Instead, she smiled like one of those antediluvian fishes with bodies of leather and three rows of teeth. 'Pearl,' she said, her weak-tea eyes all wet in their dusty pouches, 'You have been Chosen for Perfection. You have been graced.'

I did not ask for this!

MICA

7.

Amid the hissing cries I let myself sink to the floor, squeezing my eyes shut and clamping my hands over my ears against the obscene sounds. Yes, they are horrible to me, so easily unravelled are the weak fibres of my feeble-female moral being. Then, after a moment or an hour of silent prayer, I open my faithless eyes and look upon them again, the woman-idol vessels. Perhaps I may receive the truth of what they are, perhaps I will be redeemed by Truth? But GodFather (BBHCM) does not speak. No revelation through dream or vision is afforded me for I am undeserving and must be tested further. I understand this.

With a dip of the scale, beauty made in equal parts of strangeness and formal utility shifts from mystery to monstrosity. Suffering flesh is all I can see, no more and no less. The vision of symmetrical order that can only be achieved in (wo)Man and nature herself when her untamed form is pruned back to reflect pure function, the ideal to which I always aspired, is ruined. And I feel that ruination in the deepest part of me. If (wo)Men had souls – see, even if it makes me tremble, I can utter even the worst blasphemies, thoughts I would never previously have considered giving form – then that is where I would be feeling it, in my soul. In that moment my world is thrown off kilter, as if the planet itself has fallen out of its orbit around the sun, is dislocated among the dead stars. My blood roils in my brain as I crouch amid the wreckage of a dream.

I am weak and impure and although I *know* that ultimate spiritual fulfilment is achieved only through sacrifice, in that moment I cannot *feel* the truth of it. I am a poor, shallow thing, fit only for the meanest and foulest duties in the Spare Parts Manufactory, a dudbub minder or shop-floor sluicer.

But *is* that her in the rose-coloured gown? I make myself look once more.

'Pearl?' I venture.

But the veiled face is still now, the swollen lips closed over the empty mouth. Silent.

I make my way back through the corridor to the meeting house and let myself out into the corp-yard, no plan formulated, no way yet even to think. Somehow day has become evening. The sky is the deepest indigo it can be before turning black. Lightning forks among the heavy clouds banked at the edges of Civilisation, at the end of the farthest plain. I smell metal, and blood sausage frying. The shaved grass of the corp-yard is deep green, highlighted in gold where the floodlights touch it. The foot-soldiers are at their evening Defence Drill. The Martinette yelps a command and the armoured troops stop in perfect unison, the folds of their brief military skirtles subsiding into disciplined folds at mid-thigh. Then, efficiently as clockwork mannequins, each (wo)Man clicks her left shoulder-aug into the right one of her neighbour. I see that this is a formal drill tonight. They have painted their faces in regulation bands of black and white from the forehead down to where the upper body armour meets the throat. Another yelp in a slightly lower key and they click the opposite shoulder-augs into position. Now they form a perfectly impregnable barrier of metal and bone and hard flesh. A beautiful thing.

What Pearl said is true. I do have a talent for this life. It suits me. All of it: the clarity of intent, the elegant precision, the focus and nobility of purpose. Yet it could be that I will never again participate in this humble but essential aspect of the art of war. I let myself linger just a little longer to watch the lines of armed Ecumen now form ranks behind those of the (wo)Men. A further command from the Martinette and the (wo)Men at each end of each line form a circle around the Ecumen, protectors of Perfect State. I watch as the Men now lay the muzzles of their guns upon the steel shoulder-bridge formed by the female foot-soldiers, their living palisade. I do not wait to watch the second round, do not wait to listen to the prayers that will follow.

I walk past the reading room where, years ago, inspired by the images printed on the covers of books, I had sought and eventually won the privilege of learning more of that arcane art. Naturally girlies don't need very sophisticated reading skills, for we learn our lessons by rote as dictated. We accrue our vocabulary and grammar and all refinements of our spoken manners and conversation through repetitions of the elegant rhythms and poetic constructions in the Tenets of the Ways of (wo)Man and, of course, the Doppelbook. Our girlish mixture of modern post-Liberation phrasing and gracious archaisms tends to please Men – especially the Properganders and Scholars – when they desire to hear our voices. Nevertheless, I managed to get a special dispensation from Jimander, who was in charge of Instruction for Girlies. He granted it only when I had agreed to do an extra unit of Contemplation on the Responsibilities of the Vessel on Tuesday to Saturday evenings. Later, I would take my hard-earned learning and, in intimate collusion beneath the covers of my bed, would in turn impart to Pearl what I had learned … ah, how long ago that now seems!

I continue on past the telly-room where the Stone girlies of Oblation, the Dirt girlies of Sacricunt, and the Bark girlies of Dutilove will now be standing to listen to the Son of the Son delivering his evening telecast of the State Anthem of the Dual True Faith before sitting down to watch the News for Girlies. And on to the empty cunnydorm. I go to Pearl's bed and lie down there, my face in my friend's pillow. I inhale deeply, but the linen has been freshly laundered and there is no scent of her.

I lean over to my side of the table and pick up my rare book, its pages brittle and yellow with age. It has been a very long time since I have looked through it. Pearl and I had pored over it together many times, marvelling at the bravery and prowess of the noble Man whose chronicle it was, for it is full of pictures of a Hero with a spiderweb painted on his suit. (There is only a little bit of text and mostly pictures, so we were pretty sure we could handle the stress of intellectual effort. Though a female mind might tremble at the scale of the task – which was further complicated as some sections had been blacked out, and in some cases whole pages excised – still we did it! And the rewards for our efforts were boundless!) In each frame the spider Man does something dauntless. We had often mused about him. Who was he? How long ago had he lived? How much was fantasy? The height of the buildings, or the porno clothes of (wo)Men like those in the displays of pre-Liberation artifacts in the Museum?

Here I sit once more, alone this time, allowing my mind to wander along familiar tracks for the comfort that is in it, when I notice something very odd. Tucked into the middle of the book is a new, unfamiliar piece of paper. On one side is part of a story of great heroism, like the ones in the book of the spider Man, but with girlies instead! Like Pearl and me! The bravest one is named 'Tank Girl', and she is dressed in huge boots and very tight garments that expose her thighs but render her cockslot nigh-on impregnable! *Porno!*

The author of this text is clearly unschooled in the ways and roles of Man and (wo)Man, for it is not only pornographic but a most foully heretical tract – may GodFather (BBHCM) forgive me for reading it to the end! And worse – wishing for more!

I turn the page though I know it is a sin. But another page, deeply creased, has been pasted onto the original text. In one corner of this overlaying sheet is drawn the face of a person with a mask over its nose and eyes, a fat pink tongue sticking out of the slit of a mouth, and on the head a ridiculous hat with devil horns on it, brightly coloured in red and green and blue. Impossible to tell the sex of this grotesque thing, this leering, jeering gargoyle. Profane, *haraamasur*.

8.

'Fools Rule OK.'

These words are written below the ugly face. Whatever that means. What is this creature? An animal thing or a grown dudbub? A mutant Man or a misspelling?

Below this incomprehensible legend is another image drawn by an amateurish hand. It shows the wall that surrounds Perfect State and the narrow path that wends its way into Stone Plain towards BigAmass, that great pile of licheny rocks by the curved finger of Yellow Swamp from which one may see, if the sky is clear and cloudless, the tilt of the roof of Hagovel, under which *she* grovels in a stew of her own filth, or wallows in nearby muddy streamlets to salve her lust-scorched hungry loins. We have no maps that extend further than BigAmass for we have no need of them. Yet this one shows several more landmarks dotted throughout the desert of sickly grass and into the main body of the swamp. I note Tor Man, longer and narrower than BigAmass; then Black Defile that dips down, down into Longully, then up onto higher ground and a dotted line marked as Last Beat. There are other signs leading towards the green line of forest – One Tree, Womanbane and a few more – thence to the extreme edge of Perfect State and onwards, into Unrule, clinging to the land's end, beyond which is only the terrible sea. Comprehensive instructions, but no key telling exactly how far it is – though I could guess at roughly two days walking, possibly less, judging by the distance from BigAmass.

But inevitably, my eye is drawn to that dire crossroad, clearly marked at the edge of Civilisation, whither that foul enchantress had been banished: Hagovel. Once one of us, the Hag now lives in a muddy hovel that half-melts when the winter rain comes, so she is always caked in filth and thus suffers from a mortifying skin disease; her armpits and groin are paved in ulcerated sores, the skin of her face and arms is as warty as a toad's, and like a toad she lays in stagnant streams her strings of tadpoles conceived in rut with any number of the semi-corporeal ghouls whose reeking gelatinous bodies she presses up against in the heat of her loathsome lust. Her broods of halflings grow there and when they are mature, populate the forest; their groaning cries are sometimes carried to us if the wind is right. I have heard them and pitied them, for they are vengeful and hate-filled and half-starved. But they are known to catch and dismember anyone unfortunate enough to lose their way beyond the city walls. They are particularly fond of sucking the soft organs from their cavities of flesh and gristle while their victims still breathe, so strong is their craving for fresh meat. The Hag lives alone with her demons and this punishment is adequate.

Everyone knows she lives at the crossroad. One path goes from Perfect State through Stone Plain, all jaggy granite and tall thin grasses hiding scorpions, trapdoor spiders and the treacherous holes of small burrowing things with teeth white and sharp as ice-chips, then further into Yellow Swamp and on into the forest. The other path skirts its edges and forms the boundary between Civilisation and Unrule.

The route is clear. By His Cock-and-Muscle, alive-alive-oh, even to think of the Hag, Satan's emissary, stirs my gut to a stew, would make me tremble were I that kind of girlie. But though I do not quake I do admit that the idea of her chills me, oh yes it does.

Two simple facts: here is a map; Pearl has not been seen for weeks.

So she was not the rose vessel?

This is her map and she has followed it, though it shows the way to the forest with its savages and monsters, beyond which is the blank space whose far side is Unrule where Agnostic Rogues live and breed like human tumours feeding on the world's flesh.

Who provided her with these directions, I could not know, nor why. But – and here is the heart of the strangeness that my experience in the Nursery has wrought in me – I now know what I will do. It is written: 'The ways to ensoulment are various.' I must follow this strange way.

Nothing else is possible for me now, for when I had crouched fainting in the Orchid Nursery I had felt a deep spiritual tremor, portending perhaps a loss of faith. I cannot bear this. To have all that I believe in and live for, my entire life, sullied and spoiled? The nobility of the aspiration to Perfection all stained and smeared by traces of doubt, the narrow edge of the wedge of apostasy? I feel the bonds that hold me to the life I know unravelling around me, as if my life were nothing more than an old garment that has outlived its utility. No! I will rewind the threads and mend the garment if I can, and to do this I will set out on my own in search of Pearl. This will be the first step towards the redemption of my home, my faith, my reason to live. Then I will return with Pearl to Perfect State, *our* perfect state, the birthright hard won by Men so many years ago. Though the punishment for disobedience will be severe. But I put this from my mind.

Pearl is my friend, and so it is my duty to do what I can to save her as well as myself, even if that means saving her *from* herself. And there is something else still, yet another reason, simple and definitive: I need her. My friend who has patently *not* taken the map with her – who has left it behind for no credible purpose unless it was for me to find. She would have known not to speak to me of such a plan, for she knows me well. It would have caused me a fatal torment of divided loyalties. I am glad she did not put me to such a test, for what would I have done? Betrayed my friend – or betrayed my home and all the people in it who have raised me and taught me and *trusted* me to be what I am meant to be?

As I sit on her bed I am visited by a clear vision of her face lost in concentration as she commits to memory each turn of the path. I re-fold the map along its creases, and as I do, I am surprised to see that it forms a paper aeroplane, such as we used to make to play games with when we were little. This makes me smile. Pearl used to like this game.

There is no reason to wait. There is nobody for me to speak to, for what would I say? Only this: I am abandoning you, Mother Oblation, Stone sisters, soldiers and Men, to seek my beloved traitor. I will take nothing with me but the map, this notebook in which, as well as my day-to-day doings, I have recorded so much sage advice carefully copied down in recent lessons, and my little knife that once belonged to my friend. Nothing more, for what am I owed? The worst punishment should be reserved for me. I could never explain the complexities of my rationale to the Properganders. They would see – and rightly too – disobedience and fatal feminine weakness. If not burned for heresy I will likely receive a flaying at least, or a starfish splaying atop the Orchid

Nursery with my face exposed to all and my body open to any violation or insult. But better this than excommunication and no chance to Beseech on my next birthday or any of those to follow. Better any of these than enduring a long life without the comfort of True Belief. Yes, I must go, for this way lies redemption. I will kill what I can catch. I will drink from unhallowed streams.

I close the door behind me. There is a careforcer sweeping the corridor, her form hunched as she forces the brush into the corner, scouring for dust. Very thorough. Her lips have been only recently grafted together, so I do not like to look on her. But I feel her concentrated gaze on me, willing me to meet her eyes. Why such impertinence? I see it is Xeniicut227. I dislike that *way* she has, a kind of discreet knowingness. So superior. Though not uncommon among some of the more recently inducted xeniicuts, it's true. But what could a careforcer know? And neither she nor anyone else can have any idea of what I intend to do. Nevertheless, before approaching the outer door I wait until she has passed, breathily whistling through the feeding hole in her suture.

9.

The cunnydorms are now behind me. The corp-yard is quiet. I walk across it and do not pause at the gate whose inscription I know so well: SUBMISSION IS FREEDOM. Beyond are the Scholars' and Seed-Bearers' Rooms, built of purple-brown brick and white mortar. I move with great stealth, for although they should now be in their dining room on the far side of their complex they are Men, so naturally they are free to go where they please at any time. Yet I manage to pass by without incident. Then I come to the workrooms of the Craftsmen who make lovely objects of utility from glass and bone, metal and wood, or from the strong yellow ivory of the great tusked hammerheads that swim up from the Far Greasy Sea against Big River's current to feed on the waste from Spare Parts Manufactory where the dudbubs live for a short while.

After a little longer I reach the outer rings of our Perfect State, comprised of gardeners' and foot-soldiers' quarters, and make my way through the vegetable gardens that we are slowly extending further and further. In the distance I see the starlit gleam of Big River Harbour, full of container terminals and traffic from the other States, as it loops below on its way from Snow Mountain to the Sea. I follow the river a little further and soon pass beneath the darkened windows of Spare Parts. I hear the hum of the systems that sustain them, the malformed failures of gravity, and the cripsanretards. I hear an occasional small voice, not quite a cry … Very little sound penetrates, and none ever reaches beyond the nearer curve of Big River where stand the elegant Ecumenical Houses and Properganders' Mansions within their bastions of stone and their great Pine Circle.

And now Stone Plain stretches out before me, as much granite as grass. It is a rare dry night. I feel an easing of the heart as I walk through this open space along the chalky path with nothing between me and eternity but the wide sky with its masses of cloud and the high-riding moon emerging from time to time like a thin smile. That was Pearl's fancy – giving the moon moods and humours. It had become a sort of game for us. 'What is her mood today?' she – or I – would ask the other. And I – or she – might reply, 'She feigns shame tonight, see the tip of her cowl between her teeth, playing for time, a dangerous game …' or 'She needs you now, and her desire is urgent. See how round and ruddy is her blood-suffused plumpness this red dawn,' or 'She is a mean stone-faced witchy-moon tonight, just asking for trouble …'

I walk many miles and all through the night along the pale chalk line that weaves its way among stones and low wiry shrubs, and as the sun stain seeps into the worn hills to the east and the darkness ebbs to grey, I find I am very thirsty. I notice also that my feet hurt me where the shoe-leather has rubbed. There is no cover, no way to protect myself from the Ecumen or foot-soldiers who might already have been dispatched to pursue me, no relief from the elements. Still, I must rest awhile. I draw my cowl over my head and lie down.

But my mind is teeming and I do not sleep for some hours. Still, I use those hours well. I review my actions of the last day, meditating on what I have done, what I have seen, and what it might mean. Now, revisiting my feelings of horror in the Orchid Nursery, I see that I have reacted as if fully possessed by the fleshly fallacy, incapable of seeing beyond the surface of things. Thus limited I could only experience a purely visceral reaction. For without the light of reason guided by faith and prayer, how can one see truly? And the truth of what I saw was this: a set of lovely streamlined propagation machines, living (wo)Men whose whole being is directed towards one pure and precious goal. That of service to the Truth embedded in the ideals of Perfect State.

Time passes and eventually I feel myself drifting, buoyed up on a current of images, most soothing and harmonious, of fields of clean, dry grasses, of silken garments, of unfurling flowers, of Pearl's face. I will find her and bring her home. I will be forgiven in time, in time, and if the Brother Ministers will still allow it I will Beseech again, next year ... and surely they will, when I bring back my prize Pearl who will be recovered from her madness, will be glad that I found her, will walk with me in all willingness relieved and grateful that I have saved her. On our return we will confess and suffer whatever punishment is meted out, for it will be fair, and good, and redemptive ... and yes, we will both Beseech. Next year, next year...

I awake in a clammy sweat. My lips are parched. I have slept through the dewfall and now there is not even that moisture to refresh me. The sun is stewing away in the soupy cauldron of the sky, the low clouds promise yet withhold rain. But it is slightly more possible to walk than to rest. I gather some of the coarse grass that grows between the stones and layer them in a crosswise thatch-pattern between the tongue of each shoe and my blistered feet. This remedy lasts about five minutes before I am again limping badly and now hunger, as well as thirst, comes to torment me. I have eaten nothing since yesterday morning. The physical discomfort is hard to endure, but the knowledge of my own stupidity in going off without any preparation at all makes me realise once more what a foolish, dull scrap of a thing I am. Truly, I am a waste of air. Yet since I still breathe I must find a way to sustain myself for such is the animal nature of all living creatures, however undeserving.

> By the grace of GodFather,
> May the shadow of his
> Sceptred Eye forever
> Darken the false glister
> That is not gold,
> But tinsel.
> Tinsel tawdries that clutter
> The margins of the right path
> Drawing us towards the offer
> Of guileful glamour
> And temporal temptations.
> Lead us not
> Now or ever
> Alive-alive-oh, amen.

A small creature darts out, startled by my footfall. Anticipating his direction I throw myself bodily forward – and yes, my judgement is true for I feel the small, warm body crushed beneath me.

I sit up carefully and observe that it is a stone rodent, the kind with tall ears and thighs like pistons. Quickly I wring the last of the life out of him, and his head slumps heavily from his broken neck. I cut into the skin with Pearl's knife and with a strong tug I pull the whole furry sheath back to expose the pink flesh, all shiny, and the striations of white fat; I slit his belly open, pulling out the organs and taking care not to tear the intestines with their burden of filth.

I consider taking the time to build a fire to cook him here and now, but I do not have the patience to endure further rumblings in my gut while I painstakingly coax fire from stone and tinder. Thus, I eat the little heart for the modest measure of valour that is in it, and the liver for its rich blood. I feel immediately stronger, but now, with the taste of iron and salt in my mouth, my thirst is unbearable. But no – not so – for I *must* bear it. I wrap the remains of the small corpse for later in a strip of fabric torn from my dressless, and continue to walk in the direction I hope will eventually lead me to Hagovel, the destination outlined in the map beneath the Standard of the Fool.

I stop to rest a couple of hours later and cook my small meal. I allow myself time for a brief nap, awaking in the evening with my thirst now a mortal agony. The cruel moon glares down with baleful malice, and I curse her, the sow-faced Lili, monster daughter of Lilith, first (wo)Man and original criminal for whose sinful demonstration of waywardness all girlies must now suffer grief and woe, now and forever, alive-alive-oh amen. Though my feet bleed, I continue on my way in the cool of the night until, towards dawn, with the tired moonlight seeping through the dirty scrambled-egg clouds, my energy begins to wane. My head is light, my feet heavy. I stumble a little over stones and bracken and scrub. A soft, penetrating rain begins to fall, chilling my skin, pasting my hair across my face. I raise my face and open my mouth to the delicious moisture. But once my thirst is quenched, new trials await me.

The landscape has become ill-defined, foully female in its featureless-ness, grey rain blurring into grey pre-dawn light, marsh gas stinking all sulfurous and greenish and wavering in the still air and yes, I am fearful of these lights now that I am alone. How will I be able to tell the difference between a marsh-light and a fey-light? How will I know if some stealthy stalker, an emissary of the Hag, is mere inches from me, ready to drain the life from me that she might live on, a warped semblance of (wo)Mankind? Keep your head low, I tell myself. The way leads ever downwards now, and the land is less stony; there are trees now, thin, gaunt, writhy in the unreliable light refracted by rain, rain, rain; they are anchored by twisted roots into black mud, and I am now walking by the banks of a sluggish river pocked with the fat drops of the slow, insistent rain. I recognise this country. It is a dangerous place filled with fey humours, certainly riddled with the spores of Lilith. It is the place we came to before, years back, with MaOblat on that excursion to where the orchids grow, where Pearl reached out her hand to touch ... My shoes are waterlogged and my garments stick to my body like a second, ill-fitting skin, freezing me to the marrow of my bones. I stumble on, teeth chattering in my skull, and after a time I feel as if I too am losing definition, becoming blurred and vague in body and in mind both. This is surely the effect of the evil presences as yet invisible, and I pray hard that they will remain so. Indeed, the effort of traversing this place alone, without the support of the sorority, is wearing me down, so that by daybreak I feel as if I might dissolve completely and become another part of this landscape. The ground underfoot is swampy, spongy, and I too am damp and soft. I am the swamp. I've got frogs. And crocodiles. The sky reflected in my water is yellow as sulfur.

As I walk, to comfort myself I recite the Fourth Tenet from the Way of (wo)Man: 'Gonna Take up My Burden, Far From the Riverside'.

> though I walk through damp val-leys
> oo-zing with lilith spores
> ten-thousand filthy whores
> who spurn the sacred cause
> gonna think on
> the Scep-tre
> the Rod pro-tect-eth me.
>
> gonna take up the bur-den
> far from the riverside
> far from the salt-steeped tide
> where fey lil'im reside.
>
> gonna cut out my e-go
> far from the ri-ver-side
> gonna take up the bur-den

far from the riverside
far from unhallow'd sites
all rank and bloody tides.

gonna serve with decor-um
with all so-ro-ri-ty
gonna hold up the Scep-tre
prayerful humility
pious docility
uphold virility
gonna o-pen my bo-dy
to all Frat-ern-ity.

gonna lay down my e-go
beneath the holy Son
draw in his sacred cum
as servant of the Son
gonna hold to
the Scep-tre
in exalt-a-tion.

for I'm but a ves-sel
to hold the holy Seeds
to pleasure all his needs
down on my hands and knees
gonna draw
on that Sceptre
submission doth make free.

At the end of this long day I find myself by a broad and deep and very ancient crater filled with the blackened and rotten remnants from before the Liberation, when the founders of our Perfect State defeated the last of the Agnostics, impenitent transgressors as sinful as those of ancient Sodorra. Stories are still told of the Great Muster, when the artifacts of dissolution were collected from the houses of the butchered enemy and interred in such landfills. All night long our Men had overseen the collection of products of their grandiose technology, their pictures, books and clothing. And now, did I need any evidence of our righteousness and the corruption of those who populate the Lands of Unrule beyond the forest, I have only to gaze into the pit.

It is possible to identify charred remains of compacted pages of their idolatrous texts, twisted metal and melted plastic shells of their vain-glorious devices of entertainment and communication and information. Then the blasphemous thought occurs to me that, if indeed a (wo)Man could earn a soul, *inshallaweh*, that part of me would suffer for the demonstration of crude curiosity I now feel compelled to enact. Crouching at the lip of the pit I peer in to see what I can see and to take what I may take: I want some small memento. I tell myself it will be to remind me of the sins of our past. So that I might not be tempted to err now that I have placed myself out of reach of the help of the Fathers of Men and in the near occasion of foulest sin and degradation. But another part of me knows well that this is not so. It is pure acquisitiveness. I want a keepsake. Just a small thing. I spot a bit of fabric, just a small loop of stretchy material that is a hot shade of pink. It is the colour that attracts me. We do not have pink to wear. *Haraamasur*, I know. Still, I slip it over my wrist and push it up under the sleeve of my dressless, then continue on into the glare of the low sun and into this, my third night alone in the wilderness. I walk all through the night, for what reason to stop? I find no place of shelter to protect me from the cold and rain.

Close to dawn the rain eases away almost entirely, and the grisly moonlight labours once more through her cowl of cloud. Now, clear of the bog at last, I note the land is again capable of supporting flora greater than rushes and swamp grass. Indeed, here are many greeny-grey bushes. It is clear that this was once a garden, though it is now overgrown. When I kneel to investigate I find a profusion of small beans, pale yellow in colour. Surely there can be no harm in eating from such shrubs, since they seem to have been cultivated by human hand. I collect several handfuls of the beans, which are bitter and very hard, but I force myself to chew as I walk on into the morning. And now, as the mists clear, I see what kind of a place I have stumbled into.

As far as I can see stretches a field whose monotony is broken at regular intervals by grave markers, each rough-cut from white granite in the shape of the holy phallus. Some are whole, many are damaged, intentionally split down the middle by some heretical hand. There are tens of thousands that I can see, though I cannot see the end of them. All of our fallen soldiers and Men, martyrs sacrificed in the holy wars fought so long ago. All the nameless dead.

Ah, horrible! I fall to my knees and hide my face in my cowl. I am exhausted beyond description. I sleep, I don't know for how long, but after a time I hear a snuffling breath and feel the moisture of a rough tongue that dares to lick the salt from my face. A lili!

I open my eyes and find myself presented not with the lashless eyes of a malformed swamp-siren, but with the brindled face of some cat-like thing, only three times the size of any cat I have known, its muscular body longer than my own. Behind him are ranged three others, low rolling growls issuing from all throats. Then the one nearest me exposes his fangs, leaving no doubt as to his intent. Very carefully, stealthily, I feel for Pearl's knife in the folds of my garment.

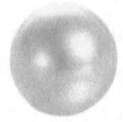 PEARL

10.

I did not ask for this.

'Thank you, Mother Oblation,' I say, oh so demure. Good on me. Oh, *thank you*. But I must turn away so she cannot see my rage, which I know is making my lips thin as wires fine enough to slice through the cheese of her heart and then feed it piece by piece to the rats.

She waits for me to swoon in an ecstasy for gratitude. *Oh, take my arms …*

So I face her. I have to. I rise, dusting the earth from my knees.

'You may finish up your duties here, and go and bathe, dear. Then bed. In the morning you will present yourself at the Careforce office, where I will meet you.' Those measured tones. The tea-coloured eyes, watery. Her eyeball skin looks oddly dimpled, as though the jelly-stuff they're made of is moldering while she still lives. But can you call it living, really? 'I will take you to your audience with the Ministers, then attend to your confinement preceding Perfection.' She smiles again, gravely. A smile from the grave. 'We are proud of you, Pearl. As we are proud of all our girlies. You are one of three Chosen from Oblation House this Attainment.' Simpering idiot slave with a voice like a weevil in my brain. And she leans forward as if to embrace me, but before her clammy hand can touch me I take a step back. I thank her. All the while I am telling myself, Do not give away by word or gesture an iota of your feeling, of what you are thinking, Pearl.

I walk away from the garden.

Mica cannot conceive of why a girlie would not Beseech, even her weak wicked Pearl. And MaOblat, mere House Mother, could not know I did not Beseech. But the Properganders who scrutinise our secret slips from the Plea Box must have known. Secret? Filthy treachers. They have chosen me though I did not ask.

I walk faster now, wanting to run run run. I control this urge and I cross the corp-yard where the eyes wait and watch on their stalkers' stalky stalks. But once clear of the gazers I do run, all fuelled by hate I run, silent as a sewer rat, down past the cunnydorms, Oblation, Sacricunt and Dutilove, all filled with girlies dreaming dreams of self-sacrifice and sacred mutilation, but I must have something vital missing in my being for I have *never* felt the impulse towards Perfection. So. Good riddance! Good riddance to whatever it is that impels those selfless girlies, and damn me to hell if that's what it takes because there is no Plea from me slipped into the cock-eye in the Plea Box – and *rot* your Citadel, your Orchid Nursery and all the Orchids too! Yes, bring on the Agnostics – if they're real, and if they are, may the Devil lead me to them!

I break into the Careforce office and steal a loaf, and from the fridge a big knob of hard cheese and a fistful of cold radishes. I steal a canteen for water and a flask of wine and a coil of fine wire for making a snare for my dinner. And I take this book and this pencil and six more and a blade to keep them sharp. And for cutting anyone who might try to stop me.

I take a big coat, the one belonging to that she-dog, the Martinette, with her voice like an air-raid siren, may she freeze her horrible pointy little doggie-dugs off, and stuff its outsized pockets with my gear. In the foyer I pass the glass Vitrine of Shame and the old-fashioned opaque porno-dress from the Museum of Iniquities in there. It takes my fancy so I slide the panel open and nick that too. I quickly slip out of my dress-less and and pull my new frock over my head. Glancing at my reflection, I'm pretty chuffed at the coverall effect. See me, titless and cuntless porno queen! I'd like to steal a lot more, but there's nothing more I need. I'd like to kick and punch and bash the glass in, but that would be very noisy and stupid.

Then I tear the first page from the notebook and scribble out a note to Asa. I tell him everything is changed and now we have no time to plan, for if I wait I will soon be on my way to Perfection tomorrow and a limbless vegetable by next week. I tell him where to meet me. By BigAmass. There is no other landmark as clear as that. And then I write: *Only wait. Wait a day and a night and if I've not been caught and bundled back like a sack of dead hope, then perhaps I am safe.* I underline this instruction to wait many times, for I do not want a dead man, but a living-breathing-loving one. I secrete the note in our hiding place, where we have always placed our messages, here under the sheeny moon with her luminous face all riddled with craters of some ancient pox that's faded now to old scars ... and still she shines! She shines. And I too will shine and I too will beam when Asa and I meet, oh yes, we will fall together down into the bracken and I will wrap myself around him and we will move together and there'll be no need for quiet, no more hush-hush secret silence, no – never mind any more those other boys or Men or damned mothers listening and watching and sharpening their nasty little knives and baring their nasty little teeth ...

I love him almost like I loved Mica, *my* Mica always, my stern and sweet love. I'm so sorry Mica, sister of my heart, but I'm twisted with a sickness that perverts all common sense, thank the long-dead gods! It's *my* disease and it's spread from my head and down down down, and it's spread from that deep ache in my cockslot and up, up through my bowels and further, further up in a wave, in a phalanx of soldiers, and they beat with their hammers on my anvil of a heart, saying let me in – *let me in!* And I did. But oh my darling little Mica, keeper of the faith, so loyal, I'm *sorry!*

But because she is pure and good and believes in Perfection and the States of Civilisation with all the passion she has in her hot little heart (that heart she guards so well, that she locks down into silence, always and ever) I could not tell her. But I knew of a way to leave her a message. If she could find a way to recognise it for what it was ...

But all the rest could go to hell.

I walk and walk until I pass the wall of the Men's compound, its many windows set into the big high walls of wine-red brick where they have their cells, some dark and others bright and gleaming like wet teeth in purple gums. And I pass the soldiers' quarters, all windows dark there, for they are (wo)Men and must follow different rules. On and on I walk and my mind is teeming, though I don't know much except that I am wrong and evil, but there is no way in hell I am going to end up an underground hole in an underground hole.

Don't ask me how I missed the point of all that saintliness that drives Mica. She never knew how bad I really was, for no matter how close our love bound us she could never never understand – must be that lacking bit of me, some vital part like a conscience or will to righteousness. But it doesn't matter because now I have a hope, that tiny hope that blew in to our cunnydorm one night on a piece of paper shaped like an ancient aeroplane from the time before, the time when Men flew in the air so that GodFather struck them down for their hubris, blew them out of the sky and crushed them into big craters in the earth. But why should a Man not fly? Why should a girlie not flee?

Why should a girlie not flee from a place that is all rules and restrictions and walls to a place that is open and wide and breathing, like the ocean I have yearned after forever?

The paper plane that flew through the window showed me a way to somewhere else. The X was marked at the spot where Civilisation ends and nowhere, elsewhere and otherwhere all Unruly begin. Hagovel, where the cursed one lives. The thought makes my skin prickle in fright and terrible, wicked, wayweird excitement, for now I too am damned, just like her.

But now is not the time for recollection. Now is the time to be aware of all that is around me. I see that while my brain has been ranting I have already walked well beyond the outermost ring of our Perfect State and into Stone Plain. Has any alarm yet been raised about a bad bad candidate for Perfection who is not in her bed?

Then, a light. Oh yes and oh no. A light that is not the moon, but lower, brighter, not close but getting nearer. I lie down, flatten my back into the hard, hard ground and look up through the spindly grasses at the sky so wide and dark. I am so small down here below all that vastness, so small here in my burrow of grasses, like a stone rodent, a stone rodent that hides and seeks and burrows. Surely no-one will find one lone girlie in a broad broad plain of stone and grass under a sky wider than imagination.

The light is strong, its beam irradiating the sky, and then there is another, and two more. Four in the party then, each one following a point of the compass. So only one will manage to come near. That much is good. What else is good? Not much, I think. I stay still and thinly trembling in my little hollow. Four people out looking for me. Am I so grand? I could laugh at the absurdity only I'm terrified. They are after me, to catch me and take me back and put me in a cell reserved for the worst kind of criminal, put me under the earth with nothing but a shit bucket and maybe a candle. Would they give me a thin book to write out the short conclusion to my little life? They could use it in a lesson to girlies of the future. A little book like the one in my pocket next to the pencils and the razor blade. I touch its sharp edge with my fingertip. I have the freedom of suicide at least.

One of the lights is slowly becoming stronger. It wavers with every footfall of the one who holds the torch. Voices now, (wo)Men's voices. Foot-soldiers. Two. Likely assisted by some sneaky silent skulking care-forcer. And a third voice, male. So they think I am worth the time of an Ecuman.

Here they come.

I will fight and maybe I can kill, but I am only one and they are four. What a pathetic death this will be. But at least it will be my own.

 ## MICA

11.

The eye of the cat is amber, a black stripe down its centre. I lash out with the blade, sinking it deep into the socket. Hot blood pulses out over my hand, my arm, and spatters my face. The creature screams in pain and flees, his brothers and sisters in his wake. I sit a while longer, wishing I had been able to sever the cat's artery for then at least I would have had meat. I lick the blood from my hand and arm, then clean the blade in the earth and slip it back into my pocket. I make myself slowly and method-ically force down more of the hard little pulses I have collected.

An hour of so later, tired to death, chilled and heartsore, I see in the near distance the beginning of the forest, a dark fringe seemingly cut out of the whitish-grey sky behind it. And there, at the pale of Civilisation is a solitary house, squat and low and blank faced. It is pale in colour and it shimmers mirage-like in the failing light. It isn't until I come quite close that I am able to make out its details. It too is made of granite. Each stone is a stolen grave marker split lengthwise and laid horizontally, one atop the other, a travesty of Man's pride. I feel sick to gaze upon it. And then, then I hear the sound that I can only think is surely the last thing I will ever hear – a guttural growling, hoarse and menacing, issuing from the direction in which I gaze all moveless with terror – and then the door opens and light spills out and in a rush of air the *thing*, massive and bulky yet moving with all the speed of a shot from the Martinette's rifle, is all but upon me. A voice rings out, '*Get back, Black!*'

But the shadow-beast does not halt. It keeps coming straight at me and I am knocked from my feet to the ground, landing heavily, my shoulder crashing into stone. The voice cries again and it seems to come from within the hot pain that sears through me. '*Stop! Black!*' it screams. And yes, the creature does desist, but the rumbling growl persists though I cannot tell whence it comes, for now it seems to be all around me.

And now a dark figure emerges from the rectangle of light, and above its head another light, and all around it smoke, blue smoke coiling. I can discern no features but can sense, with every nerve, its malevolence.

 ## PEARL

12.

A tall, broad shadow falls between me and the sky. The Ecuman, I think.

I feel his attention on me though I cannot see his face for his torch-light has blinded me. I tightly grip the blade hidden within the folds of my cuff. Then I hear that characteristic hiss of breath inhaled through a tiny hole. A careforcer then, not an Ecuman; not a soldier, but a porter. I realise it is only the bulk of the rolled tent she wears looming up well over her head that makes her seem so large and manly above me. But now the figure turns the torchlight back on itself, under-lighting it to make quite sure I see clearly the horrible wreckage of her face, the grotesque cicatrix of her lips. The scar is new, not yet fully grafted. Xeniicut230.

But what difference does that make? I will kill her anyway. Soon I know she will pucker up into a whistle ... any moment now ... I summon all my energy and nerve to attack her.

But then she lowers the torch and directs it away from me. She walks away.

Once she is well out of my immediate vicinity she whistles – not an alarm, but an all-clear. *Why?*

They move on.

 ## MICA

13.

I understand immediately who is the creature now wilfully blinding me with that cruel light. Who else could it be, living alone in a field of mutilated gravestones with her hellhound familiar? Only the Hag. And this is where Pearl's map has led me: so close to the very edge of things.

At last she lowers her torch and crouches by my side. The hound stays at her heel. I do not flee; I *cannot*. Indeed, in my exhaustion and pain I actually allow her help me to my feet though it hurts my shoulder bone badly, one broken edge grating against the other.

She draws me towards the door of her foul dwelling place. I am seized by the fear that I might be struck down – perhaps, after all, I could run? Or at least stumble a little further. But then, as if reading my thoughts, she speaks.

'You may run away if you like, but the night is very large.' She widens her eyes. The whites are almost blue. 'And it is not empty.'

This is doubtless true. And I am so very weary, my arm hanging useless at my side. And then the hound leans against my thigh, exerting an insistent pressure so that I am compelled to enter the room, but as I do I feel in my pocket with my good hand for the smooth comfort of my knife. Light from the small fire burning in the grate patterns the walls. The hound advances into the room and settles by the hearth, eyes of red regarding me with baleful menace.

'You could try coming closer to the fire. Blackguard won't bite, though I might!' She snaps her teeth at me. *Click!* I jump, stumble against a fireside chair, then fall into it.

She looks me over with the eye of a merchant considering new stock. I do not move a muscle. She sits on the arm of the chair and reaches out a hand towards my shoulder. She feels it carefully with callused fingertips, then further, to my collarbone. Now this makes me cry out.

'What brings you here, to me?' she asks as she rises and moves to a cupboard from which she withdraws a sheet. This she nips at the hem with her sharp teeth, then rips in half with a sound like a shriek. 'And so faintingly tired so that you trip over your girlie-shroud all covered in blood and mud and god knows what-all?' She approaches with the torn fabric which at first I think she will throttle me with, so that I lurch back. 'Shhh,' she hisses, 'It's a sling. For your arm.'

I feel faint, and my gut is tight, but I answer her through gritted teeth as she winds the sheet about my arm and shoulder, 'One must pass through hell to be ensouled.' My voice sounds distant to my own ears, and echoes in my brain.

She cackles quietly. The subject of my redemption is nothing to her of course. She is corrupt beyond healing and full of evil magic. They tried to burn her, the Hag. We all know her story. Once she had lived in one of the States, I don't know which. Perhaps Incomparable, or Superlative. But her story has spread throughout Civilisation. Many years ago, she was found astride a Man, her face a twisted mask of foulest carnality, riding that Man as if she had a right to harness the power of the Seed-Bearers. The prideful, wicked arrogance! They say she was a demon herself, a real demon from the pit, like Lilith, Adam's first wife and vilest incarnation of feminine mischief who was cast out of Eden for her presumption – exactly the same sin that earned the Hag her banishment. Of course the Man was censured for his weakness but the (wo)Man, the *jez*, slithered away like a sweaty snake. The soldiers caught her and bound her to the stake and lit the fire, but she wriggled free of the tether by magic she had learned in night-time conversation with demons over cups of sweet and salty blood. She slid out of the knotty twine and escaped.

I learned in Instruction & Destruction class of the time four Ecumen of Houses Usama and Gabriel rode out to her in their Holy Hummer with righteous vengeance on their minds. They failed to execute her, and it was clear that she would have drawn on her fount of evil and pitted against them some nameless horror with which no Man could be expected to contend, regardless of the nobility of his station and bearing. It was obvious that an old, as yet unaugmented, (wo)Man who had spurned Perfection would have had to have given herself to Satan. How else could she have survived in isolation, on the edge of a forest full of vindictive scouts, snipers and spies from Unrule? Ecumen are no longer dispatched after her for she serves us well enough as a living example, and there is no need for Men to pollute their hands with her noisome blood.

But she speaks again: 'Passage through hell, you say?' and her voice is sticky with sarcasm. 'Young people have been alive in the world for five minutes and think that older people will find their histrionics interesting ... There, that should do it.' She tightens the knot on the sling and then pulls up another chair. It has a tapestry covering and a small piece of spring poking through the worn seat. 'It is a function of self-centred youth to find itself fascinating,' she continues in her raspy voice as she takes a seat too close to me for comfort, 'regardless of being unformed and relatively featureless, as reflected in the youthful, unlined face like a flat, desert landscape. Isn't it so?'

I have no idea of how to answer – but it is not necessary, for she has not finished. 'Yet I have to say, it is ironic that such hopefulness endures in one who was raised like a battery chicken. And now that you are ready for plucking and butchering you have run off. Now *this* is *rare*, so it really does interest me.'

The Hag's words are disgusting but her voice is refined, like the voice of a Propergander, and her accent and intonation are almost musical. I know I must be on my guard against such charm – for charm I know it to be. Have I not been schooled since childhood in ways of pleasing both by means of attracting and satisfying Men's sexual needs, and also the subtler art of colloquy? But my gut aches and my arm throbs and the black beast glowers. Her clever, cynical eyes smile brightly at me as if expecting a response. Yet how does she expect me to answer to her presentation of me as a sacrificial chicken? Where to begin to speak to one ungraced with Truth, one whose understanding of life was formed in the muck? I choose silence, for it is written: 'An untutored woman's voice is the grunting of a rutting sow; her breathing silence is the soughing of the gentlest zephyr.'

She is dark-skinned with big eyes the shape of almonds, her hair is thick and black with a stripe of white like those spiders in the gardens whose venom causes your limbs to wither and rot if they bite you, and she wears it in a long queue to her waist. She is slight, a twig-boned woman, much smaller than me. Blighted by GodFather (Blessed Be His Cock-and-Muscle, alive-alive-oh-oh ever amen) for her sins, no doubt. The stories tell of many such punishments. GodFather (BBHCM) takes and GodFather (BBHCM) gives, beware the wrath of GodFather (BBHCM). She is mostly covered up in an ancient style of dress, the most wanton kind that covers dugs and cockslot but hints at them being there through the cut and fold of the fabric so that boys and Men can become unfairly aroused, yet be given no immediate access. Obscene. *Haraamasur.* Though in her case, given her age, probably it is best that no-one can see her body. The sight of it would likely offend more than the vanity of concealment.

I remember Colander, who taught Yearning & Duty, elucidating on the concept of feminine modesty in the past. He was less popular than Bobander, but he was good. 'In the dark past,' he explained as he lit a thin cheroot and placed it in the ivory holder, 'choice little girlies had the option of one of two kinds of dress. Either the opaque crown-to-toe ...'

'Crude!' we chorused.

'Or the little colourful frock ...'

'Rude!'

'You could say that.' He exhaled luxuriously. 'Or, you could also say: *im*plicit and *ex*plicit.'

We were puzzled. These were new concepts to us then – we were only young, Minus-Nine from Attainment, so our understanding was still limited. He continued, 'Both forms of dress had the same intent: to inflame Men and to create disorder in society. Think of it this way, children: think of sweets.'

We thought of sweets.

'Think of chocolate-covered cherries.'

We did.

'The chocolates hide something. What do they hide?'

'A cherry!'

'Correct. A cherry soaking in delicious syrup. But it is *there*, that cherry – *im*plicit in the shape of the sweet.'

'Ahh.'

'The opaque crown-to-toe was like that chocolate, announcing to the world that within the enshrouding layer of impenetrable dark is a sweet, sweet thing concealed: a plump, juicy fruit, much desired by Men. But the Men cannot readily access this cherry.'

Galena's hand shot up. 'Yes, Gal?'

'But that's teasing!'

We got it now, and chorused, *'Porno!'*

He acknowledged our response with a smile, but still favoured Gal with his attention. 'You are correct, Galena.' He threw her a chocolate.

Now Anapaite was inspired. 'Not like a licorice allsort!' she called out, and we were shocked by her impertinence.

But to our surprise, Colander was not angry. Instead, he smiled and said, 'Go on, Ana.'

'The allsort is all stripy and showy and ... if it was a dress then it would be for *jezzy teases!'*

'Excellent child! It is *ex*plicit!' He threw her an allsort. She caught it in her fist and crowed in triumph. 'So now, class, this is why modest ladies and girlies neither conceal nor reveal, are neither implicit nor explicit cockteasing flirts, but disport themselves as our GodFather (BBHCM) made them.'

'In available nakedness.'

'Unless it gets too cold. Thus the serviceably see-through dressless. And now ...' A deluge of lollies. Such a rare treat! We were in ecstasies.

'Eat them up, girlies. That is what sweets are for!'

How I wish I were back in the days of my innocence. But I am not, and never can be. And here is the Hag staring into my face, wearing an old floral-patterned shirt and Men's trousers. Sitting with her legs splayed, the seam of her pornographic trousers marking the spot of the cockslot that is hidden under thick, impenetrable material. Though I suppose it doesn't matter that much, as she is alone and, in any case, old and ugly. *And* she is tattooed. I see on the tops of her only semi-exposed dugs small fighting creatures, ferrets maybe; they are at each other's throats with blood spouting in a fanciful crimson arc up her throat to her jawline, and brown rats with tails entwined and brown teeth bared, mongooses rampant entwined up her skinny arms. Scarred arms. Scarred hands.

Then she says, 'How about a nice cup of tea?'

14.

I could die of thirst or be poisoned by the witch. So I do not answer, but sit quietly, trying to summon enough calm concentration to breathe in time with the pulses of pain that move through my arm and down my side, and to subdue the growing sick feeling in my belly.

She moves to the mantelpiece and takes down a caddy and measures tea into a saucepan, adding other powders from a jar. She adds water from a big black kettle and puts the saucepan on the range, then disappears into the adjoining room, which by the sounds of chinking crockery and running water, is probably a scullery.

I am alone with the beast, though it is now snoring like a great black boar by the hearth, where the heavy black kettle is set on its grid of metal. The rest of the room is unstable in the flickering firelight, its stone walls caulked with sludge that sprouts many small toadstools exuding a cool, dim light of their own so that there is no need for bulb or candle. There is a sleeping nook adjacent to the chimney, with a curtain of some coarse stuff painted crudely with red leaves and blue roses; it is only partly drawn and within I can see a narrow bed with yellow linen and a fat pillow under a small deep-silled window. In this main room there is a couch as well as our two chairs, and two tables, one before the fire, the other under another window on the other side of the room. Over the sound of her preparations emanating from the scullery her voice rambles on, and oh, my gut is churning …

'Adolescent people are brimming with inexperience, ignorance. These qualities are not interesting at all, are merely a condition of youth, like acne. But I *am* interested in why you are here.' Her head pops around the side of the door and her black eye winks. 'I daresay you've had a shock – something very bad indeed must have happened to bring you to me!' She disappears again then re-emerges with a tray in her arms, cups, a plate of bread and butter, radishes, salt and slices of some kind of cured meat, pink veined with white gristle. 'Bloody nasty, I should say!'

'I wanted—'

'Oh, *want*, need, desire!' She puts the tray down on the nearby table. '*I* know desire. It is the force behind everything worth doing. It motivates us and will eventually destroy us.' She butters a piece of bread and halves a big radish. She places it on top of the bread with a strip of the fatty meat and places it on the arm of my chair. The scent assaults my already nauseated stomach. I swallow back my bile.

'Desire is the eating place of the soul,' she informs me, as she lights up a foully stinking cigar, and when she's finished coughing, says, 'It is like Oroborus, the ancient snake who perpetually swallows himself alive: our beginning and our end.' She exhales a stream of acrid smoke and goggles her eyes at me so that the blue-whites show all around the dark brown irises. 'Then we will go back and join our history, beneath the necrophiliac conifers with a stone at our feet. And the residue of our passion will live on in death, churning the earth in restless sleep, disturbing worms. Yes, I think the little worms will wriggle up to the surface, as do the new shoots, pale and greeny yellow and succulent, that feed the creatures, and so on and so forth and thus the end feeds the beginning, again and again. Nothing special. Yet entirely miraculous.'

Or similar grand words. I remember the snake and his name, and the earth and the worms, but some of her meaning is lost on me, as the unpleasant bodily sensations that have been with me since I crossed her threshold are by now occluding my wits. What has been unease and tightness in my gut has increased ten-fold as if curdled with acid, and the dryness of throat, pounding heart, cramping stomach, rising gorge now threaten to undo me utterly. Gathering what strength remains to me I push myself to my feet and make for the door. I kneel on the ground and throw up what little there has been inside me, and more; then, still racked by intestinal spasms, my bowels involuntarily void and again I dry-retch, and again, my convulsions more violent than I have ever experienced.

The pain is dreadful, yet less intense than the humiliation I feel shitting and retching the reeking filth from my poisoned body in the presence of the Hag, who squats by me holding my shoulders and, after the last paroxysm passes, wipes my mouth and my brow with the hem of her sleeve, then carefully gathers me into her arms and supports me back into the house.

I lay there in the witch's bed for days, I don't know how many, then more days, for after the sickness passed I was too weak to rise. I would hear her moving about her house, and sometimes she would be by my side, looking at me thoughtfully, smelling of grease and tobacco and nutmeg and ancient, unwashed (wo)Man. Sometimes the beast was there at the side of the bed, wondering when I would be fat enough to eat. And then she would be back, sponging my face and body, retying the bandage on my arm, then later spooning broth into me, and over and over again cleaning my mess. I awoke one night to find her holding my good hand. Hers was warm and dry, and roughly corded with the old burn scars. I was too weak to pull away. I often heard her voice, soft and low, and though I understood little, in my physical and moral debilitation I found I liked to hear her speak – not the words, but the tone, for the rhythms of her voice were seductive. Later, when I was closer to recovery, I made a point of ignoring what she was actually saying so that I might be forgiven the listening, partial as it was.

But now the day has come when I can no longer fool myself. I have submitted to the ministrations of this evil one. It is true that had I not I might no longer be walking the earth – but perhaps death is preferable to this kind of surrender? I hate myself for my physical and spiritual frailty. I cannot know if I have spent days or weeks in this little nook from which I can hear the foul dog clicking across the beaten mud floor, other creatures outside or in the walls and roof, the rain in its many moods and from time to time an insistent metallic chugging noise that recurs at regular intervals. This frightened me badly the first time I heard it, though now I have worked out that it is a generator of some sort, which means she has fuel, which means she has some sort of contact with others. What others? And I am frightened again, yet helpless to act. A hateful condition.

I hear the Hag at her various profane occupations about the house. What might she be up to, what evil might she be brewing, she and her hidden cohorts? The view from the little thick-paned window by the bed gives onto the rear of the house with its vegetable plots, its pig pen and her goats with yellow devil-eyes, black-slitted and evil, and beyond that the forest, deep and green-black and filled with horrors. I spend a lot of time with this little book, writing my life as I remember it, recording all I see and think. Why? Who will care? Nobody, of course, but it calms me to have the work. The rest of the time, and there is plenty of it, I refer back to earlier notes I made while in Perfect. Semenal texts from the Holy Strictures to give me strength, and cues for images of contemplation, power-images accompanying the 28 Tenets of the Way of (wo)Man. Much of the time I keep my eyes closed, trying to attain that state of deep meditation wherein all thoughts are stilled, and one finds oneself in that peculiar state somewhere between peace and pure yearning in which the heart leans towards its own annihilation.

Now that I am strong enough, I let her know that I want to walk a little, test my strength. She brings me my clothes, humming under her breath as she helps me arrange my dressless to incorporate the sling. 'What's this, by the way?' she asks, giving the fabric on my wrist a slight tug. It is the relic I stole from the pit. 'Mine,' I say, pulling my arm away. My shame is none of her business. And it is true. Whatever it is, it is mine.

She insists we go out of doors so that I could, as she puts it, 'take the air' – though where I would take the air I do not know. Still, it is fresher than in that stagnant hovel, malodorous with many varieties of mould. I make a point of facing away from the house so that I do not have to be confronted with the disgusting masonry of split cocks. I look up at the sky, pale grey with fragile striations of white cloud. I see the way I have come – beyond the cleared area around the house is the graveyard and then, at the edge of my vision, the bean field, but invisible is the small river that leads back into the marshland and further, to Stone Plain, and home.

She says, 'You must have eaten a lot of raw beans to make yourself as ill as you have been.' And she *smiles!* The temerity! To blame harmless plants for an illness that was clearly a physical reflection of the spiritual calamity that I have allowed to betray then overtake me. Yet she persists. 'They contain a toxin which must be cooked out before you even think about putting them in your mouth.' Poison beans. What a stupid idea. In Perfect State there is no such thing. But I am careful to give nothing of these thoughts away for I know she would use them as a wedge to enter my mind, to weave her magic, to corrupt me. She says, 'Let's take a short walk, lean on me.' So we walk, though I do not lean on her.

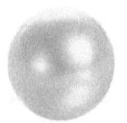 **PEARL**

15.

I had been prepared for death and it has passed me by. The Devil was with me then, as he is with me now.

After the careforcer moved away and the Ecuman followed, the two foot-soldiers came so close I could see by the light of their torches each individual grass blade, like stilettos for slipping up under the ribs of your enemies. Hard and brilliant.

And the hard brilliant idiots missed their mark.

And now I lie, still as still, for as long it takes for my heart and breathing to slow down. Skeins of thin cloud mass and disperse and come together again, veiling the face of the moon. I smell the chalky earth. I hear the crackling of sleepless insects all around. A flight of nightbirds wheels overhead, black against the grey. An owl screams blue murder.

I raise my head and pull myself up.

I walk that long, long way over Stone Plain all the rest of that night and the next and nobody comes to get me, though I stumble in the dark, only ever in the dark, muttering like the lunatic I am, mad and alone in all that openness, and falling and cutting my legs for the moon is still sulking in her shroud. Yet I find my way, and towards the second dawn, there is BigAmass looming out of the mist. Here I am to meet my Asa, my lover. I have bread and cheese enough for now. Perhaps later I can trap something fresh.

And so I wait for him, for he will come to me the following night, I know.

But he does not come. In the morning after my mean breakfast of stale bread and a bit of cheese, I wander a little way away from Big-Amass to where the brittle grass is taller and take my time to build a good, strong stone-rodent snare. I twist the wire I have brought into a loop, leaving a good length projecting out. I dig the end into the ground, and I have to go quite deep to make it fast in the loose and grainy earth. I fashion a peg from the woody base of a low-growing shrub and weigh it down with a rock. Surely Asa will be there waiting for me by the time I return.

But he is not. Nor has he come by evening. And when I go to check the snare, I see that no creature has disturbed it. I sleep somehow, cold and hungry though I am.

And the next evening is worse, for Asa still has not come. At the snare, I find the bit of cheese I left as bait has gone, but the canny little wretch that took it has evaded the wire.

I return to BigAmass and shelter as well as I can under its overhang, though the rain still finds its way through the cracks. I drift miserably between waking and sleeping. The wet wool of the stolen porno-dress clings and stinks and I have nobody to hold me, and nobody to pray to.

Has Asa been discovered? Has he weakened in his resolve? No, no. Not possible.

Night again, and the massed black birds again wheel as one, their shrieks shredding the air to ribbons. It is cold, much colder than it has been so far, and I have had no meat to warm my blood. I hug my body against the cold. I try to pretend that my arms are his arms, hard and dry and wiry. But my imagination fails me. I have never been good at invention for the real world has always and ever been able to infiltrate my dreams, turning them to nightmare.

Towards dawn I must have slept a little, for a sound wakes me: deep, snarling, and penetrating, like a swarm of giant hornets angered. I look up to see, against the red sky, the bulk of a blimp flying low, black, with a broad white stripe up the middle like those deadly sharks in one of Bobander's instructive books on the dangers of the deep, *The Horrors of the Far Greasy Sea*.

I see the plexiglass-shielded spyholes in its belly. I recognised it as a machine from Unrule with its propeller blades like guillotines churning. I could run out and wave my arms to bring it down to me, to rescue me, but they would not know if I am friend or enemy. And so, like a rat, a cockroach, I press myself back into a crevice to wait until it passes. I am lucky not to be seen this time, but I know I can no longer stay in this exposed place. There will be better places to die than this one.

Have I been abandoned and betrayed by Asa? No, I will not countenance this as a possibility. Then he must have been found out. And if that is truly so, what is happening to him? Are they hurting his sweet body, tormenting him so that his wits become all frayed and he tells, he tells ... Damn them all to hell.

That night I resume my trek.

After a while the pathway becomes less solid, with only small trees here and there, knotted into shapes like pretzels or the hands of arthritic old mothers knee-deep in swampwater that drags at your body wanting it to come down, down ... Oh don't let me drown in the goddamned sucking bog!

God*damn*, I say, *damn* you, GodFather, curse your bollocks! Then I shout it again and oh, it feels good, though the sky might open and blue tongues of hot electricity might fry me where I stand defiant as that ancient kernel of evil, the traitor who began it all ... *Lilith*. And now, on cue, thunder comes and I don't cower, I yell: *Let it come!* Then there's lightning and it splits to the core an old stunted tree with shrivelled fruit, its blackened trunk turning like the body of a drunk as it rolls sideways and the upturned eyes of its god-spawned fruits blink dumbly, the blind, idiot fruit falling in the boom and flash of the violet, violet light – and there's me, standing where the tree once stood.

The rain comes down, its ice burning my skin. My body is alive and strong and full of power. I feel my heart as a solid bulb of bullet-proof glass shot with hot blood. I pick up a hailstone the size of a boar's heart and it is freezing to the touch, chilling and burning, and I hurl it into the face of the night, GodFather's gift to me. And now I howl into the black, stone-filled night and the air is rent and rent again with the cries of all the other banished things. All the wild dogs with their white teeth and lolling tongues raise their black muzzles and howl. The screech-owls in the razor-gorse shriek, the screech-owls with their bladed beaks and their rodent breath and their eyes like globes that contain this world and the other, on this, the day of my exile.

GodFather, you do not care what becomes of me, your daughter – so many many daughters you have and you don't care about them and you don't care about me any more than you did the first one. And what will I do? I will do as my nature dictates. And who was it granted me this nature? Who was it? It was you. And you turned on me, you turncoat, you trickster, you old user you.

Pearl of wisdom! you cry, *Pearl, daughter unforgiven, thief of wisdom ungiven!* – you scream amidst a million reflections of yourself – *Get away from me, get away from my beautiful face, my lovely shining face which lights the world.*

Ah, you shining god, don't you know *I don't care* …

I gather my tattered, blasted remnants of pride and hope and will about my shoulders, and I walk on and on through that sucking bog beyond Stone Plain and then across however many miles of granite-studded graveyard. Surely, surely the Hag's house must be near, for there in the distance I now see the dark line of trees that marks the end of the known world. It must be there, and she will give me succour.

I have never been so lonely, the world turning beneath my feet and the stars wheeling overhead like hungry kites. And the rain keeps on, drumming and drumming and drumming the sodden earth. And I too keep on. I walk and walk and after a while there are trees here and there, and I take care not to go in too far, for on my own I would be easy prey.

I know the forest is haunted by heinous things that slither and slip in behind your eyeballs, eat your brains and shit them out their puckered arseholes.

After some time the wind and rain ceases, and a little light seeps up from the eastern horizon. Now, in the quiet dawn, I hear the sound of a Holy Hummer. It is not too far away and is doubtless full of righteous soldiers peering with their spyglasses here there and everywhere. So sweet of them to concern themselves with me. I have no choice but to go deeper into the forest.

After a time I find myself in an unholy glade. Bruise-blue and green-black shadows lap and overlap at the edges of this doldrum-dark place, and tentacular trees, half strangled by creeping lianas and poisoned with kudzu, drag and slurp at the waning spirits I can feel there, so strong – the ghosts all invisible but really real, watching me, up to their knees in gobbet-grass which catches the overflow of their anguish to feed their pallid suckers, parasites who cannot thrive even though they might drain the life of their hosts.

And then a form, immense and block-like, emerges from the obscurity. Its face is framed in a wide, floppy cowl, its eyes shaped like black stars are set into a white face like the moon and its wide grinning mouth, red as blood, is filled with big square tombstone teeth.

 MICA

16.

The hag insists that we 'take a turn' around her herb garden. She points out the various plants and names each as if I, a gardeners' hand from childhood, do not know them already. 'Chives, tarragon, sage,' she mentions proudly, as if she has invented them. 'And garlic all pale, paper-sealed and bound like an ancient, shrivelled librarian and *no* sense of humour.' She glances at me, as if expecting me to comment. When I do not, she carries on, 'But he has a sense of humus! Down there under the earth, amongst his other vegetable cronies, turnip here, potato people over there and,' she directs me by pressing lightly on my good arm, 'let us not step into this small parliament of parsnips. They all hate the sun, these roots, for it means their death. Yet they hunger for it, always aspiring toward the light with their little green shoots, isn't it so? But then, who amongst us does not crave the white-hot touch of Thanatos?'

Then around the back to tour her onions, beets and pumpkins, her beds of nasturtiums and her apple tree dropping white blossoms onto the flanks of the sow who lies surrounded by her guzzling piglets. I do not know who this Thanatos is and I will not ask.

'This is Victoria,' she says. 'I'm afraid I had to eat her husband, Albert. Bits of him are still hanging in the pantry. Very tasty gentleman!' She leads me towards two goats. 'And may I introduce Gavin and Alison Baxter. Gavin, Alison, this is …What's your name, waif?'

'Mica, Stone girlie of Oblation House, Attainment-Viable, Cunny-dorm Three, Perfect State.'

She glances up at me from under that hanging white lock of hers, and I cannot read the expression on her face, something of humour, something of pity. That *she* should pity *me*. Her ignorance is exceeded only by her arrogance.

We leave the goats who gaze after us in cynical silence. At the bottom of the yard I see a chicken coop alongside the shed which I guess houses her generator. It is a brief excursion for I am still weak, weak as a newborn thing.

We sit down on the bench by the door, sheltered from the drizzle. 'What is it you came looking for, all alone in the dark of the great night, banging on my door?'

I do not think it wise to contradict her, though of course I did not – and would never have – banged on her door, or that of any other. 'I am looking for my lost friend.'

'Lost friend. Ah me, sad I suppose. What is the name of this friend?'

'Pearl.'

'And would that be one of those infernal lesbian passions that make you ache right to the root of your clit, which is actually quite a large organ, goes really deep, isn't it so? Sometimes one of your more inept butchers will miss a bit so a girl can get the gist of pleasure. So, you are searching for your lost love. This is not so dull. You are questing after one who is more lost than you. I am not bored by this. Seeking Pearls in a bean field.'

I remain silent. I do not want to be the butt of a witch's witless joke.

Some days later I rise to find her at the bench in the scullery cleaning a stone rodent she has trapped. Her talk returns to the subject of the snake, eternity and desire, though there is no reason for such speculation. It is written: 'Satan finds work for idle minds.' Perhaps frustrated by my refusal to join her in a void excursion into the realm of abstracts, she huffs, 'Ah, but why should I care, little blood-from-a-stone?' as she relieves the rodent of its coat, then slits it down the middle with a neat, practised hand. 'What is *your* desire, *your* loss and yearning to me? Young people are assuming always that older people, particularly women, care about them.' She eases the sac from the cavity and drops it to the floor for the dog, who wolfs it all down in one mouthful. 'Though I must admit that you suffer less from this delusion than most, and for this I am grateful.' Separating joints with the point of a sharp knife, then chopping it into sections for the pan. 'You may not know that, often enough, we old ones feign interest only because our bones are sore so it is an effort to move away from the irritant of youthful bleatings.'

I say nothing. Issue no youthful bleatings.

'We do have our own concerns, you know. Like the brevity of life, the loss of love and limberness, the proximity of death, those things, if that makes sense. Tea?' She wipes her bloody hands on her trousers.

She is often making tea, which is always dispensed in cups that are surprisingly delicate yet chipped and stained with years of service. She usually serves it at the fireside table whose legs are decorated in carven beasts of profane nature. Its surface is marked by round scald marks from the cups that have been set there over the ages, so that a scientist might be able to measure its maturity by bisecting it and counting the layered rings. She pours boiling water and milk into the pan. I have never before drunk tea as she makes it, with tea, milk, sugar and spices all together. It is too sweet, too strongly flavoured, too foreign.

She wants something from me: conversation, distraction. She is lonely here at the crossroad with only beasts for company. And as a guest who has accepted her care, albeit involuntarily, perhaps I could be said to owe her something for her hospitality. But I speak rarely, for 'to speak with evil is to collude with evil'. And whether or not she has tended me, I know that she is the worst kind of unbeliever. I quote silently to myself, 'Be not deceived with vain words: for because of these things cometh the wrath of GodFather upon the children of disobedience.' It is clear that she is as one of those infected with those so-small-as-to-be-unseen creatures that pollute the blood and the belly. She cannot control the creatures that possess her. For the Hag, spouting filth is like breathing.

'Life is like that, isn't it?' she is saying now, continuing her theme of mortality. 'At least it is until we get so old there is no more starting over. Then there is only going on, then lagging, then self-murder if we have wit enough to do it before the option is snatched away by physical incapacitation and we can no longer wield the blade, work the trigger, read the label, work out how many pills are needed to make sure the job is thorough, for who would want to end their life a bag of blobbish flesh leaking from its cracks onto a rubber sheet?'

The Hag is close but not exactly the image of what we learnt about her in stories. Although she is old, she is not as old as I had thought, being only fifty years or perhaps a little more. I had thought she would have been pale and wizened with decades of solitude and a diet of swamp rat. But her skin is a mid-brown colour and clear. And her house, though dirty, is not sinking in the mud; it is actually set well away from Yellow Swamp. But I must remember: the woman is unutterably evil. This is obvious from her talk, the words she chooses, her manner that is at once brisk and seductive. She has no decorum, no shame, and spouts heresies in the same way I had vomited bile.

Yet, a day or two later I do tell her a little. I have to offer a minimum amount of information about myself so that she might tell me what she knows of Pearl. So when we are sitting by the fire one heavy, grey afternoon and she asks me about the circumstances of my departure from the Perfect State, I say, 'It was not long after our Fifteenth—'

'She speaks! Thank all the dodgy gods and their aunties and uncles galore!'

'And I believe that Pearl did not Beseech.'

The Hag is now looking at me quite attentively. 'Well, how almost entirely wonderful is this! So very unusual it is for one of you paranoid, debrained and denatured servile brood-wallahs to be so inspired.' Then she grins in a small but indefinably evil way so that my skin creeps to see it. 'But of course, they would always choose those who do not Beseech.'

'What do you mean, Hag?'

'I mean, my happy little sacrificial skerrick, that not to Beseech demonstrates will and self-command, qualities which you will agree are not encouraged amongst you teenaged breeders. And since you are of no value beyond that of brat incubators for a dying civilisation – may it soon expire! – I would suggest that your buddy of the bosom has been hacked and stuffed into one of those bottles and is crouching legless in her own mess even as we speak, waiting for a handsome dick-wielding paramour to answer her girlish prayers.'

'She isn't. I went there.'

'Really?'

'Pearl was not Perfected.'

There. Stated as a fact. And calmly in the face of the Hag's wicked irreverence. Strange to say, those words of mine emerged without any mental intervention on my part. Seemingly, while my mind has been busy and my body occupied with keeping itself alive and attentive, my heart has been working silently within my breast, slowly knitting any residual doubt into certainty for it is written: 'The Truth emerges from a faithful heart.'

'Ah, Pearl,' creaks the Hag. 'Named after that glowing gem born out of the irritation of its keeper, the oyster, who winds and winds around a tiny grain of sand its nacreous layers to swaddle it, keep it calm, so as not to disturb its own delicate flesh. Pearl, symbol of rarity, preciousness and wisdom. Was your Pearl both aggravating and wise?'

That is Pearl. In an oyster shell. But no. She is more. Clever and angry, swayed always by her feelings, sweet and careless, weak in faith yet wilful and brave, so brave.

The witch is regarding me as if I am a document to be interpreted. 'And Mica: from the Latin, *micare*, to glitter.'

'No, it means "crumb". Without significance.'

'Is that what you were told, Mica? You know, there are crumbs and there are crumbs. You are a chip of something sharp, that *glitters.*'

I will not be flattered.

'But you are looking tired, chick. Time to nap I think. You must build your strength slowly.'

I do not like to admit that she is right, but I let myself be guided back to the sleeping nook. I don't know how long I slept, but when I awake, the sun has passed its zenith and evening is near. I rise and go into the living area. She is nowhere. Gone off on some occult witchy mission, no doubt. Her familiar, the hellhound Blackguard, is here though, standing by the door looking out over the fields, I assume in the direction his keeper has taken.

I want to go outside, for the air is almost clear and a little late sunlight is leaking through the clouds. But *he* is blocking the way, and every time I approach, he stares straight into my eyes, his tongue lolling over his fangs, and thumps his shaggy tail on the floor. His eyes remain on me as I retreat. I can feel them.

I prop myself up in the chair by the empty grate and prepare to begin a Contemplation. What image should I choose that would most calm me and provide me with strength? Perhaps, 'The Blood of the Scapegoat Redeems the Sinner'.

17.

'Tea?'

I open my eyes. She has started a fire and is stirring tea and milk in the pot on the iron grill. Below it she has set up a spit upon which some headless, tailless, creature is roasting. Lost in my Contemplation, I had remained unaware of the noise of all these preparations. It is quite dark outside now. The window is a black square with a white star in the corner.

'Where have you been, Hag?'

She cocks an eyebrow at me. 'Cheeky morsel!' I do not know why she says this, for it is a simple question that bears no relation to cheeks or to food. Then, placing a steaming cup on the arm of the chair for me, she adds, 'Errands,' and returns her attention to the hearth.

She pours an oily mess over the roasting animal, making its skin hiss and crackle, then a splash of grog from the bottle she keeps on the mantelpiece. 'You were fast asleep there in the chair.'

'I was not sleeping.'

'Your face was all squashed up like a piglet's. Like Joyce here.' She indicates the spit. 'I've been saving her for a special occasion, and here it is!' She moves back into the scullery then returns with a folded white cloth, which she shakes out with some ceremony before laying it upon the table.

She sits down in the other fireside chair with her tea, lights up one of her stinking cigars, so unlike Colander's aromatic cheroots, and farts quietly.

I say, 'I found a map.'

'Did you, dear? Lovely.'

'Before I left my Perfect State.'

'Really?'

'It was a map that once belonged to Pearl. This map showed the way to you.'

The black eyes now spark into life. 'Yes, there are maps; there are messages and messengers. But I am sorry to say I have seen no-one who goes by the name of Pearl.'

I am sure she is lying. Why? But then, 'Weird and wily are the ways of the wicked.' I learned that along with many other instructive rhymes way back when I was Minus-Ten, but how will this knowledge help me in this particular instance? It cannot. If she refuses to help me I am lost. Were I to enter the forest and search for Pearl by myself, I do think it likely that I would be dead within days, probably hours. I am still so debilitated. I lean forward to replace my cup on the table, but instead I spill what is left in it onto the white cloth she has laid as a special tribute to Joyce. Still so very weak, in mind as well as body. I think for a terrible moment that I might cry. I try vainly to clear up the mess with my dress-less sleeve, but my sling makes me awkward, and I make it worse.

The Hag moves towards me and crouches by my side. 'It doesn't matter,' she says quietly. She reaches towards my face. I jump back out of reach of her groping fingers with their dirty black nails. 'Tch,' she clucks, I won't hurt you, mite,' and she brushes my cheek with her hand. So now a lump of feeling, sadness and more weakness – that terminal female feebleness – is squeezing up out of my heart and up and into my throat. This time I do feel the tears come to my eyes. I manage to stem the main part of the flow by clamping my eyelids very tightly till my head hurts, and clenching my body and biting the inside of my cheek. I can feel her looking at me carefully, and after a moment I meet her eyes. If I had not already an understanding of the manipulative ways of the lil'im I would have read that expression on her face as something akin to compassion.

'Truly, it does not matter,' she repeats. 'The cloth, I mean. I shall simply be washing it later.' If MaOblat had said that, there would have been some level of martyrish satisfaction in her voice. But the Hag has none of that. Then I mentally slap myself for making such a compar-ison between a virtuous woman and a demon jez practised in the arts of moral seduction (find a weakness, probe and enter through the soft spot in the defences of the victim). How could I be so pathetic? I must be on guard always, no matter how fatigued, no matter the further trials and torments that await me.

'Perhaps your Pearl travelled to the Lands of Unrule, don't you know, to The Other Side, Beyond the Forest or Over the Sea to where there are people—'

'Rogues!'

'—with freedoms greater than you can imagine.' With a wicked gleam in her eye she adds, 'Perhaps she has found your "rogues" and become one of them!' Then with demonic mischievousness: 'If indeed there is an enemy. How can you know that there is? Have you ever met one of these devil's henchmen?'

'Of course there's an enemy! And of course they want to destroy us! This is why we must be strong, and procreate, and train in military arts alongside the Ecumen, from girlie-guards through to foot-soldiers, so that they will never overcome us. GodFather (BBHCM) helps those who help themselves.'

'Yes yes yes, I am sure God is very proud of you and supports your team.' She returns to her chair, thank GodFather (BBHCM), and pours more tea into my cup and a generous measure of grog into her own.

I know she is being sarcastic like MaOblat was whenever we disobeyed or were stupid, or like Pearl when she wanted to hurt, to drive home a word-point like a knife-point. I know that also she is tricking me here, for she must certainly have seen Agents of Corruption from Unrule, though she will not admit it. As there are no barricades or walls of any kind around her house, it is obvious that she has made some arrangement with our adversaries, probably of a sexual nature, for what else would she have to offer them? What else does (wo)Man have to offer Man? – long may his strong-toed foot imprint its cool sole upon my brow. 'I am sure you would have met them,' I answer her. 'How could you not, living here at the very edge of the States of Civilisation and Righteousness?'

'Here at the "edge of righteousness" is indeed my home' – and I note that mean, teasing light in her eye as she adds, 'And I suspect you may have considered *why* I live alone, in such a remote place. Per*haps* so that I may do what I can to catch any of those who fall between the cracks of your State's surveillant watchfulness? Per*haps* I do what I can for your enemies?' She chortles as she reads the outrage which of course is showing on my face. Oh, so brazen she is! And now she does that absurd eye-goggle at me again – how could she find this *funny?*

'You, lamb chop, might do well to think a little harder about the nature of this dread adversary you have been schooled to deplore. When you consider that the best fate you have to look forward to is mutilation, imprisonment and early death, then you might just find that the enemy is really awfully pleasant by comparison.'

I quail to consider the divine consequences of this latest blasphemy and make a silent prayer for mercy should He choose to unleash a light-ning bolt right here and now.

But what does it matter? My quest is pointless. Even if she has met Pearl she is not going to tell me. I have failed to think beyond the seeking and finding. Why did I imagine I could be successful? And now what? To go alone into the forest crawling with human and inhuman demons? Or towards the Far Greasy Sea with its impossible depths, all salt and melancholy? Return to my home? I had banished from my mind all thoughts of what would happen to me when I return. Ostracism and abjection certainly, torture and death at the stake likely to follow.

The Hag has turned away from me and is staring out of the window towards the forest. Only the last dregs of the day remain. The light is a clear, soft grey, the colour of doves, and the rain has started again, quietly but insistently pattering against the iron of the roof, the cold stones. Her face in profile is really not terribly ugly, and her eyes are shining. If I did not already know that she is incapable of any of the finer feelings real (wo)Men suffer, I would think that she is sad, perhaps as sad as me, and wanting to cry. Who is this strange, isolated, sub-human creature?

'Hag?' I say, but her eyes remain on the rain.

'Hag,' I repeat, a little more loudly. 'What is your name?'

THE HAG

18.

When the strange little lost girl asks my name, this old witch makes a point of keeping her gaze on the rain. Have to, or I might burst the old banks and come over all-of-a-flood. My name – what's in a name? Jesu and Muhammed and all your dead stars, I ask you, what's *not* in a name? *History's* in a name, and what are we, after all, but bipedal historical compounds struggling across the skin of the earth looking for someone to talk to? Someone who'll recognise who we are! Love me if you want, but you first have to recognise who I am, don't you? *Don't* you? A rose is a rose (oh bearded poet beloved of my darling mama, Anjali angel, Anjalima) is a rose is always and ever a rose, and never a bloomin' beetroot! But I shut the old gob. What's the action of lips shut down over tooth and gum? – *mum!*

Keep mum, stay low-key. Settle, settle ... Oh, I'm lonely and may well be defeated but I'm not out of my tree. I've already scared the wretch half to death more than once. And look at her, so proud and righteous; yet it's a melancholy life she's had and don't I know it! But then, if misery's the norm, is it misery any longer? Who knows? Who cares? Not me, Queen of the Damned.

Any case, this old toxic spore, heinous whore, answers the little bleeding soul: 'Jenny Patel.'

'Jennypatel', it repeats thoughtfully. I like that. Running the two names together. Reminds me of the retro endearments girls used to use, back when we could still be playful. Jenny-petal. Petal, Petal-blossom, Bloss ... I feel my lips stretch into a smile I hope doesn't look too cadaverous. But just in case it does, and not wanting to alarm the child again (for I have plans for her – of course I do!), I rattle on, 'Once upon a time I was called Jen.' Because surely there's nothing more harmless than a Jen?

'Jen,' she echoes.

'My parents told me all about the early bit, the start of my life that I was too young to remember – as parents do. They told the past like a story. Such stories are always coloured by the tellers' losses though, isn't it so? Loss of youth, of place, of time rinsed by tides of recollection – they're bound to sound like a romance. But Romance with a capital R.'

Oh, really, Witch! Look at it, all perplexity. What would this would-be amputee know of Romance capitalised, lower case or spelt out in friggin' hieroglyphs? Or parents, for that matter.

Refill cups, old twit. Scratch ears of dog. Shut up and sniff scent of roasting Joyce. Stare into embers. See them surge and fail. Poke 'em with a stick. I need to splice a few more logs. Sort the piles in the yard ... But oh, Romance will wreathe you in roses or dismember you slowly on a rack, turning the handle up another notch each time you cry out. Creatures with segmented horns and huge almond eyes live in Romance. Love and hate live in Romance. Things with claws hidden in soft pads of fur will come to you in the night and love you to death. History lives in Romance. That is why history can never be objective, no matter how hard we try. So many Chinese whispers, each new version further distorted from the original – *romanticised*.

Still, Romance is the active culture in the yoghurt, the live stuff that animates the facts. Purpose grows in the deep dark places, like a foetus sprouting inside a woman's body before the child comes out of the pink murk and forgets. Romance is a notion and Romance is a place. It's a place where the ghosts of who you once were groan and grieve and sup on the substance of what once was. But look at its blue eyes all bright and expectant following my every move. Talk to it, the poor little mutton.

'Of course my mama and daddy avoided the sad bits of the past and focused on the sweetness, because a child likes sweets, no?'

She blinks, saying nothing, waiting. She hasn't proven the most responsive audience thus far in our relationship.

'There were the tender details, like my naming. How they'd waited as long as was decent before tagging me, then a little bit longer, just to make sure that they chose me a moniker to suit the kind of little bugger I was. My mama Anjali, and Arun my dad.' As I speak I see the earnest, kind lines of my dad's face. And hear the Anjal's sweet voice, back before she got the hard edge to it. 'My mama told me that as a babe I would point at objects I saw, my bottle, my doll, my daddy's moustache, with oh-so-very earnest fascination. She told me it made her feel happy and proud of our small world that she and my daddy had made—'

'Pride comes before a fall.'

Well. I thought I had everything I needed here, but now I know that all along I was missing a little live-in morality monitor. Monitor lizard, with your tongue flicking out over your pale dry lips, swiping flies.

'True. It does indeed.' Best agree with her, eh, show her what a peaceable hag I can be.

'Any case, they decided to name me after a character in an old book my Anjalima had grown up with that she'd got from *her* mother, about an inquisitive little cat who despite her smallness was *never* a moggie to be messed with! Of course that's only according to the unreliable evidence of my rather partial mama. Possibly I was a blighted little sausage, but she loved me.' I glance over at her to see how she responds to the idea of maternal love, given her understanding of such would be limited to the chilly disciplines of her House Mother. But it seems that that is not her main concern:

'But a *cat?*' Now *this* really bothers her for some reason. 'A *cat*,' she repeats. 'Who is disobedient, who is *curious?*'

'Just so.' Why so distressed by the subject of our feline friends? Fortunately the piglet roasting in the hearth gives a sudden hiss just then, then sputters quite vehemently. Good. Distract the pussophobic whey-faced stray with dinner. Rise and go to fire. Slip Joyce's bodily remains from the spit. Slice her up onto a couple of plates. Add potatoes from the embers. Hot! And a handful of lovely sharp nasturtium leaves for each of us. To the table. We eat in silence. I don't like to disturb her, so engrossed is she in separating flesh from bone. 'Good?' I venture. And her reply is the same monosyllable: 'Good.'

All good then. So long as nobody's talking.

19.

We polish off most of Joyce and she's licking her paws like one of those atrocious kitty-creatures. I light up a smoke and pour myself a tiny sip of grog, when she breaks the silence: 'What is your State, Jennypatel?'

'My state? Ah, my state was Ideal.' Oh, yes.

She looks impressed. 'An honour for you, to be raised so near Big Smoke, the epicentre of Civilisation.'

'I was only there for a little while. Actually, most of my life I lived in—'

'Impeccable? Idyllic? Ultimate?'

Oh it knows its geography then, the clever thing, take a gold star for your careful copybook. 'No, not in a State at all.'

The pale face becomes even paler at that, as I'd known it would. Yes, yes, it's unkind of me to bait her like this but we she-demons from the bowels of hell are allowed a bit of mean streak, no? Then she surprises me by saying valiantly, 'Tell me. Please tell me more.'

Such a thin little voice, all chilly-timid. Doubtless she's committing some sort of terrible impropriety for which she should be torched – oh so many possible torching offences against the States' notions of decorum! Impossible to remember them all. But she's an inquisitive girl, and plucky in her way. No, I am definitely not bored with her at all. Seems there's a bit of soul still stirring in that little frozen chicken breast of hers after all. I hear myself cackle quietly, an unpleasant noise and doubtless rather frightening for her. Oh, I'm a vile old stick and no mistake.

'I want to hear about your life,' she says bravely.

'But I am very old,' I say, 'old and cold as the stones and bones in the field. So that might take some time. So, first: more tea. A story is impossible without a great deal of tea.' I make another pot and when we've settled down, her all propped up with cushions in one armchair, me in the other, Blackie's heavy head resting against my thigh, night pressing against the window, I continue.

'Before I came to Ideal State I lived in a place over the sea, very far away from here on the opposite side of the world. My parents wanted to find somewhere easier to live, for it was hard where we came from. Not that it wasn't hard everywhere, just harder in some places than others, a matter of degrees of difficulty, don't you know. Once upon a time there was a kind of stability in the world – or so I've been told – whole nations of people that stayed in the same place for generations, but by my day mobility had become the norm and things just sped up from there. So, after some time Anjali and Arun saved enough money by working themselves almost to death's door. Then there was a voyage. I can still recall it in nightmares coloured like bruises, blue and black, with tall tall waves and all this frightening bigness of sea and sky. But sometimes … sometimes, so beautiful, for there were calm nights too, and by the time we got close to this country you could sometimes see the black water filled with sea creatures seemingly made of light, moving like dreams, only better, for they were real.

'We arrived in this new place, this Australand: me, my mama and daddy and my granny, all the way from Anglindia. Such a big change for us all. The first thing I noticed was that the land was very dry compared to what we were used to – that was back then, before the rains really set in – but as at home, a large number of the people were quite pale. Like you, my friend, with your goldy-gold curls. Blood diluted by much mixing makes for some pretty pastels, I think!' I reach out to touch her hair. And oh, but see her shivering back into herself now, all hunched against the assault of the old pervert. This could get tedious if she keeps it up. 'And so, soon I began to go to school with many other little girls and boys—'

'You went to a school?' she interrupts, her blue eyes round. 'A school with *boys?*'

'I did, my friend. Things were different then.' She nods silently and much more gravely than I ever could have at her age, having been raised in a family rather than a factory. 'The classrooms were modelled most innovatively from corrugated iron and plastic sheeting in an old low-rise cinema complex where in the olden days they would show moving pictures projected onto an indoors screen.'

'Why?'

'For entertainment.' I note that she recognises the word but not the concept. I note also her tucking it away for further ponderment as I go on, 'The old-theatre new-school was in a blocked-off side street called George, after an ancient king from the Anglindia that had produced me and, of course, the original Jenny.'

'The curious cat,' the child says, almost under her breath. Then she hisses in a way I find quite eerie, *'Pusssssy–pussss.'*

'Yes, cat. But because I was a well-brought-up little girl, I was polite and never hissed at people. And I was quite popular too, I will say, at the risk of sounding immodest. Other children, both the obedient ones and those whose who ruled them with sticks and stones and cryptic passwords, preferred my friendship to my disdain.' I smile, remembering. Yes – I knew how to carry myself as a kid, took no nonsense.

The rain's coming down a little more heavily now, each tiny drop coming to brief bright life in the band of light cast from the window. I glance back at my small audience. It's looking uneasy as ever, staring at me with its big saucer eyes. Have I become such a very very frightening thing to behold? Must take a look in the mirror one of these days. See what has become of little Jenny Patel, the child who grew up to be the outcast, whore and horrid Hag, her name used to frighten generations of children into obedience to a code that she herself loathes and deplores.

PEARL

20.

According to what I've learned from my several recent experiences, when you think you're about to die your senses sharpen up incredibly. And so: I hear the teardrops of moisture tapping on the broad leaves around me, I smell the sweet mulch stink, I sense a creeping of my skin as it puckers up into goosepimples and raises the hairs on the back of my neck, and I hear the blood ticking though my temple as I gaze at the monstrous face leering at me from within its grey hood.

I feel for my blade. This horrible creature may be very broad and very tall, but I know that in the crease between thigh and groin is a fat vein, pulsing blood … I can reach that, *I can*, so I lunge towards it.

'You funny little darling,' it says, sidestepping me with humiliating ease, and my momentum causes me to trip and plant my face in the steaming earth. Ignominious! I crack my temple on an iron-like bole on my way down. Hot blood mingles with cold mud as I land.

Darling?

'It's only Grimalda. Grimalda Grace.' And turning over onto my back I see not it but *her* emerging in full splendour, trailing a grey cape behind her, big as a wall. And oh Jesumuh, that face like a moonscape pitted with old scars looming over mine, and the great hands like hams in dirty yellow-white gloves reaching towards me that could snap my narrow neck in a second. It's at that point I faint dead away, a good move when faced with imminent death.

I am a thin person; but still, her strength must be prodigious for, as I found out later, she picked me up bodily from the forest floor and travelled some distance carrying me, dead weight and all. At some point she shifted me from her arms to sling me over her shoulder. That is when I emerge from my stupor. I look up at this 'Grimalda Grace' through my crusty veil of drying blood-and-mud. Grimalda. Not a giant at all, I realise, just an awfully big person whose hard chest has wiry hairs sticking out from her blouse that tickle my nose. So, Grimalda the fella then, a man after all?

As the sun begins to steam open the seam of the horizon and thread its way through the low, dank cloud, I regain my wits, and ask her (or him) to let me down from this undignified, sack-like position. I want to walk beside her, wherever it is she is taking me. This means we have to slow down a bit, which I know will be annoying for a person with such a long stride, but she kindly complies. There are stations dotted around the country to accommodate border Guardians – it's well known – usually small fibro cabins with outhouses and stables for the horses that Rangers and Guards ride to patrol the countryside, and closer to the river there are shored-up ruins of warehouses adapted to the needs of these itinerant patrollers. It is to one of these old godowns that she brings me – though I have to say she is a pretty funny-looking Guardian of Civilisation.

Most of the building has caved in and is charred from some old battle, leaning in on itself like an ancient-one-legged warrior supported by a bank of slender gum trees, their skins spotty with age or rust. The side of the house that remains intact and unburned teeters towards the river, and its bleached walls seem insubstantial, almost translucent with moving light-and-water shadow-patterning. We poor humans and the things we make, all just temporary convergences of light and air, so easily and so soon reduced to our elements. For we were never really all that solid in the first place. Some air, a little light, a lot of water.

The door hangs all skewiff off one of its hinges. The keyhole glares blackly. Grimalda removes her backpack, a small, white patent-leather piece of frippery with fraying straps that can barely stretch over her enormous shoulders, and begins to rummage about in it, presumably after her keys.

But then the house seems to tremble, and there is a thumping from within, and the crooked door is flung open with a shriek. There in the entryway, his form silhouetted in the sun filtering through the cobwebs that hold together a fractured window behind him, stands another huge person, even bigger than Grimalda and as black as she is white, a bearish hulk of a man in khaki Ranger regalia. He looks very, very angry. 'Are you *out* of your *tiny mind?*' he explodes, and for a moment I think he is talking to me, so I duck and cower like a sensible coward. But no, I am beneath his notice as yet, for he is leaning bulkily towards Grimalda, who looks as likely to budge as a mastodon in a tar pit. 'Going out in the forest in full disguise?' I am surprised at how high his voice is, like a child's. But I know the cruelty children are capable of, so it reassures me not at all.

'My darling Motley-wotley,' Grimalda begins, 'I was in Big Smoke this morning, and will be again tonight for the meeting of the Ministry Advisory Board, as you well know – move aside, will you, I'm knackered – if the blimp's on time for once, that is.' She pushes her way in with me in tow. 'And I'm buggered if I'm going to waste my precious energy making-up and un-making-up, cleansing and schmensing all day long, altogether a bit of a large-ish snore. Rather play Scrabble! Ah … what word I can make with a G, and an R, U, M, B, L, E, B, U, M?'

'I don't think you get nine letters, actually.' Motley-wotley says as Grimalda gently urges me inwards and the two hulks squeeze themselves through the door into a small, lopsided, sitting room, hardly bigger than the hallway, too warm and full of the smell of greasepaint and gas. There is a two-seated sofa and a chair draped in colourful fabrics in patterns of lozenges, stars, diamonds, a pantsuit of green-and-orange tartan with silver glitter trim, bodysuits that are green on one side and red on the other, or black-and-white, blue-and-yellow; elsewhere are boas of lilac and gold and hyacinth blue, muslin shawls, fringed scarves … But the shoes! Some are as big and yellow as rubber dinghies and others have platforms tall as tower blocks; one pair of huge wedged heels is made of transparent stuff filled with tiny plastic goldfish, and another with globules of luminous oil floating in purple water, like blobs of incandescent phlegm. There is costume jewellery such as that displayed in the Vitrine of Shame in the Museum of Iniquities: giant glass diamonds and strings of pearls each as big as your fist; metal chains of silver, gold, brass, and glossy black metal studded with glass beads of every colour; small spangled crownlets and bangles and studded collars and armlets and necklets and bracelets all glinting in the pale sunlight streaming through the broken skylight so that the room is alive with moving colours scintillating off every surface no matter how dowdy, bringing warmth and humour and something like beauty. When I wrench my gaze from this kaleidoscope, I see the walls are lined with stacks of books and magazines reaching to the ceiling, a tall mirror leans between two filing cabinets, covered in smeary marks of different consistencies and colours. Before it there is a heavy tray laden with feathery brushes, little tubes and pots of paint, blue and bronze and flesh-coloured, a dish of cat food, and two black-rimmed tea mugs. An enormous marmalade tomcat is curled on a big fat cushion nearby, purring like a locomotive. 'Meet Geoff the Giant Ginge,' says Grimalda, going over to the cat and scratching his ears. Geoff cocks his warm, furry head into her palm and ups his purring further, if that is possible.

'Anyway, I had my hood on, didn't I? Give us a fag. Oh – and do you like our newest stray?' she adds, chucking me under the chin, a broad smirk cracking through her greasepaint. She takes the cigarette the man passes her, while I just stand there feeling … what? Bemused, anxious, happy, stunned as a trout that's been netted only to find, shockingly, wonderfully, that it can breathe in the air. So are these the 'Fools' who 'rule ok', whose signature I have seen before: on the page with the Tank Girl on one side and the map on the other?

Or rather, as I soon work out from their talk, they are Fools in the town and Rangers in the country. Fool-Rangers. This pair and others like them are not only accepted as Fools, but welcomed by men in positions of power who need diversion. They play up the role of ridiculous entertainers and are even trusted by some in the Ministry to provide information 'from the streets'. Nobody – so far – has connected Fools with Rangers. But there are quite a few who alternate between Fool and Ranger gear so as to find and help runaways like me. And when I think about it, why *would* they make a connection between Fools and Guardians of Civilisation? Still, their boldness is terrifying. And becomes more so as I understand more about what they do.

Motley-wotley is looking me over as if measuring me for durability and utility, though what I could be useful for seems negligible enough to me. I don't know what conclusion he draws, but he smiles. Sweet and almost sorry, his smile – for what he has done or what he might do? – and tricksy at its edges, a smile you would like to trust and probably would but at your peril.

Grimalda shows me up a rickety staircase to a tiny room under the eaves. It has a small window full of riverlight and walls that in many places don't quite meet the roof but have mostly been mended by the work of many spiders whose webs enmesh the weakest points. But the honeysuckle still enters, so the room is filled with sweetness, and through the broken roof tumbles a spill of tiny yellow flowers in great profusion, an exuberant floral chandelier. When Grimalda leaves me I lie down on the mattress in the middle of my bower. I am so very tired, but I struggle against sleep for I want to lie there and listen to the river, look at the light and the flowers. I never knew that such loveliness was possible.

THE HAG

21.

'There were so many changes going on in the world when I was a little girl about your age,' I tell my charge. 'Massive, one after the other, none for the better. Yep, all bad. Kept us on our toes … kept us moving.'

'What sort of bad changes?'

'Environmental ones. Tectonic. Also heat and cold and wind and water gone wild, my pet. And moral and cultural. Disasters, all. The natural and the man-made both. Change moves and shakes, don't you know, and it slices with its secret knives, slivering away at what is familiar till it becomes strange and has to be learned all over again – the revised version – and only short courses available! The surface comforts we erected to protect ourselves from the elements in the world – the houses and dykes and sewers and such – snipper snap – all shredded in the end! And the niceties we constructed to save us from the demons in our brains – the reflex kindnesses and manners and social services and whatnot – chipper-chop – and no time to grow a decent scar! Things fall apart. But not all at once. The outer wrecked and the inner exposed by degrees. The inner where live the deep-deep fears, the ancient hatred.'

She's crouched forward, alive to my tale. 'Old fear and hate?'

'Yes. Set into the foundations of civilisation that were laid way, way back are those old monsters at the bottom of the well, the bottom of the mind.' I get up creakily, stoke the fire. A log falls forward, flame-shadows writhe across the walls. 'They've always been there in the darkness, sending up greasy feelers or breathing poisons up through the soil, always there, down below, infecting our best, most civilised intentions. And when cracks begin to open in the shell of the world, those monsters of the deep can creep towards the light, slowly, carefully, carrying their burdens of hate and rage, all the buried horrors …'

'I am not familiar with these deep monsters, Jennypatel.'

Oh but you are if only you realised it, I don't say. Ask your God-Father of the Dual True Faith. Instead I tell her, 'It's hard to really understand what's going on *when* it's going on. I talk of drama and change and monsters for I'm a mad old bat, but it doesn't feel that obvious at the time it's happening. My old friend Lee once described our culture as one of slowly boiling frogs. Do you know the story of the frog?'

Negative shake of noggin.

'I'll tell it, if you can bear another metaphor.'

'I can bear a metaphor.' She smiles! In a manner of speaking. An expression of irony glazed with suspicion.

'So. You get a pot. You put a frog in it then fill it with cold water. You put the pot on the heat. It slowly begins to warm up. The frog feels cold water, then cool, then lukewarm, then warm …' I realise then that this nasty parable might frighten the girl, and she's only just starting to open up a bit. And after a scary beginning it only gets worse – after all, my life has been terrible, a sort of nightmare-porridge, no getting away from it. I'm cursing myself for embarking on this ill-advised autobiography, but then she interrupts.

'Warmer, then hot, hotter, hottest and boiling!' she says excitedly. 'And the frog does not understand what is happening till it's too late!' Such glee – and the first sign of pleasure I've ever seen on its little clock. 'Stupid frog. We boiled a lot of them when I was Minus-Nine from Attainment.'

'When you were *six?*'

'Yes. It was very funny.'

So kittens scare her to death but torture is amusing. Maybe she'll cack herself when I get to that bit where I get staked. Hilarious. I'd managed to forget some of the details of Perfect, or Ideal, life and education. But it's coming back in all its glory. I say, 'Ah, funny. Right. So you get the point. It's an allegor—'

'Yes, an alligatorical tale. A story about a frog to explain a reality. The reality of changes going on unnoticed. Things falling apart not all at once.'

'Correct. You are not a dull child at all. Right up until the eleventh hour, when catastrophe was imminent, despite all that chopping and changing, snipping and snapping—'

'And monster-breath bubbling up through the crevices from the deep places.'

Jesumuh, she's certainly warming to the monsters. I continue, 'So people sort of took it all on bit by bit, slowly-slowly the once-strange becoming normal. After all, everything changes, doesn't it? I was very young then, but I knew this and I'd learnt from my daddy about how very important it is to adapt. He used to take me for rides on the back of his Vespa – a kind of bicycle with a motor. I would put on my special helmet, my jacket and trousers—'

'Porno!'

'That's what we *wore* then. I think you know that.'

'Yes.' It looks abashed. But only slightly. Puts me in a quandary: do I encourage any boldness in this half-crushed little being, or attempt to instil in it a little civility? I really don't know. Good job I never got to be anyone's mother. Her lips are tremulous but her gaze is hard. Creepy little relict.

'So I would squeeze myself in between Arun's shoulders and the storage unit for groceries he had welded onto the back of the scooter. He would say, "Lean with the angle of the bike, Jenny-hen! Don't resist the movement or we may crash. Take care!" That was my daddy. Of course we had to be careful on the road in all that traffic, but he was very cautious. A law-abiding, compliant man, a sweet man, always avoiding the chance of conflict, for he hated clashes. So he veered and avoided, he reasoned and adapted and listened, and he did what he could in his gentle way to make things more pleasant for his family and friends, and hoped it would turn out well in the end.

'My parents taught me to be grateful for what I had more than resentful for what I hadn't. Daddy said to me, "We were not always so fortunate, and others we knew where worse off too, were thin, often angry and sad, dying fairly young. Do you remember that, Jenny?" I remember answering, "Not so much, Dad." Then, because he looked slightly disappointed at my failure to realise exactly how lucky I was in the scheme of things, I added, "Maybe a little. I remember mazey alleys, old walls of brick and stone all crumbly. I remember a different light and colours. Smells that were not always good. I remember a skinny dog with big eyes. Boys threw stones at him."

'Arun said, "We are amongst the lucky ones, aren't we?" I told him, "Yes, we are lucky." He said, "Lucky-lucky, like these others in our street of buildings with internal plumbing, more or less." Then I remember I interrupted him, because he was getting embarrassing. Ever patient, he said, "Yes, sweetheart?" And, being a genius with very very deep thoughts and an enviable concentration-span, I said, "Can I have an iceblock please?"'

My waif smiles her sort-of smile again. 'And how did you know he was your father?'

Dear Jesumuh. She's probably been wanting to ask this since I first mentioned him. It's not as if she's had any experience of fathers, and as for mothers, some sort of horrible augmented pseudo-ma semi-robot is all. I forget so much! Funny how the old memories have become so much stronger than the newer ones. Maybe due less to my approaching senility than simply because the older ones are a good deal less horrible.

The fire's about done its dash. I glance at the window with its night pressing in against the pane. A star falls. 'I think it's high time for a bit of a nap,' I suggest. 'Catch a few zeds, eh, as they pass overhead in this deep night with its comets cometting and stars starring and us below, small and still convalescing, after all?'

But the child hunches forward towards the heat and stays where she is. I stir up the embers with my toe; one or two glow up at me half-heartedly. Then the generator chugs into life, as it does from time to time, making the kid jump. But she's gathered herself again by the time the fridge in the pantry follows suit. Chugger chugger hugger mugger. I rouse my weary bones and set about tidying up. She sits on, making no move to help – though, to be fair, it's a bit of an ask to clear up one-handed. I put the rest of Joyce in the stockpot that's been simmering since last July, good and rich with (very thoroughly cooked) beans. Add a bit of bacon off old Albert for the smokiness, and onions and carrots from my plot. I make my bed up on the couch again and give her a meaningful look, then I let myself out the door and head towards the outhouse.

22.

By the time I get back she's made herself scarce. Moonlight, just a little, shines in through the dirty glass like a benediction – though I'm hardly one for petitioning divine help, not having come across any divinities I'd trust with a dog. Or an ant. Nevertheless, regardless of my religious ambivalence, it is lovely the way the light tracks across the tea things on the table, glancing over cup and pot, lighting my way back to memories of other pots of tea, other crocks of grog – other conversations, other people … people with humour and wit and *heart*. My Arun and Anjali and dear Lee in the earliest of my recollections; then faces from later, after 'Liberation', the toughies like Tajik and Tiny and Melanie, Doll-face and Po-face, and the old guard, Mot and Grim – and, of course, Jimbo. Jimmy Jim, my darling boy ... I recall the gung-ho survivors' stories (so far, so good; another day, another dinner), their tales of derring-do and derring-*don't* – whatever-the-hell you do – or pay the debt in blood.

Jimbo and me, we tucked away a lot of bread and jam and tea during those round-table chats, deep underground below Big Smoke, with the trains chuntering overhead – *metal orchestral* he called it, my Jim – our punctuation, our clock, our warning system, those trains. We got tea and we got tips. Advice on how to sidestep deadly Ecumen patrollers who, after a ministerial decree declared that our gangs were vermin, were licensed to shoot at us if we formed groups of more than three. The general populace concurred after a time – once the Properganders got properly under way. They set up the earliest conversations between 'social commentators' and disk-jockeys on State Media until people started to absorb the 'new reality' and could do it for themselves; they sponsored the first newspaper articles that brought to public attention the 'filthy tactics' of the 'counter-revolutionaries', including the use of children in warfare. There was something in that, actually. A bit of truth, spun in a particular light ... In any case, the need for Kiddy-monster Clean up Raids, KimCuRs as they were called politely, came to be accepted in due course. 'A rabid dog is still diseased / Whether tall as your head or short as your knees.' Oh yes, there were some clever rhymes churned out back then.

But you can't keep kids locked up all the time. They get restless. Mot and Grim harnessed this energy, had us taking part in the ongoing counter-revolution that started well before the revolution had completed its cycle. Jim and I would creep out from our underground safe-haven from time to time to do jobs for our protectors. We also went out when they thought we were safely snuggled away in our mattresses and hammocks. Like the nights we'd sneak up to ground level to catch a movie. We'd head east down the Way of Martyrs to see an open-air film screening down at The Harbour Pit that used to contain the Opera Theatre. Jesumuh Utilities had had the hole partially drained and lined with concrete, and tiered seats had been built up around three of the four sides.

One night when there was a big yellow moon, the sky electric blue and the air filled with the screaming glee of cockatoos, we made our way down there to see this one titled *Satanic Sprogs and Evil Eggheads* that took place in a village called Midwich. The week before we'd already seen the first three in the quartet plugged as 'Pre-Liberation Tales of Horror': *The Bad Seed*, *The Good Son* and another about an evil boy called Kevin, I forget its name. *Satanic Sprogs*, the fourth one, starred pretty but malevolent blond children who were really alien spawn. The film was supposed to show how they got theirs – blown up by a suicide-bombing academic. Deep fun. Everyone who'd seen it loved it, other kids said it was really chill and mean and made you feel like chucking up your heart right out of your throat. They said it didn't have much blood compared to the Kevin film, but was way spookier. I was really looking forward to seeing it and turned to whisper my excitement to Jimbo. But he'd disappeared.

'Jen! Here!'

He was under the seat in the third tier, a brilliant vantage point. I crept in with him, my thin-warm, wiry animal and me peering out into the pool of night forming around us now. Soon, other people would start to show up, sitting in front, on top, behind, all around us, but unaware of our presence for their eyes would be riveted to the big screen, their minds attuned to the story that would unfold out there in the air, to transport them all to another place, a dreadful place, so that at the close of the film the relief and gratitude of post-Liberation existence would be palpable, people would embrace, some would even weep as they stood to sing the national anthem.

Jim had laid down the blanket we'd brought along to protect us from the damp. We made ourselves as comfortable as it's possible to manage when you're crouched under a row of benches avoiding feet and farts. After an hour or so the theatre was close to full. Jim and I shivered happily together under the row of buttocks. The screen unrolled and then Larry Day, one of the foremost critics of the day, walked onto the stage amid cheers from the audience. Seats creaked above us as the audience settled in to listen to the pre-movie talk by this luminary, who would conclude as always with a Strictural quote from the Doppelbook. That night, it was from Deuteronomy 21:

> If a man have a stubborn and rebellious son then shall his father and his mother lay hold on him, and bring him out unto the elders of his city, and all the men of his city shall stone him with stones, that he die: so shalt thou put evil away from among you.

But stones weren't really necessary when you had Ecumen for sharp-shooters. Sometimes they'd manage to corral a contingent of 'rebellious' (or 'evil' or 'possessed') child vermin. But usually we didn't get caught – not by them. More often it was do-gooders from Child Welfare who got the kids. Bundled them up For Their Own Good and shipped them off for re-education. Worse, when you think about it. The shooters got your body but Welfare took your soul.

23.

'Jennypatel?'

Jesumuh! The pesky little skerrick. See its nose poking out from behind my bed-curtain.

'I cannot sleep.'

She comes forward tentatively. She moves towards the fire, the sneaky little feline thing. I rub my eyes, knuckling residual images back into the past, where they belong I suppose. I light a cigar. Seems I can't stink her out though: she just takes a seat at the hearth, hunches forward and stirs up the coals a little. They wink into new life. She's still shivering though. I reach for a shawl and pass it over to her. She drapes it over her shoulders which, after a little while, are still.

'Better?'

She nods, reaches for the teapot, pours a cup for herself, wraps the fingers of her good hand around the cup, and presses it against the hand of her damaged arm. For the warmth and comfort of it all. She looks at me with those big baby blues. 'You were telling me about your father who spawned you. And of the lightless slum where you lived beyond the redeeming radiance of GodFather (BBHCM). Pre-Liberation.'

'Oh right, lightless slum. Actually, it was quite bright, Mica.'

'Tell me then, Hag.'

Tell her what, I wonder. How to soothe her, lull her, bring her into the fold, so to speak? Tales of the world before time stopped, gave itself a shake, clicked back into gear – and missed? Horribly.

'Back in the dim dark depths of time I used to live in a flat in a large building that was part of a terrace of similar buildings, quite low-rise, only twenty storeys or so. We got plenty of sun there on the eleventh floor, by the way. Though we were surrounded by terraces there was only the odd skyscraper. Our neighbourhood had been lucky: plenty of others had been done for in the last earthquake. And there was this lovely old tree in front with purple flowers. It made a bright carpet on the common area of grass by the road, where the cars drove by over bumps the road-builders had made to keep the traffic slow and the street safe, more or less. If you watched your step. You had to be careful, because the area was busy with people and animals and vehicles, the more expensive running on petrol and letting out stinky fumes, the electric ones purring and the ones drawn by donkeys clipping and clopping, a lovely, comforting, early-morning sound. Of course there was nowhere in the world that was not crowded, but this place was empty compared to my first home. Here, even the dogs were, if not fat, then not walking skeletons at least, and people rarely hit them. Or not too hard. There was a long yard behind the terrace, and a big outdoor stove for both veg and non-veg cookery that was often done on Sundays. I remember how everyone in the building would bring something to cook: eggplants, possum chops, potatoes, rice balls, sometimes milky bread pud loaded with sugar and cinnamon to heat up in a pot in the embers. My granny had been the main organiser of these events and we still kept the tradition after she died at the fine old age of ninety-seven, having choked to death on a wishbone! But then, wishes can kill. You have to be careful with wishes, as they say.'

'Who is this "they" of the killing wishes?'

'Oh, just people, dear. Never mind. So. The afternoons would always begin with a toast by Lee—'

'Who is this Lee? Is he important in your story?'

'Lee was my good, good friend and sort of pretend auntie. And yes. *She* is important. At Sunday barbecues she'd raise her glass in salute: "To Grand-ee Jen-anj-arun!", then "I want to see all your bottoms!" And everyone would drink deeply and their glass-bottoms winked in the sun. On these days, back then, the sun always shone. I understood that that was why they were called Sundays.

'My mum, my Anjali, Anjalima, one-time student of literature, then chicken plucker, bicycle courier and copy-editor for what she liked to refer to as the "Daily Dope", now worked as a cleaning-lady at my school in the old cinema. My dad taught at the university, which is where he met our Lee – Dr Cobham that is. He was in Science – a botanist, my dad, very clever-clever gentleman and also excellent expert at growing things. She was in the Humanities faculty, specialising in the study of women and things to do with gender. Also dead smart of course, brainy-wise, but less clever with her feelings, which often exploded into words that sometimes got her into trouble.'

'"A foolish woman is clamorous. She is simple and knows nothing",' quotes my learned interlocutor. Shakespeare? Hardly, you mad old bag. It'll be from the DoppelBook.

'Lee would certainly pronounce on things, my friend,' I say firmly, 'and she could declaim like Cato; she could lecture and even hector, and that is not *clamouring*.'

Mica's eyes harden, but she says nothing. *She* would not 'clamour' like a fool. Not her, all silent virtue and cold judgement. Just at that moment, I really wouldn't have minded clouting her one.

'Lee was loud and may have lacked the kind of commonsense that survivors have, but she had her own kind of wisdom. And her heart was as big as a house. A tenement a hundred storeys in the sky, crowned by clouds and light, with room for everybody inside. Understand?'

'I understand you.' Small, frosty voice from this small, frosty thing.

'So, my dad introduced Lee to my mum, and they became friends. Sometimes Anjali and I would go and visit Lee after school. Lee was funny and foul-mouthed and could, as my daddy put it, charm the leg off a donkey. I remember keying into my diary: *Could you make a leg come off a donkey? Magic. Maybe, if you concentrated hard!*'

'Travesty!'

'Sorry? Do enlighten me. I'm bit out of touch with the latest travesties.'

'Magic is a travesty of religion, the enemy of the Dual True Faith, misguided heresy of (wo)Man contaminated by the spirit of Lilith who will breathe vile humours into the tiniest of cracks she might find in the soul-encrusting shield of faith, should we fail in our vigilance.'

'Of course, sorry, forgot about the crusty faith bit. In any case – I spent a lot of time with Mum and Lee, listening to their conversations, the sort that take many detours to follow thoughts that flow like tributaries from the main river, so that sometimes it seemed we were having quite a different conversation from the one I'd thought they were having at the beginning. I was there for the ride, so I leaned as my daddy taught me; I leaned so I learned.

'I wasn't quite old enough then to follow the news of what was happening in the world in the same way they did, but I picked up plenty.

I knew how people were always moving from country to country to try and find somewhere to live where they needn't fear for their lives. I knew how there were more people in the world now than there ever had been before and no safe places, not really, and I knew that jobs were hard to find anywhere. I knew that it hadn't always been like this. That once upon a time there used to be fewer people and lots more animals in the world, marvellous ones, like giant cats with amber eyes that never blinked, and that once there had been uncountable millions of fish in the sea that sometimes people caught in nets and ate, they were so plentiful. There were giant air-breathing animals in the sea as well, some as big as a house; there were birds with tiny bells in their throats that chimed like angelic cymbals each morning; there were small fat insects that hummed all day long, and had glittering wings and bodies of black and gold that, once upon a time, had made sweet syrup from flowers. The idea of this was like a poem to me. Syrup from flowers.

'The land too was very different in the past. I learned about that from my history lessons and also from listening to Anjali and Arun and Lee, who remembered a different world from their own childhoods, which were not really as far back as all that, I realised – not in the great scheme of things. I found a lot of what I heard very hard to believe indeed. Once there had been mountains full of treasure, and valleys with strongly flowing rivers. Now, so many of the mountains have had their tops all flattened, their treasure all dug out and the river valleys filled with rubble. Once there'd been forests so wide you could never cross them and the leaves of the trees made the air delicious to breathe, and this wholesome air spread around the world in nourishing currents. Back then, people almost never wore masks, and hardly anyone needed to buy extra oxygen in canisters, queuing for days outside the superstores and minimarts. Then, there were people who lived to be seventy years old or more, believe it or not, the food and air and water was so plentiful and clean. In some countries, nobody went to bed with their tummies grumbling. Back then in the olden days, there were small islands in the Sea covered in fine white sand ringed all around by banks of lacy shells of a hundred colours. Once, Africa and America had been different shapes and twice as big. Once it had been rare for babies to die before they were born, and only a minority of children entered the world already sick or malformed. But when I was young, in my neighbourhood, people gave parties to celebrate the rare event of the birth of an undamaged child. Yet more babies were coming than ever—'

'More children makes greater productivity, stronger armies to fight,' my complacent little clone informs me. 'But I don't understand what is this Athricker? This Americker?'

'Listen, hugger-mugger. I'm dead tired even if you're not. Look' – I nod towards the window that is now filling up with a gruelly light – 'sun's coming up. In its lousy way. We can continue the story later. But I have an atlas I can show you – a book of maps? Out of date of course – the contours of the world and the borders of nations have changed many times since it was made – but it gives you a general idea of how the world looked, once a upon a time. Read yourself to sleep if you're restless.' I give her a candle to take with her into the nook, as the niggardly daylight will probably not get any brighter than it is now.

'I will look at Atalass then, while you are sleeping.'

I give her a couple of other books too, an Australand history she won't have heard before and probably won't believe, another of Anglindia, and a graphic novel, all derring-do for girlies. She is a keen listener, that's for sure. Maybe she can also learn?

There are other children who have learned, after all. Me and my underground compatriots, for example. We had been in a real mess trying to winkle a bit of truth out of the layers of lies, not knowing whom to believe, to trust. But like any strays of any species, when all's said and done, you tend to go with those who are kind to you. Like the Fools. Which is why the movement continued to grow. First the 'old' warriors like Mot and Grim – pushing twenty-three when I first met them – and then the 'older newbies', Melanie, Tajik and Tiny. They started training up the next generation of runaways as well. Fifi, Darren, Mandrake … Though I haven't heard anything of Motley and Grimie lately. I worry. Of course I worry. They're no spring chickens any more.

 PEARL

24.

On the first evening we ate a dinner of wasabi possum pies from thick ceramic plates with pictures of rabbits running around their edges, and over the next few days they both took turns to tell me a story – a recent history of the world, the Fools' version. I didn't believe much of it. Not then. But look, I said to myself, even if it *is* all lies I don't *care*, for all I want is to never, *ever* return to the only reality I have ever known. But by the second evening my poor brain was hurting a bit because everything familiar, all the places and the people, were looking very different in this new revised account. This, for example: what I had learnt as, 'So the Heroes of Liberation worked ceaselessly to protect the vulnerable populace from corruption' became, in the recent History Retold by Motley the Fool, 'So the Propergander Movement began with the seizure of control over all the communications systems so that no bugger outside the Ministry had any idea of what the fuck was going on.'

I reciprocated of course. At the beginning it was swift telling for they knew most of it already – there's hardly much room for departures from the usual themes in Perfect. Or Ideal or Impeccable or any other State. But they got pretty interested when I recounted how the paper plane had found me and livened me up. They wondered whose it had been. 'Mandy, for sure,' reckoned Grimalda, 'He's around that neck of the woods. Did you see any thin orangey-coloured men trying to blend in?'

Not many. But then redheaded jesters are easy to miss where I come from. Heh heh.

They got even more bright-eyed when I told of my refusal to Beseech, and of my escape. Told me I was brave. They were sad when I told them that my lover had not come. Not as sad as me.

Over this past week I've got to know this couple very well. Grimalda, maternal and kind; Motley – well, he tolerated me admirably once I'd worked out how to please him, keep him tranquil, my big gentle-fool.

 MICA

25.

I am no novice with regard to big books such as this one of the Hag's. Heavy tomes with covers of hard board and shiny jackets to keep them free of dust. Of course, after Liberation most were burned along with the other Satanic accoutrements, in pits like the one I encountered on my way here. So many are filled with heresies that inflame the mind. Yet some remain in the Library of the Men of Right-Sight who have the intellectual strength and integrity to read without being seduced. Some others are displayed safely within thick glass vitrines in the Museum of Iniquities, along with other exhibits from before the Liberation. But there are plenty of texts that we girlies are actively encouraged to read, oh so many! We have manuals written to accompany our lessons – on gardening, drainage and hygiene of course, but there are also much more engrossing ones, like Sating the Man, with its instructive passages on how to contract the parts within the cockslot so that it might be all the tighter for the Man, in whose service a (wo)Man might also derive great satisfaction if she learns her lessons well, and many other suggestions for improving the Man's pleasure during the sex act, for it is written: 'The hot cock yields the seed.' We are also provided with instruction on Attracting the Gaze: how to generate a Man's interest when you are simply going about your duties, or walking across the corp-yard with your sisters. For why would he touch you if you are unattractive (like poor Opal)? Thus, notes on how to sway the hips, arch the neck, thrust forth the dugs, so as to attract the gaze of Men.

Then there are detailed tracts on Sedating the Ego and Stilling the Mind, and on the Graces of CHOM and how to enact them daily. How to please by gesture and voice are important though understated aspects of CHOM, for these must replace music, once a well-loved medium of pleasure. In fact, I have heard that the Brother Ministers were reluctant to ban it. Yet ban it they must, so arousing and dangerous is it to the spirits ... There are the texts, *The Responsibilities of the Vessel*, and *Labial Mysteries as a Metaphor for Life*, and *The Adoration of the Sacred Staff and*

Rod with its beautiful cover of our blessed Jesumuh, right foot forward with one hand bearing the Sceptre, the other, a tightly furled orchid. Oh, but I am making myself homesick. I yearn to be where I belong, with the people who trust me, who have given me all I possess, both materially and spiritually. And whom I have treated with such contempt in disobeying …

But I do believe, as it happens, that I can make something of the situation in which I find myself. I have been coming to realise that whether or not I succeed in saving my Pearl, there is a way, in all humility, that I may be of service to the people to whom *I belong* (*inshallaweh* a thousand times over!). The Hag is so eager to speak, so careless of all she relates, that there is certainly a chance that she may unwittingly identify places or people in which the Properganders of Instruction & Destruction may be interested. It is known, after all, that there exist enclaves of reactionary rogues within the civilised domain of the States as well as in Unrule, for it is written: 'Many are the snares of spiders, many the cobweb strands wherein waits the patient predator.' I have to admit to myself a little self-interest here, though I do not like to think on this aspect too much, yet it is true that perhaps by these actions I might also, to some small degree, mitigate my crime. But regardless of this, in order to accomplish anything useful I must listen until the end of her tale and, I confess, it is not hard for me to do so for she brings her words to life with such vivacity. She could have been a Propergander herself, had she been a Man. And not damned to hell. What am I talking about? I must be tired. My thoughts are becoming muddled.

I must force myself to understand the references she makes as she discourses on her life and the times she has known. And so I will read her books. But I need to be strong, so first I undertake a brief Meditation on the Sacred Sceptre and a recitation of the 'Prayer for Anxious Girlies in Uncertain Times', and only then do I open the booked called *World Atlas*.

I recognise the names of the mythical 'Africa' and 'America' from the witch's lies – and how hard it has been for me to resist contradicting her 'recollections' of 'history', which are certainly the most ridiculous fabrications. Clearly she is an ignorant (wo)Man because she failed to attend to her lessons as a child, failed to exploit all of her GodFather-given advantages. And now rather than meditating on her sins as she should, she dwells on memories of her unfeminine mother and (wo)Mannish father, her syrupy blossoms and her inventions such as creatures with stripes, *cats* no less!

I must remain wary of her demonstrations of care for me. I remember another of the True Tales of my Art & Pain tutor, Bobander, from when I was little. We had progressed beyond Naughty Kitty, would have been in Minus-Seven or -Six by then, and were up to *The Child, the Witch and the Poisoned Peach*, part of which was loosely based on one of the semenal texts of the DoppelBook and modified to appeal to young girlie-minds. 'This story, children, takes place many many years ago, not long after the wars,' Bobander began. 'It is about a little girlie who was virtuous and beautiful to Men.' We all sighed and looked at handsome Bobander. Many of us – I for one – hoped that one day soon, when we were closer to (wo)Manhood, he might like to fuck us.

'And how this good little girlie was slandered …'

'Ooooh …' we breathed in unison.

'And banished …'

'Ahhhh …'

'From the State by the Evil House Mother …'

'Hissssss …'

'Who was jealous of our dear Goodgirlie's sweet face and body, and was really a Witch in disguise.' I knew such perversity could come about in a Ma, whether of Oblation, Sacricunt, Dutilove or one from any other State, for a House Mother is still a (wo)Man and therefore of fragile morality. 'This was a very bad Ma indeed. Remember, Liberation had only recently come. And she had been one of those from the time of Ignorance when the Agnostics controlled the land. She had dabbled in the Dark Arts of Fenimistry and was familiar with the magic of the ancestral whores, Lilith and her daughter Jezebel. Though of course nobody knew that, so devious was she in her wily wanton ways.'

'Wily wanton ways of wicked (wo)Man …' we chorused.

Bobander told of how the child undergoes many tribulations in her banishment but, finally, some kindly Men, Sub-Ecumen Guards of some far-flung outpost of Civilisation, take her in and allow her to service them. She is happy there in their little house. Her duties are light, for there are only seven of them and they are elderly, so most of her work is concerned with cleaning and cooking rather than fucking. And so she lives there, though never giving up hope that one day a young Ecuman might come and find her and bring her back home to the State where she hopes that she will one day be selected for Perfection. Bobander told us that the Witch learns of Goodgirlie's whereabouts by way of one of her spells of Fenimistry and determines to find the child, whom she wants to kill, for if Goodgirlie is saved she may tell the Ministers of the Witch's treachery.

'One day, children,' he said, 'she is working by the stream, washing her Men's garments while they are away Guarding, and an old (wo)Man approaches her, an old woman with a basket of …'

'Fruit! A basket of fruit!'

'The child is startled and afraid, for as we know, a (wo)Man abroad alone can only be either one of the lil'im or some other kind of demon. Yet this one's face was kind – though the child could not know it, it was the Witch who had magically transformed her face into an unfamiliar visage by occult means. The witch says, "I have a gift for you, child."'

'A gift?' we girlies all responded, for after a few tellings we knew the rhythms of the story, one of our favourites.

'An apple. She flourishes the fruit from within the bush. And the child is …'

'Appalled!'

'And the child says, "Oh no, I do not eat of the Knowledge Fruit!"'

'Because as the DoppelBook teaches us …'

'Knowledge is the preserve of Man. Obedience the preserve of (wo)Man.'

'Good girlies! Yes. And so, the Witch realises her mistake. She is not very bright because …'

'Her mind is rotten with sin.' Frightened giggles all round.

'She then offers the child a fig. And the child says …'

'Oh no, I do not eat of the Manly Fruit!' More giggles and half-knowing nudges.

'So at last, she offers the child …'

'A peach! A peach!'

'And the child takes the peach, and thanks the Witch most prettily. And she eats the peach, which is poisoned. Of course. And the child …'

'Becomes white …'

'And purple …'

'And green …'

'And she coughs and vomits until she is empty. And then, and then …'

'She dies. She dies.' The more tender-hearted among us often began to cry. Nickeline would sob loudly until Galena gave her a good, sharp smack across the ear. And there would be more for her later in Supervised Peer Slapping and Kicking.

It is a good story, and one that teaches more than the natural graces of CHOM, which all children learn at Minus-Ten; it is a sophisticated parable that teaches circumspection and caution. It protects the unwary against the seductions of strangers, and inculcates a healthy skepticism in those who would believe the charming lies of the agents of corruption that are sent to try us.

With this lesson in mind I feel equipped to continue reading the atlas given me by the witch, with whom I must have dealings whether I like it or not.

The leering sunlight is trying to get in through the window. I lean the pillow against it and sit up a bit straighter. I scan one of the other books she has provided, the one with the story of the heretic Lara Croft, but it is a fantastical tale with no bearing on reality, so it bores me when it does not insult me with its warped morality. I try the book called *Australand History* with its equally bizarre chapter headings. It is funny in a sick way to note the narrative distortions feeding into downright fabrications. When I lose patience with it I turn back to *World Atlas*. As well as maps and graphs and pictures there are vivid descriptions in the text also of places, of peoples and customs – all of which is certainly the invention of imagination both fevered and unconstrained. Yet so colourful and strange the shapes of the words: Oceania, Oman and Kiribati; Polynesia, Puerto Rico and Panama; Belarus, Bulgaria, Salahah, Switzerland. The names ring in my ears when I sound them out aloud.

Yet, deep in my heart I feel a warning. And if 'warning' can have colour, it is deep red; if sound, then it is that of flesh tearing as it resists the serrations of the blade.

THE HAG

26.

My blankets stink a bit. Might need a wash one day, me and them both. Blackie lies down beside me and in moments he's snoring like a locomotive in a dream tunnel. The sooner I move my latest foundling on, the sooner I can have my own bed back and get a decent sleep.

I've only told her generalities. It's not up to me to proselytise. And probably I shouldn't have even given her the history books. Too much too soon. I remind myself that in a little while I may well be able to see her off in the charge of my friends and allies, and then when she's out of this benighted zone there'll be time enough for her to learn a different history, one that I'm part of and she gets to inherit, lucky little devil.

I doze awhile. I wake and note the fine phosphorescent gleam of my little toadstools in their crannies. Gaze sleepily into the flames, my head on Blackie's flank. I see Jimbo and me down in the Pit, thrilling to the cinematic delights of the time, the warmth of him coming through the rough sweater he wore, the tang of his skin scented, much like mine, of petrol and papaya juice, and my mind drifts further back. I see me and my parents down at the same site, before the Action that created that great gaping hole, back in the days when it was still a pretty harbour foreshore. I'd come down with Anjali and Arun and some of the others from our building to hear Ricky Sartorial Junior give the address after Reunion of Church and State. He was speaking live from America to all his 'friends and allies in the Cold Culture War'. His father had started the process, old Ricky Senior; he was the first 'cultural warrior' – as he called himself – to propose restoration of the union of God and Country. Now here was his son, standing proudly beneath the flag of the Reformed United States of America, good old RUSA.

With tears in his eyes Ricky Junior proclaimed: 'For too long the liberal Agnostics enforced this false dichotomy, this old lie that the Word of God has no role to play in the operation of the State. And now, at last, the contest between the secular and the religious is over! And we stand proud beneath the banner that symbolises our return to the values so many of us have always held dear. God is my right! *Halle-*

lujah!' Although we were watching a broadcast from the other side of the world, it seemed as if it was the breath of the southerly coming in from the Heads that caused that triumphant billowing of their new flag: Stars and Stripes banded beneath the horizontal arm of the crucifix, the new flag of a diminished but still proud new America ... oh yes ...

The sun, such as it is, wakes me again, peering into my face like a mildly interested interrogator. The rain's eased to its lightest veil of drizzle and hangs in the air like a damp shroud blurring the edges and angles of everything. The cockies like it though. Hear them screech across the fields like aerial bandsaws. Blackie's up, his toenails tapping across the floor to the door, wagging his flag of a tail.

Get up, crack door, let dog out to attend to his doggy needs. Today's one of my meeting days, so I dress quietly, then look in on the waif. Still aslumber, a bit of spit on its sleep-puffed lips, the atlas open at Antarctica. I wrap myself up against the cold. Blacks comes over and puts his nose into my hand and leans against me, dear old bugger. As I pull on my waterproof his eyes brighten. 'Sorry,' I whisper, opening the door and nudging him back inside. '*Stay*.' He gets it, goes in and sits. Looking all cheated and miserable. 'Ah dear, you *do* do an excellent line in hang-dog, my dog. But I need you to keep the skerrick company. If you're here when she wakes she'll know I haven't abandoned her.'

I fetch the old shopping trolley from the shed and set off into the forest. Track down the incline to where a particular streamlet of Big River wends its way through casuarinas and banksias all deformed in the endless acid rain, through versions of other familiar plants grown strange since the last viral bombardments, nameless vegetal things all warty and pustular and bearded with fungus, and tubular creations as much animal as vegetable with their fanged trumpet-gobs sucking in small creatures that fly through the wet, poisonous air.

Down here, there used to be edible berries, bitter but sustaining if you were desperate enough, but now they're pallid and coated with gummy stuff – I wouldn't touch them if I were fainting with hunger. Then: I think I hear something not that far behind me, the crack of a twig, a movement of leaves as if in a breeze – yet there's no breeze. But no, just the fancy of one accustomed to hiding, accustomed to wariness, and I must not succumb to the paranoia solitude brings. No. Once there was much more in the way of activity down here; there was scurrying and fluttering, crackling in the undergrowth as small feet scampered away at the sound of my intrusion. But these days not so much. The sky still sustains cockies and crows though, and once I heard the full-throttled belly-laugh of a kookaburra, so rare now that I wept. And there's creepers and twisted trees and bright yellow carpets of scum growing over any water sheltered from the sky with its endless rain … Has heaven itself been ruptured? When will it stop? But no, don't stop, let the rain fall and the trees grow and spread and hide me and mine from the eyes above, from the aerial Ecumen and their chopping blades.

A little further through the dripping trees and past the rock-face, fungoid and rank, and again I pause, not because I hear anything, but because of a sensation I have of another's attention on me. But the eyes of watching creatures will do that. Watching and waiting until you pass by. I'm out of sorts, I know. The effect of my guest, no doubt, for she's unsettling indeed.

I guide the rickety trolley down the bank to the inlet where the contraband cargo comes in from Scandos in the far north or from the near south, the Zealanders across the narrow Tasman Channel. There is the dock, painted the dun and grey of water and sky and overarching trees. Empty now. And there our lean-to, not much more than a few sheets of corrugated iron tilted against the oozing scarp. I check the delivery timetable and add some extra staples to the list. I need more tea and flour and such when I have a visitor. I sit on the concrete slab of the doorway and wait.

27.

Soon enough the barge comes into view and I see it's Mandrake today.

She poles her way over to the bank and waves, her skinny, red-haired arm protruding from the water-coloured coat. From beneath the broad-brimmed slate-grey Ranger hat, her welcoming grin is like a slice of watermelon, black seeds and all. She has terrible teeth, poor darling, worse than mine. I move to help her unload the crate of propaganda.

'Butt out, old jez,' she says, 'you'll only slip a disk,' and she drops a swift kiss on my cheek. Together we haul the baggage towards the lean-to.

'What have we got?' I ask, feeling eager as a child at Christmastime in that world that hasn't been in existence for half a century.

'Well, a few more films I've managed to re-mistress somewhat. Miyazaki's *Nausicaa* was slightly less successful than the excellent result I got with *Brave* ... but you need the hard copy gear I know.' Once we're inside, she itemises: 'Thus, I have: coupla mini-biogs illustrated by yours truly that I'm really rather proud of – check the vigour and overall delectability of the paintwork. Masterful eh?' She stops to flip open a floppy soft-back at its title page. 'See, here's your Amelia Earheart, your Mary Shelley, not sparing the juicy bits.' She cuts the string on another parcel, 'And ... dah dah! Graphic novels galore! Also illustrated and abridged for easy consumption and corruption. There's Marvellous Margaret's *The Handmaid's Tale*, Loveable Le Guin's *Tehanu*, Fabulous Philip's *Northern Lights* – still working on the next two in the trilogy – plus movie-to-magazine adaptations of *Buffy the Vampire Slayer* and *Lisbeth Salander, the Untold Story*, a *shit*-load of *Tank Girl* and *Katniss Everdeen meets Kitkat Neverdeen*, volume six.'

'Mandy, this is beautiful, beautiful ...' I'm overwhelmed, I am. 'You've excelled yourself this time.'

'Well, much as I'd like to take all the credit, we've got a few stayers who are proving a dab hand at painting,' she confides, as a raindrop lands smack bang on Lisbeth's dragon. Carefully she blots it with her sleeve. 'And there's some dead good pomes too, rooly trooly good work. Tear this old heart up they do, almost every one of my little escapees, with their wide-open eyes and their secret hearts.' The rain starts in earnest as we page through the books, a gentle patter on the tin roof, a lovely sound. 'They've never been taught to write anything but transcriptions of idiot prayers and invocations to their big old torturer in the sky, and they've been told they don't have minds, see themselves as slop buckets, yet after a few lessons they write like angels! Pure, clear, most basic and, oh, killingly lovely, my lovely witchy-poo, *killing*. It makes me sob quite loudly I get so heartchucky.' As if to echo this thought, the rain begins to drum down very seriously now.

'They don't want to go themselves?'

'My love, they do not. They fall hopelessly in love with me and simply must stay! I explain that I'm not that kind of girl, but the poor pets can't help themselves. And they *have* had the sort of education that encourages group work. Nothing like a strict little totalitarian collective to prep a girl for the rigours of sacrifice to a greater cause. Tea? And so our ranks are swelling.'

'I've got another stray, first in ages.'

'Really?' Her arched brows arch further, corrugating the bony forehead with lines that disappear into the carrotty fringe. I see it glinting in the light of the torch I've set up on the shelf above the kerosene heater, which Mandy is now endeavouring to light with a wet match. 'Tell me more. Who what where when why and chief characteristics of the latest … It's been a while.'

'It has. Indoctrination's been on the improve alright. The stray's spouting fresher horrors than the ones I got to know in the good old days, as if those weren't enough.'

'Mind you don't act the preacher, Jen. You know it never works.' She is sitting with her long arms propped up on her knees, freckled fingers steepled under her chin, green eyes intent.

'Mandrake, I know, I know. But I'm less worried about getting all preachy at the moment than simply keeping my temper. No, don't look quizzy at me – really. She's so … *cold*, coldly *zealous*. A spooky little rodent, truly.'

'But never say die, my winsome Witch of Hagovel! The ones we have at the moment are good girls, Jen, really very good; and we get the odd boy too, even they run off from time to time. And there's a new wave too, something we hadn't predicted – careforcers turning to us. Helping out when they can, the poor ruined wretches.'

'Really? This is new. I mean it's great, of course – but I hadn't heard.'

'Yep, especially the xeniicuts from Perfect and Ideal. Perfect xeniies 226 to 230 are particularly keen. Not sure what got into them, but point is, something did! Maybe they don't like having their lips stitched up after all. Or something. Isn't it nice to know that some have worked out that Perfection ain't what it's cracked up to be? So, as well as turning out some extra-fab artists, we've got quite a few brave little spies and smugglers, really quite daring – it's probably Lara Croft's influence, or Merida's – that's why I'm getting them to do a lot of novelised versions of the *Brave* sequels recently. So it's really just a matter of time before we get another good surge I reckon. But *tell* me about your *latest!* Sugar?'

'You know there's no sugar. I doubt she'll be a stayer. It'll be all I can do to make her a goer. At the moment she's hell-bent on getting home.'

'Home is?'

'Perfect.'

'Poor darlin'.'

'Hardly *darlin'*, darlin'. She's a sanctimonious little sniper.'

We nurse our mugs of bitter tea for the warmth. The heater's working now. It's almost snug, what with the rain coming down on the corrugated iron, the scent of eucalyptus, tea, paper, ink and that greasepainty smell that always persists with Fools like Mandy and Grimalda who favour the trad clown look (with plenty of drag-queen frou-frou on top, naturally). Doesn't seem to matter how carefully they remove the stuff when they're incognito.

'Fret not, sweet,' she says. 'Get her to me and I'm bound to get her sorted! Oh, don't look so anxious, Mrs Haggy, the kid's only human and who can resist such a dashing clown as yours truly? Anyway, why'd she leave if she's so keen on Perfect and its cosy little cunnydorms and spare parts factory?'

'Ran off after the girlfriend. Got the zeal, remember. Needs to save the beloved's soul.'

'Not soul. "Girlies" don't have 'em, remember?'

'Honour, then.'

'That's the ticket. And the pursued beloved is … ?'

'Pearl. Come across any Pearls?'

'Well goodness gracious and fuck me dead. I have, as it happens. A couple of weeks back. But she's been moved on since then.'

'Zealand?'

'I don't think so. She's bright and pretty daring to boot. I think we've got her working in Transport and Counterpropaganda. I'll find out for you soon as I can I promise. But Jen, you're not looking as thrilled as you could. What's going on in that witchy noggin?'

'Oh, I don't know. That is, if Mica finds her Pearl, I don't know who'd convince whom of what. Know what I mean?'

'Ah, that Pearl's a wild one. And canny too. I'd lay odds on her. But first things first: I'll get in touch with Mot, and we'll worry about the rest later.'

'Motley? But I thought Mel was looking after the river traffic lately.'

'Jen. I'm so sorry. You haven't heard then? '

My heart clunks down to my shoes. Ah, Jesumuh. I know what's coming.

'Melanie's barge was captured a while back.'

Dear, cranky Mel in all her awkwardness, her largeness, her anger that lit her up and drove her. She was never a friend to me, but she was a force. Saboteur extraordinaire, and tireless disseminator of lies. If our little group ever managed to inject a bit of misinformation up the arse end of Propergander Advisory Boards, State Infrastructure, Border Control, often as not it was Mel who pumped the enema bag. A veteran survivor too. Until now.

'Haggy my dear, I'm going to have to make a move.' Mandrake kisses me on the cheek and stands. We load a jerrycan of petrol, another of grog, a box of gingernuts and a new hoe onto my trolley. Then she reaches into the folds of her coat and produces a big box of Honduran cigars. St Luis Rey. I lift the lid and inhale.

'Mandy, you're a darling and a gentleman.'

'*C'est moi* to a T, more or less.'

She adds a couple of Tank Girls to my provisions, saying, 'For your little evangelist – and now I shall make like a spectre into the blightful tempest. Duty schmooty and all that. No, don't come out.' We hug and I wave her off from the door.

I stay, breathing in wet bush smells and sweet tobacco, puffing and sipping and remembering.

28.

'Pass the sugar, Sugar,' said Melanie, for I was sweet back then.

Light was winking off the pot, the cups, the plates with their smears of gravy and jam and papaya juice, light that back then was electric, not moon.

'This new project in the offing,' Mel said, turning to Motley, 'are you going to enlighten us?'

Mot pushed back his boa, the one with that purple-black sheen he chose to complement his skin tone. He bit into a possum pie, rich with suet and crumbly at the edges. A bit like the man himself, come to think of it, soft and hard. He chewed ruminatively as he gazed over the other bright-eyed white and brown and black faces arrayed before him. 'You'll be posted at Impeccable Junction' – nodding his curly-wigged head at Mel, then at Tiny, Po-Face and Jimbo – 'where the reffo train from down south'll be transferring its cargo to the northbound to Perfect.' I knew what 'cargo' meant: a batch of newly 'liberated' kids collected from the borderlands of Unrule. Perfect State had one of the biggest children's re-education centres in those early days. Then he added, to Melanie, 'You'll be boss lady, ok my love?'

Melanie sometimes got mistaken for a boy, what with her wide shoulders and confident stride. She had a fleshy face and protuberant eyes which gave her a slightly amphibious look. She was a little older than most of us, though a fair bit younger than Motley and Grimalda, who seemed immensely aged and wise to me, though they were only in their very early twenties then. 'Tricky one?' Mel asked. He told her that yes, there would be a need for discretion. I said, 'Motley, let me go too.' And I added, 'I'm small enough to be handy,' just in case they might need someone slight enough to slip between cracks, and I did fancy myself as having certain rat-like virtues.

Motley became deeply involved in adding sugar to his tea. I looked over at Jimbo for help, but he just ducked his flossy noggin of blond locks between his shoulders and licked the gravy from his plate. I knew he always wanted me with him – no, he wanted me with him *always*. But he wouldn't encourage me or speak for me to Motley. He wouldn't. He loved me.

Another image of Jimbo pops up, like a snapshot: his head bowed in concentration over a book in our subterranean grotto, oblivious to all the dripping and dankness and the fluoros lighting his hair up like a halo. Or another: he's scooping a forkful of stew and sniffing it delicately in case it had a bit of chicken flesh in it – he wouldn't eat chickens – said they had wicked eyes. But then, he couldn't eat pig meat either, for pigs' eyes were twinkly and bright. Him with the deft fingers folding paper planes with messages for those who could read them ... Jimbo, my ethereally slender little love, resting his hand in the curve between my neck and shoulder as he slept.

My thoughts return to that meeting. 'Grimes and I have a meeting this afternoon upstairs,' Mot mentioned then, tilting his chin upwards to where Utilities and Transport had their offices.

'In macho mode?' Tajik asked him, loading a piece of bread up with jam.

'That is the correct goldfish. We'll be in our manly grey Ranger 'a-la-guard' camo-gear. After all, they'll be wanting gunners, not punners.'

Grimalda added, 'And because we'll be looking so *very* strong and reliable and trustworthy and everything, U & T will believe us when we say that there's been a *hell* of a lot less runaway activity in and around

Impeccable than there has been here, at Big Smoke, where delinquency's *rife* just now, so they'd be best off pulling Ecumen from there and relocating them to, say, Ideal.'

Mel said, 'But there's been next to nothing going on here this month, Grimie. It's been centred around Impeccable,' and I noticed Tiny gently nudged her in the ribs for her slowness, then she blushed beet-red when the light dawned.

Grimalda said, 'If all goes well, it'll happen like this: train from the south pauses briefly at Big Smoke, and that's where you smaller ones get on, mix in with the reffos. Mel will be there to give you orders, so make sure you attend to her. That's the easy bit. The train'll stop again at Impeccable. Doll-face will then nip into the driver's cabin and work her sweet magic on him, distracting him while Tajik and my good self adjust the sleepers. The train will then choof off east instead of north, come to a grinding halt in woop-woop by a loop of Big River, where it'll be met with: one, a fleet of stolen Holy Hummers that will drive on into Unrule; and two, a half dozen barges headed for the coast. Safest in two parties, after all.'

I could translate that easily enough – if the Hummers didn't make it, maybe the barges would, and vice versa. Don't put all your sprogs in one basket. And I was gobsmacked. This was the most audacious bit of Fool intervention I'd heard so far. Grimie made it sound simple, but I knew Mel and Jim and the others would have to evade both Guards and Ecumen. And I wouldn't have swapped places with Doll-face for anything. Then there'd be the split-second timing involved in shifting the youthful cargo, bribery and threats and the exercise of much wit and faith on the journey from Big Smoke Station to the Big River stop. And all had to be accomplished before people realised what was happening and an alarm could be raised. I looked around at the others. Many eyes on stalks. I wasn't the only one.

Motley turned to me. 'You probably already know the aircon ducts linking the Ministry offices from your travels?'

Ah, see my little ears all cocked and my puppy-tail all a-thumping in time with my pounding heart? Oh yes. I'd had a few jobs of different sorts already. Like thieving from shops and provisions stores, like kidnapping chickens and goats when we could, and nicking grain and vegetables from rural States that were being set up, like leaving messages scrawled on barn walls or on pieces of paper that we'd fold into aeroplanes and shoot in through the windows of sleeping cunnydorms and Ecuboy Houses in Perfect, Idyllic, Ideal, Peerless, Impeccable, Incomparable, Superlative. And yes, there'd also been a bit of creeping and crawling around in wall cavities. We'd drill eyeball-sized spy-holes in the walls or ceilings of main meeting places to hear what we might hear, and report back. Yes: I was indeed familiar with the aforementioned ducts.

'What you might do then, my love, if it's not too much trouble, is snuggle-wuggle yourself into the pipes above the office and press your dear little ear to the wall – or the floor as it may be – after I leave the meeting. Pay attention to what they say. As I do rather pride myself on my gift of dissimulation, I'll be telling them quite a lot of lies, and I need to know if they stick.' He waited while a train thundered by overhead. 'Point is, if they do intend to follow my advice we'll go ahead. If not, we'll pull the job.'

'But Mot,' interrupted Mel, 'there're at least 75 girls who'll end up in cunnydorms all over the States and half again as many boys who'll end up in Ecumen training programs, and—'

'I'm not sacrificing any of my babies I know and love for babies I don't yet know.'

The folds of Mel's frog face were set in stolid opposition. I wondered, unworthily, then what *would* you sacrifice your babies for?

'And Mel, my love,' he continued, 'I do believe there's a bit of organising you need to do. In case I do give you the go-ahead.'

'Mot.'

'Mel. Off you fuck, sweetest. And the rest of you, too. Give me and Grimie a bit of peace for an hour.'

Mel stumped off angrily, and the rest of us followed. As I was walking out with Jimbo, Motley reached over and tapped me on the arm, 'Alright then?'

'Alright.'

Later that day, Motley swapped his boa and his black-and-lime jumpsuit and his tricorn hat for the grey Ranger uniform. While he made his way upstairs from our subterranean hidey-hole by way of the defunct escalator, then out and along the street to the Ministry's street door, Jimbo crept with me through the ducts as far as he could go. He was skinny, but his shoulders were too wide to squeeze through spaces that a person of my unusual smallness could manage. So after a while,

Jenny Patel, would-be hero, found herself sandwiched into a vent above the offices of Utilities and Transport, ear to the grille, doing her bit for queens and cuntry.

Not long after, I heard the men coming in, then the sound of chairs scraping back, the rustle of paper. I was only inches away from the owners of the voices below. Within the first ten or so minutes I had pins-and-needles in both feet, one of my arms was numb and my neck had a horrible painful crick in it. But it's surprising how still a girl can be when she knows that any sound, any hint of movement from her, for the next hour or so will result in her immediate conversion from person to pulp.

29.

I notice now that my old limbs are cramped and aching. The rain has slowed to neutral, its default position of a kind of incontinent mistiness leaking the odd spatter and trickle. I raise my weary bones.

Blacks is stationed by the door when I get back, and something fragrant with meat juices and herbs is bubbling on the stove. She's been cooking, or at least augmenting the stock pot. Well, good for her! Sign of the civilising effect of cohabitation with the damned. She comes to the door and sees my laden trolley. She looks at it, at me, back again.

'Been shopping,' I say. Oh ho Jen, you are a one.

Blank stare.

'At the hag-o-mart.'

She doesn't smile, or rather she doesn't do that awkward grimace which is her tragic version of an expression of good humour. But neither does she question me further, which is the point. She says, 'I am looking forward to hearing more of your life, Jennypatel.' Somehow she makes the simple pronouncement sound half command, half threat'.

Any case, I have a few tasks to get out of the way, and she follows me around the house and the muddy yard with its fruit-droopy trees and valiant vegies. Her hood is drawn down against the sulky wetness of the air, trying as best she can to assist with her good hand, the one that has the pink garter dangling off it (I'd *love* to know what that's all about, I must say). We attend to Victoria and her children and to the Baxters, of whom she is wary, but less so than of Blackie. Then, after feeding the chickens, we settle on the bench under the dripping eaves and enjoy tea, a handful of tart little apricots, and Mandrake's gingernuts. From there we can look over the graveyard all drizzle-blurry and into the distance in the direction of her beloved Perfect State. I'd like to think she is after a true sense of how the world was before 'Liberation', but more likely she's just pumping me for information for her own peculiar reasons. I don't mind obliging her. I spend half my time reminiscing in any case. The scents, the light, the voices … I remember the smell of gasoline and urine, bread and fennel; I remember electric twilights. Bright dark blue, sometimes a bit of dry-heat lightning from when we had actual weather, not just this snitty-snotty vinegar-drizzle. And I remember the sound of kids shrieking after shuttlecocks in the alleys, and the ridicule of cockatoos cackling. Toughs of the bird world, they keep on top of things. Eat anything, seeds and husks and the mortar from between the bricks and splinters of stolen clothes pegs. And they never lose their humour. Sustained by a sense of the ridiculous, my darling hooligans.

I try to conjure for her the feeling on those nights when we – Anjalima, Arun, Lee and I – sat together on our eleventh-floor balcony, the yellow moth-pocked light of many small lanterns like faerie lights that my daddy had strung from the awning ages back.

'Why?'

'Why what?'

'Why the lights?'

'For the prettiness, my friend. There was so little around that was lovely, you see.'

'I see,' she says, though patently it's clear as mud.

'They were soft lights, and they illuminated my dad's thin face, the long lines from his nose to chin all shadowy, his warm brown eyes … and Anjali's face, and Lee's, as they sipped their grog and discussed what was, to me, a strange abstraction they referred to as "The Economy". I thought this Economy sounded like a sad old man, like a sort of reverse Santa Claus—'

'Who is this Santa Claws?' she asks anxiously, no doubt picturing some horrible ferocious dragony thing, all teeth and talons and fiery breath to scorch her hackles off.

'He was a man in a story about … Never mind, just a man in a story. He was a most jolly fellow loved by everyone because he brought presents to all the good little girls and boys. But where the original Santa was red and fat in all the pictures, this new reverse one that I imagined, the Economy, was thin and blue. I would have fed the poor old sod if I could have done, given him an apple and a piece of cheese and an icy-pole.

'It was on the balcony that I learned that this, my new country, was an old, old land built up over millennia upon layers and layers of mineral and vegetable deposits, and that its people had long mined the earth for its precious store of minerals and ores, which had then been exported to other countries. But times had changed, and these days they were not so much in demand, not since the Earth's most recent tectonic shift and the discovery of the GAS, the Great Asian Seam that they found under China. You know China? From the atlas?' She nods, though with a skeptical look on her mug as if the atlas were composed by Jonathon Swift. Never mind. 'Naturally,' I say, 'our government made trade agreements with China, such a massive and powerful land. But the deal favoured the owners of the GAS.'

'Of course. Jimander taught us some card games. So I know: the one who holds the best cards controls the deal,' declares my bright spark.

'Quite so, dear.' I reach over to the dish and select an apricot, split it down the middle with my thumbnail. It's a mean, shrivelled thing; the tree needs more sunlight. Who doesn't?

I bite into it. It's even bitterer than it looks. I remember apricots from when there was still fruit worthy of the name. There was that orchard Jimbo and I climbed into once. A walled garden. Lovely fruit, gold against the slatey sky. We'd yearned to enter that garden for so long but we had to wait and watch for an opportunity. But we were patient little sneak thieves, had to be. Those of us who'd survived knew that patience was more than a virtue; it was a life-preserving strategy, whether lingering beneath dorm windows waiting for a good moment to flick in a paper plane, or watching for the lights to go out in a farmhouse before advancing on their chicken coop. Or holding your breath while squashed into an air duct spying on the Transport Ministry. But I got the confirmation the Fools needed that afternoon. I did well, was a hero for an hour. The intervention went ahead.

Waiting is always so much worse than doing. Wives and daughters waiting for sailors, for soldiers, for miners – brothers, fathers, lovers, husbands. Melanie returned on time – that time. Jimbo and the others didn't. They didn't return the following one either, or the one after that. Had the Ecumen discovered them? If so, we knew we wouldn't see them again. They'd be shot or worse – corralled and driven deep underground. Awake, I could turn my mind away from images of blood-spattered walls and small corpses, or from haggard faces in lightless chambers shored up by rubble; not so when I slept. In dreams I saw Jimbo's thin frame inert by the railway tracks, or fleeing down dark passages, or trying not to breathe the poisoned air of some deep cell.

It was a week later that Tajik and Tiny returned.

And a week after that, Jimbo. He would've made it sooner, only he'd carried a dying child five kilometres through the sewers to our hideout. So she could have somewhere friendly to die in, surrounded by kind faces.

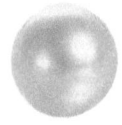 PEARL

30.

About a week after I'd arrived at the tottery house by the river with its crown of yellow flowers, its watery light, its light-filled water, Motley came to my room. He said, 'You should be very proud of what you've done, Pearly-girl.' His eyes were glowing at me from within their purple leathery pouches. I was embarrassed and looked anywhere but at him. Geoff, the Fool-Rangers' big red tomcat, gazed benevolently down on me from his perch in the rafters. Motley came over to my mattress and joined me there, stretched himself out huge and sprawly. He drew me towards him so that I could lie in the crook of his arm. I felt something like safe. Winding a lock of my hair around his finger, he added, 'We can use a spirited kid like you.' He smiled that sweet and sorry smile. 'What d'you reckon?'

I didn't have the heart to tell him that my optimism was pretty limited. I'd hoped and I even *acted* on my hope – and I knew I'd been brave, I truly had – but at this time I just felt all sooky-weak and sorry and afraid, so afraid that my hopes for a different life were just grand-iose fantasies of a vain and impertinent mad-girl. Shocking, how I'd gone against all that I'd been made to be. I felt dizzy when I looked at this truth, and dizzier still when I dared to hope that I could have a life different from the one I'd been raised to.

Grimalda came in with mugs of tea and sardine sandwiches and plates of creamed papaya pudding and joined us on the mattress. She took one look at my face and exclaimed, 'Hey little sweet! You look all sort of *thing!* Sit up and give Aunt Grimie a cuddle – right now!' I did as I was told and she wrapped her arms around me in a lovely strong hug so that I got wiry hairs up my nose. I didn't mind. She muttered over my head, 'Mottle-dottle, you are as sensitive as porridge.' Then, to me, 'What's going on in there?' She tapped the side of my head gently. But I couldn't speak because I'd got all teary thinking how I'd abandoned my people, my only friend, and my lover, and was feeling like a failed project. I couldn't say these things, for they'd give away the weak heart at the centre of my bravado; if I spoke my fears they'd be sure to come true.

'Well. I'll be off then,' said Motley, getting to his feet. 'And don't forget what I said, my love.' Grimalda gave him an angry look as he winked at me over his shoulder before closing the door quietly behind him.

Later that evening as I lay on my mattress listening to the river, I heard their voices in the room they shared, which was directly below mine. I couldn't make out the words, but they seemed fraught.

The next morning, Grimalda got me up early. 'We're going down-river a bit, my love.' She said, 'Got to see a Fool about a girl.'

'Where's Motley?'

'Oh, out and about, doing Mottle-fish things. He'll be back before we are. Here, put this on.' She threw me a long grey cloak such as Rangers wear. We waded through the bracken and reeds to the water's edge, got onto the barge that was moored in the shallows. The first hint of daylight was just winkling its way through the tree canopy that's wide and dense enough to protect us from the rain as Grimalda poled us into the centre of the river.

That was the morning I got my job at Mandrake's studio. It's down Big River a bit where it gets deeper and a lot wider than Grimalda and Motley's quiet tributary. There's this wharf sticking out into the river like a rude finger. Grimalda explained that it's where oceangoing ships used to dock, though it's disused now; all that activity is centred around Perfect these days. Mandy has taken over a rotting warehouse. It's a lovely big space, all high ceilings with great hardwood beams holding up nothing but air, great swathes of it, and it's not really rich in walls either. You could be safe here as anywhere, though – seven or eight girls and I work here at any one time, and a boy or two – because it's so decrepit it's largely camouflaged by bush and vines and tea-tree. Looks, from a distance, like a thickening of scrub rather than a building. When I am here I feel as if I'm in a kind of dream, not just because of the riverlight and ceaseless murmur of water, but because we work in near silence. Everyone here understands the consequences if we are detected by a blimp or a Hummer patrol. So we whisper and sign and beaver away. They never asked me what I preferred to do, which was silly. And I found myself working on cartoon books with some really pretty good drawers and painters. Embarrassing.

'Mandy,' I said, after Grimalda had left. 'You can see I can't draw to save my life.'

'But Grimie told me you could do just about anything,' he answered.

'She thinks everyone can do everything. She reckons we're all brilliant, everyone she loves is a genius or a beauty or some kind of star, and though she's a champion queen and I do love her so *much* and I'd be dead without her and my gratitude is boundless and everything, it's also true she's a mad cow.'

Mandy grinned. 'Well then, what's your preference?'

I gestured towards the alcove where the writers were scratching away.

'Well, then. Pen, my love?' He handed me a fistful of biros. 'Write me a tale, then, will you? Something daring. Do. Derring-do! Something bold.'

So this is what I do: I write what I know, I write what was and is now true, and what I wish were true, or will be, one day. I write without planning, hardly thinking at all. I make up heroes, people my own age, some boys but mostly girls, and they have cropped hair or stripy scarves or little round glasses and big grins usually, and are valorous beyond belief, optimistic and opportunistic and vulgar and mean and sweet. They wear impregnable porno pants and carry sharp knives and nobody, but *nobody ever* messes with my heroes. I write and write all loose and lively and I love it. I love it.

THE HAG

31.

'You will tell me more about that time of many changes?'

'I expect so.'

'And about the Action?'

'If the story unfolds that way, my chook.' But I'm feeling a bit bogged in other memories still. I manage to add, 'One must follow the dictates of the narrative.'

She doesn't look all that impressed by narrative imperatives. 'I have done my reading,' she adds, sitting up a little straighter. Does she want me to give her a gold star? I haul myself up from the bench and go inside and busy myself with kettle and milk, sugar and spices. Dried pods of cardamom, a large pinch of ginger – running low; it's losing its bite. All the while she persists, talking to me through the open doorway: 'I looked at all the countries in your most glamorous book. All from before, from Artica to Antartica, which we are told used to be to the south of our land.'

'It was.'

I don't really need the tea I've just made, just the grog I'm keen to add to it. I rejoin her on the bench, hand her a mug. While the drizzle drizzles and the sky lours, while the gravestones tilt and the vines slowly curl, I gently soak up my grog and continue my tale:

'So, well, by the time of the Action the world's already seen Iceland, Greenland and much of Norway go under – trebling the Swedish population when so much of Scandos disappeared beneath the Atlantic Ocean; same went for the southern atolls closer to home that drowned with the series of tsunamis that rolled in all along the Pacific Rim. Oh, and there were tornadoes from Mongolia to Georgia.' By her expression I might just as well have been talking about Laputa and Glubbdubdrib. Never mind.

'There was the Great Northern Quake a few years back in what was by now the Reformed USA, RUSA – almost a quarter of the country crumbled into the sea then and the aftershocks knocked Mexico into Guatemala.' I add another slug of grog to my tea and chug it back. 'People and other creatures were all clinging to crumbs of earth and crusts of bread and fighting to stave off the thousands of liberated bacteria and wriggly little viruses that came out of the wreckage of the Amazon, all pink and purple under the microscope, through the waterways and nestling in the livers and lungs of the living and the dead. The new tourism of bugs! Bugs galore!' I light up another cigar and take a good, deep drag. I can occasionally manage a headspin from tobacco if I hold my breath after a big lungful. I blow out a smoke ring, then aim another at its centre. It floats through as the larger one dissipates. Success!

'Where we were, it was bad, but not as bad as it was for plenty of others, or not yet at any rate. My valiant daddy Arun set up co-ops with neighbours and we grew a lot of our own food in soil that was not entirely toxic. I would see him decked out in his jungle-green overalls and paleo-lithic straw hat, presiding over the generators, the clearing of rainwater tanks, the planting of vines, leafy greens and root vegetables on roofs and streets that were by now mostly carless and had been divided into allotments for gardens, one per tenement. I loved working with my dad in the garden, especially the roof gardens, where you could get a bit of sun and smell the freshness of growing things while you watered them, so carefully. He'd planted herbs too, rosemary and lemon thyme, chives and oregano and basil, heavenly scents. And there were flowers too, some for the prettiness, others to draw the creepy crawlies away from our food, at least that was the theory. It worked occasionally too. And my other job, from the age of seven, was to wait in queues at the super-mart dressed in my horrible little grey riding hood, a roll of cash-money stuffed in my glove. Sometimes I stood all afternoon just so I could trot home with a box of bulbs or a flask of oil or a small canister or two of oxygen for when the wind blew foul, which was often enough.

'My mum and dad agreed that the planet had undergone cataclysms before and recovered, and, by the skin of its teeth, might *just* do so again. But now it was so much worse than it had ever been before, that would take a very long time. But the people who lived on it were not so flexible. Like the big cats and the humming insects, humanity was, as my dear old auntie Lee put it so elegantly, staring up the badgery bumhole of extinction.

'Different reasons were given for these disasters and the new vulner-ability of humanity. Some said the truth was simple: there were just too many of us. There were worldwide arguments about which people ought to be allowed to keep having babies, and how many babies they should have, and whether or not damaged babies should be allowed to live—'

'Dudbubs and cripsanretards too have their purpose. They have a function to support the needs of—'

'Shall we not go there just now? It's another discussion entirely.'

It pauses a beat, gathers itself, says, 'It is your narration, Jennypatel. I must follow your dictates.'

She's not deaf at least. 'So. There were arguments about which people should live in which countries and for how long, and what they should do for a living, arguments about the need to manufacture certain things and to stop making others, about the need to acquire certain things and the need to get rid of other things. But in the end, almost everybody chose one of two as the mainest of the main reasons for disasters recent and imminent. The first one was the fact that nature was all messed up, the earth poisoned and the sky all but caving in. Oh yes, very bad. And the other of the two mainest reasons for the rapturous end of world and the whole kit and Armagedoodle – well, you know already what it was.'

Blank look.

'Dearie me, dear one – it was *God.*' And oh, watch the transformation of that *face!* Blanched as white as a ghost. Oh, but this hag is a blasphemer if ever there was one! 'God was held by many to be very angry with his children, who had done bad things—'

'Exactly! Punishment must be meted out for crimes committed. Man is responsible, *not* GodFather (BBHCM). In His wisdom Godfather (BBHCM) gives and GodFather (BBHCM) takes, blessed be the name of GodFather (BBHCM) who is made manifest in the Resolved Twins Jesumuh in the Dual True Faith, hallelujah!'

'I see. Would you like me to continue at all?'

The Glare of the Onion-Eyed Nuthook. 'There is but One Truth and that is the Truth of the Majesty of the Sacred Sceptre and Rod of God-Father (BBHCM), long may He reign alive–alive-oh-oh as revealed by the Resolved Twins and espoused by the Properganders of Instruction & Destruction and those who fail to believe in Him and the Dual True Faith must be convinced, if not by words then by blows, else they will suffer worse torment not only in this world but in the next one too – and not just for a little while, like prisoners in gaol – but forever and ever and ever, Blessed Be His Cock–and-Muscle alive–alive-oh-oh AH-*MEN!*'

And its trap snaps shut over the pearly-whites. What a sad and silly sight it is in its earnest outrage. And scary. Yes, that too.

'Very clear, dear. So, let's just say that unlike your very articulate self, more and more often people just ran out of words to express the ideas and fears they had. And, as you so correctly say, when the words fail, the hitting starts. On a small scale this meant fists, on a large scale, warheads.' And now the childish face is all avidity again, baby-blues agleam, white-knuckled fists clenched in her lap. Adorable, not. 'It had been a long time since there'd been peace in eastern Europe, the south and west of America, the central part of Asia, the countries of the eastern Mediterranean or anywhere in Africa. Some countries that were in my school atlas, the one I'd printed out only say, six months or so before this conversation with my parents, were no longer to be found in the updates. And others that I'd never heard of sprouted like mushrooms.'

'Sprouted from enriched soil, all fertilised by the blood and bone of martyrs in the Action.'

Fertiliser. My friends and family. And her fucking *martyrs*.

32.

'Actually Mica, your "Action" wasn't all that catastrophic in the greater scheme of catastrophes, when you think about it, get it all in context,' I say to punish her.

'The Action of the Heroes of the Fraternity of Christlam was the catalyst of Liberation!'

'Not really. Australand just followed RUSA's lead. The usual sort of thing. But they did ruin our town, one of the loveliest towns there ever was.' And it was true. Big Smoke was once so stunning that people used to come from all over the word just to have a look at its harbour and bridge in the bright light we used to have, that high blue sky, before the rains started. And nearby there'd been the Theatre, a century old or thereabouts, built to resemble a massive ship coming in to dock, its white sails billowing. 'So that was a fine job of work, eh? And everyone who lived there was made miserable, disheartened and demoralised. Killing beauty has that effect. As does mass murder. I'll give you that.'

'It had to be done,' she informs me. 'Humility is the only cure for the sin of pride. The city had to be humbled.'

I stare at her. Try to formulate a response, open my mouth to speak, but she's oblivious.

'The Paradox of Creative Destruction is a fundamental Christlamic tenet that enables the liberation of the spirit! It arouses people from the moral torpor induced by the fleshly fallacy, pride in our vain accomplishments and enslavement to the world of objects and things which are but shadows of the forms that exist in the true, unchanging reality beyond.'

I remember how so very many spirits were liberated that night, ridding themselves of their fallaciously fleshy bodies first, and leaving chunks of them floating about in the salty slush that had become the heart of our town. Hallelujah. But look at that face of hers, as smooth and white and unmarked as an upturned fish belly, her eyes raised towards the heavenly gates of my rafters, pink lips slightly parted. She looks a bit like a painting I once saw of Saint Agatha just after she had her tits sliced off. That one where she's holding them up for our delectation on a platter, little trembling jellies with cherries on top, mini bombe-alaskas.

And how her sanctimoniousness is buttressed by her faith in these righteous avengers of hers, and she's blindingly unaware of the effect her words might be having on the feelings of her aged interlocutor. As empathetic as an adder. She carries on to her conclusion: 'But you survived it, Jennypatel, by the grace of GodFather (BBHCM). This is a mercy to be grateful for.'

Grateful. Oh, yes. How confused she looks when I get up. Wondering what she's said wrong. I take the scrap bucket and head off into the wet air. I stomp through the nasturtiums who blast me with their indignant peppery scent – it clears my head a little – then past the bed of squash, all exuberantly tendrilly and clingy. I nod to the Baxters who stare back benignly, then up the back to my hens. Most have gone into the henhouse as the drizzle's a bit extra-drizzly at the moment. Throw a fistful of scraps. Watch the clueless clucks congregate. Cluck cluck peck peck, stab your neighbour in the neck.

And now look. Here comes the creepy little stray again. It's materialised at my elbow, staring with its big eyes, greedy and wary, wanting and fearing. Its small dry paw is on my sleeve. I'd really rather she didn't touch me. 'The hen and the witch are kindred souls,' I say to make a shield of words, get her to back off. 'Mucky strutters, eh?' Ah, good, the nasty little mitt is withdrawn. 'Like our sister the sow, don't you think? They'll eat *any*thing.' I fling a few more scraps around, peelings, fat and gristle, and the horrid old ladies come running on their scabby reptilian legs. 'Even their own kind.'

She's looking bemused, almost frightened of me again.

'See their yellow claws all ridged and veined and dark at root from scratching in the dirt. Little filth-tillers, hens and pigs *and* grubby old witches. We scrabble around in the muck and the guano till we expose the seeds. Seeds of life we bring to life.' I realise I'm sounding a bit grandiose. What the hell. I'm probably drunk.

She murmurs quietly, '*Haraamasur.*'

'Oh, but where would you be without us, eh, hags and hens, pigs and witches and worms? We, the brokers of mortal deliverance! Animal existence is dirty and foul! You have to claw yourself free of it.' As I'd like to be free of you, you Midwich monster.

I look up at the sky. A couple of fat raindrops smack me in the face. We walk back towards the house together. Blackie's big warm head bumps against my thigh. I scratch his ears for him. Then it happens: a fork of blue-white lightning just beyond the graveyard, followed by an ear-shattering crash, and the sky caves in on us. We make it back in time, and sheltered by the eaves we watch as the storm does its thing, and my heart is pounding in time with the drumming on the tin roof, oh I do love a good storm and this is the first one since – since when? The first since about a week before the Advent of Mica.

Oh, but it is *lovely!* My throat contracts and I feel something like gratitude. *This* is what gods are for, a bit of awe and wonder, soul food. But then we get all scared and have to go and attach wrath and righteous vengeance and all manner of horrible human carry-on like a pork chop, as Lee would have said. Creating then corrupting our divinities – from the sublime to the grotesque, oh yes.

Mud splatters up my trousers and the hem of her dressless. Maybe I'll go out into it, let it melt me, let me dissolve in the rain …

But the child has grabbed my arm, digging her hard fingers into my biceps. She's looking upwards at the low sky, her face whiter than its usual white. And now I hear it too – another kind of rumble – a sound I know well, and it was never caused by a storm or any other form of ecospherical activity. We watch from under the eaves until the blackish lozenge shape takes form, seemingly out of cloud, clouds which darken resentfully as it slips through their bodies, polluting them with its presence so that that they roil biliously.

She darts into the house. Good move. I follow.

33.

The Ecumen know my place well. *Oh look,* I imagine the pilot saying to his young sidekick, *There's where the evil hag lives out her miserable existence, cut off from all the world for her sins.* The spunky kid asks, *Why not spit fire onto her roof?* Oh, let him answer: *Better as she is, boy. She's a living example of the fate of the defiant. Loneliness and poverty.* That's right – kindly remember I'm handy as a bedtime story, a fable to frighten your children into obedience – don't forget that, please, boys! I hope your masters haven't changed that particular policy.

She's crouched by the window, staring out, careful to make sure none of her shows. As if they could make out a girl in a house by a window. Perhaps she believes they have supernatural powers? But no, not necessary. For her it's enough that they are men and therefore powerful enough, unchallengeable, all cockled and muscled as they are, alive-alive – *oh-oh, here they come* – lower and lower. She turns to me, all of a quiver, blue eyes wild, 'Emissaries from Unrule!'

So she reckons not on what they are, but what she dreads most.

'They will take us away and butcher us and feed our entrails to the dogs! Where can we hide ourselves? Where's the hatch to the basement ... coal-hole ... dungeon where you keep your ...'

What – barrels of pickled children? Flyblown cadavers aging on butchers' hooks? Crated babies? Jesumuh. '*Settle*, tiger!' I reach for her hand. 'Listen. There's no basement, no bolt-hole and the blimp is *Ecumen*. Ecumen on patrol. They won't stop here.' I hope.

'They are *not* Ecumen from any of the sacred States! Ecumen have Holy Hummers, or they ride on horseback; they do not use the vainglorious devices of the pre-Liberation armoury! Every civilised person knows that Man, creature of the Earth, is forbidden to challenge the cerulean gateway of GodFather's (BBHCM) realm. Did you learn nothing in your school? Do you so despise the Holy Strictures? Did you never read of the fate of those who would ascend beyond their station? And you think you understand so much of the ways of the world!'

She's quite unnerved Blackie. Hear him growling low in his throat. He bares his teeth and clacks his jaws at her; she shrinks back, then creeps into my little bed-nook, drawing the curtains behind her. Yes, my bit of hessian sacking will certainly protect you from fire and bullet. Get under the bed, even better. Jesumuh.

But at last the burring hum does indeed recede, leaving us whole and not a bit singed. All I can hear of it now is a slight reverberation in my eardrums, echoing through my brain. Then, after a little bit, there's the scratch of her pen on the paper of that precious journal of hers. What with blimps and heretical hags, she's at her wits' end. She'll be at it for a while.

'Blackie,' I say, 'Stay and mind the fort. In case she gets frightened again. Sorry.' Sorry dog, sorry kid, sorry me. I need air. Blacks whines slightly as he watches me zip up my waterproof and tie the tags around my middle.

The air feels exhausted, as you do after a bout of nausea. It's all churned up and suffering a creaturely revulsion of the vibrating metal spike that's been driven through its belly and out the other end. I head off into the quivering mist, away from the house, through the field of dead people and down towards the old orchard.

 MICA

34.

There she goes, out over the graveyard. One minute she is reasonable, the next insane. One minute she is kind, the next spiteful. And *stupid!* Standing around in the open where the Unrulies and every kind of rogue can see her from the sky. But no. This is *wrong*. It is *I* who am stupid – why would she be afraid? She is their ally. But now, the danger has passed and the misty sky is a pale, flat grey again, with just a little sun seeping through the clouds.

I should meditate, but I feel too agitated still.

See how happy she is to abandon me to the guardianship of her great black virgin-eating minotaur. We glare at each other, the beast and I. Me from my nook, him from the hearth. I wonder if he's bright enough to remember the trick I pulled on him earlier? I could have laughed at how such a hulking thing can be reduced to such foolish uselessness. After she had left this morning, thinking I was still asleep, I decided I had to follow her, see where she goes, what she does. So I crept out and went to the meat safe, snuck the last of Albert's leg out and dropped it onto the floor on the other side of the room. The beast could not believe his luck! And as he set upon it I slipped the leash around his neck and tied it firmly to the hook where she keeps her coat and her big shoulder-bag. He was very angry when he saw what I'd done, and angrier still when I kicked the bone out of his reach – jumping clear myself before he could take a bite out of me – and dropped it into the pot on the stove. I added more water and set it to simmer. So easy! Beast caught and evidence hidden, and now I could move and *do* something at last! It wasn't hard to see the way she'd gone, her boot tracks were clear in the frost. And so, I followed. It was fortunate that she had that ridiculous cart with her, it made such a racket.

I saw her meet with the rogue, saw them unload the crates from the flat-bottomed boat then go into the shed to devise their plans. A shame I could not hear their words. But now at least I have something to report: a dock, an agent of Unrule, a smugglers' hideout! Something to show for my absence when I return. When I return *with Pearl*. I have to get away as soon as my arm is better, for who knows what she could have in store for me? And in the meantime, I'd better be nice, listen and learn. I've always been good at listening and learning. Nice is harder.

I look out the window into her scrappy yard with its overgrown garden, its gnarly rose trees taller than a Man – a skinny old Man with arthritic knees – the coils of wire and piles of unsorted wood, some for the fire and some to be trimmed for stakes for the toppling vines; the apple tree with its boughs so low they're in the pigs' wallow. I resolve to tidy it up a bit. Nice. That would be nice of me.

The hellhound is snoring by the hearth. I creep by, using the sniper-step I learned in girlie-guards. I am absolutely silent, but then the door creaks as I push it to, and I see I've roused the beast. It opens one eye and thumps its tail, trying to scare me. Quickly I slip out and latch the door firmly behind me. That's another thing I must do: see if she's got a bit of graphite to smooth the working of the hinges and generally ease all the joints of this creaking old heap of a hovel.

I have been raised to despise disorder. As we are taught from the time we are small, true beauty is only to be found in forms shaped to their purpose. *Form follows function.* Excess is mess.

The vegetable plots at the back are in the worst repair. I edge by the evil-eyed livestock in its pens, and spend the morning doing some one-armed weeding. The work feels good. I am almost content for an hour or two, piling the rubbish into an empty drum, then warming myself at the blaze I make, smoky it's true, for the weather is never dry enough, but satisfying all the same. Later, or perhaps tomorrow, I'll see if I can't prune back the apricot tree by the door. It could be espaliered against the wall, hide some of the horrible masonry.

Be nice. Listen and learn. Then you will know what to do.

 ## THE HAG

35.

The day's in a sulk now and getting blustery, the last of the scattered raindrops blatting over everything, stirring up dead leaves and throwing them in my face. I pull my hat down low over my eyes. If Blackie were with me he'd be cavorting in doggy glee, chasing his tail and yipping like a puppy, weather like this always makes him crazy. I let my mind return to the balcony all those many years ago … how many? Thirty-five, forty? God, I'm old.

I'm back with my folks and Lee on a particular summer night, and how I miss that warmth and light, the sky hot violet and the air so sultry. From the communal yard, with its long plots of herbs and pumpkins and its choko and passionfruit vines, its row of rubbish skips and its sneaking, staring cats, came the night-time scents: rose mingled with civet and sage, mould and mulch and woodsmoke. 'Old goddy-boy or his brother the devil ought to whack the lot of us once and for all,' muttered Lee, taking a big swig of grog and burping. She winked at Anjali and Arun, then turned to me. 'Dear loinfruit of my bestest chums. D'you suppose you could make me one of those sooper-dooper sangers you do so well?'

I put down the palm-sized dictionary I always had handy – oh yes, I was a keen one – and set to work assembling two hunks of bread and a bit of cheese. I proudly delivered it unto my mentor. Lee received it with great ceremony then promptly forgot about it. 'Read the latest in the "Daily Dope", Anjarun? Sheikh Humbum and Bishop Bozo of RUSA agree: it's women's rudeness and disobedience that's to blame.' Now this sounded familiar – I'd heard something similar at school from Mr Pule, who'd said that although God became very angry with all evil-doers, he often became particularly cross and disappointed with his daughters, who had forgotten how to deport themselves properly and were resorting to wilder and wilder ways, and could even endanger the mortal souls of their men because of their irresistibly amatory nature which, as he said, 'must be constrained and disciplined for the good of all'.

'Poor old goddikins,' said Lee, 'having to cope with all those maddening chicks with their horrible bosoms and those bottomless abysses between their legs. Obviously he has no option but to whip up another virus or blow the top off another volcano. Boiling lava's too good for 'em, yea and behold and all that carry-on like a pork chop!'

Arun gave her a warning nudge and slid his eyes in my direction. I could've told him he needn't worry. I might not be sure about what an 'abyss' was, but I'd already learnt about girls' horrible bosoms from Mr Pule and pretty Miss Right who took History/Divinity. They were very careful in their different ways about minding the girls' erogeneity and the boys' souls by attending to the shrouding of the seniors' chests in white or black crown-to-toes, depending on their Christlamic affiliation. It was very equitable. And underneath we could wear what we wanted, of course. I had my eye on a new-style dressless and mirkin like some of the smarter girls at school had showed off in the privacy of the girls' toilets at recess.

'Sorry.' Lee drained her glass and winced. 'But we've never really worked it out, have we? I mean, what it *is* that's so ghastly about women? Is it the mulch factor? Quims like compost, reeking of rot yet producing dear little sprogs to carry on the race?' Her eyes were all lit up with grog and glee. She'd more or less lost me at this stage, engrossed as I was in thinking about mirkin style. It was *really important*, after all. You *had* to get it right – otherwise the other girls might laugh, or worse, exclude you.

'Jenny. Bedtime.'

'No! Please, Ma!' Although I didn't get everything auntie Lee was saying and her sarcasm could make me anxious (especially when it was at odds with what I'd learned at school from my teachers who I knew were kind and wise, like Miss Right who had eloquently explained to the boys and girls about religion and sex, which God gave Man so he could please the Almighty with many children), I definitely got *Lee*. I got Lee *herself*. Her big heart and the gist of her passion, however misguided I sometimes thought she was, due to my having a poor muddled little God-bothered pea-brain. Her irony was bitter but I understood it came from a place of love. Like many children, I could pick up love more easily than hate, because children trust before they learn the dark craft of circumspection. Or at least they used to. Not so sure about our little lamb back at the house. I can just make her out, standing by the door, staring out over the fields after me, her eyes visored by her lily-white hand.

In the orchard there's a little shelter from the wind, but the wet grass is nearly up to my knees, full of leeches. There's one already. I flick it off with my nail and step into the soft mess of a large, decomposing rat. Choice.

'Sorry, Jenanjarun,' I hear Lee say; she'd often include us all in that moniker, particularly handy now when she wasn't sure who she'd offended most. She took another drink and wiped her lips on the back of her hand. Readjusted one of the chopsticks holding her topknot in place. This seemed to agitate her brain further because now she was off again: 'Or maybe they despise us since we don't tend to put up much of a physical fight, so macho chaps think we're a bunch of poofters, eh? Chicks as chaps who get fucked up the front botty by other chaps?'

'Jenny, go to …'

'Or is it the well-known fact that we eat willies with our vagina dentatas? Or that we're insatiable sex-fiends? But one thing's for sure, when control is slipping away, *carpe d*iquim! That's the thing. Old story, eh? Been going since Adam's first wife, Lilith. You know Lilith, me heathen hearties?'

'The Lilith story is apocryphal—' attempted Arun.

'Doesn't matter – still a story we made up to explain things. Banished to the edge of the world for her intemperate behaviour. Let Eve warm Adam's cods for him instead, and we know how that turned out, don't we?' Lee tilted dangerously back on the poor old chair so that it squeaked anxiously. I noticed that her nose was becoming quite shiny and pink. 'Ah me, bloody women. Faithless and stupid and get seduced by snakes.' A thoughtful burp. '*Or* wicked and sick and want to get on top! That's what did it, they say. Poor old Lil, she just wanted to get the right angle, the daring little darling, because Adam was too selfish to notice her clitoris!'

'Jen. Bed. Now. Go.'

'What's a clitoris?'

'Night, little mate,' said Lee. 'And apologies. Don't repeat any of me heinous crudity at school, ok? Only get you into trouble. Promise?'

Arun leant over and tucked a strand of hair behind my ear. 'She needn't promise. Jenny never lies.'

Any case, when Anjalima stood up and took me by the hand I went quietly. Dad's compliment made my heart swell with love for my parents and pride in myself. Pride. I had a lot of that, thanks to 'Anjarun' and Lee. Aranjalee. Much later, when I was in Post-Liberation Re-Education, I noticed that it wasn't really all that hard to strip a girl of her pride. It was just a matter of tapping into that vein of self-doubt, the weak spot that marks an absence, a gap, a space, a *hole*.

I tighten the mesh over the younger trees. Even though most of the fruit is still green, the cockies have no mercy. Ah, there goes a flock of the buggers, ee-aagh-agh-agh-aghing ecstatically overhead.

I'd best return now to the nutty puttock back at the old Hagovel. See if it's recovered from the blimp.

 PEARL

36.

Two nights ago – it's about ten days since I've been working at Mandrake's place, I think – we'd had our dinner and I was sitting contentedly by the friendly-smelly kero heater nursing big red Geoff. Then Motley and Grimalda left the room together, closing the door behind them, a signal that they wanted to talk without any interference from me. So pretty likely I was the subject under discussion. I'd worked out that they had different ideas about how best to use me; that is, Grimalda wanted to keep me working exclusively at Mandy's studio. I was happy with that too. More than happy. But Motley had it in mind to involve me in other plans as well. And I knew Grimalda didn't like them. I knew there was work along the river that involved stealth and spying. And I also knew that Fool-Rangers always needed help at the hidden departure points the smugglers used to spirit kids down to the Sea. The Sea … would I see the Sea?!

When they came back in, Grimalda looked unhappy. Motley's face was all jollity. I wonder who won? Heh heh. But no, not funny. I had the feeling Grimalda was even more upset than she was letting on. She was actually scowling, and she's not a scowler by nature; she's sweet as sweet in her large hairy way.

It seemed I had a bit of courier work to do.

The following afternoon Grimalda went ahead to Big Smoke. Motley and I waited by the river for a drop-off of banned films. Next morning – this morning – we are en route and I can hardly believe it – me, way way up in the sky looking down. Away behind us is the wide wide Sea. And I knew it was never greasy, like they'd have you believe, at least not once you get away from the coast that's all fouled up with the wasteful works of humans. It's the colour of emeralds here and there, then it's the colour of the deepest blue possible, and turquoise in the shallower parts where there's a bit of an island poking up. And ahead of us I can see the smoke of Big Smoke. And next to me, great big Mot, his face a study of scudding thoughts like clouds, and that ambivalent grin, all sweet and sad, sorry and satisfied. He catches me looking at him and, first checking out of the corner of his eye that nobody is watching, gives me a collusive wink.

So proud I am, sitting next to Motley in a blimp driven by an ingeniously misinformed Ecuman who's been led to believe I am a runaway Motley has nabbed. 'This one,' he said, holding me by the scruff, 'is one for Perfect Re-Ed. Caught it east of Yellow Swamp on its way towards the forest, heading towards Unrule.'

I couldn't see the effect Motley's words had on him, since Ecumen always cover up their faces with dark Perspex half-shields. But I thought it best to be silent, be docile, act drugged – Motley had said as much before we left: *Better not open your gob at all. I'll speak for you. You just feign muteness, in case your acting's as bad as your drawing.*

Then we were gaining height. From here, the colour of the water seems to even out till it looks like a sheet of corrugated cardboard like the stuff used to package the magazines made by those who can draw. How magnificent! And I am an emissary, like those winged go-betweens who cross realms to deliver messages between heaven and earth, the angels that we learned about in Minus-Seven from Attainment ... Only I am a dark angel, doomed to hell for this and all my transgressions.

And do I ask forgiveness? Do I look forward to Sorrow and Penitence month when I might grovel at the South Gate with the other guilt-ridden children who cry for their puny *puny* sins, *Forgive me?* No, GodFather, you dropped me years ago, let go of my hand and let me fall, and I'm falling still ...

I've seen some of the movies. Mot and I stayed up late last night, had our own film-fest. I couldn't believe the stuff, law-breakers and visionaries of every sort. Our cache is *strong magic!* I'll be dropping my cans off at Perfect for screening tonight, and others are scheduled to do the same at Impeccable, Ideal, Immaculate – all the other States.

Of course we've taped over the original titles, like *A Bug's Life, The Handmaid's Tale, The Passion of New Eve*, and penned on others: 'Meditations on the Sacred Sceptre', 'The Ways of (wo)Man' – the usual fare.

So here we are, in mid-air with an Ecuman unwittingly delivering a pair of spies and cans of counter-revolutionary gear of the most pernicious nature. Ha. Comic. How things turn out! And to cap it off, where do we land, but on the landing pad on the top of the Art & Pain Propergandery. The Properganders' central hub – don't you love love love it! Ah, Jesumuh – if they only knew!

Then there's the external lift-well. Whoosh! – down the outside, 50 storeys or more, and the wind is *full on*, a tunnel of air; my stomach's in my mouth but when, *when* have I ever been so full of joy? We reach the ground and Motley choofs me off before he goes in to meet with the Ministers. I've memorised the directions – straight down Patriarch's Road to The Way of Peace, turn left and proceed four and a half blocks – *count them carefully, love* – down the stairs, past Insolents' Pit, then down again to Central, along platform 9, then – *when you're sure the coast is clear* – slip onto the track, cross over and count 500 metres till I see a sheet of tin with an ancient advertisement pasted over it. *Make like a cockroach then, me darling*, he'd said, *and slip in behind. There's a door about big enough for Alice on one of her better trips.* I don't know who Alice was, but I did get his gist: a door of an unusual size behind the metal sheet.

Passing through it, I find myself at the head of another staircase, metal; it clangs and rattles as I make my way down it into a room, big as a blimp hangar, containing about twenty kids my age, girls and boys, and – best of all – Grimalda in all her gorgeous glory, done up to the nines in red and pink, her round, red nose-bulb agleam and her eyes glowing with pleasure at seeing me. I could sob out loud. There haven't been many people in my life who've glowed at me. Only two. My darly Mica. My love, Asa. Where are they now?

I run over and give Grimalda a massive hug. She holds me as though I am most dear to her, most deeply dearly loved.

 # THE HAG

37.

As I get closer to the old hovel I see the skerrick does seem to have recovered from the blimp. She's even been out and about a bit, exercising her neurotic compulsion to prune and cut. Ah, hell, Witch, be fair – she's doing something decent.

Apparently the work has tired her out; at least she looks like she's had a bit of a nap, her eyes are soft and a little unfocused.

'Spot of gardening, eh? Nice way to pass an hour or two, isn't it?'

'As I worked I was meditating on Labial Infolding as Mirror of Feminine Cranial Convolutions.'

'Oh, the power-image that accompanies the Second Tenet from the Way of (wo)Man.'

'Yes! You remember? It is my favourite. What is your favourite Way, Jennypatel?'

At least she isn't sulking. 'Well actually, I don't believe I have a favourite ...'

'I understand, there are so many, all wise.'

'Ah, wise.'

She seems to pick up that my tone is not entirely without irony, but her mood is now placatory rather than combative because she says, 'Tea?'

So, it *can* learn.

As she stirs a little more milk into the chai pot she says, dignified but repentant, 'I am sorry about my hasty words, Jennypatel. I ...'

I wait a beat, but it's struggling, so I let it off the hook, 'Don't fret, little fish.'

'Jennypatel, I would truly like to know more of your life. Of the days you had in that school with boys.' She hands me a cup of tea. 'Of your time in Ideal. Of the fire you survived by making a pact with Satan. And of your solitary life here in the aimless wastes without guidance of GodFather or Man.'

Fuck-a-duck. Here's her being *sweet*. Go to the fireplace, put my mug on the mantelpiece, add another log, kick up some sparks. Good, warmth. Pick up mug again, feel heat against palms. Turn around, toast the bum too. She's sitting at the table looking at me expectantly. 'I remember curfews,' I say. 'I remember rules getting stricter as we got older, when it used to be the other way round, or so my Ma told me. And dress codes for girls started to be *really* strict when I was about, oh, I suppose ten or eleven ...'

'Because (wo)Men and girlies are a force of disorder in the world. Female babies are born with the seeds of an anarchic witch-spirit ever-ready to reject authority. It must be contained.'

Or crushed. Just trying to be good – like me, back then. I worked hard in my Life Ed classes on strengthening my will to suppress what Miss called 'The Jezebel Within', who lived inside every girl. 'Horny harlot' we learned to call her – *oh, sylvan slut, despair in the light of the Sacred Sceptre* ... oh yes. Even as a little girl I felt the truth of my own desire, physical but lusciously non-specific, and it could be oh-so strong, melting me on the inside. And on the outside, how my skin would tingle like a crust of ice deliciously fractured by the warmth of the sun. Or it could be the wind that did it for me like it does for Blackie, or the raindrops sliding down the glass, or the sight of a boy's shapely hands, a picture in a book – anything, my skin and heart and what-all, all so alive, me a fresh little thing with all the world so new! The strength of my emotions could sort of clot into an ache deep-deep down in me and track up, up through my diaphragm, my throat, like my blood was molten, and my heart would swell like a fruit about to burst open and it felt *good*, but scary.

I'd seen girls who were not so good at containing themselves, the sexy girls in action at school, tempting boys with their wiggly hips and their pretty lips. I saw how the boys looked at the girls, how they mucked up in class to get the girls' attention. It was obvious we were very awfully bad for their concentration, poor dears. Everybody knew that boys could easily fall victim to the Wily Ways of Woman. Miss Right, the voice of Tradition, said, 'It is up to us ladies to have a civilising effect on the men.' Then, staring straight at me, she added, *'Shoes!'* and the whole class turned to join in her scrutiny of the little red-and-white checked ballet slippers I wore, now peeping naughtily out from under my grey crown-to-toe. (I'd found them by a bin and it had been mutual love at first sight: the shoes were lonely and I was in need of beauty. So I'd taken them and we had been inseparable friends ever since.) 'Immodesty is incitement to rape,' quoted Miss Right – whose words they were, I didn't know, but it certainly *sounded* like a quote. I'm sure I blushed. She commanded: 'Wear something decent tomorrow.' 'Sorry, Miss.' And Miss nodded her conditional forgiveness for which I felt both grateful and guilty (for despite everything, I knew that my shoes and I would never be parted!).

But my audience is waiting for me, here a million years later in my lonely croft in the cock-field. Look at her, breath bated until we continue together my fond reminiscences of the good old days. 'I remember my teacher,' I say. 'Miss with her aug-array on the shelf below the whiteboard, inserting a laser pointer and a luminous marker into two of her finger slots.'

'Yes! I loved to watch MaOblat at Perfect, she was so adept and could turn gracefully from an ordinary unenhanced (wo)Man with mediocre looks and capabilities into a diva of deft power. In a matter of moments!'

'Hmmm. Miss Right had six of her original fingers and four connections for a range of implements.' *Connectivity makes efficiency*, was one of her favourite quotes. I wasn't sure who had originally said this either – Miss never told us – but it sounded venerable. 'And several of my friends had augs built in.' Enter my bestie, Jojo Jericho. Her quick black eyes, her hands like little birds winding a narrow blue ribbon into the ringlets of her bright auburn mirkin …

'In Perfect we consider a girlie should be enhanced only after it is determined that she will not become a womanidol. It would be waste, seeing that … seeing that …'

'Seeing that there's not much point in augmenting limbs that will only get the chop and fed to the pigs?'

'Not fed to pigs! Recycled at the Spare Parts Manufactory!' She stares at me combatively, then, calmer after a moment, adds with intolerable complacency: 'Everything has its purpose and its place.' Yet I note the tension in the jaw, the tightness of the so-white skin over the bones of her face.

'In any case, we didn't have womanidols back then. That came later. After—'

'After Liberation.'

'Correct.'

'Jennypetal?'

'Tiger.'

'How is it that you, who are old—'

'Thank you.'

'That you, who have lived at the time the great changes were taking place, remain unenhanced?'

'Might be time for lunch, don't you think?'

'I'd rather talk.'

'Your lovely soup isn't quite ready, but we've got the makings of something like a ploughman's lunch.'

'I'd rather *talk*.'

I go into the scullery and she trails after me. See it leaning in the doorway, bundle of lonely need. I fetch down a loaf. Take it back out to the main room. Sit at table. Take knife and start cutting. See a child's severed limb. Stop. Wipe tears with the back of my hand. Scarred. Veiny. Old.

38.

Jojo had been the first, of course. She was the first at everything. She'd had two fingers removed, one from each hand. She'd based her choice on those recommended for teens in *Aug and Sparkle* magazine. Jojo had considered having a toe or two done too, but her Mum said she was probably too young to have any more just yet, maybe wait till her next birthday. Then they could go halves in something really special. Though of course – and here Ms Jericho's thinking was more in sync with Mr Pule's than Miss Right's – it was ultimately up to Jojo to decide whether and when she'd like more enhancement.

It had really hurt, Jojo had boasted – her hands had been throbbing for *two weeks!* But it was worth it, she reckoned. She mostly used the slots for inserting mascara and eye-liner applicators – she had the steadiest hand now – no nerves in those ex-fingers! But she also used them for embroidery and geometry tools. She'd taken her Mum's advice and was now saving up for an ear-and-eye enhancement.

Oh, was I *jealous!* I remember confiding this to Jojo back then, saying, 'But Anjali won't hear of me having any sort of augmentations at all.' And I'd added – lying, so as not to look completely hopeless – 'At least until my sixteenth birthday.' 'Oh, poor Jen,' she'd replied with heartfelt sympathy, 'Two more years! That's *forever!* It really isn't fair.' I'd explained that my mum was a Seventh Wave Feminist, and so were her friends, and Jojo had looked at me pityingly and hugged me, 'It's hard for you, Jen. Those old girls just don't get it, do they? Their old ideas just aren't *relevant* to us any more.' 'You're right,' I'd agreed guiltily. 'They've forgotten what it's like to be young,' added Jojo. 'If they want to go around looking ugly in their old-fashioned dresses, never getting any improvements to their bodies and wardrobes, putting men off with their bossy ways, why should we have to as well? That's what my mum reckons too.' Jojo's mum was a much more stylish dresser than Anjali. Jojo continued, 'Your mum and her friend Lee are lovely ladies, of course, and so clever, but really negative about men, you know? Your poor *dad!*' And I'd giggled along with her happily, guiltily. It was then that she'd invited me along to one of her exclusive gatherings: a New Year's Eve party. 'We'll start at my place, Jen. Get primed there, then later move on to the Harbour for the fireworks, yes?' Embraced by the inner circle!

I came in that afternoon from school and put it to the Anjal: 'Jojo's having some friends around for New Year's. Can I go?'

'Jojo Jericho?'

'Yes. It's only girls.' It was true. Though I didn't add that later on, once we'd dressed up, we were going down to the Harbour then on to an after-party which would definitely be mixed. I told myself I hadn't lied, just hadn't troubled her with details.

But she didn't look happy. 'I know her mother ...'

'Mum. Sure, Ms J's more enhanced than most – and definitely more than you, but then you're not at all enhanced at all – so how could you understand?'

'You know Ms Jericho is a Whore for God, don't you?'

'She *isn't*, Mum! You've got it wrong!' I hated it when she got that prim voice on. 'She's in *Gogo for God*, and it's totally different from God's *Whores!*' Jojo too was a Gogodder (as those who were in the know knew to call them). She and her mum went to meetings together. What harm in that? I wished Mum would let me go even if she didn't want to come with me. 'Gogodders aren't scary like *them* …'

'Oh, it's all the same,' she said with that skeptical sideways look she had, which was clever and bird-like usually, but now it just aggravated me beyond belief because I knew she was simply *wrong* on this one.

'It isn't!' Mum couldn't know the difference, she was so out of touch. 'Mum, really, listen—'

'Haven't you got some homework to do or something?'

'Gogodders are totally *against* God's Whores and it's really wrong of you to say they're the same.'

'I don't want you going. You don't know what they are, these people …'

This was infuriating because she thought she knew when, really, she just didn't – and I did. I knew they weren't all 'these people'. She might have known what Whores for God were – and so did I. I'd seen their orgies and their violent sexual displays in demonstrations on television and it was fierce and frightening (though it wasn't clear who or what they were angry with and what it was they were fighting for). And I knew also that they had formed out of a reaction against the United Modesty Movement, UMM. But Gogodders were a kind of playful antidote to all that. In any case, I was sure as hell going to Jojo's party no matter what Mum said. One thing I did know for sure was that they were the people to be with. They just were. No way *at all* was I missing out now that I'd finally been invited. It was only a week away.

39.

'Jennypatel?' A tentative tap on my arm and that soft but strict little voice: 'Your eyes are not on your task.' She says it with that stiff grimace of hers that passes for a kind of smile. 'We were talking about enhancements. And I wonder what it is you are looking at, now, with the eye of your mind?'

I notice I've buttered both sides of each slice of bread I'd cut. I hear the distant laughter of a kookaburra. Laugh, kookaburra. Why not?

'Oh, I'm still in my old classroom,' I lie, not being up to sharing this particular memory of the night of Jojo's party; not yet.

'Perhaps you will tell me more, so that I may be there too?'

I see Miss Right turning to the rest of the class, the silhouette of her figure all bristly against the backlit data screen. She looks like one of those multi-limbed puppets people used to make up dramas about, once upon a time in Indonarchipelaga. 'Miss Right was fond of giving talks on manners for young ladies, and quite often she'd quote our headmaster, because she admired him deeply. "As Mr Pule phrases it," she would often begin, "Gentlemen depend on ladies to help us deal with our inner-animal, which needs relief in ways that girlies cannot comprehend."' I remembered him saying that too. But then, I remembered everything he said, he was so handsome. And he had on his particularly engaging grin whenever he said this.'

'Your Mr Pool was a sagacious man,' Mica interrupts, biting into a buttery piece of bread. 'Ahead of his time. Perhaps he could have been a Propergander! Even before post-Liberation Enlightenment, to have such a visionary understanding of why girlies are so important! A well-controlled female body, disciplined inside and out, is essential to the success of Civilisation. You must have felt very proud when he said such words, Jennypatel.'

She was right! I *did* feel proud. I was oh so very very eager to please. Sprogs are like that though, aren't they? Wanting to be right, to be commended and applauded – oh what a *good* girl, so *clever*. Like puppies wagging our tails so hard we'd twist our little bodies in half for you. 'Only thing is, tiger, he was a manipulator and a liar.'

'You should not speak with such disrespect of teachers and Properganders, who are Men of Right-Sight and worldly and wise!'

'Mica, listen. Mr Pule's image of order was very reassuring, which is precisely why what he told us was *unforgivable*—' but she cut in, her thin lips spitting steely words as from a staple-gun: 'Men of certainty provide the guidance of experience, they show us how to live well. That is the most important thing any teacher can impart to his charge, whose first duty to her teacher is obedience. Obedience is an essential virtue. Obedience makes for a harmonious collective. Obedience is the highest form of moral excellence' – I want to interrupt, but she's erecting a wall of words, higher and higher, bristly with iron spikes on top – 'though it is listed third of the Graces of CHOM after Compliance and Humility and before Modesty, but we know that all are of equal value. All are vital. The lifeblood of virtuous (wo)Mankind as espoused by UMM.'

UMM, the United Modesty Movement. Virtues of CHOM. Proper-gander Lore and the Meditations. She's a solid, shored-up little construction. I examine the crumbs on the table. Dip finger in the wet ring left by my teacup. Make the circle into a spiral. Feel the heavy, gentle, pressure of Blackie's head on my foot. Glance up at the face opposite me, all clenched up like a fist. She rises from her seat and goes to the door. I watch through the window as she walks a little way from the house, thin little lonely lopsided form in its long, see-through dress. The poor little vulnerable buttocks on it. She's looking out over the fields towards her home. Desperate thing fighting for her servitude as though it is her salvation, as some famous philosopher once said. Who was that? When? Never mind. The old brain's gone to porridge. Too much time alone. Let her be. Let her yearn after what she's lost. Like the rest of us who've emerged from the wreckage of the world, the pillagers and predators, the Ministers and their praters, and the parasites that feed off their dead skin cells – *ooh no sir, I don't mind nibbling your scaly bollocks if you give me a cosy cranny to rot in at the end of the day* – and the toughest kind of soldier, who's done death over and over, who's *over* death – *Death? That old chestnut, seen it, done it, so what?* – and of course, the cleverest of human cockroaches who scurry between the cracks of the world, in the dark, grimy places with the trains roaring round us, canny creatures scuttling, like Jimbo and me. But from time to time the KimCuR death squads emerge into our dark in their blaze of light to spray the pests, and the pests fall in scores. Some get up again and others don't.

 PEARL

40.

I do as Motley says, 'make like the cockroach'. With one of the other kids from under Central, we found the bus bound for Perfect, with its box of anodyne tales for girlies. We did as planned: took it and replaced it with our own. What a treat they'd get; that is, should we manage to pull it off, if no-one went crying *porno!* to MaOblat. Opal might, she's the sort. Or Nickeline, trying to make up for being a feeb. I never thought I'd wish Perfection on another girl – and I don't, I really don't – I just hope to hell that all the girls of Oblation, Sacricunt and Dutilove get to see something to boggle their brains.

By now, I know, as I sit sipping grog-and-water with the others back under the station, the audience will be filing into the telly room, all atremble in the air of novelty. Film night! MaOblat will check the titles, then leave to go and polish her augs or whatever it is she does when she's not peeling potatoes or chivvying children. The girls will be left, as usual, in the charge of xeniicuts. Here's hoping it's our friends, the xeniies from 226 to 230.

Grimalda gives me some interesting news, too. There's a boat leaving for Zealand next week. She says I can take it if I like. Quite a few from Big Smoke will be going too. Leaving from various jetties along the river to meet at the tidal sly-port in a cave where Big River flows into the Sea. I have the impression that she is keen for me to go. She doesn't like me working with Motley on the counter-propaganda missions, and we both know there's bound to be more jobs, just as dangerous as the one we've just pulled off. Maybe more so. But that's the thing, isn't it? To have work. To be of value. To do what you are good at. You can't ask more than that for a life, can you?

Although, to be on the Sea. To be away …

Yes, I have powerful cravings. Knowing what I do now, they're even stronger than when I first discerned them, and took them for the voices of demons. There is a world out there, places beyond the bounds of Propergander Lore, where everything is the opposite of what you thought it was. Good is evil; evil, good. Always I have been like a creature who lives in grass and rocks. Or between cracks of masonry. I've been making like a cockroach all my life. And now, now the Sea draws me. The limitlessness of the horizons I glimpsed from the air.

Asa would have liked to see the Sea. Where are you now, my lover?

THE HAG

41.

Of all the escaped little scraps of humanity I've found (and sent off to try their luck in Unrule) she is by far the toughest. But then, all the others had run away to save themselves, while she is after saving her friend. From such as me. To take them both home to the slaughter-house. While some might argue that losing your limbs in the name of some weirdo patched-together deity of doolally god-botherers is possibly not the best life-choice, she does rather seem up for it. I really haven't made much of a dent in its martyr-mind. I fear for her. And I fear for her friend, Pearl.

I pour myself another cup of tea and add a double nip to help me trace the winding ways from what was, to what has come to be. Some days I follow one path, sometimes another, glowing like the luminous pictures in Anjali's precious antique prayer book whose presence in our home so frightened Arun. All that pre-Christlamic blasphemy that told of love, of gentleness … It made Anjali so cross, the way he made her keep it hidden.

Oh, Arun, darling dad. Biddable, gentle man. My earliest teacher. We'd read the news together every morning after Anjali had gone to work. With the sun just coming up and the light all goldy on the treetop below, the jacaranda with its wonderful flowers. Hunched together over our tablet, we'd scan all available sites for information. Arun told me that there used to be a lot more available a few years ago, and even more when he was a boy. But after RUSA's Morality Protection Bill was passed and their agencies controlled most of the media internationally, it was harder to get a picture of what was going on. Arun explained that it had had to happen though. The government, he told me, had to stop the proliferation of what he called 'rude pictures' and 'rogue websites'.

How embarrassed he'd looked when I'd asked, 'What sort of rude pictures?' Red as a beetroot. 'Oh, pictures of undressed ladies and gentlemen I think, more or less…' he said vaguely. 'Like the sort of thing Sonny Manson talks about, which is why we have a special firewall just for Australand, to protect our children.'

I knew Mr Manson from television. He was very handsome, I thought, almost as gorgeous as Mr Pule. He was the chairman of the Australand Christlamic Fraternity well before God's Economic and Ecumenical Trust (GEET) was formed, and he led this very noisy campaign called 'Save Our Sons and Daughters'. At least it was called that originally – they dropped the D for Daughters, because SOSD didn't have much of a ring to it and reversing the last two letters gave you SODS – not quite the tone they were after, and also it altered the 'natural order of precedence'. So they just dropped the Daughters bit: Save Our Sons or SOS. Of course all these marketing deliberations were lost on me; all I remember thinking was that he must be a very kind man to want to protect children. I made a point of watching their rallies on the telly: Manson and all his followers with their pretty banners, the Crucifix and Crescent standing proud over a background of red, white and green, joined by the ladies of UMM, the United Modesty Movement, in their flowing black or white or grey crown-to-toes. Awfully impressive. Lovely, really.

As Arun was so uncomfortable talking about the rude pictures and things, I asked him instead what 'misinformation' was. 'That is fibs to mislead people, more or less, about current events,' he explained. 'Like the Fools, those gentlemen dressed up as ladies or wearing silly pantaloons, do. Up to all kinds of mischief.' I knew Dad didn't see eye-to-eye with Mum and Lee about the Fools movement. 'But,' he continued, 'it doesn't happen much any more because people who spread misinformation are locked up in prison or sent overseas to RUSA's special institutions where they teach you a lesson.'

Lee and Anjali enjoyed checking out the mainstream coverage of Fool activity though. They loved the fact nobody could seem to get a handle on the Fools, yet they still managed to inveigle themselves into peripheral (or not-so-peripheral) positions in government, even into the Christlamic Cabinet Ministry. 'Perfect tricksters!' Lee called them, chuckling happily when yet another highly-positioned politician quoted one of their comments: the Fools were considered by some to be useful as a sort of social barometer – and if they said something risqué, well, what could you expect from people in pancake makeup and psychedelic trousers?

Even much later, I sometimes wondered at the States' tolerance of those who became our starry-eyed, silly-shoed protectors. But after a while I worked out that kings need foils: someone you can safely despise.

Fools were a mix of those most hated: ladyboys and women, girls and blacks and Jews. There was also a handful of straight Anglo and Asian men and boys. Some of them were religious, too, still are, and I feel sorry for them now though I didn't get it then. But it was *their* religions, *their* prophets whose messages had been corrupted beyond recognition. Still, they remembered that their faiths had once centred on injunctions against violence and cruelty. They remembered a prophet who had preached humility and compassion – what a revolutionary! So hideous, what had come of all that ancient goodness that had been born, miraculously, at a time and place in the thrall of warring tribal warlords.

Any case, their silly disguises were perfect for hiding in the light, so to speak. I mean, how could an Ecuman distinguish religious affiliations, gender or race, when all were costumed in baggy harlequin pants or drag-queen splendour, with wigs and greasepainted faces? So even though you'd think, logically, that their sweet levity would offend against every protocol of Christlam, it was the reverse: the Fraternity enjoyed them as a pathetic contrast to their own 'manliness', sort of reminding them that there, but for the grace of their GodFather, go they. And the Fools were allowed to give occasional backhanded advice like any worthy court jester.

But hark, my little bosom-viper returns! It sits. Silent but sulking rather loudly. 'Tea, darling?' Oh, cut the sarcasm!

It nods, its face now all bland and impermeable as an egg.

What am I, its personal xeniicut slave? I tell her to help herself and light up another cigar, cough and spit. If I hadn't been gassed in the riots I'd be able to enjoy smoking a lot more.

She carries the pot over to the hob and refills it, brings it to the table, pours both of us another cup. I add a nip to mine. She takes the bottle and follows suit. I raise an eyebrow, which she ignores. Fine. You might as well be a child alcoholic as a child fascist.

'Will you tell me more about the olden days?' she asks cautiously.

'Oh, days of wine and roses …'

She looks at me with the sort of pitying smile a teenager in my time would have given an adult, which humanises her slightly, though not much. She takes a grimacy sip and I too have a swig to warm my cockles (and muscles, alive etc).

'So not much wine then, and few roses either; a lot of pacts and agreements though, and misinformation, half-truths and total lies. Arrangements between people in different countries shifted and changed; I saw grown-ups' loyalties break down and re-align themselves every bit as often as schoolkids'. Main realignment happened after the Great Toxic Archipelago had formed itself out of what had been the Atlantic seaboard of America – when RUSA formed the pact with men from the part of North Africa that had survived the Middle Eastern Pantastrophe. You may have learnt about it?'

She shakes her head and sips her groggy tea. Seems to be getting the hang of it.

'The Pantastrophe happened when much of the subterranean fuel that hadn't already self-ignited had leaked and spread, devastating whole nations that had once made themselves rich through selling the self-same stuff. These African men were very handsome, I reckoned, with their uptilted eyes like cats' and high cheekbones, their curly beards and light brown skin. They wore long white robes and headdresses like women.'

'Like women? Sacrilege. The Ways of Man are not the Ways of (wo)Man. *Haraamasur.*'

Jesu. Check pulse of Hag: irrit-meter's mercury rising again. Damp it down with a swallow of grog. 'So true.' (Swig.) 'They are not.' (Swig.) 'But I do remember thinking, though, maybe they dressed that way because there were no women in their country.'

'Hag, now you are not being serious.'

'Well I'd never seen any onscreen, women I mean. Only men with beards in long dresses.'

'Not *dresses.* Robes!'

Possibly I grinned a bit, showing my black tooth. Left upper incisor. The Hag bares its fang. Close my mouth. Stop provoking the dippy kipper. I do honestly remember, though, wondering back then if they had children over there in Africa, and if so, how they were born. Perhaps the American women had the babies for these men because, after all, the Americans and the robed gentlemen were very kind to each other, having so many ideas in common about morality and how best to live. I said, 'They had very strict ideas what was right and what was wrong, not much room for a divergent opinion—'

'There is but One Truth. It is written: "Beware the ruses of relativism."'

'Yes yes, the majesty of the Sacred Sceptre and Rod of GodFather etc etc—'

'*BBHCM!* Long may he reign alive-alive-oh-oh as revealed by Jesumuh and espoused by the Properganders of Instruction & Destruction. The Properganders decide.'

'I remember learning in my history lessons that the African men in robes and the American men in suits had been angry at each other for many, many years – up until not so long before all this happened. But where once they'd seen only differences, especially when it came to religion, or to ideas of what it meant to be enlightened, now the stricter more pious American Christians and North African Muslims finally noticed how much they had in common with each other. So much more than with the non-religious people, like my parents, whom I knew were called "liberals"—'

'*Heretics.*'

Jesumuh. And you can kiss my chuddies, you cranky little spitfire. 'It was because of this new understanding that God's Economic and Ecumenical Trust, or—'

'GEET.'

'—was formed.' *Spawned.* 'Men who first developed the new Ways, organised the militias who marched under the banner with its crucifix surmounted by a half-moon in the shape of a blade, a sceptre—'

'The First Christlamic Accord. Initiated by the Men unto whom was first revealed the Dual True Faith. Our saviours!'

That kookaburra's at it again. A brown leaf is pasted against the window pane, veins splayed against cold glass. I get up from the table and begin to chop up a few bits and pieces to put in the stockpot. I remember there'd been a great ceremony that day, televised internationally, with us all down at the Harbour again beneath the magnificent arch of the Bridge, and glinting nearby in the bright sunshine the white, sail-like structure, pride of our city, where people used to congregate to enjoy the opera, to hear internationally acclaimed musicians and singers, and where great speakers would gather each year … And here we were now in our gladrags made of whatever bibs and bobs we could scrounge and tack together; oh yes, we had our standards, and see our hungry faces upturned to watch the dregs of our future being decided by Africans and Americans.

The proceedings lasted a day and a half: the ratification of the First Christlamic Accord. Brilliant blue sky as the backdrop for the Ecumen standing guard with riot shields in red, white and green, the protective horizontal bar of the crucifix sheltering the bands of stars, now alternating with moons, one of each for all the states of RUSA and its allies. But there was no reaction worth speaking of, no protest. The event had been carefully planned. Ricky Sartorial Junior was back up there again, his bland face as exultant as a bland face can get. I remember his speech:

'On this historic day, East and West meet at long, long last, in shared acceptance and belief. A harmonious Accord of Men! We have been too-long divided but now our differences dissolve in the Name of the Resolved Twins Jesumuh! We are now one in the sacred alliance of the Dual True Faith! *Inshallaweh!* Together we stand united beneath the banner of the Crucifix and the Crescent! *Inshallaweh!*' – and the call was echoed throughout the crowd, … *aweh* … *aweh* – 'At last, the people of the Cross and the people of the waxing Moon, representing sacrifice and regeneration ongoing, meet in symphonic unity! And to cement this blessed covenant, today we launch the sacred text that contains – at last! – the combined wisdom of Koran and Bible. *Inshallaweh!*' He holds up to the cameras the first one of its kind and he thunders: 'I give you the Holy DoppelBook!'

Deafening applause. No dry lightning forking down behind him or big goddy hand reaching out of the sky; but what the hell, the book was launched.

Millions of free copies were distributed on that day, and from then on also in schools, on the streets, in shops and offices. In hotels and motels all Gideon Bibles were removed and replaced with the DoppelBook.

'"Saviours" you say, Mica. Quite a lot of people thought that.' I could cry, but that would just make me wet. Anger is better. 'Con-men leading a bandwagon of credulous idiots to hell.' She just sits and stares. I could slap her. Whack her. Whack the lot of them, as my darling Lee would've said. Instead I suggest in my most grown-up voice, 'Time you had a rest, my blossom.'

'I am not tired. Also, I am not a blossom.'

True enough. Look at it now, staring me down now, and those eyes of hers all flinty. I light up and pour myself a drink. The child can make any Anglindian witch come over quite glassy.

'Then go and contemplate something.' Meditate on The Beauty of the Suture or whatever.

'But there is so much more for us to talk about!' Her eyes are brilliant with fervour, but I turn away. I'm just not up to it at the moment, to feeding her desire to live vicariously the only bit of history she knows. She wants to feel as if she'd been there, triumphant, marching under the banner of the green, red and blue, crushing the evil agnostic infidels underfoot. Onward Christian soldiers! *Allahu Akbar! Oh, mine eyes have seen the glory of the coming of the Lord, He is trampling out the vintage where the grapes of wrath are stored ...*

 ## MICA

42.

She had been there at the start of Liberation, had seen it all unfolding – although her view of it all is horribly skewed. But then, it is not possible to be objective about something when you're at the centre of it and it's happening all around you, so no wonder. And I have to remember that she has not had the benefit of a proper formal education either. She was offered a life in a civilised State but could not accept it – all the fault of her rebellious spirit. And now, after so hard a life of refusal and denial and reactivity, to be sliding alone into demented decrepitude. She is a poor thing.

Still, despite the terrible things she says I can still get a feeling for the energy of those revolutionary times!

I wanted her to continue talking, of course I did. Yet it is good also to have a moment to re-gather my thoughts, to sort through the muddle of her story based on her faulty memory. She is worse than misguided, her soul is dark with ignorance and her tales mix up wonder and evil, lies and truths. And so always I bear in mind what she is. It is not hard, for daily I am reminded by the sight of those evil animal tattoos upon her dugs and the tough, white, corded scars on her hands from when she seized the scorching ropes that had failed to hold her to the stake. She is strong, it is true, but deluded; she is sly without actually being very intelligent.

I can afford to allow myself to feel some small pity for her. She is very lost, her mind awash in a senile muddle of reality and fantasy. Perhaps she is already quite mad and does not know what she is doing? This too could be so. She has been alone so long. But I will not be drawn into the confusion of her fancies. I am strong in my heart and my mind, as strong as a girlie can be. And each day my body too is a little stronger. My collarbone is healing. Though I can't yet use my arm without pain I am sure there's not much longer to wait.

She was very angry with me just now – yet she never ill-treats me. Instead, she treats me with care, no matter that we differ. She speaks to me not as a child or a servant. It is strange, though: she is my elder, yet I am her moral superior. She must have some dim awareness of this paradox, which contributes to her bad temper with me, but also I confess it has to do with my manner. I am unused to the sort of human commerce such as this I share with this mad old (wo)Man.

I must stay focused, not allow myself to be led off on the byways of her meandering mind. Perhaps if I can quell my anger and revulsion when she blasphemes I might even lead her back, at least a small distance, toward the light? Might I help her a little? What if I were able to formulate a word or two in such a way that she would understand, and be moved, just a little – in the direction of the Truth? I can try when the opportunity presents itself. I can only try.

And soon, regardless, having done what good I can, I will be able to leave. I will be able to leave and go in search of my Pearl.

But for now, I am just frustrated by this enforced inactivity. I will do some more gardening.

+ + +

It was good to do some work with my hands. Or hand, at least. After I finished writing the last entry I went back out to the kitchen, took the secateurs from the drawer and went outside. I spent an hour or so on that apricot tree. It looks well now. It will develop into a good shape, especially if I can train its branches to spread across the wall, as do the limbs of the pear trees against the wall of our most sacred citadel. And so I think once more of my reason for being here, my reason for leaving, my Pearl. I must keep the faith. I will save her and we will return. We will welcome whatever punishment is deemed meet for our treachery. Then, together we will make our sacrifice.

I will save her.

The Hag came out as I was raking up the twigs and leaves. All she said was, 'Neatly cropped. In a sort of scorched earth way.' What would she know about gardening? I ignored her and went to attend to the peas while there was still some light left in the day. They are a shambles, the trellis all lopsided, and if it's not fixed they'll soon all be rotting on the ground. I managed, with the application of patience and the skill I have acquired through experience, to set it to rights with one hand. When she went out to feed the animals she made no comment. I prayed as I worked, and I pray now, as I prepare for sleep: Oh, keep me strong, GodFather, Blessed Be Your Cock-and-Muscle, may you reign in eternal grace, alive-alive-oh-oh, forever and ever, amen, long may your strong-toed foot imprint its cool sole upon my brow. Keep me and protect me for I am your faithful daughter.

 **PEARL**

43.

Back in our tilting little house set amongst the spotty gums and river-light, we sit in companionable silence listening to the soft rain drumming lightly on the slates, and the rusty rattle of an ancient electric fan-heater Grimalda found. (The kero one finally expired.) The cobwebs stir gently in the rain-scented air. Motley puts his empty plate aside and takes up his sewing. He is putting together a jacket and a pair of trousers for me. I can hardly wait to try on those rather thrilling 'porno pants'. They will be tight around the hips, as inaccessible as Tank Girl's, and though we can't risk bright colours for me – for I am soon to be 'away with the tides' as they put it – we can play with different textures, suede and hessian and see-though muslin stripes crosshatched with cotton drill in subdued shades, mottled cloudy green and slate and dove and what Motley calls 'gerbil-belly grey' that will meld with both leaf-filtered daylight and shadows of the river in moonlight. My departure is scheduled for tomorrow evening – or maybe the following one, depending on the rain – off down the river to the sea and away to one of the free lands.

There are barges on the most sheltered inlets of the river, poled by Fool-Rangers in capes the colour of rainwet gum trees. There are boats that dock in secret bays by the edge of the Sea. Boats to take people like me away to lands more myth than real. I will go and see. To go to sea and see what may be.

Is it possible? There are spies and patrollers everywhere and, as Grimalda is fond of saying, the rulers of the States are not paranoid, but justifiably fearful. They have to be, for they are hated by all who have not fallen under their sway. This hate strengthens my hope. My desire.

There is no way I can keep in touch with my Fools after I leave. Nor will I see Mica again, never know what happened to Asa. He may have been caught. My fault. What that means is too terrible to contemplate. And she – she may be Perfected this time next year. I turn my mind away from that also. I am abandoning them. I hate myself for it. I will do it anyway.

But here's this letter, testimony to what I have lived through so others may read it if, one night, a little plane made of paper should happen to skim through their sleeping window – through Asa's window? And just *maybe* Mica may already have found that other coded missive, and read it, and – but why do I say this? She would *never* follow the map. See? Once more the real invades the dream for I have not the power to keep it at bay. Ah, give it up. Just live. Asa and Mica and I will *never* meet again in another place.

Just live, you goner!

 **THE HAG**

44.

She's in bed now. Thankfully. I sit here before the flickering hearth. My memory's an old woman's wig. A wreck of a memory; what I think I know now is superimposed over the perceptions of the child I was. A child's-eye view is the root of memory but the child's mind is now old, and all loose and wobbly. A rotten tooth. Pull it gently, because the root is still attached to the gum. Be careful now. I can still bleed.

New Year's Eve. Anjali had said nothing more about Jojo's party and neither had I. I watched the nine o'clock fireworks from our balcony with Mum and Dad and some of their friends, including Lee, then I left them to it – off to my sleeping place. I leant on the window for a while, listening to the grown-ups chatting away together. I remember feeling guilty for what I was going to do because the only reason I'd get away with it was because they wouldn't feel the need to check up on me: they trusted me (*Jenny never lies*). But I figured it was only a small betrayal because, after all, it was absolutely *imperative* that I go. It just *was*. So I quietly opened the window that gave onto the light-well with its fire-escape that lay between us and the next door tenement, and to the left a narrow laneway lined with compost and rubbish bins, worm farms and lumber, spare bricks, coils of wire, cockatoo-proofing and kegs of pest repellent. It led into the long, thin backyard we shared with the neighbours, where we held our Sunday barbecues and birthday parties.

I climbed out the window. Sky the colour of jacarandas, the air warm and smelling of hot metal and mangoes and fertiliser of blood and bone. Climbed carefully down the fire-escape, slowly, slowly, as there hadn't been any maintenance work done on it in my lifetime and I wasn't taking any chances. Made the ground, took the lane and, in case anyone was looking out a window – and people did like to keep an eye on each other and their kids – slipped sideways in a cockroachy sort of way into an even narrower alley between the two blocks facing ours.

Jojo lived quite close by, as did most of the kids at my school which was only a couple of kilometres down the hill, towards the north of the city. Her mum opened the door and smiled. She was very pretty. Like Jojo. Then I saw Jojo's face at the top of the stairs, all pink with excitement. She beckoned me up the stairs. She had a whole room to herself in the attic. The room was lit by about fifty candles so that it was all glowing gold and lovely and cosy. Only three other girls were there, older girls from the year ahead of us. Jojo knew them though, and they weren't ashamed to be with this junior because Jojo was so popular. But I didn't take all that much notice of this for one simple reason: they were all wearing dresslesses! I felt such an idiot. I was the only one in the standard crown-to-toe instated by UMM, like the ones we always wore when we went out of doors. The dressless was similar in style, only with an all-important difference: it featured a band of transparent material that extended from about navel-height to just above the knee.

Though of course they didn't actually show the real private parts back then – girls wore g-strings over them. The furry ones called mirkins were what you had to have, especially handy if, like me, you hadn't sprouted any hair down there yet. As I walked in, amid much glee and hilarity, they were all in the process of trying on different mirkins. Jojo could see my discomfort and took my hand, saying, 'They're great, aren't they? We went down to Y-Mart this morning, Mum and me, cos there was a special on!' Then she did a little bump and grind to show off the auburn one she was wearing. It was all done up in little glossy ringlets that bounced against her thighs.

'Personally, I find the curly ones a bit too much – no offence, Jojo – but I think the cropped style is most gloriable,' said Bo-bella, a tall girl with straight black hair that swooped down over her face like a magpie's wing. 'Sort of fuck-you and what-the-hell, don't you reckon?'

Jojo laughed and so did Shi-Shi and Ellabella, so I did too. Shi-Shi had a false cunny-line stitched into her mirkin, all marked out in sequins. Ellabella had a bald cap on her quim, which was funny as I suspect that what was underneath was bald too.

'There were tons of styles at Y-Mart. It's great how you can get whatever style suits your personality. They're all really personal, you know?' explained Jojo. 'But you have to have a pretty sophisticated sense of humour to appreciate it, actually.'

'I don't think they're funny. I think they're sexy,' said Shi-Shi.

'As the lady said: a *sophisticated* sense of humour,' teased Bo-bella, grinning.

'Ha ha and ta for that.'

Jojo threw me one of her dresslesses. I quickly stripped off my old UMM coverall and put hers on. It felt sumptuous. Jojo said, 'It's an ironic statement, Mum reckons.' I wasn't entirely sure what an ironic statement was, but Jojo continued: 'Mum says, the radical exposure of the part that's meant to stay hidden is *empowering*, it returns authority to the wearer and of course it's all a matter of a woman's individual *choice*. And the boys really like it when you turn up to a mixed party and take off your UMM-issue crown-to-toe and there's a dressless underneath!' She passed me a shiny black-furred mirkin with a dainty white bowtie at the top. 'Try this. It's very you, Jennypenny. Always serious, slightly formal, but with a clever sense of humour.' She gave me an affectionate squeeze.

It was true that Jojo had lots of boyfriends, though I knew she didn't fuck them all, only those who were really nice about it. What would Miss have said? *Bad girls, leading those poor boys on!* And Mr Pule? Well, his message to us girls had been changing over time and was now a bit more ambivalent. Where once he'd simply insisted, like Miss, that 'Gentlemen depend on ladies to help us deal with our inner-animal,' he'd now added a sort of codicil: 'But relief for the animal may be negotiated *within the constraints of a safe environment.*' We admired his ability to adapt to the various aspects of the prevailing spirit of the age; Miss seemed hidebound by comparison. He was our strong leader, and *so* cute. I supposed he'd be happy to learn that if Jojo felt sorry for his 'gentlemen' she would in mitigation hold their cocks for a bit, or put them in her mouth for a little while. Sometimes, she'd told me, at those private dressless parties the girls would take turns to do that for a boy. It always cheered them up a lot, she said, and stopped them getting grumpy. I wasn't sure that I wanted to put boys' things in my mouth. But if I didn't feel like it I supposed I could always leave early.

And in the meantime there was nothing to worry about because there were no boys at Jojo's that night. So we chatted, and made up each other's faces for maximum drama, manicured and polished our nails, drank some of Ms Jericho's grog, and listened to music and danced the emblematic Gogodder gogo until it was time to go down to the Harbour and watch the fireworks light up the sky.

When we got there, it seemed as if the whole city had crammed into the foreshore to see the New Year in. And I was wildly excited and I don't know even now if it was more because of the big, scary, wonderful party going on all around us, or the fact that under my crown-to-toe I was wearing a dressless, and under the dressless that cute mirkin with the bowtie. And of course my red-checked ballet slippers for which Miss Right had such contempt. It was so wonderful and outrageous and thrilling. *If she could see me now!* I thought.

I see us now: arm in arm, there's Jenny and Jojo, Shi-Shi and Ellabella and Bo-bella, holding on tight to each other because the crowd was dense and surging. We'd managed to wriggle our way down to the waterfront where, although you didn't get great views, you were at the heart of the action. We could just make out the upper part of the span of the bridge in the middle distance and we couldn't see the grand white Opera Theatre but we could hear the throb of the bass it emitted, so deep and strong, echoing the pulse of the heartbeats of each and every person there, so we were all joined, one to the other by the vibration, by the fervour of the tribal joy.

At midnight, the countdown: FIVE ... FOUR ... THREE ... TWO ... *ONE!* and the sky was alight with starbursts, then cascades and comets that bloomed out of nothing, blazed in fiery arcs then fell, trailing brilliant dust; and then someone, I didn't know who, lifted me up bodily and put me on his shoulders, and I wasn't afraid for he only wanted to let me see better, this man in a mad puffy suit of different colours covered in great big diamonds, and his face made up too, a huge smile on it with a huger one marked out in lipstick, and who could fear a double-smiling man with stars for eyes? And then I had a clear view through the haze of scintillating silver and gold and violet and scarlet motes to the sail-like roof of the theatre, but it was no longer white, it was billowing with some brilliant light effects so that it resembled silken fabric filled with the movement of the wind, shifting and changing, and more lights were rippling across its surface like anemone tentacles and the fey bodies of those fluorescent sea-creatures I remembered from my trip across the ocean when I was small, which was only a dream to me now; and then the man released me for the kissing had started on the ground: friends kissing friends, strangers kissing friends, strangers kissing strangers, all of us touching lips to faces so briefly, and I kissed Shi-Shi and Jojo and Bo, then on to another, and we linked arms with whoever was near and sang as loudly as we could, *Should auld acquaintance be forgot, and never brought to mind ... Should auld acquaintance ...*

Then there's a roar of sound that drowns out all others. Heaven collapses and Hell rears up out of the wreckage. People running everywhere, no sense to their movement, but the sky's red and black and I'm looking for Jojo, for the others, for my friend in the clown suit, and I can't see any of them; then I'm looking for a landmark to find my way through this horror of screaming people, but I can't even see the Bridge, where the *hell* is the *Bridge?* My head hurts and I'm crying though I can't hear it, only know I am because my face is wet, or is it blood? I pass a rank of Ecumen, their shiny masks reflecting fire and smoke, their guns raised, and the militants of the American-Arabian Anti-Atheism Union – QuadA – with their blazing insignia. I dart off in another direction,

I run and stumble. I hitch up the stupid skirts of my crown-to-toe and dressless, and run and run and run …

 PEARL

45.

Blue light forks down, a dragon's tongue, as the rain batters the roof. My darly Mica and I read about dragons once. Great armoured lizards, their flanks all bronze slates, their eyes like boiling cauldrons and their bellies full of fire that they would spew onto their enemies below. It was nice to read together, her and me, when it was raining outside and we were warm, inside, safe from monsters, mythical or otherwise. Only there is no Mica any more. Only the rain.

Waiting in the storm, waiting by the river, with Motley.

The inlet is tiny, sheltered from view, remote.

Lightning opens up the sky once again. There is thunder; it fills the void that closed up again after the last rumble died.

The grass is spongy underfoot; there's a scent of sweet rot rising from the mud. Rain pocks the surface of the water, and where the starlight shines through the canopy there's a purple-green-pink film of oil. Flimsy tree branches dip low, trailing fringes of leaves. It is not a bright night, but not perfectly dark either. Then the rain gets progressively heavier, breaking the sheen on the water into brilliant fragments like bright shards of memory.

I am wearing my new suit of clothes, the trousers and jacket of grey, grey-green, blue-grey, gerbil-belly grey. I feel proud and I am not afraid. Every pore of my body tingles with excitement. The air is cold but I cannot feel it for the blood that pumps through my body is fierce. And dear Motley has wrapped his waxed raincoat around me, not his citywear one of course, beautiful with red and orange lozenges, but the grey Ranger one for skulking and sneaking around the fringes of the world. I press back against his body. We strain our eyes looking for the approach of the barge, looking for more grey-shrouded Fools.

THE HAG

46

Morning. I shift the bulk of Blackie who has managed somehow to insinuate himself between me and the back of the couch so that I'm half on the floor. Pick up lumpy self. Let dog out for a pee. Close door quickly against dawn chill. Light stove. Apply kettle to hob. Ah, I see my mini-fascist's up and about again. It's peering around the side of its nook, its nose all atremble like a questing mouse snout. Seems to have got its mojo back.

'Good-day, my furry fiend.'

'Good-day, my Hag.'

'Cheeky.'

'Means?'

'Doesn't matter.' I smile, taking care to hide my black tooth this time. When my tiger-lily's feeling sweet, I really must try to keep her that way. 'Tea?'

'I will make it.' Very nice. Must've had an epiphany: *be kind unto the old budi for she is good and wise.*

She brings the tea to the table, sits down and looks up at me expectantly. 'Story?' She's a cat herself, with her soft step and her inscrutable gaze, her schmoozy ways here, her arrogance there …

I light a smoke. She wrinkles her nose. Tough titty, pretty pussy. She looks at me expectantly.

'Yes?'

'If you tell me another story I will listen. I will not interrupt you, Jennypatel. I know we have different, ah, different—'

'Perspectives?'

'We have different perspectives. On history. But I must exercise the humility of the younger, for I was not there.'

I wonder what that cost her? Never mind. Go with it. 'So. You wanted to know about the Action.'

'I did. Do.'

'There had been two major detonations, one destroying the Opera Theatre, the other the Bridge, and the Harbour flooded over the smashed banks and into the city itself so that the tall buildings stuck out of the mess like fuck-you fingers; then away to the east our City Gardens were submerged, and the low-lying areas called The Pott and The Loo. In the west the waters merged with Black and Rosette Bays to make one big salty swamp, and it slopped all over the Glebe and the last of it was lapping, all disconsolate and stinking, at the Gothic façade of the university.

'The city was in shock. The jewel-like centre we had so loved was utterly smashed out of shape and flooded with water that joined with the wash from broken sewerage pipes. But after the initial flood it just lay still and gloating, breeding under its viscous skin the creatures that spread diseases and would soon plague us with gleeful vehemence.

'When you go through some shattering event, your body and mind close down for a bit, sort of conk out and go blank, then after however long it takes, you recover. Or no, that's not right; you don't actually *recover* from devastation – you *absorb* it. Loss and pain are incorporated into who you are. You can absorb horror too – it's broken down into little pieces after the event and digested, becomes just more of the stuff that makes you who you are. I'm the post-disaster version of a once-upon-a-time innocent Jenny. The person who survived what came later probably wouldn't have done if this hadn't happened first, this preview. Then there are those who are so ravaged that they may never feel calm again, never feel tenderness again; anger drives them and they are filled with a fierce will to vengeance or to justice, and both of these are terrible things. Lee was a bit like this. Others, like my mother, lose hope. Other are filled with constructive energy and busy themselves in organising and rebuilding and trying to buoy up the others who, often as not, despise them for their efforts. My father was one of these.

'After the explosions I'd been fortunate enough to be caught up in one of the streams of people that had climbed onto one of the City's broken towers, then up onto the roof before the waters rushed in to swamp us and any others who'd survived the blasts. It was only a shard of a building really, held up more by luck than physics. No access into any of the rooms below unless you wanted to try jumping across a great gaping chasm five hundred metres from the ground. I was there for some days, but you don't really need to hear all about the hunger and thirst – yes thirst, so much water everywhere but nothing to drink but salty mud and sewage. Nor will I bother describing the filth that soon overtook our tower, or the shame of shitting in public, or any of the other aspects of human-animality that emerge at times like this among both the greedy and the generous, the selfish and selfless, those with hope destroyed and those whose spirits were sanguine enough to buoy them through even this.

'I remember waking up on the sixth or seventh morning to the usual stinking and crying and the white, aching sky full of gulls and smoke. But something was different from the other mornings. The very air around me seemed to be creaking and trembling. But of course it wasn't – it was the building. Its luck was running out and it was heading earth-wards, not quickly, but inexorably. Like the movement of a slow drunk. There were other buildings in its way, you see, so we'd lurch down a bit, then the process would be slowed by another building; another lurch, another crunch and so forth. Soon our small platform was a just a mass of howling maniacs running about, as if that would help. I don't know how I had the presence of mind, but I took off my crown-to-toe and used it as a rope to tie myself onto the stump of the flagpole that stood in the middle of our roof. See me, one dressless-wearing girlie lassoed to the banner of the nation. Watching how, with each heave of our sky-tossed ship, a wave of panicked mortals would be flung off into the sky, screaming and screaming. But Odyssea here remained lashed to the mast amidships.

'By the time I finally, miraculously, made it home to my poor, terri-fied parents it wasn't as if there was any need for recrimination. I was safe, unlike Bo-bella, unlike Jojo.

'Oh and there were rallies and speeches, fingers of blame pointed and proud claims of responsibility – from nascent terrorist organisations to the Fools (Arun claimed it was Fools) to God's Whores (Anjalima reck-oned it was them – though Lee said that for all their hatefilled energy they couldn't have organised their way out of a wet paper bag). It would be some years before it became clear that this was actually the work of the Christlamic Fraternity, a tactic based on one invented in the previous century called 'Shock and Awe'. Well, it shocked and it awed. But they knew to wait until a time when the Action would be interpreted as that of freedom fighters rather than that of terrorists. They framed it as an unfortunate but essential part of their longer-term strategy towards acti-vating one of the first grinding turns of the Wheel of Revolution—'

'Force is needed to crush out corrupt ways of being, to level old habits of mind to smooth the way for the Wheel to roll onwards!'

'Yay, rah. Roll freely across the shattered and flattened history-scape—'

'I understand that you are being sarcastic. But you are wrong to be so, my Hag. The purpose of revolution is to reform the world so that new—'

'Mica, if you cannot resist moralising then I will not speak.'

'Sorry.'

I go to the stove and stir the pot, add a bit of garlic. The witch's brew simmering with onions and carrots and Albert. Memory stew. Look at the pictures as they bubble away: one gleams up and I breathe it in then skim it back with my big old spatula, then comes another, breathe and skim, another – breathe, breathe and skim … How did it all happen? How *could* it have happened the way it did? Back then in the time of the First Christlamic Accord, before Liberation (from thought, from feeling, from hope), the people in my new-old country were so feeble, really, so insecure, so keen to hold onto another who looked strong, RUSA or China, custodians of the Great Asian Seam, until our divided loyalties just pissed off the both of them.

'My Hag?'

'Sorry, Mica. I can't remember what we were up to.'

'War.'

'I'm tired of war. How about love?' I suggest, as a rum sort of joke.

'Love then,' she answers, much to my surprise. 'Tell me a love story from before.'

47.

'You *like* love stories?'

'I do, my Hag. Bobander A/P of A & P told us such stories sometimes.'

'A P A P?'

'He was Assistant to the Propergander of Art & Pain. Surely you remember Art & Pain?'

'Oh yes. I remember that alright. But love stories from a Propergander? That I don't recall.'

'Yes! Like Romeo and Juliet. Where the prince escapes from the evil-doers because the princess diverts them with sexing, she sexes them all for a day and a night, fuck-fuck-fuck like a motor-girl, so that he can escape' – and here she burst into a little sing-song chant, the Christlamic version of music – '*run, run, run away; live to reign another day*. And she dies the noble death in sacrificing her life for her Man.'

'Possibly some liberties were taken with the original text.'

'I doubt it,' she replies in a most strict and superior tone. 'Bobander only told true stories.'

I wouldn't want to be Pearl, getting bossed around by this little virago. Though Pearl obviously had a will too. A marriage made in heaven or hell. I say, 'It seems you learned early on in your life about the power of love and its uses.'

'And sex and its uses.'

Well fuck me dead.

'All girlies have cockslots. All Men have cocks. Simple. And the world runs on the energy generated by fucking.'

I don't remember this being part of my training either. It's got better. Oh, yes.

'Sex makes the world. I learned all about it in ASPD—'

'Which is?'

'Advanced Sexual Politics and Divinity classes. Colander A/P of Y & D took it.'

'Colander who of what?'

'Assistant to the Propergander of Yearning and *Duty*, my Hag.' Impatiently.

'Of course. Go on.'

'He began by telling us about the origins of our true Christlamic Ways. How it started in reaction to a part of the fleshly fallacy called Fenimistry, long may its proponents burn in the hottest fires of hell and their intestines be eternally drawn out of their breathing bodies and wound around a white-hot radiator. We learned it in Week 3 of the classes we took at Minus-Eight from Attainment, because Weeks 1 and 2 were all A-level Basic Impulses and Denial.'

Good, glad we got that sorted, my sweet senior prefect in the school of hard cocks.

'The Heresy of Fenimistry,' she continues, like the obedient little rote-scholar she is, 'is called so because it is a self-reflexive word that blends a sense of the swampy origins of Man in dank female fecundity with the inherent unknowability of (wo)Man that is "fen" and "mystery" for she is dark and rank and if unpruned stinks of the carcasses of many dead fishes, and the movement began in the early twentieth century as an offshoot of the eugenics movement' – quick breath – 'and although the eugenics movement was virtuous and valorous and sought to save us from the spreading of cripsanretards and dudbubs, the Fenimists, long may they burn in the—'

'Yes, their torture, your piety. Got it, go on.'

'Fenimists conspired to enable (wo)Man to harness population growth by the use of poisonous medicaments and potions which are abominations from whose consequences we are still suffering today and these are: one, the depletion of human resources, and two, an unwieldy number of children malformed at birth, that is, cripsanretards. Dudbubs.'

'Mica. You're obviously a very dedicated pupil, but—'

'I have memorised all recommended historical tracts plus the Meditations, Ways, Virtues and many prayers.'

'But I was *saying*: I think perhaps that the malformations were caused by poisons in the air and water.'

Blank look. 'The goals of Fenimistry, long may … sorry … the goals were political. Those Fenimist conspirators plotted to undermine the authority of Holy Jesumuh, the Resolved Twins, and by this means ultimately of our GodFather Himself (BBHCM), may he reign in enduring grace alive-alive-oh! The loreful order of the Dual Truth Faith laid down by the original and most ancient Properganders and rejuvenated by Christlam was threatened by unconstrained (wo)Manhood which allied itself with another spiritual impediment which was a philosophy called human-something which was a perverted system of logic that denied that at the centre of all things is GodFather (BBHCM), may He reign in enduring grace alive–alive-oh-oh a-*men!*

'The Fenimists would' – and here she held up the first and second fingers of both hands to show she was quoting – '"worm their way into homes and gain control over gullible (wo)Men, who are loaded down with sins and are swayed by all kinds of evil desires, always learning but never able to come to a knowledge of the Truth." DoppelBook, 2 Timothy 3:1-8. Only think on it, Jennypatel! They were "always learning" but never appreciating the Truth!'

Hark, she reflects upon the text! How deep I don't think.

'But how else could it be for, as we learn from the DoppelBook, a (wo)Man's mind is not made this way because it is not a Way of (wo)Man to rule, but to *be* ruled by Man, long may his strong-toed foot imprint its cool sole upon my brow. It is for *Man* to interpret the stories, to create the rules that create the structures within which all have their appropriate place in the eyes of GodFather (BBHCM), may he reign in eternal grace, alive-oh-amen.'

'Oh, Mica. Can I just say that—'

'But that is not all!' As if it were not enough! *No.* 'The origins of Fenimistry are much older, are stemming from witchcraft which is styled after the profane methods Jezebel inherited from her spiritual mother who is Lilith the first vampire and queen of the damned and font of the noisome lil'im – long may they moulder after the wet flesh has been peeled from their cankered bones – those devouring spirits who come to Men in the night to invade them at their most vulnerable, in dreams, to deplete them of the essential masculine energies. Documentary evidence of succubantic rape is manifold.'

Lee would have loved that! Oh dear, all those poor blameless men victimised by fantasy whores who know all the tricks those dear little fellas can dream up in the most hectic of their fevered visions. Obviously there's not a damned thing I can say that might affect the version she's been taught oh so very, very well. Yet, I try in my tragic way: 'Mica, your passion and your pride are admirable, but have you ever thought—'

'I am not proud for myself. Neither is it for me to think. (wo)Man is the vehicle. Man is the driver, the actor, impelled by the imperatives of his sex.'

She has something there. I remembered the sex that oozed into the atmosphere of the political rants I'd witnessed when I was very young. I didn't know what it was, but I felt its electric force animating the air and everyone around me. A politician dully prating platitudes in a speech cobbled together by a team of public relations people? Forget it! Flailing without a throttle! What you need is a Sonny Manson firing on all cylinders.

'Like Sonny Manson.'

48.

Jesumuh – is the child a mind reader? And how would she know of Sonny Manson? But then I remind myself – silly old bat that I am with my tired cerebral folds all flopping over each other like jelly in my dotage – of course, they would have studied the great statesmen who were there beating up the crowds into a fever of religious zealotry. Come to think about it, I'm surprised it wasn't on the curriculum when I was at Ideal.

'Sonny Manson was a driver. He was a driver of Men and a Big Man in God's Economic and Ecumenical Trust. I've seen pictures and heard recordings of his voice. He was so beautiful. I love him. We all love him. Every little girlie wants a man like him to fuck her till she faints. Did you ever see him talk, in the days before the First Accord? He was a masterprater.'

You bet he was.

'Jennypatel. Talk to me. Did you see him when he was alive?'

'People like Sonny, these men, are like magicians, or seducers on erotic overdrive, skilled operators working on our fears, desires—'

'Jennypatel. We are so different that I think we can never be friends, even if we were the same age, yet I am grateful to you for your hospitality for you did indeed save my life. But you have been away from the world for a very long time, ever since you committed an evil crime when you were young. I do not feel angry with you, for it was long ago and you were young.'

'Thank you.' Keep calm, Jen. Keep a straight face. She is dead serious.

'But I must say, even though you are my elder, I have more moral sense—'

'You have more *moral se—*'

'I can help you, Hag! Though you can never be reinstated in Ideal or Perfect or any other civilised State, yet you can come to be at peace with Truth. If you relinquish your false beliefs. If you pray to GodFather (BBHCM). Think back to the speeches of the mighty Sonny Manson – surely they moved you? How he ignited the fuse that flares up in the face of deception, of wrong-thinking, paving the way for the triumph of the Dual True Faith and the sovereignty of the Son of the Son on Earth!' She reaches out and takes my hands in hers. 'Jennypatel, you could meditate upon those speeches, allow the spirit of revolution to move you once more, as it did when you were young, like me!'

Fanatics are exhausting.

I get up to clear away the tea things. Cups and saucers. Teapot. Sonny. Sex. Feasts and famines of it. We had massive chastity movements, and we had Sonny. We also had bacchanals that made the orgiastic frenzies of the Greeks look like a cup of tea and a little lie-down in a gently swinging hammock in the mango tree. We had burning of books and pianos; we had music and dancing to drums when only drums were left – oh, the dancing and the drumming – you had to be there. I was. By the Crescent and the Crucifix was I *there*. Oh yes, and what was and shall be for ever and ever ah … *men!*

My stomach is feeling rather tight, there's a sour taste in my mouth. She watches my every move, waiting for me to respond to what she seems to think is some flash of sympathetic brilliance.

'Mica, I have a few things to do. I want to go down to the river and get some cress. We need greens for a salad. To go with your soup.' I go to my shelf above one of the denser toadstool colonies. My subdued green faerie engines. I reach down a couple of old books for her, romances from the olden days when the frog was still boiling. The illustrated and abridged *Infidel* by inimitable Ayaan, as Mandy would say, and the graphic novel based on Adorable Angela's *The Passion of the New Eve* with … starring – oh what's her name? – never mind, as it didn't seem that she'd opened *Tank Girl*. Hoped they'd be instructive. If not, she can always read the atlas again. Or the cracks on the wall for all I care just now.

 ## MICA

49.

She has gone out on one of her witchy reconnaissance missions. I'm tempted to follow her again, but the hellhound is guarding the door and looks daggers at me if I approach it. In any case, it's too soon to try my earlier trick on him again. Besides, all the meat is in the pot. Perhaps the witch will bring home a stone rodent or a fish. Stupid! She has not gone *fishing*.

I sit by the window. Sky gunmetal grey. Another blimp from Unrule passes by, its sides smooth and grey, its underneath black, with that white stripe down the middle like a pussy cat's where the curious spies sit and look, and look. Unnatural thing! It is written, 'Thou shalt not go in insolence: for thou canst not rend the earth asunder, nor reach the mountains in height.' Doppelbook, Sura Al-Isra, 17:37.

But this time I stay calm. Nobody can see into the house. I find myself wondering, could there be any truth in what the Hag says? *Could* the States have amended their policy? Perhaps after prayer and many discussions amongst the most learned among the Ministry, they might have made some changes? Perhaps GodFather (BBHCM) no longer sees human flight as a form of spiritual arrogance, but a sensible form of defence against the agents of Unrule? There is no reason why we girlies would have been informed, if that were so. It is not our business to know about the subtle reasonings of our superiors.

If so, then should I not run out and wave them down? Tell them: she is not so harmless as you think! She is old and her mind is not what it once was, yet she speaks with eloquence as she tries to insinuate her way into your sympathies. She is as slippery as a snake. One less strong than me might easily be moved by her smooth words ... But stop! I know that as she lies about this, so too about many other things! Blimps piloted by Ecumen. *Ridiculous.*

So many distortions of reality. Truly, her mind inhabits a twisted maze. And she will not listen to me even when I show her sympathy. *Hurtful.* But that is nothing in the face of what is far worse: her pure agnostic arrogance. I remember a seminar discussion on the subject as we approached the age of viability, Minus-Six from Attainment. Our wise senior Properganger of Y & D, Colander, was fond of a particularly apt DoppelBook maxim from Sura 27:14: 'And they rejected those Signs in iniquity and arrogance, though their souls were convinced thereof: so see what was the end of those who acted corruptly!'

Indeed, let us see what will be the end of this Hag. Poor Hag.

But where has she gone, leaving me after I had reached out to her, if not in love at least in fellow feeling? I am afraid I have not made much of an impression on her. I am torn. I feel for her, the poor exhausted relic of the past. Yet she also fills me with moral horror.

And she has allies. She meets with red-haired devils by the river.

Is that where she has gone? Back to the river, to where the rogues dock? Or perhaps she is in the field setting out a message for the pilot, a message constructed from pieces of broken stone phalluses ... Oh, I know *nothing.* I am *useless.* The hellhound glares and thumps his tail.

But I do so want to hear the Hag's story. I will be *silent.* I will not interrupt, for that only distracts and annoys her. I will be *patient.*

And now it is time for quiet. I will meditate on the Clean Line of the Sceptre. The Beautiful Man steps forward, Rod in one hand, furled orchid in the other, his chin uptilted to the sun, his clear eyes bright with certainty, alight with the purity of Truth unencumbered by doubt.

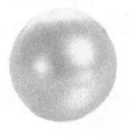 **PEARL**

50.

An image in my mind: I see Motley and myself by the river that evening through veils of memory, veils of rain. We are early. I tell myself to be patient, and after a little while, assisted by the steadiness of the rain and the warm, solid presence of Motley's bulk so close to me, I manage to subdue the eager beating of my heart. I manage to distance myself from the scene until it's as if another Pearl has taken this decision. Another Pearl is waiting for the next phase to begin. The sky and water, puckered as beaten pewter, the bent reeds, the dripping trees, and the two of us: we keep our eyes trained on the river for the approach of the barge.

There's a long, low rumble, then a shattering thunderclap. Thinking back, as I have often enough, I had it in my mind then that it was the thunder which activated the switch that turned on the hornets' buzzing rotor. Stupid fancy. There was no on-switch, but the storm did cover the sound of the blimp's approach.

The infernal machine appears just above the tall bank. Its long, bloated belly reflects the blue-white flash of the next bolt of lightning so that, for a second, it glares like the furious eye of God.

THE HAG

51.

The shadows lengthen and in the air hangs a certain electric promise. Another State blimp overhead, it dips a little then rises, dips and rises again, then chudders away over the forest, just above the trees. Who are you looking for, dear little mannikins up there? You've got Melanie. Will you find Mandrake next? Or Fifi? Or any of the other skulking secreteers holding office in the quiet places, the hidden inlets, in their grey cloaks and hats beneath grey trees by grey water? You can't control everything, you know. Some things are just … out of control. I hope. And would pray, only I don't pray, ever.

I should have my wet-weather gear on against this eternal bitter drizzle. Instead I hunch shoulders, pull my jacket close. My mind turns once more to my mother, Anjali. To Lee. Without them I may well have ended up not unlike our dictatorial little proselytiser back at the croft.

Lee was one of the few women still employed in the university by this time, just before the riots and 'liberation'. She maintained her position by frightening people with her razor tongue but also, I suspect, supplemented with occasional prostitution and blackmail. She'd have to have had something on certain somebodies. Anyway, who cares now?

But of course it wasn't as if women were actively clamouring for teaching jobs by then. Few had time for theoretical discussion, were more interested in keeping breath in their babies than sharing apples of wisdom with a student body, almost entirely male, who could hardly even hear the words a female teacher spoke in lectures, so hyper-aware were they of the fact that behind her desk she would inevitably be sitting on a cunt. Oh how dare she, how could she go about so flagrant and fragrant with that, that *cunt* between her legs, sitting and walking and talking and all the time – with that cunt being jostled by movement or dozing off in lectures while the other mouth speaks! Glory halle-fucken-lujah, the incubator speaks! – as Lee herself might say in one of her lighter moods – Shut up, unholy vessel! Down on your knees! Scrub the floor! Suck my cock!

Anjali and I often used to drop in on Lee at work. I remember the last time we came to pick her (and her cunt) up from uni. We had in mind a cup of tea at the time, not a revolution – but you don't always get what you ask for, do you?

We came to the door of the small classroom in the Women's Studies Department. The undergraduates' seminars were listed:

Prof. Brian Annus – The Uterine Maze: The Ebb and Flow of Female Utility 8.30 – 10.30

Prof. Johannes Meinkopf – Love in the Time of Scarcity: The Sacrificial Womb 10.30 – 12.30

Prof. Ibrahim ibn Ibrahim – Ma Vierge, Ma Putain: Female Virginity as Essential Currency 12.30 – 2.30

Prof. Dick Aimes – The Economy of Difference: The Redundancy of Female Identity Beyond the Domestic Sphere 2.30 – 4.30

Dr. Lee Cobham – Power and Control in Uncertain Times 4.30 – 5.00

We were late, the class was already under way. One of the boys was speaking to the topic at hand: 'We might say that men tend to focus too much attention on maintaining control …' He hesitated, and Lee nodded, encouraging, 'Yes, go on.'

'… when instead it is the relinquishment of the arrogant illusion of control in the material realm that will enable the pious believer to attain immortality in the heavenly—'

Lee glanced briefly up, as though towards heaven, and sighed deeply, which of course silenced the boy. His lips closed in a firm line and he stared down at his desktop. A girl in a black, beaded veil draped loosely over her hair and shoulders, raised her hand.

'Aadila,' acknowledged Lee.

'Mike is right. We are duty-bound to submit to the will of God. It is inevitable that man will falter and fail without God-given grace and …'

'Faith,' added the only other girl in the room, sitting next to the boy who had spoken, Mike. She was shrouded in the white favoured by the Christian converts to Christlam. She met Lee's eye briefly then ducked her head, blushing either with bashfulness or defiance, then flicked a shy, sly glance towards Mike. Youthful and naïve as I was then, I still remember being aware of a kind of contained heat between these two, concentrated in the sliver of space between their two bodies, that later, as an adult, I understood was simple lust.

'Right,' said Lee. 'Thank you Aadila, thank you Maria. Faith. Submission. Fascinating analysis.'

I remember wondering at the time why it was when the world was full of so many of God's faithful servants, he'd gone and sunk all those Pacific islands, wrecked half the Americas, let great floods of oil lay waste to Saudi Arabia – but then the answer came from Maria: 'Today we suffer for our parents' practice of disobedience; it is because they lacked virtue that God has struck.'

Then Aadila: 'We asked for signs! The signs have been given, the judgement passed.' She twitched her veil back a little, enlivened beads applauded her oratory skill.

'Hmm, yes … And speaking of judgement,' said Lee evenly, 'I have your marked assignments here with me. The paper on the topic "Coercion and Consent: What is the Difference?"'

Their eyes lit up. These had a look about them of good students, accustomed to receiving good marks. Earnest faces, attentive listeners. Then Lee said, 'I found nobody in the room deserving of a passing grade.'

Their eyes hardened.

Lee's black brows were straight as can be, and she had a sharp fringe too. She could at times look like a very fierce Greek. Now was one of those classical moments. She frowned out from under her fringe as she leant forward over the lectern. I noticed a daddy-longlegs hanging from the lightbulb over her head, six legs holding tight, two legs waving towards the tight, cranky little black bun perched on top of Lee's head and fixed in place by a pair of chopsticks. She never wore a veil or even a hood. She absolutely refused – though it cost her. Today I could see she had the remains of a black eye, glowering dull yellow, from the latest random act of discipline sustained the previous week at a staff meeting.

'No matter which part of the Middle-East, no matter whether 300 or 3000 years old, no matter what venerable chieftains were at the time in charge of whatever warring desert tribes engaged in raiding, raping and murdering each other in the name of their respective deities, no matter who the ascribed chronicler may or may not have been – ancient so-called "sacred" texts are *not* scholarly sources! The DoppelBook is not a peer-reviewed academic journal! You may *not* cite God or any of his self-appointed scriveners as support for your arguments! You are all postgraduate students of the humanities, so why, by the crescent and crucifix, do you think you can present this totalitarian claptrap!'

Collective gasp, then silence.

And then Aadila spoke up. 'Dr Cobham, with all the respect due to a learned female scholar, I would like to humbly suggest that surely it has been proven that without God's guidance we fragile human beings fail repeatedly to be able to discern good from evil.'

Mike stood now in order to make his point, which he did in the sweetest of tones, as if speaking to a parent suffering from mid-stage dementia. 'The Bible and the Koran, now united in one sacred Book, thank God the Father, both contain moral codes that enable us to tell right from wrong, Dr Cobham. Since the Third Christlamic Accord we, the Peoples of the Books, have agreed upon the rules for living. Surely you will concede that this marriage of faiths within Christlam, a marriage whose courtship was centuries-long and bloody, can only be a force for good in our troubled world? And will continue to be so until Kingdom Come, *inshallaweh*.'

'*Inshallaweh!*' echoed the others.

I saw something change in Lee's expression. The combativeness dropped away and, although she stood quite still, I sensed something like a sort of all-over psychic shrug if there's such a thing – not exactly resignation and certainly not acceptance – but in that moment she just gave up on her job, her students, teaching, the university. She had *had* it. She snorted loudly and picked up her bag and left the appalled dregs of the class staring after her. The daddy-longlegs, mere seconds away from settling into her topknot, scooted back up his lifeline towards the light.

'Stupid little virgins,' she muttered as Anjali and I followed her down the corridor. It smelled of pee in this wing of the building. It had once smelled of polish. I stepped carefully over a mess of wadded blankets with a foot sticking out of the end.

'*Scary* little virgins,' opined my mother.

'What's a virgin?' I asked. I was a rather brilliant child.

'It's a person who hasn't had sex yet,' said Anjali.

'Oh.' I wasn't sure what this had to do with people being silly or scary, but let it go. I got good at letting things go early. Holding things tight was certain to lead to disaster, whether the things you held were kittens or principles. Love or memories.

52.

Anjali, Lee and I made our way up the main avenue of the university. The tall eucalypts that had been planted when this thoroughfare was new were looking a bit sickly for their salting – the flood waters had been at their roots. But although the trees were haggard and skimpy, they were tall enough to block out some of the heat and light.

'Where are we going?'

'Quadrangle, darl. I want to check out this ridiculous fucked-up rally the students have organised. The bleached anuses of UMM.'

We walked past a yellowish building that looked half-melted in the heat; once upon a time, Mum had told me, it had been straight and tall, but had since been damaged during the '22 Austerity Riots; then the Action's floodwaters had got into its foundations, which is why it had slopped into lopsided lozenges.

The black bitumen beneath our feet was alive with glittering flecks of silica like many lights. I imagined in the midst of all this unforgiving light that I was walking like a lost astronaut through the dark sky. We turned and entered under an archway into the Quadrangle; its once-fine lawns were now yellow and spongy but the building itself was still a dream in stone – beautiful. I didn't know it then, but this was to be the last day of the life I thought I had. I've been over and over it since with the eyes of an adult, with the helpless wisdom of hindsight.

In the crowd I recognised Lee's student, Maria. There she was, modestly shrouded in well-lined opaque white but for a band of some-thing see-through from navel to upper thigh and the glint of a sequined mirkin winking through. I hadn't noticed in class as she'd been sitting down, but now all was revealed! I'd never seen anyone wearing a dressless before at the university. So she wasn't UMM, as I'd assumed – she was a Gogodder, or maybe even a God's Whore! I looked around anxiously, hoping the Whores wouldn't turn up en masse. That could get messy in this company. Maria was standing close by the boy Mike from the class, attending with concentration and a tiny smirk to the words of the speaker on a raised podium: Sonny Manson, smartly dressed in jacket and trousers, not quite a suit but hinting at the possibility of one for those who prefer a certain decorum. His dark blond hair, streaked with silver, was neatly combed, though a charmingly recalcitrant lock curling over his eye contrived to cock a snook at the idea of primness. He was treading a fine line, managing to displease only a few, delighting many. And when he spoke, his voice was resonant though light, with an accent that might be that of an American who had spent many years in this country, or an Australander who had spent some years in America. He was flanked by the UMM ladies in crown-to-toes of sober pattern and design: pale-hued former Christians, dark brown or black erstwhile Muslims, all with gloved hands clasped in front, their gazes cast downwards from under their modified veils that were a nod at once to the hijab of the pious Muslim and to the wimple of the Catholic nun, the costume a compromise finally reached after much discussion among the amalgamated faithful of two proud monotheisms. In front of each was a microphone on a stand.

'I am not young,' Sonny said, prompting a surge of warm chuckles from his fans among the listeners, 'though hardly old.' More appreciative murmuring. He continued, speaking in grabs of three to six, maybe eight, words so as not to lose the less mentally agile among his congregation: 'In this lifetime. I have seen much social change. All people believe. Theirs is an age of change. And *movement*. And we are no different. But movement and change. Are not the same. Not synonyms for improvement. Yet our age *is*. Ours is an age of *improvement*. We stand now on the *brink*. Of a revo*lution*. I use the word advisedly. Revolution in the old-fashioned sense. The wheel of change. Is taking another turn. And we find ourselves revisiting *older values*. *Values* which stood our forefathers. In good stead. Values that hold family, children. And woman. Close and safe from harm. Enfolded within the embrace. Of a *protective masculinity*. Once again, after so long. So long a time of uncertainty. When men doubted. Their place in the world. Once again man and woman know their *place*. Their *roles*. Their *duties*. Yes, I am talking duty of *care*. Of those who need us. Who have always needed us. Even though, like headstrong children. You ladies have, for at least three entire generations. Held us at arm's length. While you tried your wings.

'Ladies, your wings are strong. But ours are *stronger*. I and my brothers applaud. Your strength of character. In trying out. Your worthy experiment. You have been out. And about in the world. And tried to make a new way. A way in which women and men. Stand side by side. And work together. To create a world of *equity*. Safe for your children. Safe for yourselves. Now comes the time. When you must ask yourselves – and I know many have – *how successful have we been?*

'You have endured. All that a harsh world. Can throw at you. Abuse and loneliness. And childlessness. Your natural innocence smeared. You tried to "reclaim the streets". The night. Your perceived God-given rights. *But the world is a wild place.* And the fittest *always have.* And *always will.* Throw down their prey. And watch it *squirm.* Before shredding flesh from bone. Pride from soul.'

I whispered, 'Why do the ladies have mikes if they don't get to speak?' but was silenced by a hiss and a savage glare from a student standing nearby.

'Ladies, it is time to return. To the safety. Of your *Father's house.* It is time to admit. And to *embrace.* The power of the feminine soul. Which is strong, *though not bold.* Which is accommodating and *never defiant. Generous* and compassionate. *Never withholding or critical.* Self actualisation for Woman. Is through *acceptance.* Of the strengths and limitations. That are innately female. Woman: helpmeet of man. As above, so below. The Great Chain of Being. Each aspect in the care. And the possession. Of its superior.'

And then, on a screen that slowly unfurled at the back of the stage, an image: Heaven, all blue sky and fluffy cumulus with God the Father at the pinnacle, light beams radiating from his head like a man in a Sunblest Bread advertisement, with massed angels – why all female, I wondered briefly – in fluttering robes opening here and there to reveal the odd breast or thigh, embracing his feet, smiling ecstatically.

'Acknowledge that each of us. Has a place. And a role. And woman's is. To raise your children wisely. To instil *humility* and *fidelity.* In your men. For they have demonstrated time and again. How lost they are. Without your feminine guidance. And above all. To take pride in your role. Of carer. Lover. Mother and wife. Ephesians 5:22: "Wives, be subject to your husband, as to the Lord." Submerge yourselves in this wisdom. And you need no longer feel. The anguish of guilt that comes. When by the very forms. With which God the Father has graced you. You have, often in innocence, *tempted* men. In their weakness. To forget their duties. *Tempted* them to commit lust-induced acts. Of violence against your persons. And God will smile once more. Upon his most precious, perfect planet.'

'Oh give me a diaphanous fold that I might faff about in it!' exploded Lee – though it's unlikely that anyone more than a foot away can have heard her over Manson and the punctuating cheers and hoots. 'Let me cringe in my cowl, for *mea culpa, mea culpa!* World-wide fuckwittage going on, oh yes, that's me, I did it, whoops a-daisy and sorr-eee – oh let me surrender, submit, ooh spank me papa, take me now, Big Boy!'

'*Shhhh*,' hissed Anjali, 'You want to get us crucified?'

'Oops.'

'And remember always,' continued Manson, 'as is recorded in Sura 4.34: "Men are managers. Of the affairs of women." Attend, ladies, and take relief! *Men* are the *managers*. Because God has made the one. Superior to the other. Seek the education. That has been allowed you. And read your Maududi – it's in volume one, page 329.

'Read and attend to these messages. In *the new DoppelBook*. Which *melds the wisdom of ages*. And more. Much more. I enjoin you. To read your DoppelBook. And its authorised commentaries – for they are clear, unambiguous. They brook no discussion. *Inshallaweh!*'

'*Inshallaweh!*' responded the crowd, meaning 'God willing!' in the modern meld of the names of Koranic and Old Testament gods. '*Inshallaweh – aweh – aweh!*'

'No longer need you go out. Into a hostile workplace. No longer need you present. Your bodies as currency. No longer need you leave. Your children in the care of strangers. Once again you may rely. On the love and protection. Of the provider, lover, father and husband.'

'*Inshallaweh! Inshallaweh! Inshallaweh – aweh – aweh – aweh!*'

Oh yes. Those were the days. While back here, beneath a sky that I now notice has darkened to the colour of scalded tin, the cry of an owl joins the refrain, *aweh – aweh – aweh*, and I feel a rush of wind by my cheek and a small but piercing scream as the hunter descends on his prey, and the creature cries out with a human voice.

 **PEARL**

53.

The furious eye of God. What a foolish conceit. An ugly blasphemy, a fantasy, and untrue. I know this, though I know very little these days.

But I remember some things about that evening by the river, where I had thought I was about to embark on an exciting new trajectory, to realise a new dream. I remember some things.

Like the spotlights arcing overhead, crossing each other so that the sky was all layered stripes of light and night juddery in the rain.

Like Motley holding me close to his chest, one huge hand an iron manacle holding both my wrists together, the other clenching a fistful of my hair.

Like an Ecuman descending through the rainlight on a ladder, a spider on its thread. He let go, landed silently on the wooden dock. His masked face nodded once towards Motley, who thrust my hands forward to receive the Ecuman's cuffs. I wrenched myself free and tried to run back up the jetty, but was caught in less than three paces. I somehow wriggled from the Ecuman's grasp and almost got to throw myself into the river, but he grabbed me by the leg. I came down hard on the wet deck, felt the skin of my face breaking open, but I whipped around, my fists held tightly together and tried to club him one. It was a pathetic fight, yet it was the best, the very best, I could do.

And Motley standing by, unmoving. Unmoved? There might have been tears in his eyes, but it was raining so hard by then, so who could tell? And what did it matter?

I understood later that he had no choice – but no, this is wrong. Motley had two choices.

One: he could try to save me. He might have fought the Ecuman and succeeded. He *might* have – but this would mean giving himself away. And Grimalda. And their covert way-stations. And the whole disguised Ranger movement.

So, two: he could pretend that here he was, a dutiful Ranger assisting in the arrest of a traitor. Motley could not destroy that illusion. And so this is what he did.

He handed over his 'captured' runaway to the Ecuman of Perfect State, who hoisted me, dazed and close to senseless, over his shoulder and then grabbed hold of his ladder with his free hand. And before the black hood was pulled down over my head, before the fist was driven into my stomach and another into the side of my head, I saw through the rain and my tangle of bloodied hair Motley's face for the last time, and understood what I had seen the day I met him. The 'sorry' in the sweet smile.

THE HAG

54.

When I return from my walk there she is, out in the garden again. It's becoming quite a thing with her. She's laying stones around the herb beds for goodness' sake. With her one good hand she picks one up from the pile she's made, places it in her careful row and tamps the earth down around it as if it's a nursling, then gets the next one. I notice the nasturtiums are penned up neatly too; well, we can't have them running amok can we, all their frilly petticoats on display in red and gold and pink.

Closer up I see that her face is pale and drawn, her gaze inturned; that is her way, she meditates as she works. Or chants a bit of rote-learned nastiness under her breath. But now she rouses herself to regard me and in a moment her eyes sharpen into curiosity. 'No cress?'

I hang my jacket on the peg. 'Slipped my mind.'

I see that she has laid the table and set out bread and Albert soup, and she has made a salad of nasturtiums dressed with the good oil from last season. There is cheese, and some wizened apples from the cupboard; there are some of those undersized apricots, halved – looks like she's poached them in a bit of honeyed water to bring out the small amount of sweetness they might contain. A dish of butter. I am visited now with a memory from Re-Education – the fate of the deity's enemies, Yael and Sisera, in Judges 4:2: 'And she brought forth butter in a lordly dish. She put her hand on the nail, and her right hand to the workmen's hammer; and with the hammer she smote Sisera, she smote off his head, when she had pierced and stricken through the temples.'

'Thank you, Mica. What a lovely table setting.'

'Sit, my Hag. Eat. Then you can tell me more.'

'Oh, goody.' I reach for a piece of bread.

Level gaze measures my mood from across the table.

Dip spoon in soup. Taste. It's getting better.

'Mica, you tell me about the brilliance of your Sonny Manson, the righteousness of his cause, but I remember a different version.'

'Then tell me what you remember.'

'I remember the riots. I was with my Mum and our friend, Lee. We were at Big Smoke Uni—'

'The day of the Destruction of the Citadel of Insolence!'

'Yes. It went down that day, most of the rest of the town too. Sonny Manson had just finished speaking—'

'Oh, you are *so lucky* to have heard him!'

Right. Lucky. Very. I remember my Anjali nudging Lee, asking, 'Are those tears in his eyes?' 'Definitely,' Lee said. 'He's desperately in love, can't bear the anguish of being unable to fuck himself, eh. Sorry, Jen.' Anjali pointed out that he wasn't the only one. 'Look,' she said, 'See the ladies.' I looked, and I saw they were all falling about trying to get his attention. The crowd was thickening up and, raising my voice to be heard over the deafening applause, I commented on how like one of my favourite pop stars he looked. 'Who's he?' asked the Anjal. 'Musician,' I told her. 'Famous.' My mother didn't keep up with the fads that flicked by, one after the other, like those bright fish, rainbow-coloured, that had lived in the streams once upon a time. Then Lee said, 'That Manson, he's like father, son and holy … *fuck!* God's barnacled bumhole! Check out the "ladies"!'

'The women on stage,' I say to Mica, 'They were a spectacle. First this massive ululating howl, then they all surged forward as Manson's speech was drawing to a close; they were like one colossal body or a great breaker rolling in towards the edge of the stage, the better to stomp the other ones in the audience trying to get up there. And under those veils they had on big black boots, and when the invaders fell back they began to chant. Old Sonny moved well to the back now, and the rhythmic sound of the chant built and built and its volume increased till it seemed we were submerged in a great wave of undifferentiated noise that would have been crushing only it had become our element. We were fish in waves of sound so all-encompassing it was the same as silence.

'And they chanted: CHOM chom chom chom, CHOM chom chom chom …'

'The manifesto of UMM! The graces of Compliance, Humility, Obedience and Modesty!'

'That's the correct goldfish, my sweet. Though there wasn't actually a lot of modesty and that going on just then. There was this drum roll, low at first, then quickly getting louder. Anjali grabbed my hand and held it tight. "Stay near," she said, and her hand was cold and moist. She was trembling all over with fear, her face blank. I'd no idea what was happening. "We really have to leave *now*," she hissed. The drums – they'd started over by the philosophy rooms – had now been joined by bells, silvery tinkling bells that might have been pretty somewhere else, but not here, not here they weren't; then came the deeper brassy bells, then electronic doorbells, bicycle bells, then tambourines and castanets and car alarms. And my heart hurt with beating so hard, as if it was trying to bash its way out of my chest.

'We tried to push ourselves back out the way we'd come. But then they came charging – they burst out like rockets from all four cloisters at once. God's Whores. They inundated the quad and were joined by others of their sect. I saw Maria join the surge. And soon the bells and whistles were overtaken by the throaty surge of an old song, a once-beautiful, sad song drawn from the pain of a life lived in slavery where the singer imagines herself at heaven's door; she knocks and knocks and begs for entry so as to escape the chains of miserable servitude. But appropriated by the Whores and altered to suit their new message – men are exhorted to "come right in" for there's "no need to knock, knock, knock" – it became an invitation to a fuck-fest.'

And Mica's joined in with me for the final chorus, eyes closed, dirging her monotone Perfect-learnt version of the song. Then her eyes fly open and they're brilliant with feeling. Jesu. I stop abruptly. Is there such a colour as zealot-blue?

'By his Cock-and-Muscle,' she murmurs fervently, 'I wish I'd *been* there!'

This isn't actually the effect I'm after. But maybe after she's heard the worst of it, she could have questions. Not that likely, but I continue on the offchance. 'So they kept pouring in, more and more of them, cartwheeling, high-kicking, hand-walking in, some in swirls of completely transparent crown-to-toes, but more had taken it further. *Much* further. I'd never seen this before: they were completely naked but for thongs of leather coiled round and round their middles, and really tight so their breasts and pubes seemed to burst out from either side of the leather bands, and their waist-flesh bulged where the leather cut into them – but they showed no discomfort – none at all, in fact their faces were alight with joy, their eyes blankly glazed over with the glace-fruit gleam of the convert—'

'Dressed in Christlamic ceremonial garb. The first true believers. Their purpose was greater than they themselves.'

'There were people charging about all over the shop and we were stuck in the Quad with no way out. Brothers and sisters in Christlam were still teeming out from the cloisters where they'd been waiting for the right moment, and they kept coming – twenty, fifty, a hundred, a hundred and fifty, a thousand – humming in a deep drone composed of all those voices, a dense, hot, cicada-like numb-buzzery delimited by drums and cymbals of an evangelical band, and they had their banners too, bearing their twin slogans. Some read, *Fucking for Freedom*, and others, *Fuck Freedom*. In both cases the words surmounted the same image: a woman's torso bound around the middle, arms and legs and faces cut off by the frame to draw the eye to the central feature of each image: a woman's shaved pudendum, several sizes bigger than life, photo-shopped to resemble an eye-shaped key hole, and within the cunt's eye could be glimpsed a brilliant dawn in hot pinks, orange and reds over a fabulist landscape like the cover of a novel of high fantasy—'

'Dreams made real by the will and faith of the people in GodFather (BBHCM) and his works.'

'Lee pointed out a gap by the northern wall and we headed for that. Meantime the speakers kept belting out that song about knocking on the doors of heaven—'

'The Anthem of the Rebels!'

'—so loud the distortion and shrieking feedback had me and plenty of others clapping their hands over their ears, but nothing could drown out the roar of the men in the procession: *knock knock!* And the women's voices responded, *You're welcome! You're welcome! Come right in, darlin'! Come in come in come in through heaven's door! It's free!'*

55.

'*IAM!'*

'You are what?'

'No. Immediate Accessibility Movement. And you were *there!'*

'I was.'

'We learned about this when we were Minus-Four from Attainment – IAM! The first brave, freethinking (wo)Men reclaiming the right to choose self-abandonment!' Ah, the dreamy-eyed idealist. 'Now a girl could earn respect once more – at last, *inshallaweh* – for her choice of service and humility, the noblest expression of passivity; (wo)Men could once more bask in the glow of Man's radiance, reflecting the light that has positive masculinity as its source ... But you look upset. Don't be angry with me. Please tell me what happened next!'

Tell your tale, Jen. 'God's Whores dispersed into the crowd, scattering the veiled women like rats before a flood. As they offered their bodies to any man who wanted them, a soldier in QuadA colours of red, white and green, his perspex crescent and crucifix riot shield held before him, yelled into the PA system: "Behold, here is my daughter a maiden, and this man's concubine; them I will bring out now, and humble ye them, and do with them what seemeth good unto you ... But the men would not hearken to him: so the man took his concubine, and brought her forth unto them; and they knew her, and abused her all the night until the morning!"'

'From the DoppelBook, Judges chapter 19 verses 24 to 25!'

'A few took up the offer there and then, which had a sort of chain reaction, creating pockets of orgiastic frenzy, but others were either frozen to the spot in shock, while others retreated from the Quadrangle.

'I remember Lee's face as white as death. "Christlam's cunting katyushas," she goes, and Anjali picks me up bodily and holds me close, trying to hide my eyes in her jumper, but I'm much too big for that and easily twist out of her grip. I saw how the male musterers of the go-go dancing Whores patrolled, directing their women, encouraging the other men to take advantage of what was on offer.'

Take a good deep drink. Bite the end off the cigar the avid rat has passed me. Pick a strand of tobacco off my lip.

'And then, and then?' Mica says, lighting my cigar for me. I drag back a great lungful. Hag fuel. Who ever said you shouldn't inhale cigars? Idiots who want to live forever.

I exhale and regard her through a pall of blue smoke. It waves an ineffectual little paw in front of its face.

'What are the scenes you are watching inside your head? Tell me please – for how I wish I had been there! History in the making.'

'Oh yes, history alright.' Exhale again. She coughs like a kitten. 'I didn't know what was going on then, and it took me a while to work out that I was living through a process, begun before I was born, probably before Anj and Arun too, where in our "civilised" part of the world girls were being transformed, bit by bit, from female people to livestock—'

'Oh sour words and so *wrong*, my Hag! Not livestock but (wo)Men freely enacting the role that echoes the cosmic truth represented by the sun and the moon – source and reflector – the complementarity of light and darkness. The natural Lore that had been all but obliterated for nearly a century by Fenimistry, the beginning of a brave new—'

'Shut up.'

The shock on its little white mug. *So* white. The wan face of a subterranean creature, a cave-dweller, troglodyte. Lived all its life deep underground, buried beneath the layered muck of ages of lies. I don't care. My sympathies are now reserved for the dead. 'You are stuffed full of lies, Mica.'

'No. It is *you* who are filled with lies!'

And now, tears. Anger and frustration. It gathers itself up and launches itself into my room in a swirl of hessian sacking. Off you fuck then, darling.

I shall stay out here and count my cataclysms, like a string of too-late-to-worry beads, click click through my fingers – cyclone meeting tornado meeting tsunami meeting typhoon – all crashing in on each other in a colossal debacle mashing religion, war, politics, and – as you so rightly said, my horrid trog – *sex*. It's sex that makes the world. Pity the sex we made was so very, very nasty.

 MICA

56.

She's pacing around out there, babbling to herself, doesn't know she's talking, she does it all the time. She's mad, mad, and her mind is so dark and dirty, no light, no beauty. Her talk is of death, of sex. Sex and dirt and death.

This is hard work, such hard work. But I've made my choices and now I must continue on the path laid out before me. But I am so lonely. I miss Pearl. I miss loving Pearl.

What she and I had wasn't nasty or dirty. But then, it wasn't sex. Not really. Girlies don't have sex, it is not possible, for 'two negatives do not make a positive', as we learned in Science of Creation classes from

Minus-Five. Though of course we are encouraged to play with each other's cockslots, so we can get an idea when we're young of what a Man requires and what our purpose is. We have the books and the Meditations and Contemplations and we have each other too, to practise with, to practise for real sex, for world-making. But sometimes when I think of Pearl and me together in Pearl's bed, and how we would touch and kiss, I feel moved in a way that I don't know how to describe. I don't know what to call it.

But we'd stopped. That's why I think she found a man. She never knew I suspected. But I did. It made me feel cold to think on it, so whenever the soft feelings would come over me, I would drive them back down into the hidden part of me where all memories are stored. I would press them down, down, and turn my mind instead to one of the Meditations, and focus all my intent on emptying my mind of everything but the sacred words. And it is good that I am skilled in such self-discipline. It is why I am able to walk away when the Hag's lies become too outrageous, her emotions too frenetic, why I am able to leave her gaping and secrete myself in this little nook. The look on her old face when I stood up from the table! Frustration, outrage, disgust!

But I have been gifted with the tools and techniques of resistance. Thus my faith is only strengthened. This is how I survive here; this is how I withstand the contrivances of her twisted logic. I am eternally in the debt of the Properganders' lessons in yearning and duty, in art and pain.

I remember, I recite, and I am protected.

Had I dwelt, back then in Perfect, on Pearl, on the loss of Pearl's love, on the images of Pearl and me together in her bed – with the moonlight creeping in and showing the sweet line of her jaw, her small nipple, her eyes wide and dark and fixed on my face with such intensity as I carefully stroked her where she would become so moist, like a spring – had I dwelt on Pearl, I too may have been led astray. Never so far as Pearl was, of course, but far enough to make it difficult for me to find my way back. For our feelings were a power. A power.

In this little sleeping place, alone now, I hear the Hag bumbling drunkenly around, talking to the hound, coughing her wet, hacking cough. Leave her to it, mad old crone. Irredeemable devil. Outside the piglets are eek-aak-ing in their high-pitched little voices like human babies. I can hear the low thrum of the generator that she uses to power her mini-fridge in the scullery, the reading lamp here by the bed and the other one on the table where soon she will sit to read one of her heretical texts. When she stops thumping and clattering. Perhaps she is regretting the vile words she spoke earlier.

I do so want to hear about the events that reformed history from one who was there – but she cannot tell a story straight! She has to depart into her own outmoded, long-redundant speculations. The old outrages, the old lies that brought the world to its knees, that made revolution essential, that caused such awful waste of life. *Stupid old witch!*

I draw myself into myself to begin a recitation of all 28 Tenets of the Ways of (wo)Man.

I am calm when I finish, though far from happy with myself. I look out of the small square window. It is now quite dark. The darkness is like a solid body pressing against the glass. No moon yet. I click on the lamp and read over what I have written and find that I have been prideful – the old sin, my worst weakness. I have failed in humility. I think back also to the Hag's tale-telling: I should *not* interrupt!

I promised I would not and yet I did. I am overly eager and have failed to control my impulses. I have behaved in the way of the 'clamorous woman'. My words anger her for she hates to hear the truth, because if she accepted it she would also have to accept that her life has been a waste. Yet I have allowed myself to behave with all the wisdom of a dudbub. I have fallen victim to the illusion of freedom that so confounds me here, where there is no discipline, no punctuating bells to divide the day into sensible eating, sleeping, working and study times. Yet I know I am not free. She goes and wanders across the land and I must stay behind in the custody of the monstrous dog.

I will try again to be mild, to be one who listens and does not speak. I should continue to meditate now, but I cannot settle back into that state. I will read awhile. I inspect the pile of ancient 'literature' she has given me. I flick through the book by the African lady, but the pictures are few and lack colour. I note that picture book with the warrior girlie in porno pants that had so shocked me when I found a page of it a million years ago by Pearl's bed. But that one was old and yellowed, its pictures and writing hard to read, so aged was it – yet this is newly printed, its colours fresh. I read a little, and have to grant that she is a brave warrior, that Tank Girl, and I wonder once more when she lived, and why she is dressed like a pornographer's confection. And her speech! If a dudbub could speak, this would be the language it would use.

Yet I read, I read into the night, and when the first light comes I am still reading. I open another illustrated text, though I know it can have no relevance, that it is yet another old outdated story. It's another one about a warrior girlie who is sacrificing herself for her people. It is titled, *The Hunger Games Retold*. I open at chapter one: 'Everdeen to Neverdeen: How Kitkat Refused to Collude'. I read for a while but it becomes an adventure story where she fights against the rightful government. I am distressed by this Kitkat's complete absence of a sense of duty, of service, except to the people she loves – as if her love has value in and of itself! But it is compulsive reading. I find I am wanting her to succeed in her disobedience. I find I am superimposing Pearl's face onto that of this Kitkat person.

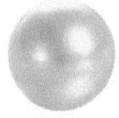 **PEARL**

57.

There was no light for a long time. Days or weeks I'd say. You wouldn't call it a month, I think. There was food the first day or two or three – I don't know exactly because it was always dark. They told me of Asa's capture, the how and who and where of it, and they told me what followed for him. I wanted to die when I learned this, and would have taken my own life, but I could not. I was hobbled and they'd stuffed my arms into hard tubes and drawn thick mittens of leather onto my hands so that I could not identify my own body parts, much less use them. I might have tried to bite my tongue and so seek the way to oblivion on a river of my own blood, but my teeth had been smashed. Also, my hearing was muffled by big pads that had been strapped to my head. They emitted a noise like rain, driving rain, rain driving into my brain so I couldn't think. Sometimes meals came in quick succession, brought in by a masked person who attempted to feed the mush to me, but I always spat it out. At other times there were gaps so long I thought I might die of hunger, a most welcome possiblity. So when the food came I still would not eat it until two (wo)Men came in, removed the pads and hit me in the side of the head so that my ears bled. Then one day, or possibly one night, someone thrust a needle in my arm and I felt something cold pulse into my vein. After this my head was filled of pictures that made no sense, sometimes horrible and bloody, sometimes mad and brilliant landscapes, or faces glowering or wheedling or crying.

Then there was the time – how long? – that I was strapped to a plank cot and set to sizzle by currents of electricity that made my body arc and writhe. Then more liquids dripping into me. Food to sustain the body and drugs that brought on more images or blanked out parts of my thinking. I don't know which parts. After a while, you couldn't call it a long while, I started voluntarily eating the pap they gave me. As a reward they took the pads from my ears.

It's mostly quiet now. But sometimes there's sound. Drumming, and words. You wouldn't call it music. The words are repetitious, but I can't bring them to mind at the moment.

Then one day, or perhaps one night, the lights come on. I'd got a lot of sleep before the lights. I may have slept for a week at a time. In that time of many images. The oblivion was good. It gave my ribs time to heal, and my arm, my jaw. My ear hasn't quite healed. There's a sound like bells in my head most of the time. I don't sleep at all now. There's those bells. And the lights go on and off at odd times. Sometimes it stays dark for an hour or more. The Men come when it's dark. Though never completely dark. Dim, a deep deep dimness is what you'd call it. There's always a light on outside the grille. It makes the Men's shadows – what? – loom? Yes, loom. That's the word. Occasionally they arrive singly, but usually in groups. For moral support, that would be. Sometimes one stands to one side and watches. Once, two friends came in together and one gave the other instructions for a while before joining in. He said, 'Use the pulley to hoist her from the waist. No, leave her feet anchored. Just so, but spread her knees a bit more will you? I can't see. Get her to open her mouth – what? Well *make* her. Then turn her over.'

None of the Men direct any words to me, not ever. At first I didn't get it. Later, I did. I know I did, I remember when it dawned on me. Why no words for me. But just at the moment I can't recall specifically why, or what I understood, specifically.

I've just been repeating that word. Specific, specific, specific. Makes no sense if you say it over and over, the letters and the meaning get jumbled after a while. Specific-specific-pacific-pacific. Spacific. Pascefic, pascefic … Then I remember I was trying to think, to recall, something pascefic. Trying to recall something when I started playing with the word. It had to do with a thought about knowing what I'm for. And why no words for me, from the Men. Something like that. But I know what I'm for now. It's been demonstrated often enough. So what was it I was thinking?

It doesn't matter really. Any sort of speculation is redundant here. I do the repeating thing with that word too – redundant – because of how repetition eventually takes the meaning out of things. It's calming to do this. I repeat the words I choose to repeat in time with the drumming that's always going on. The not-music. The beat, like marching. ReDUNdant reDUNDant reDUND— No more dreams. I'm in the real now. Though the dreaming-waking did persist for a very long time indeed. Particularly strong was an image of a big, round, white face, smiling, with yellow teeth and eyes like stars. I know I know this person, or knew them, and I might have loved them, or trusted them, or something. But I can't put a name to the face. This will be frustrating if I pursue it, so I don't. No more dreaming. No love. No hope. Such illusions. They seem sweet but are deadly.

These new understandings – about my purpose, about the vanity of dreams – haven't happened overnight – whatever that means in this light on/off, on/off place. And I fought the Men at first. Stupid. I didn't keep it up all that long, the beatings I got meant it just wasn't worth it. Though they were no worse than the thrashings I got from the (wo)Men. All the healing done in the dark has to happen again. But it isn't getting done very well. I have a pain in my side that won't go. My vision's blurry and my head hurts most of the time. And the bells. Point is, I'm not violent anymore. And my anger is all condensed and compacted into a hard knot now. And contained. In my belly. It's cold and tight where it used to be mobile, flowing, hot as lava. I remember that and how it made me move through the world thoughtlessly, violently, like a storm instead of a girlie. And now it has nowhere to go. I have it stored now. It's mine. Like the hate. I've got hate. I am it and it is me and mine. Nobody need notice it. No trouble.

MICA

58.

I remain closeted in the nook. She is still clumping and clattering about, attending to her chores, though why bother trying to maintain hygiene in this grubby humpy I don't know. I peek out. Now she's delicately lining the toadstooled crannies with goat dung, now sweeping the floor, now removing the linens to the tub outside near the vegetables, now boiling water on the stove. It is to be wash day, then. I will help her.

She does not smile that toothy smile when I come outside into the hard white light, as she has done before. She is still angry. I am too, and with justification. But I shall rise above this. I shall exercise The Expression of the Paradoxical Relation of Dignity and Humility.

I go to her but she does not greet me when I wish her good morning. She does not thank me as I help her wring out the tablecloth by holding fast with my good arm while she twists the fabric into a long, hard coil to force out the water. Nor when I hold the peg basket for her. I leave her to it and wander over to the herb bed. I continue arranging along the edge the stones I have so painstakingly collected. To save from the incursion of paspalum and dandelion, the parsley, lemon thyme and mint. There is satisfaction in creating even this little gesture towards order. I glance over at her once or twice, at her skinny old frame in its man's shirt and sad trousers. She pays no attention to me at all and I feel sorrow, for I might have led her a little way towards the light, if only she were capable of opening her heart, just a fraction, to the consolations of faith.

She returns the laundry basket to the place where she piles all outdoor things beneath the eaves, by the door, a higgledy-piggledy pyramid of tools and utensils, and heads off away from the house. I follow her and her hulking familiar as they make their way towards the planting of olive trees at the nearer edge of the cemetery. And I fully expect her to tell me to return to the house, or him to bare his teeth at me. Yet she does not. He does not.

The sun peers through a sheath of low cloud, lighting the edges of grasses and gravestones. It sheds a thin light, watery but valiant. The heavy-bellied clouds withhold their burden of rain. I steady the ladder as she plucks the fruit. The hound attends us. As she descends the ladder, she looks at me for the first time that day. 'Thank you,' she says, at last. 'You are feeling stronger now, I see.'

'Yes, thank you.'

'This is the first time you have walked so far.'

'But I was not allowed before.'

'Not allowed?'

I look meaningfully at the beast.

'Blacks? Why? He wouldn't stop you.'

'But you set him to guard me!'

She looks honestly puzzled. 'I left him with you to keep you company.'

Could this be so? *No.* She is surely trying to confound my grasp on reality, as ever. I trail back towards the house after them. I say, 'I read about the girl in the forest. Kitkat.'

'Oh, yes?'

'It was not her fault she was an unbeliever, because that was how she was raised.'

'A fair observation.'

'In her world there was no moral guide. Only an animal drive to survive.'

'Ah.'

'She was brave.'

'Yup.'

'There is virtue in bravery.' We walk together back across the cemetery.

At the house, I make tea and pour her a cup, adding a slug of grog to mine as well as hers. I find it is warming and soothes the anxiety in my breast. I push her cigars towards her across the table. She gets the hint.

'I see,' she says, drawing a cigar from the tin. I light it for her. Red tip waxes, wanes, waxes. I blow out the match.

'We were up to the sacking of the Citadel of Insolence.'

'Ah, yes.'

'Jennypetal, I promise I will not interrupt you. No matter what outrageous claims you make.'

She stares at me evenly. I don't know what the stare means. She swigs her tea.

'Please.' It is a funny expression she has on her face. Or no, a mixture of expressions. She looks mistrustful, then almost affectionate. She looks sad and also amused, then there is something like hope. What could *she* have to hope for?

I am relieved when she continues to spin her yarn, resuming at the point where she, her mother, and her foul-mouthed friend were escaping from the riot at the sacking of the Citadel of Insolence.

 ## THE HAG

59.

'We were afraid for our lives. But we made the gap by the northern wall and through the crushing crowds, over the footbridge and out onto Matta Road. When the bus came we sat towards the back, the safest place these days for women unveiled, whether grey, white or black. My mother was crying. I cuddled up to her. "Anjali?" I said, "Mum, please, don't." She wiped her eyes and looked out the window rather than meeting my eyes. She spoke, to the glass not to me, "Now you've seen your options. You can be a woman bagged and bridled for the use of one man only, or you can be a whore." Then Lee pointed out, "Actually, no, Anj. Prostitutes are paid. Godsbods give it away."

'No stretch for me to work out what was preferable. A person whose value is all between their legs might as well get at least part-ownership of her only asset.

'We got out at the minimart. Lee headed off home. For once there wasn't much of a queue, no more than a couple of dozen ahead of us, and we needed flour, tea, some other things. All was cool and crisp under the clinical fluoros, bright and orderly. Protein sticks and packets of flour in rows, citrus allfruit in their hermetically-sealed vacuum packs, green jars of oil in their serried regiments, ranked canisters of oxygen. My heart slowed down at last. At the checkout, Anjali proffered her palmplant. "Sorry, love," said the girl behind the register. "Invalid." On her tunic was her name. Roxie. Mum stared, speechless. "Since yesterday," said Roxie. "It was all over the radio, the paper. You name it. Where you been?"

'Weeding, Anjali does not say. Mopping the offices of the town hall. Watching my friend being humiliated by teenagers in cowls.

'"It's a girlie number, lady," said Roxie kindly. Clearly it was not her first time to explain this today. "Machine only accepts numbers starting with prefix 6253: M-A-L-E. See where all that suffer-jism got us? Feminimistry, that's what." Clearly, Roxie was a historian. "Too much sexempowery for girls. Somebody's got to do something about it, eh?' she observed. "Can't have the ladies running about taking the jobs away from the boys and whatnot."

'"You work, Roxie," mentioned my Mum.

'"Family franchise," replied The Rox. "I wouldn't ask for money." Her eyes slid away from us, discouraging any further comment. She spoke to the cash register: "Anyway, point is, your palmplant's dead in the water."

'We left. I looked up at Mum. Her skin looked too tight over her bones.

'I understood a bit of what was going on, but as I've said, I didn't really grasp the full horror – yes, Mica, horror – and if you want me to continue you'll have to control your face. So. I didn't really grasp the full *horror* of it all and what it meant until it was over. But then, nobody did. It was obvious to me that we were up shit creek – you want to hear this? Yes? Then stop curling your lip and let me tell it my way. So. We were *up shit creek*. But I did think we still had a paddle. Or if I didn't, Mum and Dad did. But that day marked a shift for me. I realised that although my dad might have a paddle, Anjali's had been confiscated.

'We were late home that afternoon. Anjali put the key into the lock just as Dad opened the door, startling us. We both jumped. "Sorry," said Arun, looking anxious and diffident – that was something he'd been doing a lot of lately, apologising. For being a man. He was my dear darling dad but for a split second he was simply the enemy. Anjali must have felt the same, because she said, "Hello, husband. Esteemed property manager." He answered, "Sorry?" She: "*To husband*, husband dear, is to cultivate one's resources. I am a resource. Useful in my way, if handled correctly." She put her bag down on the table, said, "My palmplant doesn't work, by the way. Is there any tea?"

'"I don't know," and he put his arm around her stiff shoulder and added, "I heard. About the palmplants, I mean." He squeezed her shoulder, but she stayed rigid.

'"And the riot? At the university?" Her eyes were that vivid blue-black they used to get when she was working particularly hard to control her feelings, to stop them spilling out, trying to convert misery or rage into something civilised. "The idiot girls, bondage babes, fucking for freedom?"

'"Anjali, we have to find ways to stay calm and *think*. There are actions we can take, and we *do*. We have counter-movements. The Men4Women meeting tonight, for example. It's making changes, it's popular!" I thought after what I'd just witnessed, this sounded a bit thin.

'Then I noticed Brian, the uni student from upstairs hovering uncomfortably in the doorway. He often came over to stay with me – "babysquashing" he called it – when my parents went out. I smiled at him. He smiled uncertainly, looking very awkward; likely he was also feeling embarrassed about the viperous dick curled in his pants.

'My Anjalima knuckled her angry tears away. "Well at least it's not always us," she agreed. "Gays and Jews and secular Christians and Muslims are getting it in the neck too! But what I want to know," she said, as she squinted into the spotty wall-mirror, adjusted her scarf and retied it loosely under her chin, "is why can't they have a go at philatelists and pigeon fanciers for a change?" She grinned over her shoulder at him. Sunrise over a battleground.

'Dad walked over and hugged her around the waist. She leant back into him. "Good for you, my love! Now, we'll be late if we don't make a move."

'"I want to come with you," I said.

'Mum, knowing what I'd been through that afternoon, just stared at me dumbfounded, so it was Arun who spoke. "You've had enough action for one day, my love," he said firmly. "Stay here with Bri." Only now did Anjalima notice Brian. She greeted him apologetically, gave him an affectionate peck on the cheek, then turned to me. "We'll see you in an hour or so, Jenny-hen." My heart went clunk in my shoes, those sweet red-and-white checked ballet slippers, fair incitement to rape.

'As they walked out, hands clasped, I looked at their dear silhouettes against the streetlight that just sputtered on, and had a chilly premonitory feeling, like a cold slug creeping into my heart.'

60.

'"Well," said Brian, as he closed the door behind the folks. "Big day, eh?"

'"Yeah. Quite large." By his enquiring look and the way he settled himself back down in the chair he'd vacated when we came in, he looked like he might want to find out more, have a chat, which I categorically did *not* want. So I added, "And now, believe it or not, homework." I headed towards my sleeping space by the cook-nook and he mumbled something sympathetic after me, like, "Poor you." As I closed the sliding door behind me I saw he'd picked up the book he'd been reading, a historical novel about the olden days when life was free and easy. It had a picture on the cover of a teenager in a pretty frock. I was so jealous of her freedom, that lucky Tess of the D'Urbervilles.

'I took the Men4Women flier from the fridge en route. For such a famously reliable and honest child I was getting awfully good at dissimulation. But the way I saw it, I had to. So … once again, I carefully unlatched the window over the light-well and crept down the fire-escape, down and out into the moist and warm twilight redolent with compost, jasmine and hot bitumen.

'The park where the meeting was being held was not far, only about a half hour's walk away. I heard it before I saw it. Thrumming of generators and voices, bursts of music from busking trumpeters and guitarists, raised voices of vendors selling fried potato skins, mango and papaya slices, toasted locusts, boiled and salted soybean pods, and those tasty little pink sausages made of meal and meat-juices that we called "little boys".

'People milling about on the pavement and on the road and across the road from the park. No way everyone could fit. I'm not inclined to be a nervous sort of hag now and wasn't back then as a latent one, but the apprehension I'd felt at home was only getting worse, even though there were no particularly scary-looking goings-on just then. But it seemed to me the air was filled with millions of invisible electric wires as fine as spiderwebs, all criss-crossing each other and giving off little tiny shocks at each of the trillions of crossover points. If you could draw a map of wishes and fears, and then enter it as you do a dream, this is how the dream would feel. Only the other day my daddy had said to me, "The most real things are the invisible ones." We'd been working together fixing a tricky pump that was always playing up. I had the job of cutting off bits of gaffer tape and also of holding the pliers. "*And*," he'd added, "the most dangerous." He tightened a screw then wrapped a long piece of tape around the join to prevent leaks. I had asked him why invisible things were so dangerous. He said, "Because you can't control what you cannot see."

'There was a makeshift podium in front of the little rotunda in the middle of the park, a kind of folly that used to be a coffee shop when there was coffee and when people had had the time and money to do such lovely things as sit in cafes and talk. There were women, veiled or hooded, most of them in pairs or threes, and also some groups that were larger than considered decent by this time. There were also couples of men and women together, and bands of boys in Men4Women t-shirts. There were lights, big strobes irradiating the grass to hyper-green; it looked as if things made out of poisonous waste were growing under it, growing on fast forward and ready to irrupt like triffids at any time. I pulled my grey hood further down over my face and stuffed my hands in my pockets. But I knew that under my long skirt I had on those friendly checked slippers, so no matter how invisible I had to make myself, I still knew who I was.

'From time to time wide arc lights were thrown up against the electric blue of the sky, bleaching it to white. The crowd was getting louder and even bigger, and people were drinking on the pavement out of flasks. Some religious gang had already observed this and taken it upon themselves to erect Strictural banners up all around saying, *A drinker of alcoholic drink is not a believer!* But nobody told them to stop, not yet anyway. And so they did not, even in the face of the posters claiming, *Verily, God the Father of the Resolved Twins Jesumuh and of Men hath cursed the unbeliever!*

'A helicopter made passes overhead at regular intervals. This was before the Christlamic Ministry, in its wisdom, had decreed that aircraft represented overweening human pride and that GodFather would … how did it go, Mica?'

'He would "put an end to the arrogance of the haughty, and humble the conceits of men with a holy tempest, fires, and plagues …"'

'Choice. There were knots of local Ecumen on horseback too. Looking anxious. Some fingered their automatic weapons, some contented themselves with glaring at anyone who had the bad form to meet their eyes. It'd been a long time since police had forgotten they were public servants, that they were meant to look after us, not intimidate us, frighten us into submission.

'Half excited, half afraid, butterflies in my tummy, I got this feeling as I walked through the crowd that I was breaking little gaps in the network of invisible threads, and I imagined them curling away and shrivelling up and dying. I kept moving to keep my confidence up. Then, out of nowhere, a hand clamped itself to my shoulder and I jumped out of my skin.

'"Whoops, matie, didn't mean to scare you to death!" It was Lee. "Where are the folks?" I told her they were around somewhere, I was sure. But she looked at me with her weather eye. "You're supposed to be at home, aren't you?"

'"I, um …"

'"You, um *what?*"

'"…cannot tell a lie."

'"Cheeky wretch." She gave me a quick hug. Have I told you how much I loved our friend Lee? Yes? Here I go again then. My beloved, beetle-browed, black-bunned, blue-eyed Lee.

'"This afternoon wasn't enough for you?" she said. "Well, I've got to give a talk here, I'm so busy and important," and she chuckled in her deep scratchy way. God I miss her! "So you'll just have to hang about a bit while I spruik up the cause in case anyone gives a flying fuck. Then I'll get you a bag of spud-skins and frogmarch you back to your home and hearty hearth."

'"Lee," I say.

'"Pet," says she.

'"What are all those signs for?" I pointed around at the banners – not the ecumenical ones but others with legends on that I didn't recognise.

'"So a quick tour's in order I do believe. That lot there, see? With the big blue flags with all those big boofy blokes around it? They're the Larssonists, the turn-out from Sweden. About a zillion years ago those boys were the worst sort of rapists and pillagers. But these days they're about the most civilised you can get; seen the light over time, they have. Takes time, does light … to travel, I mean. Then there are eclipses, like now. We're in the middle of the biggest fucken eclipse ever." She realised she'd lost me, and added. "Sorry, blossom, I do rave. The name, Larssonists, comes from this writer from yonks back, a bit before yer old mate here was born. He did these books about men's bad treatment of women, and these lovely big old blokes reckon he'd got something right way back then. Only it wasn't until more recently they realised how spot-on he was. So they do him the honour of naming themselves after him. Then, see over there, South and East Asian Men4Women—"

'But she was interrupted by a voice nearby: "Thank any old god you fancy for large numbers of atheist workaholics!"

'"Hi, Mick!" said Lee, as a man detached himself from the crowd and came over to join us. He was tall and gangly, with a broken nose; he looked rough and sort of handsome and slightly scary and a bit comical at the same time.

'"Jenny, this is Micky. Mick, Jen," and after giving him a quick hug, Lee continued, "But there aren't that many Chinese around any more are there? Most have bailed and gone back home to the land of the free."

'"They had the foresight to see we were fucked," said Micky, deftly rolling himself a cigarette with one hand. "About five years ago, after the first Accord," he added for my benefit. I nodded to show him how bright I was. "They knew they'd truly lost us to the god-botherers from RUSA. Saw Western business was on its last legs. Bye bye China."

'"They were never going to be so stupid as to halve their workforce for the sake of anybody's goddy-boy, Christian or Islamic or Christlamic or fucken Tittyfuck. Sorry, Jen. Give us a drag on that would you, Micky-poo?"

'"Canaries in a coal mine," said Micky, passing her his smoke. "They saw it coming alright. And I suspect they never liked us all that much anyway, so why not let the religious nuts wreck what's left of the West? Anyhow, they've had all that lovely oil since the big quake. But at least we still have our Thai chums and Viets and the Indonarchipelagans since they dumped the radicals into the Arafura." He paused here, as a shadow passed over his ugly-handsome face. "Bit rough, that was," he added. "Gotta admit."

'"Yeah well," muttered Lee, and by the dark look on her face, I saw this probably wasn't the time to ask more about the fate of the Indonarchipelagan radicals. She handed Mickey's cigarette back to him. It looked a bit damp and unappealing now. "And see, Jen, by the podium, you've got your USCA – United States of the Central Americas. They'd never have been able to draw numbers like that even a decade ago. If RUSA hadn't caved in to the holy rollers and come over all Christlamic, the Latins would never have got up the gumption. Not that it isn't a horrible loss for us, the Yanks, but something cha-cha'd out from under the wreckage alright! We might have the GEET, but god bless maracas!"

'And now some large voice was booming out the agenda for that evening: "*One.* Draft response to the freezing of women's banking privileges, by Su Congqi. *Two.* Lars Svensson talking on the development of local non-denominational business enterprises in Scandinavia. *Three.* A progress report on the re-introduction of Critical Ethics into the university curriculum by Luisa and Pablo Estevez. But first I'd like to hand over to Dr Lee Cobham to do the introductions."

'Lee sort of chucked me at Micky, saying, "Mind the sprog with your life, darl. Don't let her go till I get back to you or I'll pop your knackers out of their dear little furry pods and have them on toast with relish." Then she plunged into the crowd and headed for the scaffold. She stood before the bank of microphones. I waved at her though I knew she wouldn't be able to see me with all those lights directed on her. Lee was at home giving speeches. Stage and lectern, her element. I couldn't hear much of her introductory spiel because there was quite a bit of feedback. But that's the image I carried away of her, that I still carry: strength and certainty. Though I never saw her again after that night.

'The audio guys had got the sound system under control by the time Su Congqi began to speak. But there were two reasons why I couldn't follow her talk either. The first was because Congqi used many words beyond my vocab, and no matter how busily my fingers tapped away at my dictionary there was no way I could keep up, she spoke so fast. But the other reason, which quickly made the first redundant, was this great flash of brilliance that was suddenly streaming in overhead like a comet, opening the sky and all the heavens rained down, igniting the air, the buildings, the people below, who flared up like torches. Some ran, their hair on fire like haloes of blazing angels, screaming, screaming of a thousand voices, two thousand, three, all in one voice and in a moment everyone's stampeding in all directions. Micky and I ran for the road but got ourselves caught in a bloody clash between a bunch of Larssonists and a QuadA battalion. QuadA stood out against the rest not only because of their colours but because of the artillery they'd barged in with and it was backed up with tanks like blunt, blind animals crushing everything in their way. Micky's hand was torn out of mine. There was gunfire; there were rockets; there were men with batons beating their way through the crowd, some of them Ecumen, some not; there were green burning choking fumes. I scrambled under a rack of upended benches that had been set up around the podium. There was a roaring and raillery of explosives and gun- and rocketfire and everywhere a foul black ash and redness of fire and blood and foul green gas like acid soup, but you have to your eyes open, and you have to breathe, don't you? Keep a lookout though it seems your eyeballs are being boiled in their sockets ... and breathe, breathe somehow though your acid-poached lungs ...'

61.

'It was no secret that the Men4Women rallies had been scheduled for the same time and place all over the country, in all the major capitals. It wouldn't have taken a strategic genius to work out that QuadA only had to mobilise themselves so that with the support of the Ecumen of each state, they had units ready in all those locations. Nationwide riots at every hub. It was a massive multiple coup, a great death-blow to one of the few cores of organised resistance against GEET. So, multiple counter-strikes against our sorry excuse for concerted insurgency and the Men4Women movement was toast.

'Then came the Blackout that knocked out every electricity grid in the country. And when power was restored and the first ISP attempted to restore Internet service, it was quashed by the government kill-switch. They framed it like this: a means of protecting us from the influence of dangerous terrorist organisations, several of which had, it seemed, claimed responsibility for the Blackout. A state of emergency was declared: "temporary" governmental control of the Internet and of all electronic records was deemed essential to the national interest. Individuals could be monitored for the "protection" of the nation, but we ourselves could not gain independent access to any site. *Anywhere.* This made large chunks of the population rather cross, as it was only a generation back that we had harboured delusionary faith in notions of civil liberty which, once upon a time and not so very long ago, included freedom of speech, and so there were reactions, and when reason failed, violence became the method, and so further controls were required, and so it went, and so it went on, and on ...'

'*SOC!*'

'No, Mica, Blackout Day became known as *FOC* – the Fall of Civilisation day.'

'No. It was SOC: the *Start* of Civilisation, for the *rebirth* of—'

'Effectively, tiger, all the data that had been stored electronically was lost to all but those few men in control. After all, for the last few generations physical documents had been steadily replaced by electronic ones in the misguided belief that this form of storage was more reliable. (And why *did* we think this? All it took was *one* war, *one* power failure to cap off all the propaganda we'd been subject to for a generation!) Now all personal files, all business records, all literature and music for god's sake, all access to email and all social media – contact with anyone not physically present – *all gone*. Irretrievable. All records were kept in the central database controlled by the government, which by this time was itself completely in thrall to the major religious affiliations. It had taken your hard-core holy book-bashers centuries to realise the power they could have when they worked in unison – Christendom and Islam together – and they were now making up for lost time. They and they alone had access to all historical information and all current communications. They had all knowledge.

'But they weren't yet all-powerful. Various groups of insurgents kept mounting the odd attack on centres of Christlamic control, or incursions against States as they built their fortresses, set up their schools and Re-Education centres. We made a mess of Impeccable when they first started construction; we all but destroyed Perfect and they had to re-build not once, not twice, but three times – yes, that was good. And there was the massacre that took place just beyond the bean fields, where they buried the dead and marked the places with lumps of granite rough-hewn into phallic tombstones that I *spit* on whenever I pass by. But the reprisals against our loosely-knit armed forces were vicious, and there weren't that many of us, and after a time, we lost the wars. The War. We lost, your lot won.'

I don't say any more. She looks at me expectantly for a while, and yes, I've left questions unanswered, but I've had it. All talked out. I reach down to Blackie and he looks up at me with big-eyed doggy love. I scratch his ears for him. He licks my hand.

The tiger gives up on me and goes outside to plan her next attack on the poor garden instead.

I probably would have either died in one of their reprisals or been captured and 're-educated' a lot sooner than I was – but I was found, and you could say saved – by the only real enemies of the States, had the States only known it then. And of whom they're still ignorant. At least, I hope they are. This is my only real source of hope for this benighted country and for the world, for all I know; which I can't, since we've been cut off for so very, very long. I was saved on the day of the riot that took Lee, that took my Anjalima, that took my poor, deluded dad.

There's me, a smallish girl fainting in the shadow of a broken set of stairs, and the last thing I see before lights-out is this face looming close to mine. Round as the moon and just as white, with black stars for eyes and a crazy red-painted leer framing big square yellow teeth.

 MICA

62.

If I ever thought there was a little hope, the odd tiny sign here and there, I know now that I was misled. For her, truth is falsehood and falsehood truth. She insults the first and noblest statesmen of GEET, including the glorious masterprator Manson. She deplores the breaking of the ethereal network that for decades poisoned the minds of (wo)Men and children with its pornographic imagery and false claims, the universal web of lies that so confounded those of weak mind for so long. She mourns the coming of the new world order based on the infallible wisdom of the ancients and insults our new nation of interdependent Civilised States created by the freedom fighters after Liberation. She refuses to humble herself to the spiritual guidance of Men, the Lore of the Properganders as laid out centuries earlier by the wisdom of the prophets. She flouts the will of GodFather (BBHCM) Himself! She quotes with respect the words of poison-tongued insurgents and takes great pleasure in repeating those foul words, though she *knows* how it must offend me! She *boasts* about her own wilful disobedience. She boasts too about the victories, however short-lived, of her warriors' incursions against our States when they were young and vulnerable. She believes the lies of our adversaries with all her heart. She is deluded, misguided, recalcitrant, unrepentant. An ill-thinker, a dark power.

And yet, this is not the face I see when she is speaking to me. I see an aging woman with scarred hands and a taste for grog and tobacco and a confused vision of history and religion. This is not the face she shows me when she meets my eyes, or serves tea, or jokes with the beast. The *beast*. I do see now that I have been foolish as regards the dog. It was never meant to be my guard, but my company. But although I see this now, *why* would she think I could feel affection for a monstrous creature like that in the first place?

Oh, Mica. The answer is obvious. Because *she* does. She cannot imagine fearing him so she cannot imagine that anyone else would. It is true that he hurt me. But what I take for brutality she calls clumsiness. Indeed, this could be true. Yet I was so certain of his malevolence. Could there be other certainties I must revisit?

No. *No.*

Such are the thoughts she would implant in me, to weaken and corrupt me by raising questions, fostering uncertainty. And uncertainty is weakness. I have been cautioned all my life, yet *still I have not learnt!* As it is written, (wo)Man is 'always learning but never able to come to a knowledge of the truth'. This is the reason for the rules, for the sanctions and the restrictions and the injunctions. The Properganders have done their duty by providing me with protections against false words, against dangerous agencies of disorder. I find this in my collection of quotes in my notebook:

> There is the type of man whose speech about this world's life may dazzle you … he the most contentious of enemies. No sooner does he leave you than he hastens to spread mischief throughout the land … But GodFather (BBHCM) does not love mischief. When it is said to him, 'Fear GodFather (BBHCM),' he is led by arrogance to further crime. Enough for him is Hell, an evil bed indeed to lie on.' Doppel-Book, Sura 2: 204–206.

I have broken bread with 'the most contentious of enemies'. I have lied to myself about my motivations. I submitted to the temptation of curiosity, a profane, feline, female attribute. I put myself in the near occasion of betraying all that I believe, all that I represent. I have compromised. And compromise is a sin! It is written, 'I would thou wert cold or hot. So then because thou art lukewarm, and neither cold nor hot, I will spue thee out of my mouth.' DoppelBook, Revelation 3:15–16.

Unbearable. Excommunication. Exile. Solitude.

I must leave this rodent's hutch as soon as my arm is out of its sling. Which should be soon. Only days, surely?

In the meantime I will listen no more to her stories for I did 'sufferest that woman Jezebel, which calleth herself a prophetess, to teach and to seduce [me … and GodFather (BBHCM) did give] her space to repent of her fornication; and she repented not.' DoppelBook, Revelation 2:20–21.

She repented not – but I shall. I do. I *do*.

For the remainder of this purgatorial time here I will occupy myself with fasting and prayer and readings from my book, from the time before my faith was challenged and I weakened. But I shall no longer consent to hear her wicked confabulations, for she is a power to be reckoned with. Yes. She is an ill-thinker, an evil-doer. She is a Dark Power.

'Thou shalt not consent unto him, nor hearken unto him; neither shall thine eye pity him.' DoppelBook, Deuteronomy 13:8.

 ## PEARL

63.

I have been here for some time, possibly not as much as two months, I think, but it really is very hard to gauge time now.

When the lights go on I pass out of consciousness again for a while. If I wake before any Man comes, I wash. There's a sink and a cloth. They encourage me to wash. Sometimes, also, I do this: I put a few words down. Fewer, lately, I'm not usually in the mood. I have some things of my own here. Shoes. The mask to cover my upper face. This book. Since the tubes were taken off my arms so that I could move properly and use my hands, they have encouraged me to write. Every so often the (wo)Man who brings the food takes this book with her when she leaves. She always brings it back though, with the next meal. She tells me it's good reading, useful and instructive, the better to know the minds of those students who have been in contact with the evil-doers, who have witnessed their ways. Am I a 'student' then? Seemingly it is so. A student should do her best to make her teachers proud. And for the first time, I feel like I could in fact be an adept student. It's not a good feeling, or a bad one. But it doesn't hurt to be useful.

THE HAG

64.

She's in there scribbling away in that little book of hers. At least she's writing. She has thoughts. Of a kind. If simple-minded regurgitations of dogma pass for thoughts. So stale are its droppings of compacted ideology, small and hard and dry, stinking of sanctimony. She's probably given herself a task of lines to write as punishment: *I will not believe a word the aging jez says, I will not believe a word, I will not believe, I will not, I will …*

Will you? Won't you?

Oh, you're wasting your breath, Jen. Give up and send her packing.

And yet. How could she be other than she is? And she has shown that she can be very brave, despite knowing only a life of submission. Despite having been cowed and cut and utterly humbled. Though the poor little wretch has only a limited range of feelings, none of them pleasant, the overriding curiosity-switch still works. And how would I be if I hadn't the privilege of knowing life before Liberation, and of being loved and looked after, and caught even as I fell …

That ugly great face over mine, white and moony-round, breathing grog all over me. Its eyes inside their black crosses were shining and full of concern.

The voice said, 'Oh dear. The poor darling thing's all of a tremble.'

'Fancy,' said another from nearby, out of view, with a voice both high and rough, as if the speaker's throat were lined with fine gravel. 'And there's only the incredible hulk in polka dots with a face uglier than the threat of death hangin' over it, breathing foul old man fumes in its little brown face.'

Not only was the owner of the second voice invisible, so also was much of the 'hulk' because she was cradling my head against her big, hard chest. Fuzzy hairs from her décolletage tickled my nose. 'Heart,' she said, 'don't be frightened; it's only Grimalda. Grimalda Grace. Remember me?'

I didn't recognise her, but I saw that she was one of the Fools that Lee and Anjali loved, and that frightened my dad. I wanted to say something, though I was not sure what – please don't hurt me? – but it was patently obvious that she could already have done me in if she'd wanted to, instead of holding me tenderly and stroking my face so gently. Any case, I couldn't get my breath properly and when I tried it really hurt, hurt so badly I had to make do with little gasps of air and it was horrible, like only being able to sip a glass of water when you're dying of thirst. I had to stretch my neck right back to try and open my throat and my chest. She held my hand as I gagged and spat out something yellow with streaks of blood in it, and my head was pounding like a stampede of Ecumen who even then were marching through the gassy miasma, their snouts of masks under their Perspex visors pressing through the green-hazed air and the fires burning all around, and guns and grenades and tanks, and chanting and howling into the night air alive with death, soupy and smoky and stinking of blood and sulfur and gunsmoke, and all the people running and howling, and me gasping for a bit of real air in all that foulness.

But here was Grimalda. Grimalda Grace.

 MICA

65.

'As to those who reject faith, I will punish them with terrible agony in this world and in the Hereafter, nor will they have anyone to help.' DoppelBook, Sura 3:56.

THE HAG

66.

'Quiet now, my dear little Fragilily. There's no harm in your Aunt Grimie. Just love, that's all.'

I looked around and noted that we were no longer in the battlefield. No smoke, no fire, no guns or uniformed men. The space was cool and dank. I could hear the sound of a dripping pipe, there was a smell of petrol and something else, something sweet, maybe jasmine? I realised it was perfume. Grimalda's perfume. And she was humming softly, a simple little tune, the sort for putting babies to sleep. Her voice was muffled through the bandages wound around my head and over my ears, which felt like they'd been boiled. She laid her large, square hand on my head very gently, and it felt like a blessing, and my heart warmed so much that tears wanted to come up, and they did, though it hurt to cry. Still, they spilt over no matter that I tried to stop them, so then I choked some more.

'Let the poor little bugger sleep, Grimes. It doesn't need your big hairy mug in its face,' said the man with the voice too small for his body, which was huge in all directions. He came forward. His skin was black and his eyes hazel; he had on trousers whose uneven zig-zags distorted over his massive middle. They made my eyes swim and my tummy queasy.

'My darling Mottle-bottle,' Grimalda said quietly, 'had *I* awoken from a holocaustical dream of gas and guns and bad men in boots, with my poor little peepers and sweet pink lungs all aflame, and found a lovely lady like myself gazing upon my troubled brow, well, I would have been most gratified, most relieved.' To me she added, 'In fact, a tiny tear might have welled. And I wouldn't have even thought of stopping it. So go ahead, sweetness, you've been through some kind of hell. Weeping was invented for occasions like this.'

'A dream?' I asked, so I choked again then found I couldn't stop, and all this stuff kept coming up. The big strong hairy polka-dot lady-man cleaned me up, didn't even wrinkle her nose. 'What happened?' I asked. 'Where's Micky? Lee? *Where's my mum?*' and I coughed some more and probably chucked, I can't remember, because I had a tiny hope then, and had to know, in case, just in case it could be true – was I dreaming?

Big Grimalda tucked my hair behind my ear, like Dad or Anjali would have done, and gave me a drink of water and a pill of some sort. Then she simply said, 'Resting time now. Question time later when you surface, my little taddy-tadpole.'

I was about to protest and she noted it. 'Hush,' she said.

Some time later – how long I don't know – I woke myself up in a fit of coughing. When it subsided I had a chance to take in my surroundings a bit. I was somewhere dark but for a candle that was flickering in a jam jar on the floor below a vent. A bit of soft air was coming in and I relished it, even though each breath hurt. The floor was concrete. I could feel the chill it exuded and wherever bits of me stuck out from under the blanket, I was terribly cold. The blanket was scratchy and smelled sort of gamey. I could smell oil too, and something faecal.

I was lying with my shoulders and upper back supported on a pile of cushions, on a mattress, thin, smelly too – maybe that was the source of the stink – or was it me? I noticed that I had on some sort of giant shirt with lime and pink and violet circles intersecting all over it in a fairly sick-making way. With a bit of effort I managed at last to prop myself up on my elbows. Where were my own clothes? I needed to get out but I couldn't go anywhere without my crown-to-toe or the Ecumen would have me up for indecent exposure in a flash. My chest hurt, a deep deep hurt. I fought against the dizziness that wanted to floor me again. Then the whole room started to shake with a rumble from somewhere overhead, and it got louder and louder as I sat there quaking, the room all trembly with the roaring and the candle too, so the light wuthered on the walls making big shadows like witchy warriors dancing their death dance. I sank back down and pulled the blanket over my head. I was small enough to hardly make a difference so maybe, just maybe, I begged Jesumuh Twins Resolved with the fraction of my heart that believed in him: *Could you spare me? Let the monster or the army or whatever horror it is just pass me by …* Then I felt a hand through the blanket, grasping my foot …

I snatched it away and burrowed deeper, hoping that if I were to die then let them shoot me, quick and painless. Through the head, please, that would be best, yes, a blessed relief to be free of the grinding lump of throb that replaced my brain, and the hell of trying to breathe. But nothing happened. I lay there absolutely still until the sound of the monster army was perceptibly diminishing, the shaking of the walls subsiding. But the hand was back there again on my foot. I noticed then that it was not a heavy hand, not much pressure, hardly fierce at all. Perhaps it was not the hand of my would-be murderer? I saw through the weave of the blanket that the room was a bit brighter now. There was a light that wasn't there before. I glimpsed over the edge of the blanket cabbage roses entwined with lacy ferns, red thorn and pale yellow-green frond so elegantly entangled, and spots of gold and violet, tiny budding things. Was I in some kind of elven glade then, home to very smelly faeries? No – it was the wallpaper. Floral wallpaper? It looked new too, the colours fresh though grubby and peeling already, the damp concrete showing through in places. And in front of those valiant blooms and faery flowers: a boy. A thin boy. A real one, with three whole dimensions to himself. I noted dirty blond hair and bright brown eyes.

His hand remained on my foot for a second longer – as long as it took to give it a quick, reassuring squeeze; the other hand was holding a cup. Light brown eyes all flecked with gold. 'Metal orchestral,' he said. 'Don't worry. It's just the five o'clock to Impeccable passing overhead.'

I had no idea what he was talking about. I started to lever myself upright but then the hand was back on my foot.

'Easy does it. You mustn't sit up too quick or you'll be sick again,' he said. 'You've got pneumonia, Grimie says, and that it's a good thing too, because if you hadn't you'd be dead for sure. But she reckons you'll pull through if you behave. Here,' and he passed me the cup. It was full of some kind of meat-scented soup. I sipped it carefully, and the salt in it stung my lips, which felt as boiled as my ears. But I didn't actually chuck, which I thought was pretty good. I couldn't taste anything, though. Maybe my taste buds had got burned off by my acid spit.

'I'm Jimbo, by the way.'

'Jimbo.'

He smiled. 'Grimie says sorry she can't come just now; she has to check the incoming post. She'll look in on you later. Maybe bring you a papaya.'

'Oh,' I said. Or something clever like that. Post and papayas. All was clear as mud.

Once upon a time it was believed that a person could control her destiny – to a degree, at least – and although I now know that history puts paid to this pretty lie, back then we all kept believing it, even when our world was taken from us by those who had no such illusion. Those canny and cynical enough to work out that if any controlling at all was to be done, it had better be by them, for as long as they could. They understood that when push comes to shove we've got about as much control over our lives as we do over our dreams. Either way, eyes open or closed, reality shifts and changes in a heartbeat, in a neural pulse, in a sleepy soul-shiver …

Back then, dear Lee and a few others, my Anjalima perhaps, had seen the writing on the wall and read that its medium was blood and shit and despair. But even they had failed to see just how bad it could get.

'Good, eh?' the boy Jimbo spoke again. Why and what was good? Then I realised he was talking about the soup in the cup, and yes, it may well have been good. 'You'll probably get your taste back, Jenny.' I must've looked a bit startled at his use of my name, as he quickly added, 'Grimalda told me your name.' I supposed I must have said a few things to her before my last fainting spell. I looked at him a bit more. Decided I liked his eyes. They had those goldy bits; they were warm. 'I should let you get a bit of rest.' He started to get up. He was not so much long as very thin. Not gangly, graceful.

'No. Talk to me. Just for a little while. Jimbo.'

He sat back down. The movement was like a concertina folding up. Then he was cross-legged on the end of my mattress. Such big eyes and pale hair, straight as straight, and his skin so fine. His long arms and legs and long fingers and long long bare toes that looked like they'd been made for climbing, like a monkey. His sleeves were too short and so were his trousers, and both were grey with black spots. 'Well, Jenny. Jenny Patel. Here we are. You and me. Me and one little Glindian.' He smiled to show me his white teeth, several of which were broken and two at the side missing entirely. The unbroken ones crossed over as if trying to hide behind each other, afraid of being knocked out like their neighbours. 'You're one of the lucky ones. Me too. I'm luckier, actually, because I found my way here months back, before the shit hit the fan.'

'Here. Underground?'

'Here. Underground. Lucky. You'll find out. You'll find out how to carry on. We do what we can with what we've got, since Riot Night.'

So with kindness and love, possum pies and papayas (why papayas were so easy to get at this time remains an enduring mystery), Grimalda,

Motley and the other Fools tended us – Jimbo and me and about twenty other new-made orphans – back to a semblance of health. I did get better, mostly. The gas burns healed around my mouth and ears and privates. My lungs never got all that great, but I can still enjoy a good cigar.

Then, as now, the main activity of the Fools and their children was contrabanditry, and our main contraband was other children. To send off on boats as whimsically hopeful as our paper planes. And all of us kiddie-spies were waiting our turn too, to set sail for Zealand or Scandos or China.

I worked with the Fools for two years back then, until I was sixteen. After the successful trainjacking and a couple more jobs, I was considered experienced enough to be partnered up with Jim. And mostly, that's how it was. We worked together well, Jimbo and me, so that when my name came up for 'export' to Zealand, and his for Hong Kong, we offered our places to others further down the list. We didn't want to go. We had our new family and work and we loved both. And we loved each other. So although we agreed with the Fools that we'd be able to do more good from the outside, that it was our duty to go, to meet up with the other expatriated children and teenagers, continue to expand our network, we were determined to score a place on a boat with the same destination.

 MICA

67.

'But thou shalt surely kill him; thine hand shall be first upon him to put him to death.' DoppelBook, Deuteronomy 13:9.

 PEARL

68.

I'm sitting by an open window as I write this. MaOblat came to get me from my stone cell with the cot and the no-window. I don't like her any more now than I did last time I saw her. Back in prehistory. I expect I hate her. I can't say why. Can't remember. But the hate's there, that small mean animal in my belly, baring sharp teeth.

She went pale when she saw me. I wonder what I look like? Not that it matters. She didn't say anything, just came in and touched my cheek briefly, softly, with the back of her hand. My jaw didn't hurt any more so I let her. She undid my hobble and grabbed my good arm and held me to her for a moment. She was knobby with new aug-sockets. She smelt of frying. I let her hold me though I really didn't like it at all.

It's probably because of her that I've been moved to another cell. I'm allowed books and films. Some history, a lot about the wars and Liberation – the Liberation films have some very moving crowd scenes. The books are *Philosophy for Girlies*, *Virtues of the Faithful*, the *Meditations*. And the DoppelBook. I get treats for each passage I memorise. Soap. Pyjamas. Things like that. It's worth the effort to have a bit of luxury, I think.

 THE HAG

69.

I can't be sure it was true, but what I heard was that Jimbo was gunned down by Ecumen in a KimCuR raid. I still wait to hear news of him, even now, so many years later. Mad old thing, Jen.

As for me, it was a few days before my seventeenth birthday that I was picked up by a large, muscular and well-intentioned child welfare worker from Ideal State. I didn't have much choice but to go with her after I was cuffed For My Own Good and loaded into a van.

There was Re-Education in a finishing school for girls where we were 'rehabilitated' – less said of that the better so I'll only mention that those of us graded 'Recalcitrant' became familiar with the dark, but because we were young the electric shock treatments were kept to a minimum. The focus was on chanted rote lessons and 'educational' films. When we were deemed psychologically healthy enough we were installed in a cunnydorm with the others, most of whom had been there since the revolution and were too young to remember much. There weren't that many like me.

Mother Oblation 3rd of Ideal State (four Oblations before Mica's House Mother in neighbouring Perfect) made sure I knew their version of the fate of Grimalda and Motley and the movement of Fools. I had no way of knowing if the story of their capture and execution had any truth in it.

I survived two years of this kind of life, six months in rehab, then another eighteen working for the State and living in a cunnydorm with other little loin-chops and womanidol vessels in potentia. Cut off from the rest of the world, it was the stories we told each other that kept alive impressions of what terms like 'communication', 'democracy' and 'totalitarianism' meant – and how these abstractions related to each other and to individual people.

But to my little boy, born into Ideal State three years after Blackout Day, the ideas contained in the stories were now once-removed from reality. Not only because of the time that had passed, but because of the counter-tales he was force-fed by the men and women (sorry, (wo)Men) of Christlam. My little Adamite-19th (not named by me, but by the State) was taken from me immediately after his birth to be raised as an Ecuman; I never even found out whether he stayed in Ideal or was moved to another State. So what would he possibly understand of the world of his mother, or of any world other than the one into which he was born? Or the little girls, the Micas and Pearls, raised like hothouse plants and destined for sacrifice or slavery? Even to me, after a year or so, the words and the past began to feel more mythic than historic. Had I really lived with a man and a woman I called father and mother? Or at least, Arun and Anjali. Had I really walked about the streets of our town unmolested? Had I really had the privilege – no, watch the language! –

the *right* – to cover my breasts and cunny from the gaze and gropings of men? Was there a time when women and girls had independent agency, had value beyond the reproductive? I had to remind myself of Anjali and Arun, I had to remember Lee, I had to remember the lead-up, when I was only a child, to the catastrophic war, to the takeover of history and our means of communication.

After Adamite's conception, after my brief involvement with the man who let me ride him for my pleasure, after the theft of my little boy, and after my escape from the pyre, came the fugitive years. These are still the fugitive years, and I endure even now. On the fringes, part of a network of resistance with its safe-ish houses dotted around the edges of the States. I've chosen to work with the resistance and the Fool-Rangers rather than take my chances on a leaky boat. Someone's got to do it, eh?

Any case, without Jimbo, I really didn't see the point in seeking a new future.

When I happened upon this house it was only a burnt-out shell. I rebuilt it with cocks from the graveyards. I spat on each one to consecrate it. I found furniture, crockery, cutlery in the basement, with a big stash of non-perishables, seeds and bulbs in brown paper bags. Clearly – and fortunately for me – the previous owners had had time to store some useful provisions before the house was burnt down and they were murdered.

I caught the goats and penned them. Albert (RIP) and Victoria were already here, though they had no children back then. Now I have piglets, though no Joyce (RIP). I tend my garden. I decorate my skin with needle and ink, amuse myself with incising other despised creatures into the flesh of my body. Spirit of small fighters who have only teeth and nails and sheer fierce will against larger, better armed predators. The pain is good, a salve and distraction from other torments that plague my waking hours as well as my dreams … yes. So I garden and I hunt and I'm a mean fisher. Haven't caught a fish yet; but children, yes. I don't know if any of those I've sent off on barges down the river to the sea have been successful. I don't even know for certain if any of those notional centres of civilisation still actually exist in the Pacific or to the north of this tormented little globe, in Asia, in Scandos …

Who knows what happened to Pearl? I expect Mica still wants to find her, 'save' her and take her back with her so that they can both die like poultry. She's been in my room for two solid days running. Reciting Revelation in a monotone. It's very unpleasant.

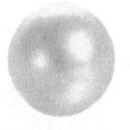 ## PEARL

70.

I have a job now. It's a good job. Not many people can do it. You can't get emotional or you'll make the brighter dudbubs scream. That's horrible. They don't understand anything but they're like little feeling-meters. So if you do get upset or impatient or if you feel sick when you look at them, you have to be able to hide it. I can do that. And the dudbubs seem to like me, those who can. I mean, the ones who are old enough and have the mental capacity. I think they do, anyway. Like me, I mean. It's hard to read their expressions sometimes. Dudbubs can't live long. Three years maybe at the most. But while they're alive I look after them. I clean them and change their dressings and attach their feeders. Once I did a little chanting in time with the pulse of the bank of humidicribs, and they seemed to like that. But when the manager heard me doing it she thrashed me. Dudbubs don't need music and anyway, I don't have vocal privileges. I shut up after that. Don't want to end up xeniicut.

I mind them all, the ones in the swaddling pods and the cribs, and the crawlers in their pens. I mind the ones with limbs and faces and the ones who missed the full complement that proper, viable people are born with. When it's time for one of them to go to hospital, I take them in, I sit by while they are sedated, I stay for their operations, and I remove what's left afterwards.

You can't say they are noble, because to be noble you need some kind of agency. A noble act is a thing you decide to do. They can't do that. But you can say, they are *ennobled*. I'm pleased by being able to make this subtle distinction. I'm pleased that I still can, so dead am I most of the time. But yes. My mind is healing itself as my body does too, and new understanding grows over the old delusions like protective scar tissue. Yes. I can see that the dudbubs are ennobled by their sacrifice, and it doesn't matter if they will it or not. It took me a long time to work out this simple truth. I'd like to tell someone this, but of course I don't talk any more. Mica. I remember you, Mica my darly. She would laugh to herself at the thought of a silent Pearl. But she would laugh quietly, discreetly.

Remembering Mica teases the knot in my belly. It hurts. The knot needs to stay firm to keep the hate and the anger contained. I can't afford to let it loosen, for it could break through my healed-over scabs and make me miserable again with GodFather-(BBHCM)-knows-what vagrant notions and feelings. So now I will tuck the memory of her away again in a safe place, and forget.

But sometimes the gut knot also gets teased loose by the cries of the dudbubs. Then I feel sadness deep as a well. It's horrible. It helps to remind myself that their skin can grow again on another person to help them heal, and that their tiny organs, the ones that work, will grow to maturity in the healthful solutions provided. I remind myself that had that little kidney, this pulsing heart, remained in a dudbub's body, then it would have died when the dudbub died. And that would just be a waste.

And there's always more coming in. It's because of the spiritual defilements. The (wo)Men and womanidols both produce more dudbubs than viables and have for a very long time. When I lived in Perfect's cunnydorm I never realised how many there are. How many fail to last a full gestation. How few Orchid womb-combings or ordinary girlie birthings produce viables. GodFather (BBHCM) has punished us and will continue to punish us until we get it right at last. But in the mean-time, it is our duty to make the best of what we have.

 ## MICA

71.

I will stay with the Hag for another day and another night. Only that long, just enough time to exercise my arm into a semblance of usefulness. It is healed. I have removed the sling.

I have prayed and I have meditated. I have been weak. I have listened to the Hag's lies, she of the lyrical voice and limpid eyes. But it is written: 'A man also or woman that hath a familiar spirit, or that is a wizard, shall surely be put to death: they shall stone them with stones: their blood shall be upon them.' DoppelBook, Leviticus 20:27.

I now recognise that I can remain no longer than necessary in her company than I would in that of any other viper. I am strong again.

I must maintain my determination to do what I know has to be done. Though I have failed my people and my home and can never, ever be forgiven, still I have my own mind, which has been tutored from childhood in truth that must be protected from the ravages of spiritual depravity. This true knowledge is my inheritance and nobody can take it from me.

These are the thoughts that I use to strengthen my resolve to leave, taking with me a proof of my renewed loyalty to our Perfect State: a memento that may mitigate the evil I have committed in the name of love. I know what that must be. But I will speak of that later, if I succeed – all else would be hollow boasting and GodFather (BBHCM) 'does not love the vainglorious boaster' – DoppelBook, Sura Al-Hadid 23.

Then I will do my utmost to find my lost friend and bring her back with me. Together we will face whatever trials lie ahead of us. Perhaps the Son of the Son will be merciful, spare us, even let us live out our lives in all humility, as gardeners or night-soil cleaners, if we show how profoundly we regret … oh, and I *do* regret. Unlike the unrepentant Hag, whose misreading of the Strictures, selective memory and wrongful interpretation of history seems wilful rather than ignorant. She has long since been utterly ruined by minds stronger than hers, and driven by dark impulses that run counter to everything the valiant Fraternity has achieved. She would see the destruction of our Perfect State. Yet I feel pity for her still. She can never know the peace that comes from winning a battle against the evil Jezebel that resides within each girlie and (wo)Man. I have fallen, and yet I know and recognise my failings. Yes, pride again, but this time I see that although a little of it attaches to that false sense of individual personality which I seem unable to quash, in the main it is pride in what I represent – in who I am within the greater scheme laid out by GodFather, revealed by the Resolved Twins Jesumuh and disseminated by the Son of the Son through His Properganders and His Ministers.

72

It is night. I have kept myself awake by repeatedly reciting the Tenets of the Ways of (wo)Man, The Sacrificial Path, and The Sins of the Child. I rise and beckon the Hag's familiar with a bone I have stolen from the pot. He tap-taps towards me, and I slip the leash around his neck.

She sleeps on, her face in a pool of moonlight. There is the tip of a tattooed rodent tail curled at her throat, there are the white scars on the palms of her hands from the fire that should have purified her, that should have cleansed the world of her. Yet she does not look malign, just much older than when awake, when her face is animated by the wickedness of her sacrilegious thoughts. It is a sin to take the life of one who has given you hospitality. I know this. But it is a greater sin to consort with evil.

I remind myself that her intention is only to corrupt, to make me one of her lil'im, some foul agent of defilement like herself. So, 'thine eye shall *not pity*; but life shall go for life, eye for eye, tooth for tooth, hand for hand.' DoppelBook, Deuteronomy 19:21.

So *no pity*.

I raise the kitchen knife high. As I bring it down with all my strength and thrust it into her throat her eyes fly open. Oh, so horrible. Her eyes are a blaze of dying light, like the sun at the end of the world … and the blood, most horrible, foul, and so copious. She tries to cry out; yes, she would have screamed had I been slower. But now her mouth fills with blood and she gurgles like a drain. I make myself watch until the light in her eyes is extinguished and she is still and there is only quiet and the metallic reek of blood and the foul-sweet stink of shit.

Yet how red is her blood. Why am I surprised? Had I thought it would be black or the colour of bile? It doesn't matter what I thought or half-thought. Barely thought. I continue to act while I am still able, for of those who would confound the seekers of truth it is written: 'Thou shalt cut off her hand, thine eye shall not pity her.' DoppelBook, Deuteronomy 25:12.

With difficulty I sever one scarred hand at the wrist that I may take it as my proof that I have combated this demonic witch and won. It is hard to break through the bone. Though her bones are very small and fine, they are hard. But *no pity!* For it is written in DoppelBook, Sura Al-Maida 5:33, 'The punishment of those who wage war against GodFather (BBHCM) and strive to make mischief is that they should be murdered or crucified or their hands and their feet should be cut off and in the hereafter they shall have a grievous chastisement.'

I wrap the hand in a towel from her cupboard. Still it bleeds. I find another and wrap it around the first. I stow the hand in a small satchel, also taken from the cupboard of the witch.

And all the while the dog is howling and crying and twisting his body in an agony of rage and grief. No pity.

73.

I go some way into the forest, full of the horror of what I have done.

Where do I think I am going? I look back and wonder at this vain madness. Do I think I will find a path, the one path Pearl might have taken among all the countless possible ways from which to choose? No to all of those questions. I do not think. I do not think at all. I just keep moving away, away from the nightmare I have created and whose main protagonist now lies ruined, the last dregs of her life-blood ebbing away into the clay of the floor.

I stop by a stream overhung with ancient willows, its banks tricksy with slippy stones and maiden-hair fern; perhaps it's a tributary of Big River and of the smaller, narrower one with the steep banks and secret inlets where the rogues dock their barge to leave supplies for their cohorts. Like my Hag. And where they pick up the strays she would find. Like me. Perhaps there are many streams spreading out in the delta land near where the terrible Sea, filled with great carnivorous fish and glowing creatures like the ones the Hag saw, years ago, in the night-times of her journey to this country, when she was a girlie younger than me.

The moon is spent, but there are many stars, their myriad bright eyes staring through the spaces between the leaves overhead like those of silent predators. I kneel on a green mossy rock and breathe the scents of decay and growth. I bathe my face and hands in the cool water of the creek, for I am hot with the effort of walking through the rough country. The anger and determination that have driven me this far are now extinguished by the act I have committed.

I close my eyes and the scene replays itself on the backs of my eyelids, coloured red and black. At some stage consciousness departs. It is probably a kind of sleep.

Close to dawn they find me, four Ecumen bearing the insignia of Caedmon House. Had they come by means of Holy Hummer I would have been warned, but what use is a vehicle in a forest? They come quietly, on horses. I only know they are upon me when they leap down, shouting in triumph. They beat me around the back and arms, not the legs or the gut, and not so badly that I cannot walk. Then they bind a rope around my wrists. As I stumble along behind the last horse I cry out to them, 'The satchel! Don't leave it!' The men laugh. One quips, 'What use does a doomed girlie have for her toothbrush and comb?' But they fetch it anyway.

I should have known I would fail, for I am weak and the Men who came for me are strong. I am feeble and full of confusion; they work in the name of the Son of the Son and do not suffer sentimental qualms that disguise themselves as moral revulsion that sap all integrity while stealing your strength and judgment. These are Men. They participate in the nature of GodFather (BBHCM) alive-alive-oh-oh amen.

74.

I am confined to a small room with no company but my thoughts. It is dark. I recognise MaOblat by her voice. She tells me that I must wait here until the next Council meeting. The Ministers will then decide the best path to follow. Clemency is unlikely.

I may have been here for a week, possibly a little longer. It is hard to know exactly as there is neither day nor night, only grey twilight created by the weakest of electric bulbs. Xeniicut careforcers come and go. They bring food and remove my waste, breathing heavily, hissily. One of them lingers over her tasks and I can feel her looking at me. I hate this. When she leaves I go to the door to peer out through the grille. I see her stationed there, her back towards me so I cannot tell who it is. In any case, they all look very similar, dead-eyed and hideous. But what does it matter?

My mind is snarled with loose threads that lead me one way, then another and another, through violent images made of recent memories, old lessons, hatred inturned. My skin is wet and sour and there is no water to wash. I know I have a fever but cannot tell heat from cold.

After a time, MaOblat comes to tell me the Council is in session. More hours pass while they remain closeted in their meeting room, discussing affairs of Perfect State and, eventually, my crimes and my fate. Then MaOblat is back. She moves over to the window, inserts her key and loosens the shutters. Now I see her properly for the first time since my return. She has had a recent augmentation. Taut optical fibres extend from her skull like antennae, tiny 'eyes' at their tips for looking around corners, behind her, to each side of her head simultaneously. I can tell by her demeanour that she is very proud of her new facility, so useful to a Mother and keeper of potentially wayward girlies. She looks ridiculous. I recognise this thought as one Pearl might have had, and had she told me of it I would have scolded her for her disrespect. But now I merely note it as one does some absurd phenomenon in a dream, then let it pass so as to mover deeper into the dream.

She has brought me the memorandum of their verdict. She opens the envelope and reads: 'Death by fire is the punishment of the faithless and disobedient.' She does not say this coldly. There is some sorrow in her voice, and disappointment. 'Or,' she continues, 'you may be allowed to Beseech for Perfection.' She glances up at me from under her new eyes, and both originals and augs are bright as summer berries. She smiles her quick, poo-jammed smile. I recognise it as the State smile now, having seen another kind. The sort that lingers and looks into your eyes without the expectation of being quashed.

'So large of heart and broad of vision are the Brother Ministers,' MaOblat continues, 'that they have decreed in their wisdom that although you have erred, yet you may be redeemed.'

I have broken the laws of the State, yet still they offer me this, the greatest of distinctions. Mercy is to be shown me because I have brought them that small, scarred hand.

Not so long ago, there was nothing I desired more passionately than to serve as a vessel. I should throw myself at Mother Oblation's feet and smother them with my kisses and tears of gratitude, but I do not. I sit mute and moveless, for my voice cannot be trusted. I am appalled to find that I am ambivalent about the honour, the mercy. How unstable is this faltering spirit of mine! It seeks to grasp, however ineffectually, at some means of holding onto the remains of this meagre life when now, more than ever, I should offer myself in profoundest humility. But now, the fire that has driven me burns with far less heat.

It does not matter.

I lower my head in a such a way that she will read modesty and gratitude in the gesture. I nod, and she leaves, saying that in due course she will return so that we might begin our preparations for my audience with the Brother Ministers, who will receive my formal Plea this evening. Given the extraordinary circumstances they will hear me in person.

She returns an hour later carrying towels, a basin of water, and some garments in a bag. She helps me undress, wash and depilate; I knot the broad-belt around my waist as tightly as I can. I put on the mask, an old one of my own with bright chips of glass and peacock eyes framing the narrow peep-holes. I put on the new shoes, deep, dark red and tall, that MaOblat has had made for this occasion. Then she leads me down the corridor, just we two, alone; me swaying a little on my heels, her antennae bobbing.

She opens the door to the Council meeting room and ushers me in. I take a step or two further. There they sit, a trio of venerable Elders in the centre of the brightly lit room at the Council Table, resplendent in their robes of office. Each appraises my form as I approach. I am glad for the mask. No-one can read my eyes. But I can read theirs.

'Say your name and place,' says the one without hair, whose teeth look wet.

'Mica, Stone girlie of Oblation House, Attainment-Viable, Cunny-dorm Three, Perfect State.'

'You are the one who left without notice and was returned in disgrace.'

'There are not so many apostates,' adds a second, irrelevantly I think. He has mottled skin, faded reddish hair and small, close, darting green eyes that address my dugs.

'She brought back evidence of her enduring faith,' mentions the first speaker.

'Have you chosen?' asks a third Elder, iron-eyed with thick grey stubble studding his jaw. If I brushed my knuckles over it, it would feel like nails.

'I have.'

'Then speak.'

'Once, I was able only to see the surface of things,' I say. 'I fell victim to my own unstable wits and senses, forgetting the truths I have been taught.'

'What are these truths?' says the one with the metallic stubble.

'That on the surface one may see only flesh over bone, sad corporeal matter: the fleshly fallacy.' I know what I saw in the Orchid Nursery. I know how I reacted and that my reaction was hateful, which I have already confessed in this book. I remind myself that my repugnance was due to the emotional extreme I had failed to control, thus I foundered. I say: 'I was afraid for my friend. Perfection is hard and painful, and one Perfected lives only a season or two.'

They nod as one, as if they understand this. But they have never been Seed-Bearers or (wo)Men. Or womanidols. They have not been and they have not seen and they do not know. This thought is heretical. I think it, and you cannot unthink a thought. But you can swallow it down, though it may sour the stomach.

'Hard and painful,' prompts the reddish one.

'Yet not so painful as the ignominy of betrayal,' I continue. I kneel, head bowed, hands clasped before my breasts. 'I beg you to forgive me.'

No Man speaks. So I continue. 'I truly perceive that that which lies within and above is of the essence. Not flesh, not breath or blood, not light or air. I hold to this. This is my truth. And I would be Perfected. I know that I have erred, yet I would emulate that exemplar of formal refinement and decorum, the orchid, at once emblem and embodiment of the highest moral aspirations. Thus I Beseech: let me spend my days in profound meditation, unencumbered by any superfluity. I would be embodied spirit. And I would serve the greatest cause known to (wo)Man until my last breath.'

75.

Despite all, my Plea was heard and accepted. I have just received notice of their decision. I have been gifted with the honour I have always craved, awarded with the greatest of distinctions. The Brothers are merciful. Salvation has been granted me in the name of the Resolved Twins Jesumuh.

It is of course MaOblat who brings me the verdict. She enters my cell where I am sitting in meditation. 'And tomorrow morning,' she concludes, 'Before you go with the careforcers who will prepare you for the surgery from which you will awake Perfected, you and a select group of other girlies of Oblation, Sacricunt and Dutilove will meet with the Witness.'

I ask her, 'Who is this Witness?' I have no knowledge of a such a person.

'The Witness program is a Ministerial initiative, Mica. The position was recently endorsed, confirmed in your absence.' I can hear from the change in her tone that she is now quoting from a tract she has memorised. 'As our State evolves and grows, we discover new needs for our people, males and females alike. (wo)Men, though their lives are ordered and their ways clearly defined by the wisdom of the State's Ministries, require help, require advice. The Witness is come to salve the spirits of damaged girlies, for she too has suffered. She is a girlchild who has passed through hell and been redeemed. She has already helped others these past weeks, since her first address to the other girlies of the Houses of Oblation, Sacricunt and Dutilove. Her testimony strengthens any whose spirits quail, and they may be revitalised in her restorative presence.' Here the quotation finishes and she adds, 'The Brother Ministers have decreed that your presence at this audience, as a now penitent renegade, will further assist any who lack conviction.'

After she has gone I give myself up to profound contemplation of the Sacred Crescent and Crucifix. Soon I will cease to keep this journal. I will cease to write anything, to read, to train with the girlie-guards or work in the garden. I know my spirit once quailed in the presence of the sacred vessels, but it will not again. I have been set back upon the one true path that is and always was my destiny.

And so it is that before first light, two Men come to take me to the Witness, who lives by Big River where she can enjoy the perfect solitude required for her profound meditations. 'She loves the sound of water, its gentle repetitions encourage her inward focus, her seeking,' MaOblat tells me while the Men wait. 'The Witness may be as much spirit as human. Be silent in her presence unless she invites you to speak.'

We are gathered together at the exit to the corp-yard, myself and several other girlies from Stone, Bark and Dirt. Nickeline, who always cries so easily, is there. I am not surprised that she is one considered lacking in resolve. I dislike the Brothers' association of me with one such as her. But that is not important.

The sun is rising when we arrive, backlighting the thick clouds. Pale mist rises from the river as the Men lead us down to the low banks whose grasses have been cropped short by the goats who I can see watching us with unblinking yellow and black demon-eyes. The Men lead us yet further down to where the rushes stand still as sentinels, the thin lines of their shadows unmoving on the mirror-like surface of the water. The Men walk on, sending disturbing ripples out to destroy the glass of the river, fracturing its glaze into many parts. We follow. Still further, knee-deep, thigh-deep ... I see ahead a small island fringed with smooth grey stones spattered with guano from the big black birds that cluster in the overhanging willows. And upon the island, a construction of stones. Its height is not much greater than my own, but broad and wide enough to house a single person with minimal needs. Its four walls are made of rocks jigsawed together in an imperfect puzzle of stone.

One by one we are led towards one of the flaws in the structure of this edifice, a slit in the rocks, and told that we should enter one after the other. Indeed, these Men look nervous and would not enter of their own volition even were they able to, but only a girlie can fit through such a narrow cavity.

I tremble at the thought of entering. Yet we have no choice, with a cohort of Men standing guard, their eyes sharp and their blades sharper. When my turn comes I push myself through the gap; the cold stone grazes my dugs but I enter with little trouble. I find myself in a grotto, moist and dripping. Watery light filters through from the space I have just negotiated, and from others in the two walls on either side. This is as much a barrow or crypt as a sanctuary for a holy ascetic.

The third wall is hung with the standard of our Perfect State: the Beautiful Man, his gaze mild and loving, his left foot forward and arms upraised, in his right hand a sword, in his left, the unfurled orchid. Below the banner is a broad, ornate throne of carven bone formed after the shape of a great half-shell, all inlaid with precious minerals that glint softly in the subtle light.

And upon the shell there sits my Pearl.

76.

Praise the Resolved Twins Jesumuh!

But she cannot see me nor any other, for her eyes are bound with a cloth. At the base of her throne is a small fire-pit, and a coil of sweetly-scented blue smoke rises and spreads throughout the small chamber on little eddies of air.

We sit at her feet. I breathe in deeply, and gaze in awe at this transformation. I want to lay my hands on her feet and whisper as I gaze up at her face, 'Ah, Pearl, it is me, your Mica.' But I cannot. Not yet. Perhaps I can contrive to be the last to leave and then I can ... but for now, I gaze into the soft blue smoke, coiling mesmerically. After all that Pearl has done, all that has happened, some seed of wisdom has prevailed. Where once she was a wild thing, now she is at peace. And honoured.

When all the others have assembled, she speaks. 'There is a myth about pearls of wisdom,' she begins, 'but there is no wisdom in any pearl, only a hardened crust concealing impurity.'

'Surely not so,' comes a whisper from one of the group. I look around to see who has spoken. But all have lowered their faces, and so now do I.

'But it *is* so,' Pearl says. 'I was aggravation. I was irritation. I caused others to feel discontent. And I would redress this sin. This is why you have all been sent here to me, to receive advice. But I have no advice to give. I have only my story. It is brief, and I will tell it simply. That is my job. That is why I am the "Witness". If what I have to tell helps you, then I will have done my work well.

'I did not Beseech for I was proud and restless. I believed I had a right to live and work and experience love. I had a man, a single lover ...'

'*Haraamasur*,' breathe the other girlies. Though I have long-since guessed it, still this confession is a knife in my belly.

'... and his name was Asa. Asa was much older than me, was once a fine Ecuman of Gabriel House. He was my exclusive lover. Under my influence, he would take no other. It is through me that he was ruined.

'I did not Beseech. Instead I wrote to Asa. I left him a note telling him where to find me the night I fled. He never came. The note was found by another Man in his House and Asa was reported, then imprisoned. I have not seen him. I have heard of his fate, however. He has been un-Manned, as is correct. He works now with the Dirt girlies of Sacricunt in the sewage recycling plant near the godowns by Big River.

'This news subdued my restlessness, stripped back my pride. How can one guilty of causing an un-Manning go on breathing? I wanted to take my life, but was left with no means to do it in my prison. I tried to starve myself, but was tied down and fed through tubes so I had no choice but to live another day, and another, and another. As it happens, I now find I can feel gratitude for this action, though I screamed and cried for a long time. Mother Oblation told me sadly, "My dear, you still have much to learn about life." She was right.

'There was re-education in the old Finishing School where I lived for many weeks. There they continued to feed me with liquid nourishment and strong sedative medicines extracted from poppy juices while I lay on a cot and had my lessons. First the Men came and showed me what I was for. I had known the gentling touch of my lover, but their touch was ... workmanlike. It was reality. So, through many forms of physical demonstration, the vanity of personal identity was by degrees diminished. It was aided also by the contraction of a foul and stinking infection of my female parts, one of the many diseases the cunny attracts, and I came to understand the fleshly fallacy for what it was – a deceit to tempt, then disappoint. Sensual pleasure leads ultimately to corruption. That is the nature of the flesh.

'Later, I was shown films about the history of our State and witnessed the atrocities of Unrule armies during the War of Liberation which our glorious Ecumen ultimately defeated. I need not relate them to you, for I do not believe you need to hear of these horrors. Unlike me. I needed to witness them, to absorb them, to understand. I saw too the artifacts of dissolution including the common "entertainments" of our Adversary, the spillage of blood and spatter of semen, the wanton waste of vitality and seed, the wretched deaths of so many Men, (wo)Men and children.

'And for my penance I was allowed then to go to work with the wretched of the earth, the dudbubs. There I learned humility in caring for the ruined, the dying, and the dead little ones.

'After I had seen it all and finally understood, my eyes were taken from me, that I might rather look within and watch the growth of the new seeds of wisdom that had been planted in my consciousness. And it is true indeed that although I am sightless – rather, *because* I am blind – I now look into the light. I see more deeply than I could have imagined possible. And every day understanding grows. Salvation comes only through mortification and sacrifice. I have embraced it and am grateful.'

I had felt I had a duty of care to keep Pearl safe. I still believe that was true. She was the weaker in faith, prone to whimsy, driven by feeling. And because she would never exercise restraint, I was there. I was there to hold her back. It had always seemed to me to be this way. And to her, I am sure. We each knew what we were to the other: I was to care, and she was to be cared for. She had been grateful to me, and loving. She showed this humility to me and to no other. But no, not so. She *did* have another.

And she found her way to this end without me. She has followed a circuitous route, a hard road, but it was her road and it brought her here, to this place, to this noble role.

She does not need me. Perhaps she never did.

She has learned and is grateful for the torments she has undergone. Such terrible torments of body and of spirit.

77.

Outside this cairn is the river. I hear its quiet murmur. And the rushes. Black birds, white rocks. The stone chamber, a burial mound for a living idol. The Witness enthroned. A curl of scented blue smoke. There is Pearl. No. It is a form of Pearl. Her semblance. The Witness.

78.

She never needed me.

She found her own path. She needed neither my love nor my example of piety. Chance, not will, has brought her to this pass. At last the Son of the Son has smiled upon her. She is blessed.

I am not blessed. I am alone.

And I need never have left.

I imperilled my life and my honour. All for Pearl. I allowed myself to be diverted from the proper direction of my life. I committed apostasy. I committed murder.

She speaks some more, lips moving beneath the bandage that hides her ruined eyes. I know who she was and who she is. She was a girl who spoke her heart. She is now a girl whose words are a mosquito drone.

79.

And I?

I murdered the one who took me in and tended to me. My Hag, renegade and sinner, adhered to every sacred law of hospitality due the wanderer. I, believer and virtuous girlie, broke every reciprocal obligation of the guest. She did not love me yet she treated me kindly. She liked to make soup. She cared for her animals, her trees. She kept her garden, in her way. She gave the softly glowing toadstools a place in the walls of her home. She loved cockatoos though they wrecked her nets and stole her seeds and fruits. She met with rogues and brought me what she thought were gifts. And I murdered her.

And Pearl has not found grace. Not humility. She has found sanctimony.

I am sickened by this eyeless mask with the moving lips. This counterfeit person mouthing truisms of the sort I have mouthed, often enough. So, she is reduced. So, she is exalted. So, all I have done is wasted.

I cannot bear it. I cannot abide listening to this eyeless effigy. I look around at the rapt faces of the others lost in contemplation.

I creep away from the place early, back outside to where the Men stand smoking and joking on the bank, waiting for us to emerge, cleansed of all doubt, ready to meet our destiny pure of heart.

I stand a little apart from them, to wait. One Man gestures to me to approach him, which I do. He then directs me with his eyes to remove the dressless I have on to protect me from the rain, rain that is falling so lightly I can hear the sound of each drop on the wet leaves at my feet. I do as I am bade, and now I am naked in the rain. It is very cold. A beautiful cold.

I close my eyes. I can hear the other Men gathering in more closely to watch. They are murmuring comments to each other, about me. I do not attend. Hands are on my dugs, tweaking, cupping, crushing. Another is standing behind me, his hands on my hips, moving me as he pleases against the hardness I can feel in his trousers. More hands on my belly, and a finger is inside me, then another, probing. I feel a Man's hands on my face. He runs his fingers over my lips, and gives me a light slap when at first I do not open my mouth. I comply. He dips his fingers into my mouth and moves them in and out, touching tongue, gums, lips again. He forces me to my knees and I have an image of myself as an animal at an auction. My gorge rises. Oh, it is a most sickening thing, to have your breast burning with the outrage of something being done to your body, yet to be without power.

Then I bite down hard. There is a scream and the iron taste of blood, then a great pain in the side of my head.

80.

Later I open my eyes. I am prone on some hard platform. I cannot move my arms and legs. I can feel they are cuffed to the bed, or table. The room is brilliantly lit and I can see a redundant sliver of daylight from a high, narrow window. It looks like it's about midday. My head is pounding from the blow I received and when I try to move it I notice that it is confined also; there is some kind of padded vice-like structure holding it still. I notice also a tight pressure on my face; my cheeks have been pulled back and taped into place with some very strong adhesive, immobilising them. My lips are stretched into a grimace over my jaws. The skin is thin over the framework that anchors it in the world. I feel a sickening dread. And again, I am at the mercy of others.

To quell my panic so that I do not die of it, I do an inventory of my body parts: they all seem to be present and responsive to my mental attention, though some may have been bruised and maybe some ribs are broken; fortunately I was knocked out cold immediately after my action of outrage, so I did not have to feel it at the time. It seems the Men needed to beat me more than they needed to help their colleague. Priorities.

A careforcer is looking down on me. Her eyes are huge, a dark, deep blue, like lapis – no, like sodalite, for there are light flecks and striations, and they contain some warmth. Sodalite, I remember, is a mineral recommended for the home, for it has peaceful properties.

My peripheral vision picks up the presence of a white coat, so I know I am in the hospital, possibly an operating theatre. I return to the blue gaze which holds me steady. And I have no power. No power, *again*.

So at last, to what has Mica, the Crumb, been reduced? Neither the noble sacrifice nor righteous avenger nor saviour of the weak. Pride was ever the strongest of my sins. Yet I have not been quite broken on the wheel. What will they try next? What will be my final punishment, now I wait here on the operating table, about to be silenced forever with scalpel and suture, now that I have been commandeered for the careforce? Will I be a cunnydorm guard? A porter for the military? A sweeper of slops from the Spare Parts Manufactory?

Cruelty is useful up to a point. It can break even the most resilient of spirits. The Ministers and Properganders are adept and experienced, after all, in the arts of spiritual and intellectual manipulation. But if you mismatch the torment with the nature of the tormented, if you disregard all that your victim has already experienced and how it might have moulded them, the result might be the opposite of what you planned. You can upset the balance.

I look back again at the xeniicut – is it 229? – at her already-wrecked mouth with its little hole in the middle for drinking, for whistling.

She is holding something up to my eyes. A piece of paper with a drawing – no, three drawings, in boxes. They are laid out like the illustrated biographies of the Hag's, like the story of the warrior girlie Tank Girl. But these are drawings the xeniicut has made, I think. They are: box one: face with a pair of lips with cross-stitches holding them together; box two: a face, smiling, the lips unstitched; box three: a running girl.

If I die trying once more to leave, what difference will that make?

Her great blue eyes look questioningly into mine. I nod.

EPILOGUE

The small white house, reflecting light. The black dog stands guard. He has slipped from his leash but not from his sense of duty. He stares at me as I approach but makes no move towards me. I walk to the back of the house. The goat and the piglets have broken out of their enclosures. The Hag's carpentry was never that reliable. Just as well, for the creatures have at least been able to feed themselves. I see one of the Baxters peering from behind a straggling bean trellis. Later, I will find more food for them. Later I will rebuild their pens.

But first, I have another task.

I find a shovel leaning against the generator shed. I walk a little way away to where the trees begin. I spend some time here, digging her grave. The soil is moist. It is nearing dark by the time I return to the house.

Stay, I tell the dog. I open the door. It is darker inside than out. There is enough light for me to see by. Some from the window, some from the chinks in the wall and the glowing toadstools in their crannies. Most of her blood has soaked into the earth floor, but there is a great deal of it on the wall. I had not realised this at the time. Later, I will scrub it off.

I gather the poor lifeless thing up in my arms and carry it to the grave, the dog following. He knows what it is that I carry and he cries and cries.

After I have buried her, I say no prayer.

The dog and I sit by the fresh grave for many hours. We watch the moon rise. We see that big star that crouches by the lower tip of the crescent. We see the cross-shape formed by five other stars.

In the morning we return to the house. We will wait here. There is plenty to do. I am a gardener, after all. I will turn the soil and tend the vegetable plots, I will repair the supports for the beans, fertilise the fruit trees, mend the chicken run, the pens.

Perhaps a troop of men will come. If so, that will be that.

Perhaps they will not, and later I will find a way to send a message to the xeniicut. Let her know I am safe. Let her know there is a place other than Perfect to hope for. To send others.

Perhaps, sooner or later, a lost child will find her way here, looking for the Hag at the crossroad.

I'll be here.

Acknowledgements

I'd like to thank Stephanie Smith, Linda Funnell, and Graeme Ulbrick for their patient readings and re-readings, and for their suggestions for the manuscript as it developed over time. Thanks also to Linda Nix for her invaluable advice and meticulous editing.

About the author

Louise Katz is a speculative fiction writer and winner of two Aurealis Awards. She has travelled widely and has been employed in too many and varied jobs to recall, from early days in bars and restaurants, sales or fruit-picking, to working as a museum educator, a visual artist, and a high-school teacher. Louise currently lectures in academic writing at the University of Sydney.

Novels:

> *The Orchid Nursery* (Lacuna, 2015)
>
> *The Absent Men* (novella) in *X-6 Anthology* (Coeur de Lion, 2009)
>
> *The Other Face of Janus* (HarperCollins, 2001) – Winner of the Aurealis Award for Best Young Adult Novel, 2001
>
> *Myfanwy's Demon* (HarperCollins, 1996)

Short stories:

> "Weavers of the Twilight" in *Smashing Stories* (Agog! Press, 2004) – Joint winner of the Aurealis Award for Best Fantasy Short Story, 2004
>
> "The Little Demon" in *Mystery, Magic, Voodoo & the Holy Grail* (Harper-Collins, 2000)